CROSS MY HEART

AVERY MAXWELL

THE BEST OF US LLC

Copyright © 2020 by Avery Maxwell

All rights reserved.

No part of this book may be reproduced in any form or by any electronic or mechanical means, including information storage and retrieval systems, without written permission from the author, except for the use of brief quotations in a book review.

❦ Created with Vellum

For my Family & Friends,
Thank you.
Avery

In loving memory of my very own real-life GG

While my GG wasn't outlandish like Lanie's grandmother, my GG and I were so very much alike.

At the age of ten, my GG unintentionally passed on her love of romance novels to me. She was always a thrifty shopper, so one day while out "yard-sale-ing," she found her passion, a $5 paper bag full of romance novels. After bargaining her way down to $3.50 for the entire bag, we were on our way to go blueberry picking on the side of a random Vermont road.

After picking for about an hour, I was hot and getting sunburned, so I headed back to the car to wait for her and guess what I found while waiting? Her bag of treasures. I remember sitting there reading a book with a half-naked man on the front while continually looking over my shoulder, waiting for her to come back. It was a learning experience for sure.

GG's love of these stories is just one of the many things I inherited from her. I know she would have loved Lanie and Dex, and she would have been so proud of me. Gram, you will always be missed.

A NOTE FROM AVERY

Disclaimer & Trigger Warning

While Burke-Mountain is a very real place in Vermont's North-East Kingdom, everything else in this book is a work of fiction. All characters, scenes, and other settings were all created in my imagination.

If you ever get the chance, I highly suggest you visit Burke, Vermont and all the surrounding towns. Mimi was right when she said it's a place that builds character. Vermont is a place I'll always hold near and dear to my heart, from the people to the landscapes, it is truly a one-of-a-kind place.

*This romance novel is a work of fiction. However, Lanie has had a hard life. Before the story begins, Lanie was a victim of physical abuse. Although I tried to discuss her attack as vaguely as possible, I am aware this may be a trigger for some readers.

If this applies to you, I am genuinely sorry for all you have had to endure. I hope I was able to tell Lanie's story respectfully and if you are ever in need of help, please reach out to the National Domestic Violence Hotline: https://www.thehotline.org/

PROLOGUE

DEX

"Hey, Dad, it's me again. The doctors and nurses don't know if you can hear me, but said it's worth a shot. You were in a car accident almost two weeks ago."

Breathe, Dex. Just breathe. "Drunk driver. You never even saw him coming." I can't help the deep, painful sob that escapes from my soul.

A heavy hand lands on my shoulder, and I already know it's my best friend, Trevor. We've known each other since kindergarten and he loves my dad like he's his own. I raise my head and see my other friends, Preston and Loki, on the opposite side of the bed.

"We know you said you would do this alone, but we're here for you, man." Turning to my dad, he continues, "Mr. Cross? I promise you, Dex and his family will never be alone. We'll always be here for him."

In my peripheral vision, I see Loki and Preston nod in agreement.

"Loki and I are also here, sir," Preston chimes in.

"Dad, the doctor told me you won't wake up. Th-That I have to say good-bye, except I'm not ready. I need you."

Visions of my childhood flood my vision, and I have to wipe the memories away. "Anna was just here in the hospital, too. She had an ultrasound. The twins are both girls. We've named them Sara and Harper after your mom. Anna didn't mind either way, and I thought you would like that. She wanted to be here, but we thought it might be too much for her. I knew you'd understand." I break down with my hand in his and cry. "You're never going to meet them. You're never going to know my daughters. You won't get to see Tate grow up." My voice is thick with emotion, but I force myself to continue, "I love you so much, Dad. I'm so sorry. I wish there was something, anything I could do. Please know, I-I love you."

My head drops once more, and I cry with no shame, as if I've never cried before. I give the nod to Trevor, who calls the doctor in from the hallway. When Dr. Fox comes in, we all say our good-byes, and he's gone within the hour.

"Dex? Do you want us to take you home to Anna? I mean, I know she hates us," Trevor jokes to ease my pain, "but maybe you need someone?"

I shake my head. "Thanks, I'm all right. I'm sure it's probably better for you to wait and come over later."

"Okay. We'll stay close by, though. If you need anything, text me. I know this is hard, but the girls and Tate are going to need you. Two girls, Dex. I can't wait." Trevor hasn't even met the girls yet, and he loves them as much as I do.

Eyes red and puffy, I try not to vomit as I make my way home. Pulling up to our house, I take a moment to collect myself. As I open the car door, a man in a designer suit exits my home. I know I should wonder who he is, but my brain is too tired to think much of it.

Searching for Anna, I walk through the garage to our kitchen. On my way, I pass through the mudroom and take a minute to study all of Tate's shoes, jackets, and hats spilling out of every bin in here. I smile when I realize it will soon be covered with pink, too.

I find her in the kitchen, sitting at the island, so I lean in for a hug, hoping for comfort after all that happened. I'll need all the strength I can get to care for her and our children. I just want this moment with my wife, except she's stiff and not looking at me.

I sit beside her. "Anna, is everything okay?"

"I'm sorry about your dad," she says while frowning out the window.

"Me too." *What is going on with her?* "Are you nervous about the girls? The doctor said everything looks great."

Anna sighs. "No, Dexter, I'm not upset. Here." She hands me a manila envelope, and as I turn it over, my chest constricts more than I thought possible. "I want a divorce. I'm sorry to do this now, but it's best for everyone if I just leave before anyone gets attached."

Gets attached? I want to yell, but my mouth feels like it's full of sawdust and razor blades.

She uses my silence to continue, "I had these drawn up about three months ago. I'm not asking for anything but a little money to get me on my feet—"

I interrupt her, finding my anger. Anger at her in this situation. Anger that my father died less than an hour ago. Anger that nothing will ever be the same again. Outrage at what that means for my children.

"You're not taking my kids away from me. Do you hear me, Anna? You will not take them," I scream.

"Dexter, if you will calm down and look at the paperwork, you'll see all I'm asking for is ten thousand dollars. You'll also see I have signed away all parental rights to you." She glances at the door. "I have a ride waiting. I ask that you give me a few hours alone later this week so I can collect the rest of my clothing," she says coldly.

That's when I notice the suitcase at her feet. "You have a

ride? There's someone else, isn't there?" She doesn't have to answer; I can see it in her face. "What are you going to tell Tate?"

"I texted Preston's mom. She came and took him to the park for a few hours. I'll be gone before he returns." Anna turns her icy stare on me. "You can still be involved in this pregnancy if you'd like to be, Dexter. I'll keep you updated on all appointments, and as soon as I give birth, I'll walk away."

I don't recognize the woman before me—the woman I met when I was sixteen. This woman is cold, unfeeling. She is exactly who my friends saw when they first met her.

"You don't even have the courage to say good-bye to Tate? Don't do this to him, Anna. Please don't," I plead. "You know how my mother left. Don't do that to him, too."

I'm numb.

Anna shakes her head, then turns and walks out of our lives while I slide down the wall to the floor.

How am I going to do this? My dad is gone. My wife is gone. I have a four year old and twins on the way. Just before I have a heart-wrenching breakdown, I text Trevor.

Dexter: My house. Now.
Trevor: On my way.

CHAPTER 1

LANIE: PRESENT DAY

"*L*anie, wake up! *Lanie!*"

I feel small hands on my shoulders, shaking me. *Don't make a sound, Lanie. Stay quiet for Max. Don't let this asshole find him.* Wait ... small hands, female hands, that's not Zachary's voice. It's Julia's. My best friend, Jules. She can't be here.

"Lanie, Jesus Christ, wake up!"

Wake up. Wake up. I'm dreaming. Slowly, I open my eyes. Nothing is in focus. I jump back, and my head hits the headboard. *Headboard.* I'm not on that filthy floor. I'm in bed. *My bed, right?* But it's so dark. Jules turns the flashlight on from her phone, and I glance around.

The light, coastal-themed bedding Julia picked out for me right before I moved in is pooled at my legs. The pale gray walls are covered in pictures of Julia and me, artwork that little Charlie has made, along with all the random stuff I've been able to collect since college. A secondhand, aqua-colored armchair and an antique, white desk I found at the only antique shop in town sit under the window. This is home. I'm safe.

"Lanie, it's me ... it's Jules. The power went out again, but you're okay."

"I'm okay. Yes, I'm a survivor. I'm a protector. I'm okay. Julia's here," I say, obviously more for my benefit than hers. "Julia? I'm so sorry. I didn't wake up Charlie this time, did I?"

Charlie is Julia's ridiculously cute son. I love him like my own, but he's another of my failures. It's my fault he'll never know his dad.

"No, Lanes, you didn't." She shakes her head with sad eyes. "Are you all right here for a minute while I go get the flashlights?" She eyes me, and I nod. "Okay, hold my phone so you have some light. I'll run to the kitchen and be right back."

"Mhm. Thanks, Jules."

Julia retreats, her shoulder-length brown hair swaying behind her. She and I couldn't be more opposite. Where I'm six feet tall with dirty blonde hair and blue eyes, she's barely five foot two with dark chocolate hair and green eyes. The only similarity between us is our Irish skin and the smattering of freckles covering our faces. Regardless, I had promised her this wasn't happening anymore.

Fuck. I want to string together every four-letter word I know but refrain. Peeking around the room with the phone light, I try to determine what could have alerted her other than the power going out.

The freaking power. *Will I always be afraid of the dark now?* Glancing to my left, I realize another bedside lamp has bit the dust. I lean over the bed and see it smashed to pieces.

Well, shit. Maybe I need to go to HomeGoods and see if they have any wooden lamps or something made of concrete? Anything sturdy enough to prevent me from breaking another one. This makes the second broken lamp this month, not to mention I've lost a couple of picture frames as well. If only we didn't lose power so often up here in the mountains.

Jules is going to want to talk. Maybe she's right. Perhaps I need to get out of here.

Interrupting my train of thought, Jules walks in with a battery-operated lantern and two sleeves of thin mints. *Yup, she wants to talk, all right.*

"Don't give me that look, Lanes. It's my turn to take care of you for a change. You have been watching out for me since wretched, old Mrs. Ford yelled at me for picking up my pencil too early on the first day of school."

"Ugh, she was the worst. She had it out for you because she knew she could never teach you anything you didn't already know!" I'll never forget that day. Mrs. Ford was horrid to Julia. Her only crime was being smarter than the teacher.

Julia swings her hair over her shoulder and climbs into bed with me. "That's true! That old hag seriously had it out for me. But you never let her get to me again. I swear you probably should have been expelled for the torment you caused her."

"Hey! I was just taking the heat off you."

"I know that, Lanes ... just like I know it was you who gave Amy Warback the swirly after she told the basketball team I had herpes."

"She deserved it," I grumble.

Jules is the friend I needed when I was a poor kid from the wrong side of town, and the friend I still need to this day. She's saved me in more ways than I can ever repay her for.

"Lanes?" The nickname she gave me in fifth grade always makes my lip curl up into a smile. I earned the moniker when we started running track to get out of gym class, and I had a hard time staying in my own lane.

"Yeah?"

"We need to talk about this," Jules says. "You promised me

this wasn't happening anymore, but I've seen the broken lamps on the curb and in the recycling. I know you're trying to hide it so I don't worry, but you can't live like this."

It's been eighteen months since my attack. Six months since the doctor said I was better, that I was all healed and ready to move on. All healed. *Right*. That's the biggest crock of shit I've ever heard in my life. I roll my eyes at the memory.

Jules smiles with a mischievous glint in her eyes. "You're swearing in your head again, aren't you?"

"Like a sailor." *Damn it, Jules.* "You know me better than I know myself sometimes."

When I glance up, her sad gaze hits mine.

"Lanes, you haven't sworn out loud since you were ten years old, and your mother's douche-canoe of a boyfriend tripped you, then punished you by making you swallow that bottle of Purell."

"I didn't think you knew about that." I immediately stare at my bed, eyes downcast in shame.

"You ended up in the hospital, and your mother told them you were always doing shit like that. I knew the first day I met you that you were neither stupid nor suicidal. Your mother made you cover for him. She's done it your entire life."

Shocked and a little unsettled, I wrap my arms around my middle. "She consistently chose her boyfriends over me … she still does, actually."

"Oh, honey." Julia sits closer and wraps me in a hug. "We're your family now. Us, and GG. My parents have made you call them Mimi and Pawpaw since you were ten years old, so you're a McDowell in all but name."

Maxine and Pete McDowell never let me call them Mr. or Mrs. It's like they knew I needed them. It was my third sleepover at Julia's when my mom forgot to pick me up again, and Mrs. McDowell told me I was like a second daughter to them, so the Mr. and Mrs. business wasn't going to work anymore. I called them Mimi and Pawpaw ever since, except in front of my mother. I never knew how she would take it, and Mimi seemed to understand that.

I can't help the tears that flow. "You always did know how to cheer me up."

"Lanes, you know I love you, and this is going to break mine and Charlie's hearts so much, but I think it's time you consider getting out of here. You know I'll never kick you out, and you are always welcome. I kind of like the idea of growing old with you on the porch with unlimited Bahama Mamas, but you deserve better, and I'm not sure staying in this town, or even this state is what you need."

I laugh as I'm sure she intended. Bahama Mamas had become our drink in high school. We liked to pretend we were somewhere warm and not in this tiny, Vermont town. Don't get me wrong, I loved growing up here with Jules. The trouble is, if you're not in a large ski town, many people in Vermont live in poverty. With no real job prospects, it can make for a tough living.

"I'm so proud of you, Jules. You're so smart." Right after college, Julia landed an amazing job in Boston. It gives her the ability to work remotely to take care of her parents and Charlie. "You have your life together."

"Lanie, you graduated right behind me at BU. You're just as smart. You know me, though, I'm not great socially with most people. Everyone thinks I'm weird or quirky. I'm just too uncomfortable all the time. There's no way I could have ever lived in Boston, and I can't make that kind of money here. Plus, Mimi and Pawpaw aren't getting any younger. They'll need me soon enough."

"You better not let Mimi hear you say that! She doesn't think she's old." I laugh.

"I know, but until they're ready to retire to the beach

house, I have to be here for them." Just then, the lights flicker to life. "Here, start eating these. I'll be right back."

Julia turns off the lantern after handing me the thin mints and runs to her room. She's back a few minutes later with her computer.

"Are we making a list?" I smirk. Julia's always making lists … it's how her brain works. She can solve any equation, any work-related catastrophe in minutes flat, but she needs to see everything in black and white when it comes to life.

"Sure are! First pros and cons of living here, in Vermont, versus somewhere else. Then a list of potential places. Please remember, I'm not kicking you out and you can always come back, but you need this. You know that, right?"

It's the same conversation we've had for the last year. I know Julia loves me, and I know it will kill her when I move. I came to live with her and Charlie after I was released from the hospital. It's been everything you would expect living with your best friend to be. However, she's right. I can't stay in Vermont anymore. I have to find a way to move on from the bad memories.

"Okay. The first list will be quick. The only pro for me staying is you, your parents, and GG."

GG is my grandmother. She owns the tiny ski lodge on the mountain, and admittedly, she's a little crazy, but she was always there for me. My cousin, Lexi, and I grew up with GG in between my mother moving me from apartment to apartment. My mother, Laurel, and her twin sister had us weeks apart and chose our names together. Lanie and Lexi … I always thought they sounded like porn names, but it is what it is. My aunt died when we were two, and my mother never recovered.

"You know what, Jules? I don't think we need to make this list."

Jules looks up at me with teary eyes. *Oh shit.*

"No, Jules, I think you're right. It's time for me to get

away for a while. I don't think I can go forever, but possibly for a year? If I can find some work that will get me out of here, I might be able to get my head on straight. When I come home, maybe I can be normal."

"Oh, Lanes, for crying out loud. You are normal! What you went through is not."

This is a conversation we also have had ad nauseam. I don't argue with her anymore, although I know, in my heart, I'll never be normal again.

A few hours later, the sun has risen, and we hear the first bits of chatter coming from Charlie's room.

"I have to get Charlie ready for Mimi," Jules tells me. "I need to be on a call for work soon, but think about all of this, okay?"

I give her a hug and watch her go next door to Charlie's room. A few minutes later, I hear Mimi coming up to get him, and Jules heads to her office.

I listen as Julia carries on a conversation on the other side of my wall. She's downright scary at work. People who don't know her, and even people who do, would never believe how intimidating she is when she's working. Before the attack, it had been my goal to get that confidence she has in her career to carry over to the rest of her life. Someday, when I'm less broken, I'll find a way to show her just how amazing she is.

I stare at the list we made last night. It began with grandiose plans of Paris, LA, Seattle, and North Carolina. Paris for obvious reasons, LA, because hello? Celebrities! I chose Seattle because of Kurt Cobain, but it got nixed immediately. I wasn't starting a new life somewhere that rained more days than not. I crossed Paris out, too. I couldn't make a new life in a place where I didn't even speak the language, not to mention I've never left the United States except to go to Canada with Jules and her parents a couple of times.

That left North Carolina. The only place I ever truly felt safe and at home. Julia's parents have a beach house in the

Outer Banks, a town called Corolla, and they brought me with them for two weeks every summer. Sometimes we'd go for the week between Christmas and New Year's, too.

It was during my time visiting North Carolina that I felt whole. Real. Loved. Really loved and worthy of that love. As I stare at the screen, a wave of memories from the Outer Banks wash over me. I don't know how long I've sat here before Julia walks back into my room, scaring the crap out of me.

"North Carolina, huh?" she asks, and I nearly jump off my bed, making her laugh. "Sorry, I didn't mean to startle you."

Settling back onto the pale blue comforter, I take one last glance at our list. "I think so. It's the only place I ever truly felt at home. I mean, besides your house and GG's." I feel a stab of guilt for saying that, but it's honest, and Jules knows it.

"I know, Lanes." She rubs her hands together and sits down. "All right, let's do this."

"Do what?" I eye her cautiously.

"Well, let's figure out where in North Carolina. You know you're always welcome to stay at the beach house, but I'm not sure the Outer Banks is the best place either. It's too quiet around there in the off season."

"Jules, it's not like I plan on going clubbing. Maybe quiet is just what I need?"

Blatantly ignoring me, she gets to work. "As I said, my parents would love to have you stay there where they can keep tabs on you, but let's talk about this first. Maybe a compromise? Something by the water but still close enough that I can get to you ... ah, I mean visit you without the six-hour drive from an airport. Somewhere close enough to city life that it doesn't become a complete ghost town in the winter. Let's look along the coast." She does a little shimmy-shake; research is her drug of choice.

I know what she means. I may have been her protector all

these years, but she's become my savior in the last year and a half. She said "*get*" to me in case I break down again, and I love her for it.

"Fine, Miss Google, let's find me a job and a place to live." *I can't believe I agreed to this.*

Two hours later, Julia squeals again. "Lanie, I have the perfect town ... see how cute these pictures are? It's called Waverley-Cay, and it's only about an hour and a half away from the Coastal Carolina Airport."

It looks like a cute, little vineyard town but fancier somehow.

"You have to read their little town paper; it sounds like ours. Miss Popper, whoever she is, must be quite the town gossip, just like our Miss Rosa." She wiggles her eyebrows, and I laugh. "I don't think there's a single piece of actual news here, but I can tell you about the church dinner and who got caught on a date last week. This is too much."

Good Lord. *Do I really want to trade one small town for another?* I know what small-town life is like here, so maybe it will be nice having that same familiarity, albeit with warmer weather and the ocean.

"I've also been thinking about your job situation. You want something temporary, right? Why don't you consider nannying like you did in college?"

I bolt upright. "I hadn't even thought about that. A nanny gig for a year would be perfect."

"Mmhmm, I even found some placement agencies in between my work calls."

"You did? So, you knew I was going to pick North Carolina, huh? Am I that predictable?"

"No. You're not." Julia smiles. "But you can't know someone your entire life and not come to the same conclusions sometimes."

"This. This right here," I say, pointing between the two of us, "is one of the many reasons I luvs you, Jules."

Two weeks, and several phone conversations with the nanny placement agency later, I'm packing up my belongings into my old but trusty silver Toyota Corolla. Jules and Charlie are standing by, waiting to give me the thousandth hug of the day.

I lean in and hug them tight. "It's only a year, and you'll visit, right? We can FaceTime every day!"

Jules tries not to cry, but I see the tears. "Every day. This move will be so good for you, Lanie, really good. I can feel it."

With one more hug for each of them, I climb into my car and set off on my fifteen-hour journey to North Carolina.

CHAPTER 2

DEX

"*Molly!*"

"Yes, sir?"

My assistant walks around the corner appearing as frazzled as I feel.

Since nanny number three quit two weeks ago, I've been asking the impossible of her. Molly is in her fifties, and while she's the best damn assistant I've ever had, children are not in her wheelhouse.

"Were you just asking Emily how to shut a baby up?" I ask, knowing Emily is her partner and also happens to be a kindergarten teacher.

Molly shrugs but has the grace to look chagrined. "I didn't exactly say shut up, but Emily is much more capable of handling this ... ah, stuff ... than I am."

I get the feeling Molly is at the end of her rope; this was certainly not in her job description. I have to find a new nanny soon, and it can't just be any nanny. I'll be leaving for London in two weeks, so it has to be the perfect nanny. Hell, it needs to be someone I can trust implicitly with my children. I hate that I'll be leaving them with a virtual stranger.

I also know that if I don't make this meeting and the deal

goes south, my company is in trouble. I need this venture to be successful for my employees and my family. Christ, the company succeeding is the reason we just moved into this ridiculously large house.

It was time to move out of the townhome. Get away from all the memories of Bitchzilla—the name we've given my ex-wife. I never call her that in front of the kids, though. As much as I hate her, I'll never talk ill of her to my children.

Who the hell walks away from their children? *Your mother and your wife,* says the nagging voice inside of my head. I can't think of her right now, or ever for that matter. She's dead to me.

"What time is it?" I lost my watch in the last diaper change. I'm losing my shit here. Twins are tough, but feverish, baby twins are brutal. It's times like this that I'm so thankful for my little, six-year-old boy. Tate has always been a people pleaser.

Molly gives me an expression I can't quite read ... and I'm not sure if I want to. If I did, I'm afraid I'd learn she's five minutes away from quitting, and I can't have that, so I look away.

"4:52, sir."

"Shit, where is this girl?" I know her interview isn't until five, but I'm antsy and exhausted. Harper and Sara had me up at least six times last night. "What's her name again?" I ask Molly, and I'm pretty sure she just rolled her eyes at me.

"Lanie. Her name is Lanie," Molly says stiffly.

I glance up at her. She's in a pants suit, and it looks as though there might be green peas on the lapel. Man, I hope it's green peas and not the contents of Harper's diaper ... again. Pointing at her jacket, I cringe. "I'll pay to have that cleaned, Molly."

She peers down and grimaces. Maybe I shouldn't have said anything. It doesn't seem as if she even knew it was there.

"Yes, you will." Molly whips her head up almost like she can't believe she said that out loud, and quickly adds, "Thank you."

I give her a quick nod. "Lanie. What the hell kind of name is Lanie? Is it short for something?"

"I don't believe so, sir. They just buzzed her in at the gate, she'll be arriving momentarily." Efficient as always.

I moved us out of the townhome we lived in uptown and into a gated community. Everyone thought it was best for the safety of my family, but I still feel like a jackass every time I come through the gates.

If—no, *when*—this deal goes through, I will become more of a target, not just in Charlotte but also in New York, London, LA ... anywhere with a corporate financial presence will know me by year's end. Except, this is Waverley-Cay for Christ's sake, not the ghetto. The median home price in this neighborhood is a million-plus. Knowing I have other things I need to focus on right now, I groan.

Maybe we'll grow to love this ostentatious money pit, but I doubt it. In a year, maybe two, the company will be running smoothly. Then I can slowly bring us back down to earth and find a more realistic family home.

I sigh, and Molly turns her attention to me again, this time with concern. When I get back from London, I need to give her a raise. A big one. And maybe a vacation.

"Can you give me the quick rundown on her?" *Shit, what was her name?*

Molly lets out a sigh of her own and recites the details from memory. "Lanie Heart. Twenty-six. From Burke Mountain, Vermont. She graduated second in her class at Boston University with a degree in social work. She worked as a nanny in Brookline, Massachusetts, during her last two years of college. Once she graduated, she worked for the State of Vermont. There is no work history for the last eighteen months. From what I could find, it seems there was a major accident of some sort and she was severely injured. However, the records are sealed because a minor was involved. I asked Ryan to look into her, and the preliminary report is that she was injured trying to save the child. No more details were readily available. She has remarkable references, most notably a letter of personal reference from Maxine and Pete McDowell."

My head whips up. "The lawyers?"

I remember them from law school. They had a firm in Boston and won an unprecedented case that we studied in my first year. I became enamored with their skills in the courtroom and the way they worked together as attorneys and in life. In my second and third years, I followed their careers and became dumbfounded to learn they sold their practice when they were in their early forties and moved to some small town to practice family law.

"Yes, sir. It seems she has known them most of her life. Would you like to see the letter?"

Just then, the doorbell rings, and Harper—who is in my arms asleep—lets out a shriek that could break glass throughout the house. I need to unhook that goddamn doorbell. It plays some ridiculous song and goes on for far too long.

I look over at Molly. "Yes, please. Just put it on my desk ... ah, at some point."

Harper's screams are inconsolable. I know because I have been trying for two weeks, but once she starts, she goes on for hours. *Can kids have colic at eleven months?* I peek down at my beautiful baby girl and soften. I have to remember it's not her fault.

"Molly, can you get the door, please? I'll try to get her calmed down."

"Yes, sir."

I peek back down at Harper. "Please, baby girl, don't scare off this nanny, too. I hate to admit it, but I need help."

Harper just stares at me and keeps on screaming.

Sighing, I put her on my hip. I'm not sure when I became the man who sighs so much. I hear Molly coming down the hall, talking. When I look up, my chest constricts. *What the hell?*

"Mr. Cross, Lanie Heart to see you." Molly stares at me like I have three heads, and maybe I do, but I can't seem to form words. "Okay, well, I'll leave you two to it then?" my assistant says quizzically. "Sara is in the contraption on the kitchen floor, and Tate is sitting at the table doing homework," she reminds me as she turns, leaving me staring at Lanie Heart.

Lanie Heart is beautiful, gorgeous even. I've never hurt for a woman's attention, though it has been years since I've been affected by one. When the business took off—thankfully, after Bitchzilla left—women were continually inundating me with unwanted attention. But I'm no idiot. While I know I'm good looking, I also know they see a handsome face covered in dollar signs.

No fucking thank you!

Lanie Heart stands there with her hands on her hips and her head tilted to the side. She's staring between Harper and me, and I can't read what she's thinking. I can always read people, which makes her dangerous for all kinds of reasons.

She's wearing skinny jeans that cause her legs to continue for miles, matched with a T-shirt that says, 'The Northeast Kingdom.'

What is the Northeast Kingdom, some sort of video game? I make a mental note to Google that later. She isn't in anything fancy, and yet the perfect fitting T-shirt has my blood running south. As if I need more reasons to be attracted to her, she has long, dirty blonde hair and the bluest eyes I've ever seen.

Hiring this girl will not work. I can't have her living in my house. Nothing good will come of that.

Shit, how long have I been staring at her? She seems to be laughing at me and about to take action. Lanie heads straight for me just as Molly walks back in.

"Mr. Cross, it's nice to meet you. It seems like you have your hands full." Jesus, even her voice sounds like a melody.

I watch like a fly on the wall as she comes toe-to-toe with me. She's tall. Really fucking tall. I'm six foot five, and she has to be at least six feet. Harper, who is still screaming in my arms, reaches for her.

Wait, what the hell? The pediatrician said she is going through something called stranger danger and hasn't let anyone but me hold her in two months. That's part of the reason I keep losing nannies. Not that I can blame them, but it's their job, so they should be able to handle her.

I can't take my eyes off Lanie Heart as she scoops up Harper, scanning the room with a scrunched-up nose. I take a covert glance around to determine what she sees—boxes and boxes of shit. Toys and baby gear are covering every available surface. As I scan the room, I realize Harper has stopped crying.

Glancing down at her, then back to Lanie Heart with wide eyes, I can't help but wonder what the hell is going on. Lanie Heart is smiling at Harper and kissing her cheeks, and my daughter is ... laughing? Seriously, she's laughing? I look back to Lanie Heart, and she has apparently had enough of my blundering. She turns, again searching the room, and asks, "Which way to the kitchen?"

Molly and I both point through the doorway, dumbstruck, as Lanie Heart starts walking away, cuddling a now quiet Harper.

Molly has come up beside me, so I glance down at her and whisper, "Who is she, fucking Mary Poppins?"

Molly begins to answer when I realize I said it louder than intended because Lanie Heart turns her head over her shoulder and answers me.

"I prefer Maria, but I promise not to cut up your curtains for play clothes." She glances around the room one more time. "Unless I find you dress them in suits and party dresses twenty-four-seven." Giving me a crooked smile, she walks through the door.

"What the hell is she talking about, who is Maria?" Molly wonders out loud.

Turning to Molly, I almost smile. "I think she just made a *Sound of Music* reference." And she isn't shy about calling me out either. This could be bad. Very, very bad. I discreetly adjust myself and follow the path that Lanie 'Maria' Heart just walked.

CHAPTER 3

LANIE

Holy shit, holy shit, holy shit. Mr. Cross is hot. Like hotter than hot. Completely disheveled with dark hair a little too long and wild above his deep, green eyes. He's so tall, he makes me feel small, and that's no easy feat. I can't even describe the wall of muscle that was his chest when I grabbed Harper from his arms.

Seriously, Lanie, you just took a man's daughter out of his hands and walked away! I don't know what the heck happened back there, but I now have a calm baby on my hip, and I'm walking toward the kitchen, I think. This house is freaking nuts. Who needs a home this big? *Focus, Lanie.*

I heard the woman named Molly say Sara and Tate were in the kitchen, so I'm heading that way. I had walked into what I can only describe as a war zone. Mr. Cross was standing with a half-dressed, screaming baby. Lord knows what is covering the front of his dress shirt. Or why he was standing in the middle of hundreds of boxes. There were toys everywhere and makeshift diaper changing stations all over the room. While it looks like the house will eventually be tastefully decorated, I can't help but wonder how long they've lived here.

I don't officially have the job, but I took pity on him. The least I can do is help get the kids settled. I walk around the corner and come across the cutest little boy crouched down next to a smiling replica of the baby girl in my arms.

"Hey, buddy," I say, walking over to him.

He looks up at me and frowns.

O-kay, not the greeting I usually get with kids. I think back to the file Molly emailed me earlier. His name is Tate, and he is six years old. He's been having a tough time since his mom left. I quickly wonder where the heck she would have gone. *How can you leave Mr. Sexy Pants and these beautiful children?*

I shut that train of thought down immediately. I can't start thinking of Mr. Cross as Mr. Sexy Pants, or I'll say something inadvertently. I know myself and lack of filter at times.

Glancing around the kitchen, I notice it's similar to the disaster I found Harper in. *Oh boy, what have I gotten myself into?* Another quick scan of the room and I decide it's time to get to work.

"Hey, buddy, my name's Lanie."

He scowls again. He's so much like his father, it's scary.

"Listen, I know you're probably not psyched to be meeting someone new again, and it's okay. I get it, trust me. But here's the thing, I'm pretty sure your sister is getting her top teeth. That's pretty painful for babies, so I'm going to need you to help me out for a minute."

His big, grey-green eyes soften slightly, and he nods once.

Okay, note to self, he likes helping. I tuck that away for use later. I'm vaguely aware of eyes on me but decide to focus and get this situation handled.

"Do you know if you have any of those super soft baby washcloths?" I ask him as I'm pulling open the door to the freezer.

He doesn't answer me, just nods again and makes a move to what I'm guessing is a bathroom.

While he's on his mission, I search through the mostly empty contents of the freezer and pull out what I'm looking for—frozen peas. I hold them up in victory and hear a quick, brief bark of laughter. That's when I remember I have an audience. Taming the horrid blush rushing over my cheeks, I turn and give Tate a fist bump just as he hands me the small, pink cloths.

"Thanks, buddy! Can you open this bag of peas for me?"

He gives me a little side-eye but again nods his head.

"Lanie Heart."

I hear my name in a low, silky voice that makes me blush like a schoolgirl. I know it belongs to Mr. Cross, but I can't bring myself to face him. Jules always tells me I can't hide anything in my facial expressions, and she's probably right, so I keep my head down. Instead of glancing up at him, I interrupt whatever he was about to say by holding up my hand and hear a small gasp. This time, I think it came from Molly.

"Hold, please ... let me get this butterball settled, then we can talk." Did I seriously just basically tell this man to shut it in his own home? I dare sneak a glance, and both he and Molly stare on with open mouths. Ah, hell. I bet no one talks to Mr. Tall, Dark, and Slightly Scary this way, but I've already done it. I might as well own it, so I commit whole-heartedly.

I turn to Tate as I'm wetting the little, pink cloth. "Hey, Tate, did you just get home from school?"

He nods once.

"Have you had a snack yet?"

He shakes his head and peers at the doorway like he's checking to make sure that is all right.

Allowing myself a quick glance, I see Mr. Hot Pants smile at Tate. Oh hell. Scowling, he's sexy, but that smile leaves me breathless. Why is he affecting me like this? No one has ever gotten me worked up like this before. *Focus, Lanie, geez!*

I move the damp cloth to the counter and lay it flat. While I'm dumping a small pile of frozen peas in the center, I turn back to Tate. "Do you know where the snacks are, buddy?"

He nods.

"That's great. I can tell you're a great helper already. Why don't you grab a snack you're usually allowed to have and bring it over to the table? It looks like you're doing homework?"

Another nod of his head.

"Is it going well, or do you need help?"

He shocks me when he says very quietly, "I can do it."

I whip around and smile at him. "I thought so, but first, can you help me with one more thing?"

"Yes," he whispers, and I smile to myself. His file said he didn't talk at home to anyone but his dad, and even then, it was rare.

"Awesome-sauce." I give him a little fist bump, and his lip twitches.

"Can you pick up this cloth and twist all the ends together like a little pouch so I can wrap my hair elastic around it?" He gets to his task while I gently sway Harper from side to side and grab the elastic off my wrist. While he holds it, I wrap the elastic around until it's secure.

"Thanks, Tate-o-nator."

He smiles and walks off to the pantry, while I turn my attention to Harper.

"Ms. Lanie Heart, I—"

I cut him off again. "Almost ready, Mr. Dexter Cross. I'll be right with you." I hear Molly snort. Oh shit, I will never get this job if I can't stop sassing him. Peeking over at Tate, I see he's sitting down at the table, giggling. My gaze finds Mr. Hot Pants, and his eyes are darting everywhere with his mouth hanging open.

25

Noticing an empty baby bouncer next to him and Sara, I give Harper my makeshift teething ring and walk that way. His eyes are on me the entire way, and I'm transfixed. I can't look away even if I wanted to.

I don't know what comes over me, but as I walk past him, I place my fingers under his chin to close his mouth. His eyes snap to me, then to Molly, who appears completely flabbergasted. As I bend down to put Harper in her seat, it seems he's finally come to his senses.

"Ms. Lanie Heart, Harper won't sit in that thing. She'll just scream. Give her to me." His voice carries an edge of annoyance, and something else I can't place.

Instead of listening, I go about buckling her in, and he makes a sound that I could swear was a growl. A growl? No, now I'm just making things up, but the expression on Molly's face informs me maybe I'm not wrong. Making sure Harper has her teething ring, I turn to Sara, who I can smell from a mile away, and pick her up.

"What in the ever living fu-udge is going on?" Mr. Cross bellows. I'm impressed he caught himself before hurling an f-bomb in front of his kids, but his loud, scary demeanor immediately puts me on alert. Without a second thought, I stand between him and Harper, positioning Sara to my other side. I know I'm shaking, but I didn't even feel myself move in front of the babies. *Keep them safe.* Some instincts never go away.

Mr. Cross stares down at me and his eyes soften. He takes a step back. Julia's right. I can't hide anything in my facial expressions. He knows he has terrified me, so he puts his hands up in surrender, and softens his voice. "Ms. Lanie Heart—"

"Just Lanie," I interject, and now realize that being interrupted is something that rarely happens to Mr. Dexter Cross.

He sighs and starts again. "Lanie, I apologize for my outburst."

Now it's Molly's turn to gasp. Apparently, apologies don't fall very often from that sexy as sin mouth either, and I realize I'm smiling. Best of all, Tate is giggling again.

Mr. Cross seems to have noticed and peeks over at him. Tate stops immediately, and I see Mr. Cross's face drop. "Let me start again. You're like a whirlwind and I don't know what's going on. You don't have the job yet; we haven't even had the interview. You do realize this, yes?"

I can't help myself as I roll my eyes, which causes his to narrow in on me. Does he look pissed? Turned on? *Wishful thinking, Lanie. Wishful thinking.* I settle on pissed. Definitely pissed. I have to backtrack if I want this job. "Yes, Mr. Cross—"

"Call me Dex."

Molly takes an audible breath. If I didn't know better, I would think he's starting to blush, but as quickly as it started, it's gone.

"All right, Dex. Yes, I know I don't have the job. I do realize we have not conducted the interview yet. However, I walked in on a ship-sandwich and figured I would help you get things under control so you can undoubtedly ask every question known to man. I'm sure you'll want to check out my abilities to care for your children. Which, by the way, I would do exceptionally, but back to my point. You cannot ask me all these questions with babies crying and Tate starving." I look over to Tate, who is bug-eyed, and give him a little wink, which makes him crack up again.

"Okay, okay. Fine. Uh, thanks? Do you plan to do anything else, or can we start the interview now?"

"Well, Sara smells like a sewer, so why don't I change her and make sure all three are settled down for Molly?"

Molly's eyes widen in what I assume is fear. I reach over and squeeze her arm. She's definitely not a fan of kids.

"It's all right. I'll make sure everyone is happy and quiet before I leave them in here with you."

Molly glares at me, then gives a tight smile. "Very well," she says, taking a seat at the island, supervising.

"Now, Mr. Cross. Why don't you go into your office and I'll meet you there in five minutes?" Maybe I did come on too strong because he looks as if he's in a daze.

"Ah, okay. I'll see you in five minutes." He walks backward, eyes roaming all around the room, then bumps into the wall and quickly rights himself. "Right, five minutes."

I turn away and move to Tate so I can help him open his snack. Covertly, I scan his homework and realize he does seem to have it under control. After changing Sara, I set her up in the seat next to a sleeping Harper and take out my phone. I put on baby Mozart and leave it on the counter.

"Are you all set?" I ask Molly.

She stares at me, bewildered, and nods her head.

A lot of head nodders in this house. I laugh and head to Mr. Sexy Smirk's office.

CHAPTER 4

DEX

Before I sit down behind my large, maple desk, I have to adjust myself again, and it pisses me off.

What in the actual fuck is happening? My dick is acting like a fifteen year old seeing boobs for the first time. Thank God I have the desk to hide behind. After picking up the file on Lanie Heart, I flip through it quickly. She reads too good to be true.

"What has she been doing for the last eighteen months?" I whisper. As I read one of her many letters of recommendation, I hear music. *What the hell kind of music is that? And who turned it on?*

Well, that was a stupid question. Even if I hadn't said it out loud, it could only be the tornado of a woman who waltzed in here like she owns the place. No one else would have. Then, out of nowhere, she's standing in the doorway.

"Is that ... music?" I ask foolishly.

She tilts her head to the side, just like when she first walked into the house.

Why does she look at me like that? More importantly, why is my body having such an intense reaction to her? I can't be interested in her. In fact, she should be pissing me off. Not only did she interrupt me multiple times, but she also closed my damn mouth, for fuck's sake. And now she's staring at me with raised eyebrows like she is waiting for an answer.

Shit. Now what did she say? "I'm sorry, you're completely … unexpected. What did you say?"

She smirks, and this time it does piss me off—I wish my dick would get the memo. "I asked if you were ready to begin?" Lanie Heart asks with a hint of a smile.

Jesus, this is not how this works. She isn't interviewing me! I need to get a handle on this and quickly. "Fucking Mary Poppins."

Her laugh startles me. *Shit, did I say that out loud?*

"I told you before. I'm more of a Maria," she explains, a broad smile taking over her face.

Oh, hell. That answers my question. Something is going on with me. I'm usually more controlled than this. She cannot come in here, tilt my world, and fuck everything up. I won't allow it, so I scowl at her, and she laughs again.

Expelling a long, slow breath, I throw my pen down on the desk. Screw it. This will undoubtedly be the most unconventional interview I have ever conducted in my entire life. Something tells me if I hire Ms. Lanie Heart, my life will never be conventional again, and my spine tingles at the revelation.

I shake my head, attempting to clear it of those errant thoughts. "All right, Ms. Lanie Heart—"

"Just Lanie," she interrupts again.

Shit, why do I keep calling her by her first and last name? Sleep deprivation? That has to be it. That's why this entire encounter is so fucked up.

"Lanie, on paper, you're more than qualified to be a nanny."

She bristles at that.

I briefly wonder why she would stiffen at such a

mundane statement, but carry on, "Why aren't you interested in continuing in social work?"

She relaxes slightly. "Well, Mr. Dexter Cross ..."

Is she doing that to mess with me? She has to be. It should irritate the living hell out of me. But before I can school my features, my lip quirks up.

"The burnout rate for a social worker, especially one working with children, is exceptionally high. I love kids, and I love working with them." She turns her gaze to the floor, sadness filling her beautiful, blue eyes. When she looks up at me, the warmth in her face vanishes as she speaks. "I realized pretty quickly that I was not cut out to deal with some of the cases you, unfortunately, come across in that field."

"What is your long-term goal here?" I ask her more sharply than intended.

"Sir?"

That one word has my cock stirring in my pants again, and I realize I like her calling me sir ... a lot! This is so messed up.

She's here for you kids, Cross, not you.

"Ah," clearing my throat, I try again, "do you plan to return to social work? You're coming from Vermont, correct? Do you plan to use your degree here in the Carolinas?"

For the first time since she walked in here, she seems uneasy. *Why?* I can't help but think this should be an easy question, but her eyes shift away from me before she answers.

"Um, yes, I'm coming from Vermont, but no, I don't plan to continue in social work," Lanie replies, her voice devoid of any emotion.

"Why not?"

"I'm just not cut out for it," she says barely above a whisper.

"Why not?" I repeat.

Lanie is silent for a long minute. When she looks up, the floor drops out from below me. There are tears in her eyes and I have no doubt I can see right through to her soul.

"I'm not emotionally equipped to handle such severe cases of abuse," she states, her voice raw with feeling.

I believe her, but I also get the sense that it's not a complete answer. I won't push, though. I know from experience I couldn't handle child abuse cases either.

"Okay, Lanie, I see you're CPR and first aid certified?"

"Yes."

There's my girl. Where the fuck did that thought come from?

"And you have excellent references," I say out loud to no one in particular.

"Is that a question, Mr. Dexter Cross?" Her sass shocks me.

I stare across the desk at her, unwilling to tame the lift of my lips. "No, Ms. Lanie Heart, I suppose it's not."

"Where is the children's mother?" she asks so bluntly I don't have time to gather myself.

"She left. And she won't be coming back," I bark. Obviously, she needs to know the basics if I hire her, but who the hell does she think she is, and why do I keep letting her control this interview?

"I know the girls are too small, but does Tate know that?" she pushes.

Now I'm getting pissed again. "Yes."

"Does he know it isn't his fault?"

If I say *what the fuck* one more time today, my head might explode. She's staring at me, honestly expecting me to answer. Even my scowl doesn't seem to affect her. I can make grown men crumble in board rooms with this glare, and she doesn't even bat an eye.

"He knows what he needs to know," I finally say.

"Have you told him it's not his fault?" Lanie repeats. "I

read the file Molly sent over, and it says he rarely speaks. Do you know what his last conversation with his mother entailed? In my experience—"

"Your limited work experience or life experience?" I bark, barely containing my anger.

She stares at me for a long while before answering. I get the impression she's sizing me up. "Both," she explains quietly, and I feel like an asshole. "My mother did the best she could, but she was unstable most of my life. She said things—" She stops mid-sentence, and I can tell she's working hard to swallow.

Not only am I an asshole, but I'm also a pervert because now I can't stop thinking about her long, slender neck. How would she react to my tongue on it? I snap my gaze to her eyes and I'm caught in her spell. Completely unable to control myself, an instant later, I'm back to studying her neck. I swear I can see her pulse racing from here.

Interesting. Maybe my bizarre reaction isn't as one-sided as I thought.

My trance is broken when she speaks again. "My mother often told me all the wrongs in her life were my fault. In my *'limited work experience',*" she uses air quotes as she recites my earlier douchey comment back to me, "I saw a lot of the same behaviors with troubled mothers and their children."

"My ex-wife isn't troubled. She's just a bitch," I blurt. Immediately, I place the back of my hand to my head as I do with the kids. I must be getting sick. There's no other explanation for these uncharacteristic outbursts.

"Be that as it may, if you haven't spoken to him, I don't think it would hurt. Children rarely stick to their guns for as long as Tate has without reason." Her stubborn insistence grabs my attention.

Did I talk to him? Yes, I know I had. The night she left, we sat and talked over pizza.

But he hadn't stopped talking at that point, the asshat voice in my head reminds me. How dare she question my parenting? I've been doing the best I can. She has no right to judge me.

As if reading my mind, she speaks. "Mr. Dexter Cross?"

"Jesus. Just call me Dex," I all but yell, and gone is the confident, young woman from a moment ago. The woman before me is in fight or flight mode, so I try to backtrack.

"Look, I'm sorry. This is a challenging time for me. I shouldn't be raising my voice at you. To be honest, Ms. Lanie Heart, I'm not sure what it is about our interactions making me react like I am. I don't do outbursts. I'm generally more composed, always in complete control. I'm sorry if I've startled you. My only explanation is that my company is in the middle of acquiring, or attempting to acquire, a company in London. If I can make that happen, life will be much more comfortable for me, my family, and my employees."

I wasn't lying when I said I don't do outbursts. It's what makes me so dangerous in the boardroom. I'm controlled. I'm calm. *Jesus, maybe I caught whatever Harper has.*

Lanie's focused on her lap when she mumbles something I don't quite catch.

"What was that, Ms. Lanie Heart?"

Sighing, she aims her gaze to the ceiling. "Shiplap."

I raise an eyebrow at her in question. When she doesn't respond, I ask, "Did you just say shiplap? Didn't you also say earlier that you walked into a ship-sandwich?" I don't even try to hide the smirk taking over my face.

Jesus, this girl is unexpected. She flushes bright red from the tips of her ears down her neck to her barely visible cleavage. I snap my eyes back to hers. *Do not get caught ogling the nanny, asshat.*

"Ugh." She slaps a hand over her eyes. "Honestly?"

"I do value honesty above all else, Ms. Lanie Heart." I feel my face transforming into a full-on smile. When was the last time I smiled at someone I hadn't created like I am at Lanie

Heart? *Seriously, why does my brain insist on referring to her with both her first and last names?*

"Okay, full disclosure." She flashes an awkward smile. "I swear like a drunken sailor … in my head. I haven't sworn out loud since I was ten. Now it just comes out in the most ridiculously PG statements."

The bark of laughter that comes out of me is so surprising that I don't bother trying to contain it. Composing myself, I ask, "What happened when you were ten?"

Lanie Heart considers my question for a minute as she scans my face. "My mother's boyfriend happened." She looks away, and I suddenly have an unreasonable amount of anger toward this boyfriend. When she notices my hands balled into fists, I make a show of flexing them, forcing them to relax.

"Care to elaborate?" I ask in as calm a voice as I can muster.

"No." She looks away purposefully so I can't read her expression.

That's it, just no. Lanie stares straight ahead.

"Ms. Lanie Heart?" I need those eyes on me again.

"Just Lanie," she answers softly, and I smile.

"Okay, just Lanie. I'm entrusting my future nanny with the welfare of my children. There has to be a level of trust and understanding between myself and whomever I hire."

"I agree. I also believe there's a line between employee and employer. Not everything is for quenching an employer's curiosity." She got me there.

"Touché, Lanie, touché." Clearing my throat, I force my brain to focus. "Getting back on track. Vermont is awfully far away. How can I be sure you won't get homesick and leave me hanging?"

The smile on her face sends a bolt of sunlight straight to

my blackened heart. She gives me a sly smile before speaking, and it makes me feel like I'm about to be told her deepest, darkest secrets.

"Well, Dex, as you can assume, I didn't have the best family life growing up. That doesn't mean I didn't have examples of healthy relationships, though. My best friend's parents were always there when I needed them. Actually, they're more like the family I never had, even though my mother was physically present most of the time. Maxine and Pete McDowell, my friend's parents, took me under their wing. I don't know that I would have been able to attend college without their help and support." Her eyes shift, and I notice her hands are clasped tightly in her lap.

"Anyway," she continues, "they have a house in the Outer Banks. I have spent weeks at a time there since I was ten years old. I love North Carolina, and to be honest, I need to be here right now. I won't lie and say I'll be here forever, so don't go falling in love with me, Mr. Cross." She smirks and gives me a wink before a blush crosses her fair skin once again, and she quickly continues, "However, I will sign a contract to stay for one full year."

A lot happened to this girl when she was ten. I can't begin to imagine what her life has been like. I should also be concerned that it irritates me when she says she needs to be here, not *wants* to be here. I'll focus on that another time, though. *Most importantly, why did I feel sucker-punched when she told me not to fall in love with her?* Not that it would ever be a possibility. I'm not giving my heart away again, ever. Period. She'll stay for one year and then we'll part ways. *Stop thinking about why that makes your heart ache, Cross.*

The way she's looking at me, I realize I've been too harsh and cut her a break. "I don't know the McDowells personally, but I did study their careers when I was in law school. They're remarkable attorneys."

She nods in agreement. "They're even more amazing humans."

The warmth in her voice tells me all I need to know about her relationship with the McDowells. "Okay, Ms. Lanie Heart. I think we can agree you are extremely qualified, and we all saw how my children respond to you. That's not something I take lightly. Could you briefly fill me in on what you've been doing for the last eighteen months?"

The color drains from her face and she fidgets in her chair. Surely, she was expecting this question, right? An eighteen-month gap in your work history? *It's a reasonable question to ask, right?*

So, why do I feel like the world's biggest asshole?

Then my blood runs cold at her response.

"Recovering," she responds in a shaky voice.

Leaning forward in my chair, I force my voice to remain calm. "You were in an accident?"

Lanie shrugs. "Sure."

I feel the frown creep across my lips. *Sure? What kind of answer is that?* I can tell by her blank stare that I won't get any more information from her on this. I also know I cannot hire her to care for my children without knowing. I'll have to buy some time for my guy Ryan from EnVision Securities to dig into this further.

"What's your plan now that you're here? Are you interviewing with other families?" *Over my dead body,* the voice in my head shouts, *you're mine.* I feel my forehead again. What in the ever-living hell is going on with me?

Lanie throws her hair over one shoulder. "Not this week. When I leave here, I'm driving to Corolla to stay at my friend's beach house for a few days. I love it there. It always makes me feel at home."

"Corolla?" I almost leap from my leather chair. "That's at least six hours from here." Glancing at my phone, I see it's already six-thirty. *Has she been here that long? Shit, should I pay her?* "You won't get there until one in the morning!"

She stares at me, blinking slowly.

"Molly will get you a room in town for the night so you can leave at a reasonable hour," I insist.

Lanie's head raises to glare at me with narrowed eyes. "Wait, what?"

Oh boy, she looks pissed.

"She will do no such thing. I'm perfectly capable of taking care of myself. I will be driving to the beach. Tonight! Do you have any more questions for me, Mr. Dexter Cross?" she spits.

What can I say? I have no control over this woman. I have a feeling I would never have control of her, even if she were mine, and the thought makes my insides warm. *Mine.*

Cut the shit, Cross.

"No, Ms. Lanie Heart. No more questions. I plan to follow up with your references and will be in touch soon. Thank you for coming ... and thank you for your help today. I can't believe the girls are still sleeping. I'm not going to lie, though; it scares me for tonight."

She graces me with a small smile, and I feel like the king of the castle again.

"They're teething, Mr. Dexter Cross," she tells me kindly. "Harper's top gums are swollen. Sara looks like she has one on the bottom left just about to break the skin. Give them some infant Tylenol before bedtime. If they wake up in the middle of the night, just remake the teething pouch I showed you earlier. That will help the inflammation in their gums. I would suggest you go on to Amazon and purchase some teething rings and real pouches ASAP, though. You're going to need them, and I didn't see any in my quick look around."

I feel myself still wearing a smile as I walk her to the door. "Thank you, Lanie."

"You're welcome, Dex." Her smile doesn't quite meet her eyes as she walks out the door, and I fear it's my fault.

I hear Molly's heels coming down the hallway, but I turn to go back to my office. She watches as I head to the window and peer out just in time to see Lanie pounding her forehead on her steering wheel. And just like that, I'm smiling. Again. Good, at least I wasn't the only one to be affected by this fucked up afternoon.

"Sir?"

Tearing my gaze away from the window, I face Molly. She looks how I feel. That's when I realize "Girls Just Want to Have Fun" is blaring from a bright pink phone case.

"Lanie forgot her phone ... and if you don't hire that girl, I quit."

My head snaps to attention. She can't be serious.

As if reading my thoughts, she adds, "As a heart attack."

"Understood. But you can't quit. I need you. I'm just not sure yet if Lanie Heart is the best one for the job given her background." There are so many reasons that would make hiring Lanie Heart a colossal mistake, but I can't tell Molly that. Instead, I take the phone from Molly's hand. "She's in the driveway. I'll bring it out to her."

~

"*R*yan speaking." He always sounds like a robot. Ryan Nicoles is a private investigator I recently hired and keep on retainer. Lately, his only job has been monitoring Bitchzilla, but that will have to wait for now.

"Ryan, it's Dexter. I need a report on Lanie Heart. The full report, whatever it takes. And I need it yesterday."

"It'll cost you. I already told Molly that the state sealed most of her file," he states monotonously.

"Just do what you need to do and get it to me. I can't hire

this woman to watch my kids without knowing everything." I leave no room for error in my tone.

"Consider it done."

"Thanks." My spine tingles again as I hang up the phone. I just don't know if it's in anticipation of what I'll find out or fear.

CHAPTER 5

LANIE

Mr. Sexy Bossy Pants was wrong. It didn't take six hours, it took eight, but I'm here. I let myself in with the key Mimi gave me when I turned sixteen, and an overwhelming sense of relief washes over me. I've never felt more at peace than I do when I'm here. I set my stuff down and scan the house. Mimi knew I hated the dark. She must have had the cleaning staff leave on every light in here. God, I love that woman.

Everything is exactly the way I remembered it. They stopped renting it out a few years ago because they plan to retire here someday, so there are more personal touches now than when we were kids. I walk over to the mantel in the family room full of photos, mainly of Charlie, Jules, and me. I don't remember my mother ever even owning a picture of me. Here, it's like I have always been a part of their family.

I set the frame I was holding down, turn to the windows that take up the entire backside of the house, and gape at the ocean. The waves here always calm me. They're nothing like the waves on Cape Cod. These waves are angry yet beautiful. I have a feeling that's also how people would describe me these days.

Reaching for my hair elastic on my wrist, I come up empty. I check the other wrist and realize I left it at Mr. Dexter Cross's house.

Dexter Cross.

After grabbing a throw blanket off the back of the couch, I head out to the deck. It's not the peak season yet, but there are a few Adirondack chairs out here, each weathered from the salt air. I sit down and pull my legs under me, and my hand lands on the engraving Jules and I did when we were about fourteen. 'Julia and Lanie. BFFs always'. I let my fingers caress the work of young teenagers while I think about the day's events.

I haven't ever responded to someone the way I did to Dexter. I know he was looking for information about the last year, but I couldn't tell him. Someday, I hope I'll be able to talk about everything that happened to me, but not to him. He's too intense. Too moody. Too fucking hot. If I'm being honest with myself, I won't blame him for not hiring me. I was a hot mess in there today, and his questions were not unexpected. If they were my children, I'd want answers, too.

God, those kids were beautiful. I felt uniquely connected to Tate, even though he barely spoke. There's something about him that drew me in. I have no doubt his non-verbal status has something to do with his mother; I just hope Dexter talks to him. *Shit. I really needed that job.*

I send Jules a quick text to let her know I'm here. I'm about to put my phone on the table when it dings with a response. I pinch my brows together when I see it's from a number I don't recognize. My breath catches when I open it.

Dexter: Lanie, this is Mr. Cross. The Tylenol and frozen peas have been a lifesaver. The girls are sleeping peacefully, but I have not been as lucky. Please let me know you have arrived in Corolla safely.

A ridiculous smile washes over my face as I reply.

Lanie: Mr. Dexter Cross. You'll no doubt be disap-

pointed to know it did not take me six hours to arrive ... it took eight. I just got in, safe and sound. Thank you for your concern. I'm happy the girls are resting comfortably.

I want to add something about his sleeping problem but know that would be crossing a line, so I hit send. His response bubbles start and stop multiple times. When I'm beginning to think he won't respond, he does.

Dexter: Just Dex. Have a good night.

I smile like a middle school girl with her first crush, but don't respond. I'm not sure what to say to that. If I answered, I'm afraid of where it might lead, so I put my phone down and head into to my bedroom.

Even though I grabbed my toiletries, I'm too tired for anything but brushing my teeth. Julia would kill me if she knew I was skipping my routine of washing off my makeup and applying moisturizer. She's nothing if not rigid in her habits, but exhaustion is hitting hard. Plopping down on the bed that was bought for me by the only example of parents I've ever had, I think about all that has brought me here.

I'm driving on a dirt road. I know the trailer is back here somewhere, I've just never been. This family is not a client of mine, but it's an emergency and I'm the closest. I read the file before heading over. I'm not sure what my colleague was thinking. I would have removed this little boy from his home long before now.

Finally, I find the driveway hiding between overgrown brush and pull in. The door hanging on its hinges makes my hair stand up on the back of my neck, but I pull on my big girl panties. There might be a little boy named Max in there that needs me. Slowly, I make my way toward the door and knock.

Inside, I see a little boy sitting under a table, so I call out, "Hello? Hey, buddy, are your parents home?"

He shakes his head and climbs farther under the table before speaking.

"You b-better go. My d-dad will be back s-soon, and he will h-hurt you for being here."

I make my way over the broken door and closer to Max. When we hear a car door slam, the little boy starts shaking. I know this isn't going to be pretty. I grab for Max and instruct him to hide under the sink.

"Whatever you do, Max, do not come out of this hiding spot for anything, no matter what you hear, until I or the police come to get you. Do you understand?"

With eyes wide and terrified, he tells me, "Y-Yes."

I back away from him while reaching for my phone to call 911. Before I can hit send, the phone is knocked forcefully from my hands.

"What the fuck do you think you're doing in my house, bitch? Where's my son?"

I can tell he's drunk; he's slurring and smells like a distillery. Now I am shaking, but I try to steal my nerve.

"I'm s-sorry, someone called the police. They just took him into town. I was waiting here to explain everything. I'm sorry for the intrusion. I'll just be on my way now."

I'm pushed hard into a wall.

"You're not going anywhere, you filthy whore."

I see the blade of a knife as he walks toward me. Then I feel the first cut, not deep enough to kill, just enough to cause pain. I get a blow to the head next, and instantly everything goes black.

I sit upright, covered in sweat. Crap, I must have fallen asleep. I'm not sure what wakes me, though. I usually have a difficult time escaping those nightmares. Checking my phone, I see it's only 4:58 a.m. I know I won't be able to fall back to sleep now, so I get myself up and make some coffee. I might as well start my day off watching the sunrise over the ocean. It's my favorite way to start the day anyway.

CHAPTER 6

DEX

It's been three days since Lanie Heart was here, and two since I got the report on her from Ryan. No wonder she didn't want to talk about it. After reading her file, I ran to the bathroom and was sick for a full hour. *She's stronger than she realizes.*

I think back to our interview. It was the craziest one I've ever conducted in my entire fucking life. I'll never forget how she jumped in between my daughters and me, protecting them. I would never hurt anyone, but she didn't know that.

She's not a small woman. Still, I outweigh her by at least fifty pounds, and she stood between perceived danger and my girls. I didn't understand why she seemed so ready to run when I raised my voice. After I read Ryan's file, it all made sense. She protected Max by enduring the abuse of her attacker, doing so in complete silence so she wouldn't scare the child. All because she wanted him to stay hidden.

I wish Ryan hadn't sent the pictures that painted her attack so vividly, though. I'll never get them out of my head. *She was so broken and bruised.* The report even lists all injuries; it takes up an entire page. She wasn't lying when she said she was recovering. She must have scars, too, although I didn't see any. *The animal took a knife to her.* My stomach roils again at the thought.

I'm sitting in my office in the corner chair with a glass of scotch perched on the end table, having just put the kids to bed. I filled the bookcases with law books, but the rest of the room is still in disarray. There are fewer boxes in this room. I just haven't had the time to organize any of it.

Dropping my head in my hands, I pull at my hair. Molly thinks I should hire Lanie, and she's probably right. I've gone strictly by paper for the last three nannies, and look how they worked out. Something in my gut tells me to hire Lanie, that she's the one even though her resume may be lacking.

The one for our nanny or the one for me? the nagging voice in my head keeps repeating. I need to shut that little pecker up.

I had texted the guys to come over after I tucked Tate in. It'll be about an hour before they arrive, so I stand up and head to my room for a quick shower, confident my childhood friends will know what to do.

Preston arrives first. If I were ever to use the word suave, it would be to describe him. "Are you living at the gym these days, Pres? If you're not careful, you'll end up looking like one of those Jersey Shore meatheads." As he walks through my house, I notice he's really starting to bulk up.

"Jealous, buddy? I can get you out of that Dad-bod in no time," Preston teases. He's full of shit. All four of us are in excellent shape. It's like an unspoken competition. We're all a little intimidating in our own ways. I'm about to give Preston a man hug when Loki arrives.

"Why didn't you guys drive together? You live in the same damn building."

"Pretty boy over there was taking too long," Preston laughs.

Loki is in his normal state. His hair slightly mussed, and

the five-o'clock shadow on prominent display. His wardrobe consists entirely of cargo pants and T-shirts.

Loki scowls. "Fuck off. I was working, and I left five minutes after you. You could have waited for me, dickhead."

"Okay, true, but I might have a date later," Preston explains through a lopsided grin.

"By date, you mean late-night hook-up," Loki points out.

"I don't miss those nights," I tell them. They never held the same appeal to me, and I have even less desire for them now.

"Maybe that's your issue, dude. You need to get laid." Pres is our resident man-whore these days. Loki rolls his eyes and goes to the fridge for a beer as Trevor walks in.

"What the hell, Trev?" Preston greets him. "You're the richest son of a bitch and you look homeless."

Leave it to Preston to call people out.

Trevor has a trust fund but has never touched it. The other guys don't know the shit his father has done. I can understand why he doesn't want the money—it's tainted. At the same time, he doesn't need to live like a pauper. His tech company is about to take off, I can feel it. He's the smartest out of the four of us, and it's only a matter of time.

"Fuck off, Pres. I'm not in the mood. What's up, Dex? It's been a long time since you've sent an SOS. You okay?" Trevor asks.

He always sees through my bullshit.

"What SOS? I just got a text saying beers at his house!" I love Preston like a brother, but sometimes he's an entitled asshole with his head in the clouds.

Loki hands us all beers, and we head into the family room. I've been able to get through a few boxes, but it's still a shit show. *Maybe I should have hired unpackers, too?* I just couldn't bring myself to spend money like that yet.

Trevor glances around and shakes his head. He takes a

long gulp of his beer before setting it down on the only empty table in the room and opens a box.

"If you called us here to unpack for you, I'm going to be pissed," Preston says, annoyed.

Loki shoves him. "Fuck off, Preston. He didn't call us here to help unpack, but since we're here, the least we can do is help."

"He has three small kids, so stop being a prick and get off your ass to help," Trevor insists.

We have all been friends for years. Trevor and I met Preston and Loki in grade school, but it's Trevor that I've always counted on. Trevor is Tate's godfather; he was also the first one there the night Anna left. He turns to me and frowns. "Dex, what's up? The last SOS was when Bitchzilla left."

I can't help but smile. "How long have you called Anna Bitchzilla? I know the name started well before she left."

"Dude, you know she always hated us." Loki shrugs. "We may have given her the name after senior prom when she wouldn't ride home in the limo with us."

He's right, Anna never liked these guys, and I wasn't willing to give them up.

"Dexter. Honest to God, why do those assholes have to come over here every Friday night?"

"Anna," I coo, walking around the table I'm setting up for poker to hug her "It's once a month. We all take turns."

"Ugh, I just figured once we got married, you'd get more mature friends," she says, rolling her eyes.

"Don't start, Anna, please. I'm not sure why you have always disliked them so much, but they're my best friends. They aren't going anywhere. I don't expect you to spend all your time with them, but you do need to treat them with the same level of respect I show your friends."

"Whatever, Dexter. Just make sure they're out of here by

midnight. And if I find beer all over the counter again, I'll make sure they never want to be here again."

Trevor nudges me out of the memory, and I let out a long sigh. Again with the sighing. I want to roll my eyes at myself but answer him instead. "Nanny number three bit the dust ... two and a half weeks ago." I cringe because I know they're about to rain down on me. However, when I look up, I just see hurt faces.

Preston is the first to speak. "What? Why didn't you call us, man? We know what you have going on with the company. We would have been here in shifts to help out because we love those kids more than we love you." He gives me a wicked grin and continues somberly, "We would have been here, Dex."

"Better be careful there, Pres, or we might start to think the asshole persona is all an act," I tell him, but I feel like a prick again. It's becoming a familiar feeling for me, and I hang my head before answering. "I know, I'm sorry. I just felt like an asshole. This is my family! I should be able to handle this shit." I dare a peek around the room and see all their disappointed faces. *Fuck.*

Loki clears his throat. "Listen, man, we love you, but your family is our family, too. We're in this with you. You have to understand you're not on your own. Let us help. Have you interviewed new nannies yet? Fuck, dude, you have to be in London in what, ten days?"

"Yeah, and I did interview a woman." The grin that threatens my face raises eyebrows throughout the room, and I see my three best friends exchanging worried expressions. "What? I see you all. What's with the look?"

This time, it's Trevor to sit next to me. "You like her."

"What? I don't know her. The interview was the biggest clusterfuck of my life. She swooped in here, took Harper from my arms, and got her to stop crying immediately, might I add. Then, she essentially told me to shut up while she got my kids settled. Then, and only then, would she let me know when we could carry on with the interview."

They all bust up laughing until I add, "She got Tate to speak." I let my head droop. The shame I feel over Tate's pain is unbearable.

Trevor jumps up, and the sudden movement startles me out of my pity party for one. "What?"

"What do you mean what?" asks Preston. "She got him to speak!"

"Yeah, it wasn't like he opened up or anything. It was just a couple of words here and there. He liked helping her find stuff for the girls. When she gave me shit, he burst out laughing." I chuckle, remembering my shock.

"So, where is she? Why haven't you hired her?" Loki demands. His outburst has everyone gaping. Loki is even more locked down with his emotions than I am.

"She has some issues," I finally answer. I don't feel right telling her story. I feel like that would be betraying her. "She …" I pause, "this is just between us because I found out through Ryan." I give them all a pointed glare. "She was attacked. Severely, about a year and a half ago." I break off, debating whether I want to admit the rest. I should have known Trevor would catch on right away.

Loki asks, "You seem pretty confident in her abilities to care for the kids. What's holding you back?"

"I am. She was truly great with them." I look up at Trevor, who is now pacing as he speaks again.

"Then what aren't you telling us? Do you think she has issues from her attack that would make her unable to care for the kids?" Trevor asks gently.

"What? No, I meant it when I said I think she would take good care of them. When I yelled at her the first time, she jumped in between the girls like she was protecting them from me. She moved on instinct." I glance up to see them all exchanging expressions of concern.

Shit. Here it comes.

"What do you mean the first time you yelled at her?" asks Loki slowly.

I see the confusion on Trevor's face. He knows me better than anyone. I don't have emotional outbursts … ever.

"Well, fuck." I rest my head in my hands before I continue, "You have no idea how insane it was when she walked in here. It was like an out-of-body experience. My blood was boiling, and she was doing everything right with my kids. Even Molly was caught unawares. I told her not to put Harper down in her bouncy seat because she would just start screaming again. It was like she didn't even hear me. She just walked right past me, put her fingers under my chin, closed my mouth, then bent down to buckle Harper into the seat, anyway. When she reached over and grabbed Sara because she said she smelled like a sewer, I lost my mind." I don't have a chance to continue because I made the mistake of lifting my head, and all three assholes burst out laughing. "What the fuck? This isn't funny."

Preston, the asshole, composes himself first. "So, she's hot?"

"Yes. What? Of course, she is—wait, no, I mean …" I splutter, and their laughter starts anew. I get up to grab another beer. "You guys don't understand. I don't even know what I yelled. Before I caught myself, she had positioned herself in between the girls and me. She looked like she was two seconds away from dropping my ass. I felt bad after, but when I got Ryan's report, I felt even worse. She was hurt." I swallow hard, remembering the pictures, and continue, "She probably should have died. The entire time she didn't make a sound because she was protecting a six-year-old boy. She was afraid if he heard her cry out, he would come out of his hiding spot and the animal would have killed him, too."

The admission sobers them up quickly. I know Trevor's

past. His father often used his mom as a punching bag. He grows quiet, trying to keep his own demons at bay.

"I just don't know what to do. I'll admit I'm attracted to her. I'm really fucking attracted to her. I'd have to be blind not to be, but I just don't know if having her here is the right thing to do for any of us. At the same time, the agency doesn't have many other options this time of year, and I have to go to London. I feel like I can trust her, but going through something like that has to change a person, right?" I stare right at Trevor.

He knows I'm asking his opinion for the safety of my kids. He lets out a long sigh. "Look, man, you know about my mom. After everything she went through, she was still the best thing in my life. She would have done anything for me. What's your gut telling you about this girl?"

I don't even hesitate. "It says to trust her."

Loki sits down. "It seems like you have your answer."

I put my head in my hands again, tugging at my hair. I haven't felt this conflicted since the night I took my father off life support. I shake my head and look up as Preston speaks.

"Listen, man, you know we're here for you. Hire her. Go to London and get your shit done. We'll take turns coming by here every day to assess. If we feel like something isn't right, we'll stay here and call you right away. Your instincts are rarely wrong, though, so if you think you can trust her, you probably can. Plus, it won't be a hardship if she's as hot as you say she is." Preston gives me a shit-eating grin, and I can't help the growl that escapes my throat.

I point to each of them. "Keep your fucking paws off her. I mean it. All of you."

Preston leans back in his chair, laughing. "This is going to be a fun ride, fellas. A really fucking fun ride."

"Leave it to Pres to turn hiring a nanny into something perverted," Loki chides.

I don't suppress my chuckle. With these guys, there's no pretending.

"So, you all set?" Trevor asks.

Preston nods. "You're going to hire her, right?"

Loki asks next, "What's her name, anyway?"

Sitting back on the couch, I smile. "Lanie. Her name is Lanie Heart, and yes, I'll call her tomorrow."

We spend the rest of the night unpacking and breaking down box after box.

CHAPTER 7

LANIE

I'm washing the dishes with my gaze on the waves crashing just beyond the dunes. Mimi designed this house so you could appreciate the ocean wherever you are, but I have a hard time focusing when there's a view like this.

When I finish cleaning my last glass, I call Julia. "Hi, Jules."

"Hey, lady, what's cooking?" I love this girl. Only Julia would ask, 'what's cooking.'

"My body. It's hot as hell here, and it's only March. Maybe North Carolina wasn't such a great idea after all. My Irish skin isn't cut out for this," I tell her while fanning my face and making my way out to the deck for some ocean breeze.

Jules just laughs. "I saw online it's unseasonably hot there right now, even on the coast."

Loving the sense of calm I get hearing her voice, I say, "God, I miss your Irish face."

"I miss your Irish face, too. Any word on the job yet?"

I sigh. It's been four days and nothing. "No, Mr. Dexter Cross said he would be in touch soon, but it's been four days. I take that as a sign I didn't get it. I need to come up with a plan B. I'm going to run out of money sooner rather than later."

"I can give you money, Lanes. I've told you this."

"And I've told you, thank you, but I cannot take your money. I'll figure it out. I always do."

Julia's voice is uncharacteristically quiet. "I know you do."

"How are you and Char—" My phone beeps, cutting me off.

Mr. Dexter Cross is calling.

"Ship, Jules, I have to go. *He's* calling," I say in a rush.

"Okay, Lanes, call me later. Luvs."

"Luvs to you, too," I say as my finger slips a millisecond too soon.

The voice of Dexter Cross replaces Jules on the other end, confirming I switched over to his call too soon. "Ah, Ms. Lanie Heart?"

"Oh my God, I'm so sorry. I was talking to my best friend from home. I was telling her I loved her, too, but must have clicked over to you before I did. I mean, obviously, I don't love you. That would be crazy. Not that you're not loveable, but ... ah, man. What is wrong with me?"

I hear his rumbling low laugh through the phone. "Are you done, Ms. Lanie Heart?"

"Yes, Mr. Dexter Cross." I can't help but push his buttons.

"Just Dex," he laments.

"Okay, just Dex. Yes, I'm shutting up now." My embarrassment radiates through my voice.

He laughs again. "Excellent. I'd like to offer you the job. However, there's a lot to talk about, and I'm sort of on a time crunch here. My friends are coming over this afternoon to help with the kids. I was hoping you could come back so we could talk about the details."

"Ah, t-today?" I stammer.

"Yes, Lanie, today," he replies authoritatively.

"Okay, Dex. It'll take me a while to get there."

"That's fine. Just text me when you leave so I know when to expect you. Drive safely," his sultry voice demands.

"I will. See you soon. Oh, Dex?"

Dexter Cross responds with humor lacing his tone, "Yes, Lanie?"

"Thank you." I'm sincere and hope all traces of teasing are gone.

There's a pause before he finally responds, "See you soon, Lanie."

He hangs up before I can say good-bye, but I have a feeling he's smiling just as big as I am right now. *Shit, I have to get the house cleaned and hit the road.*

Almost an hour later, I'm in my car and on my way back to Waverley-Cay. All feels right for once.

~

"Hey, Jules, it's me. I don't need anything. I was just calling to tell you I'm about ten minutes away from Dexter's house. I'm more nervous than I was a few days ago. Maybe it's because I know how hot he is now?" *No, do not think of him as hot. He's my boss, that's it.* "Anyway, I'm rambling. I just wanted to let you know I'm all right. I'll call again when I'm settled. Give everyone hugs and kisses for me. Luvs."

As I pull up to the house, I'm once again in shock. His house is so freaking big. How does Tate not get lost in here? There are a lot more cars in the driveway today, too. Expensive cars.

Geez, that's not intimidating at all.

Putting my ten-year-old Toyota Corolla in park, I sit, taking in my surroundings for a few minutes. Is this going to be my life? Living among the rich? Peering down at my shorts and T-shirt, I know I'm going to stick out like a sore thumb. After counting to ten, I open my car door.

Here goes nothing.

CHAPTER 8

DEX

"Hey, Dex?"

"What, Pres? I'm elbow deep in diapers right now." Annoyance rings clearly in my voice.

"Ah, I think your hot-as-fuck nanny is here." Preston's tone is strained, and suddenly I'm second guessing my choice to have them here.

Trevor and Loki run to the window a second later. Shit, having them here was definitely a mistake.

"Holy hell," Loki whistles.

"What? Guys, I'm serious. If you make her feel uncomfortable, I'll rip your balls right off."

Loki chokes on a laugh, but gives me a stern look. "She isn't just pretty, Dex. I think you might be in trouble."

The doorbell rings, and I let out a groan as they trip over each other, trying to get to the door first.

"Do not f-this up for me, guys, I mean it." I glance down at Sara as I finish changing her diaper. "And keep your eyes and your hands off my goddamn girl." *Fuck*.

Three sets of eyes whip toward me. I've never been a jealous guy, but I've never had reactions like this either.

Preston shakes his head. "Hell yeah, this is going to be good. I'll get the beer and popcorn."

"Just answer the freaking door, please."

"You're getting really good at catching your cursing," Trevor acknowledges.

Their laughter fades as they head to the front door. I take a few minutes to pull myself together. Silently, I curse myself when I realize I'm still in gym shorts, but at least they're clean. I lift my arm and smell my pits. Ugh, it could be worse, I guess.

In no time, I hear the guys vying for Lanie's attention, and I roll my eyes. But then I hear her laugh. God, that laugh. *I'm in fucking trouble.*

Lanie comes walking around the corner, the guys right behind her with puppy dog eyes. They're such assholes. She walks into the room and looks around. "Hey," she says with a wave. "It almost looks like a home in here ... you've been busy!"

I see her lips moving, but I'm blinded by her smile.

Oh hell, I'm a goner. I look from her to the guys and back to her. They're all standing behind her, a little shell shocked. When I meet Trevor's eyes, he laughs.

"She's a ball buster, Dex. She called Pres out on his shit before she got both feet in the door." Trevor's laughing so hard he has tears rolling down his face.

Great, they're absolutely no help.

I narrow my eyes at Pres, though, and growl. I actually fucking growl. "I told you to cut the shit."

"Relax, Dex. It was all in good fun." His laughter is grating on my last nerve.

I try, really, I do, but I guess I'm as awestruck in Lanie Heart's presence as my goofball friends. Lanie walks over to me and attempts to close my mouth again.

"Are you planning to piss me off every single day?"

"Am I?" she asks, stepping back. "Ticking you off, I mean?"

"I don't know how to feel about you, Lanie Heart. All my other employees are scared of me." *Maybe this is a mistake.*

She steps forward again, her voice a sultry whisper when she tells me, "It's hard to be afraid of pretend monsters when you've dealt with the real thing your whole life."

I don't have an answer to that. I catch the shocked expressions of the guys in the background. *Good, now they know what I'm dealing with here.*

Trying to gain the upper hand, since this is *my* house, I scowl at Lanie, so I can get my thoughts in order.

Lanie smiles. "Oh, goody. I wasn't sure I was in the right house, but with your constant scowl back in place, I feel right at home." She strolls past me to the girls and picks not one but both of them up and walks toward the kitchen. Halfway there, she calls over her shoulder, "Hey, guys, make yourselves useful and go grab Tate for me."

All three of my friends look from her to me and back again, then as if pulled by a little string she attached to them earlier, they shrug their shoulders and go off in search of my son.

What have I done?

~

I walk into the kitchen just in time to find Lanie buckling Harper into her highchair.

"Lanie, what are you doing?" I ask with a heavy sigh while pinching the bridge of my nose. I already feel a headache coming on and she hasn't been here for five minutes. "I haven't actually hired you yet. There's paperwork, and we need to talk about salary. I also have to go to London soon. We'll need to go over schedules."

She puts her hand on her hip. "I know, and we will, but I

just spent five minutes with your friends, and while they seem nice, I don't foresee any of them knowing what or how to feed a baby dinner. Am I wrong?"

I shake my head, knowing she's right. "No, you're right. It took longer than I expected for you to arrive. The kids will melt down soon if they don't eat."

She smiles, and God how I don't want the reaction it causes in me. I scowl in return.

"I know I am." She beams. "Now, do you have a dinner plan, or are we winging it?"

"The girls have some of those mashed up meals in the pantry. I was going to order pizza for everyone else." She scrunches up her nose. I think she does that a lot, and it's fucking cute as hell. "What now, Lanie?" Exasperation laces my voice.

"Oh, nothing really. We can talk about meals later, but I'll plan to make the kids' food from now on. No more of this packaged crap." She must notice the irritation on my face. "Listen, I love myself some Kraft mac and cheese as much as the next girl, but we don't want them growing up only having taste buds for processed stuff."

I want to be mad. She's basically shitting all over my parenting again, except she's right. I scowl anyway to let her know just who the boss is around here, but my mouth doesn't connect to my brain. "You said crap," I blurt, smiling.

What the fuck? That's not ... I wanted to tell her my way is just fine. I glower and look away.

"Listen, Mr. Dexter Cross," she says with that sassy lilt to her voice, "I know you're trying hard not to like me, but I might as well tell you now, most people who try, fail."

I stalk toward Lanie Heart and watch her fold in on herself. Fuck, I don't want to scare her. Anger rises from my gut, but it's aimed at her attacker, not her. Still, I try to squash it down so I don't frighten her more. Taking a step back, I lean against the counter instead, crossing my arms so she can't see my hands balled into fists.

"Well, Ms. Lanie Heart, I'm not most people."

Her eyes drift down my body and snap back to my eyes. "No, Dex, you're not. You're definitely not."

She turns and puts all her attention on the girls for the next thirty minutes while I stand off to the side and watch. *What the hell was that look? Did she mean to do it? She's a complete mind-fuck.* Maybe it's good that I'm going to London for a while. She can get settled, and I can cool off. Get my head on straight.

The rest of the night goes smoothly. The guys are on their best behavior, for the most part. Tate sat next to Lanie at dinner. I didn't notice him talking, but he was smiling at her; that's progress. Maybe she's right ... I should speak to him about his mom.

Anna is a total bitch, but she was always a good mom, wasn't she? *A good mom wouldn't just walk away from her kids,* the asshat voice in my head chimes in.

Fuck. If she said something to Tate, I'll rip her limb from limb. I will have to come up with a plan for figuring this out when I get back from London.

Lanie takes the girls upstairs, asking Tate to show her their room. As I watch Tate climb the stairs, a memory I've tried to forget appears unbidden.

"Dexter, go upstairs and get ready for bed. Daddy will be home soon to tuck you in."

"What about you, Mama? Are you going to tuck me in, too?"

"Not today, Dex. Mama's got somewhere to be, but Daddy will take care of you."

I walk up the stairs, looking back every couple of steps. Somehow, I knew that would be the last time I would ever see my mother.

Hearing the guys give each other shit, I look up and

realize how late it is. "The kids will be in bed soon, guys, so Lanie and I can work everything out then."

They ended up getting it together enough to help unpack more boxes. Although that doesn't stop them from giving me the side-eye on their way out.

As he's walking through the door, Trevor pulls me in for a hug. Stepping back, he offers some advice, "Just let things play out. She seems like a trustworthy person. I think your instincts are right about her, but we'll still check in every day you're gone."

"Thanks, man. I think she will be good, too." My eyes dart toward the stairs she just climbed. "Maybe I just needed you guys to back me up. Single parenting is fucking hard." I say it like we don't understand the truth of that statement firsthand.

He gives me a sad smile. We're both thinking about our single parents as he claps me on the back on his way out. "You're one of the good ones, you know that, right?"

"One of the good ones?"

"Yeah, one of the good ones. A good man and a hell of a good dad. Things will get easier, and we're always here. Don't be a pecker next time, though. If Lanie goes running for the hills, call us immediately," he says, punching me in the arm.

"I will, thanks."

"I don't think she'll be running away, though."

I smile at him because I don't think she will either. Shutting the door, I hear water running, so I head for the stairs. I pass Tate's room first and notice his light on, so I step in.

"Hey, King Tate. How's it going?"

He shrugs his shoulders, and my heart cracks a little more. I miss his voice.

"What do you think of Lanie?" Talking with him lately is more of a one-sided conversation.

He peers up at me and smiles.

"You like her?"

He nods twice.

"Tate?" I let the question linger until he lifts his eyes to me. "I love you more than anything. You know that, right?"

He just stares at me.

"I will always be here for you. Always. When I have to go on these work trips, I'll always, always come back."

He nods his head again, signaling he knows, while I pick him up in a hug.

"Listen, buddy. Remember how I have to go on that trip next week? I'll be away for almost two weeks, but I promise I will call you every day, okay?"

His eyes glisten, but he doesn't speak.

I didn't think my heart could hurt anymore. "I promise I'll come back. I'll always come back." I peel away from him and look down into sad eyes. "Tate, I promise."

He nods his head again, and I feel a tear fall down my face.

How could she do this to him? How could she do this to us? I hate Anna with a new passion today.

"Lanie will be here with you while I'm gone. Uncle Trevor, Loki, and even Preston will stop in everyday to check on you. If something's not right, you tell them right away. They'll stay with you guys, and I'll be on the next flight home." I pause, pulling him in for another hug. "I hate that I have to leave, but it's important for work. I'll come home early if I can. Okay? Please let me know you'll be all right with Lanie?"

In a whisper so soft I'm not one hundred percent sure I haven't made it up, he says, "I like Lanie, Dad. We'll be okay."

I study him and know he said it, but the knot in my throat is too big to swallow down. Squeezing him a little tighter, I nod.

When he squirms, I kiss him one more time before pulling back. "Get your jammies on and climb into bed. You can read for a little bit while I check on Lanie and the girls, all right?"

He nods his head and walks to his bathroom to change.

Maybe having Lanie here will be a good thing after all. I leave Tate's room and head toward the sound of water splashing.

I find Lanie kneeling over the bathtub in the nursery and lose my breath. Her shorts are short. Really short and riding up toward her ass as she leans over Sara to wash her hair. Harper splashes and kicks her feet, so Lanie jumps back, landing right against my chest. Her scent is calming, like lilacs and baby powder.

She whips around with her hand to her chest. I know she's scared because she's in a defensive stance between the girls and me. It makes me both ridiculously happy and extremely sad at the same time. I have no doubt Lanie will protect and help piece together my little family.

Maybe I can find a way for us to protect and heal her, too.

"Shiplap," she finally says, making me chuckle.

I take a step back with my hands raised. "What are you doing, Lanie?"

"Ah, the girls needed baths?" she says as though that should be the most obvious thing in the world. "They're completely orange from the canned pasta."

I look her up and down. I cannot figure this girl out, and fuck if I know why I want to so badly. "The girls have, uh, splashed you a lot." Her shirt is slightly see-through now, allowing me to see the lace outline of her bra.

Fuck me. I spin around and dart from the room. "I'll grab you a new shirt," I call over my shoulder.

When I come back, she has both girls dry and dressed, lying on the bed with their sippy cups.

"How the hell did you do that so fast? It takes me at least forty minutes to get them both dressed."

Handing her the shirt, I can tell I've embarrassed her. The flush across her cheeks is an easy tell.

"I've been helping my friend, Julia, with her son, Charlie, since he was born. Just lots of practice, I guess," she says, making minimal eye contact.

I smile. I can't help it around her.

"I can take it from here. Why don't you go get changed? I know you weren't planning on starting tonight, but I have a lot I need to go over with you. Do you mind waiting downstairs so we can go over the details?" I ask, enjoying the way her skin has flushed a deep pink.

"Sure. I'll see you down there." Leaning in, she kisses both girls on the cheek.

They giggle and love her back with open-mouthed, wet kisses. *Have the other nannies done this with them?* Maybe that's why they're so comfortable with Lanie. She gives affection freely.

Lanie gets up with my T-shirt covering her front and heads out the door. Watching her walk out of the room, I can't help but compare her to Anna. I know the girls never had a connection with Anna. She made sure of that. *But why don't I remember Anna ever cuddling or kissing Tate? Surely, she did ... right?*

I snuggle with the girls for a few minutes, then put them both in their cribs. Heading back to Tate's room, I find Lanie on the bed with him singing a song and rubbing his hair. That darkness in my heart opens a little more, and I don't know what to make of it.

Where did this woman come from?

Finishing her song, she looks down at Tate. He's fallen asleep in her lap, so she leans down and kisses him on the cheek, too. She whispers something I can't quite make out as I watch. Tate smiles in his sleep, and I think he even mumbles something, although I can't be sure with the angle of his face.

Lanie pats his head again and scans the room, taking everything in. When she spots me in the doorway, she gives me a bashful little shrug.

My shoulders shake in silent laughter at her innocent gesture. Making my way over, I lean down to whisper, "I'm going to lift him off your lap so you can slide out."

Her eyes go wide, and she gasps as my hands come in contact with her thigh and stomach.

Now it's my turn to shrug. "Sorry, I can't get him otherwise," I whisper.

She bobbles her head again, so I slide him off her. She shimmies to the end of the bed and climbs out.

Leaning over, I kiss Tate on the cheek. "I love you, buddy."

I turn and guide Lanie out of the room with my hand on the small of her back. I don't want to acknowledge how right this feels. I've got to stay focused. She's excellent with the kids.

Do not do anything to mess that up, I scold myself as I follow Lanie downstairs.

"Want to meet me in the kitchen? I just have to run to my office to grab your folder," I say, loving how she looks in my home.

Lanie doesn't speak but heads off in the direction I sent her.

When I return, I find her sitting at the table with her bare feet tucked up under her. She has my old law school T-shirt on and damn if it doesn't make me want to think dirty thoughts. *Focus, asshole.*

"Ah, hey. Thank you for today." Running a hand through my mop of hair, I take a seat next to her. "I know you were only expecting to be here for an hour or so. I hope we didn't ruin any plans you had?"

"No. I'm just going to head to a hotel when I leave here, so it's no big deal. Plus, if you have to go on a trip soon, it's better that I spend a lot of time with the kids before you leave to learn their routines," she explains with a small yawn.

What she says makes sense, but I can feel the frown on my face. "You're going to a hotel?" I know I sound snippy, but it's too late for her to be traipsing around town, even if this is Waverley-Cay.

"Well, yeah, it's late. It was a long drive here. Corolla will take too long to go back there tonight, and I'm not ready to return to Vermont yet," Lanie defends herself, not understanding my tone.

I'm with you there, sweetheart. I don't understand a damn thing about today.

I let out a long breath. "Lanie, I want to offer you this position. Let's go over this stuff. If we can agree to the terms, you can just stay here tonight. Will you need to get your stuff from Vermont?"

"Are you sure?" she asks, surprised. "And no, I don't have a ton of stuff. Everything I'll need is in my car already."

I don't know why the thought of all her belongings fitting into her small sedan bothers me so much, but it does.

I school my features and continue, "You're going to be living in my house if you take this job. You might as well stay tonight and save money on the hotel."

"Yeah, sure." She bites her lip, still a little unsure.

I stare at her mouth for a beat too long, so I clear my throat and look away.

For the next hour and a half, we go over salary, expectations, hours, and living arrangements while Lanie fills out paperwork for things like insurance and taxes. I give her a rundown of the kids' schedules, knowing honestly that she had them on a better routine in just a couple of hours than I've been able to do in the last year. When it seems like we've answered any questions either of us has, I glance at my phone and realize it's after eleven.

"Shit, I'm sorry. I didn't realize it was so late. I didn't give the girls any medicine. Now they'll probably be up soon because of their teeth. Why don't you give me your keys and I'll grab your stuff so we can go to bed?"

Damn if I didn't like the blush that crossed both her cheeks and ran down her neck.

"Um, yeah, it's fine, though. I can get my stuff. Like I said, there isn't much." She jumps out of her chair and gets her keys. "I probably should have checked with you first, but I gave the girls their medicine after their bath. I hope that's all right?"

Smiling, I gaze at her in wonder. I'm doing that a lot around her. "Of course you did. Thank you, Lanie, but I insist, give me your keys."

"You're welcome, Dex," she replies sweetly.

I'm beginning to like the sound of my name on those sexy lips way too much. I head out to Lanie's car and grab what she said she would need. I can't help but look around; she wasn't kidding. She doesn't have much in here, and it bothers me. Then again, most things bother me much more than they should where she's concerned.

She graduated second in her class. If it weren't for the monster who cut her up and left her for dead, she would probably be on a much different path right now. I shouldn't feel this protective of her. I barely know her, yet I feel like she could know me better than anyone ever has.

I've got to get to London. My head is a mess.

Entering the house with Lanie's measly belongings, I set out to find her. She's standing at the back door, staring out at the guest house with a worried expression. *Is she scared to go out there?* Something is telling me to keep her in the house, so I act quickly.

"So, I was thinking," I start. "I know I said you'd be living in the guest house, and that's still all yours, but since I'm heading to London soon, and you need to spend as much time with the kids as possible ..." I pause, trying to read her.

"Well, while I'm still here, maybe you should just stay in the guest room for now. I'd prefer you to stay in the main house when I'm away anyway because I want you close to the kids. Then, I can put your stuff in the guest house when I return if you would be more comfortable there."

I have barely finished speaking before she replies, "The guest room would be great. Thank you."

I nod and turn her toward the stairs. Reaching the top, I guide her to the room at the end of the hall. Then I stop short and head in the other direction, mumbling a half-assed apology along the way. "Sorry, I must be more tired than I thought. Your room is down here."

The room next to the master. I'm playing with fire here. I know it, but I can't help the instinct I have to keep her close.

She can only be the nanny, nothing else. She's here for the kids, and they already love her. Do not fuck this up, Cross.

Opening the door to the guest room, I usher her inside. Suddenly, I'm incredibly grateful the guys helped me unpack a few things, the guest rooms being one of them. There's nothing special about this bedroom; it's standard and dull. Now I wish I had thought to add a few personal touches, or at least have someone else do it for her.

She deserves better than ordinary.

The walls are a light color; I'm not sure what. There are deep green drapes that cover the ceiling-to-floor windows. The bedding is all white with accents the same color as the curtains. The only luxurious thing in here is the carpet I'm walking across. Fixing her room will have to be a priority. I make a mental note to call Molly tomorrow.

The voice in my head is questioning, *Why would you do that, Cross? She isn't staying here permanently.*

I decide to ignore that voice this time.

Feeling slightly embarrassed, I cross the spacious room and open the door to the attached en suite.

"You have a private bathroom, and I hope you have towels

in here?" I check the cabinets. "The guys started helping me unpack a few days ago. While I love them, I wouldn't say they're experts in hospitality. Settle in, look around, and make a list of anything you might want. I'll run out to get whatever you require tomorrow after my meeting."

I turn to walk across her room toward the hallway but stop myself. "If there's anything else you want to change about the room to make you more comfortable, let me know, and I'll take care of it."

"Ah, yeah. I don't need much. I'm sure whatever is in there is fine. Plus, the room is lovely, but thank you."

Her response rankles me. I must be overtired because I take a slow step toward her. Then another. "Lanie, you're going to be living here. You will need things. I will be the one to provide them. Is that clear?"

Her face goes ashen, then bright red. Her eyes narrow on me, and I know she's pissed. Good. Pissed off is better than whatever the fuck has been happening for the last few hours.

"Mr. Dexter Cross," she starts, "I appreciate the offer, but as I have said before, I am perfectly capable of taking care of myself and will continue to do so."

"Ms. Lanie Heart." I mimic her body language. God, why do we revert to full names when we're angry or pushing buttons? *Maybe that's what we are doing.* "I won't fight with you. Make a list, or I will buy out the drugstore to stock your bathroom."

Before she can say another word, I pivot and head out the door. "Goodnight, Lanie."

Quickly shutting the door behind me, I take long strides to my room with a hard-on. Out of habit, I leave my door open to listen for the kids and apparently for Lanie too. Maybe having her share a wall with me wasn't my brightest idea, but it's too late now.

After changing and brushing my teeth, I climb into my bed, yet lay there wide awake. It's been at least two hours since I left Lanie's room. Her door is cracked open, and her light is on. Not that I'm watching her room or anything.

Why the hell is she still awake? Maybe I should check on her? No, that would be weird. She has told me multiple times that she can take care of herself.

"Great," I groan, "... now I'm talking to myself."

Rolling over, I try to put the thoughts of the pretty blonde next door out of my head and end up tossing and turning the rest of the night.

CHAPTER 9

LANIE

I roll over and stretch. Yawning, I realize I slept well ... so well, that it takes me a minute to remember where I am. *Dexter Cross's house.* Sitting up, I lean over to the nightstand and grab my phone when I hear it again, the sound that must have woken me.

Straining to hear, I recognize the song I sang to Tate last night. I peek at the clock. Eesh, it's early, six a.m., but I'm wide awake now.

After sliding out of bed, I creep out into the hallway. To my left, I see Dexter's door wide open. Okay, I might be drooling slightly. He's asleep on his stomach; the sheet pooled around his waist, which is such a shame. *No, no, don't think like that, you idiot.*

I sneak over and very quietly close his door. I'm up and he must be exhausted, so I let him sleep while I search for the source of singing and babbling echoing through the otherwise quiet house.

Across the hall, I find Tate on the floor with his back to me and his two baby sisters lying in his lap, looking at books. The room is decorated with little ballerinas. There's so much pink, it's hard to not think of Pepto-Bismol. Then I hear it again.

"You are my sunshine, my only sunshine..."

It's so quiet. I wonder how I could have possibly heard it from my room. One of the girls lifts her head and sees me. I think it's Sara. Staring at them makes me wonder what their mother looks like. They all look so much like Dex. He must have some strong swimmers. As soon as that thought hits my head, I groan. *Stop thinking like that!* I want to slap my forehead, but Tate turns around, offering me a small smile.

"Don't stop on my account. I love that you're so good with your sisters." I offer him an easy smile.

Tate smiles in return but doesn't continue singing.

"How come you didn't get your dad or me when you woke up?"

He studies me for a minute and just shrugs, so I take a guess.

"Were you trying to help? Maybe give your dad a little more sleep?"

Tate doesn't look up at me, he just nods his head.

Okay, I can work with this.

"That's so sweet of you, buddy. I want you to know while I'm here, you can always come to me. I won't ever get mad at you for needing something. Would you mind if I gave you a hand?"

His eyes tear up, but he shakes his head.

What did I say to upset him? My heart hurts seeing his tears. "How about if I carry the girls downstairs? I can get you guys some breakfast while your dad sleeps. You can even help me cook!"

He peeks up at me and smiles. I have the urge to reach over and hug him, so I do. He stiffens for just a moment, but then hugs me back. I feel like it's my win for the day.

"Okay, buddy, let's head to the kitchen." I settle Sara on

my left and Harper on my right before following Tate down the stairs to the kitchen. When we place the girls in their highchairs, though, they stare right at each other and start crying.

Oh boy! Think, Lanes.

"Hey, Tate, do you know if your dad has any of those baby carriers around? You know, the ones that make you look sort of like a kangaroo?"

He jumps to attention, already opening a closet door.

I'm floored by what I see. It seems like someone bought out the entire baby section on Amazon. It's all brand new. *What the hell?*

"Thanks, bubs." I start digging around and find what I'm searching for—a Baby Bjorn and a Baby Ergo. I pump my fist and yell, "Score!" causing Tate to giggle. Even the girls have quieted for a minute, so I get to work. The Bjorn goes on my front first, then I put the Ergo on my back. I can do this.

Since Sara is heavier and seems less fussy, I put her on my back and start to sway. Harper has started crying again, so I grab her, sliding her into the Bjorn on my front. For once, I am thankful I'm not a small woman. When I'm satisfied they're both secure, I twirl around for Tate. He smiles, and the girls giggle. Now we're ready to get to work.

"Hmm, Mr. Tate. What do you like for breakfast?"

He walks to the pantry and pulls out some frosted pastries, and I frown.

"Is that what you normally have for breakfast?"

He looks down and nods.

I don't want him to feel bad, so I put on a smile and crouch down the best I can while wearing two babies. "Those are okay sometimes, but there's not much you can do to help cook them. How do you feel about pancakes?"

When he raises his head and grins, I know I've got him.

"Perfect, let's get started. But first, we need some music!"

He raises his eyebrows, so much like his dad, and I feel a smile take over my whole face. I quickly glance around for a speaker but realize I don't know the passwords to sync up even if I found one. Instead, I pull out my phone and open iTunes, searching for a PG playlist. When I find what I'm looking for, I press play.

"Tate, can you find me a mixing bowl? I'll get all our ingredients ready," I ask him, swaying to the music.

I peek over my shoulder, and Sara smiles. She's so sweet. Glancing down at my chest, I find Harper fast asleep. This just feels right. I need to call Jules later and let her know how it's going.

"Ah, this is a little trickier than I thought it would be with the four extra arms and legs I have sticking out of me," I tell Tate.

As I'm turning, Sara grabs the bowl before I can stop her, resulting in Tate, the girls, and myself getting covered in flour. I shrug, trying not to laugh. "Oh well, let's just scoop the flour from the counter back into the bowl."

Tate seems slightly suspicious but follows my lead. We do our best to keep grabby fingers away from our breakfast.

"Here, buddy, you pour the milk, then you can mix." I hand him a whisk. I'm using mine as a microphone while I dance and sing around the kitchen. Every once in a while, I grab Tate's little hands and get him to move around with me. I think he finds me funny but hasn't gone full dance mode yet. *He'll get there, I'm sure of it.*

While he's whisking, I turn to the stove. Covering Harper's legs with one arm to make sure they don't reach the burner, I set the flame on low to heat the pan.

When "Uptown Funk" comes on, I turn to Tate with a grin.

He shakes his head like he knows he's in trouble, and I reach for his hand. With Sara giggling behind me, and

Harper still fast asleep, Tate and I swing and shimmy all over the kitchen.

Halfway through the song, Tate bursts out into a belly laugh, and I crumble beside him. It's now my mission in life to make him laugh like that every day.

CHAPTER 10

DEX

I wake up slowly, stretching my arms above my head, and roll over. I slept really well, better than I have in a long time. Reaching over to grab my phone, I find it's already after seven.

Shit!

Sitting up, I find my door is closed and frown. I always leave my door open so I can hear the kids. I jump out of bed and run to the hallway. The kids' doors are all open, as is Lanie's. After a quick peek inside each one, I realize they're all empty. Panic sets in until I hear the music, then I'm just confused.

I rush to the stairs and around the corner. I'm following the sounds of "Uptown Funk" and laughter, but come to an abrupt halt in the doorway of my kitchen. Rubbing my eyes, I try to make sense of what I'm witnessing. Lanie has on very short sleep shorts, although I can't see anything else because she has Sara strapped to her back and a sleeping Harper on her front. Her left hand holds Tate's while their free hands cling to the whisks they're using as microphones.

Lanie swirls them around. Sara's belly laughing, and Tate

seems like the little boy he used to be. Happy, smiling, and carefree.

I've failed him. Leaning against the doorframe, I watch Lanie shimmy her ass in time to the music, and fuck, if all the blood in my body doesn't rush south. *Insta lust is a real thing, folks.*

As the song ends, Tate spots me and gives me a wide grin and a little wave. Lanie twirls around to follow his line of sight, still kind of dancing—if you can call that dancing. She stops short, right leg lifted in the air, and the whisk frozen inches from her mouth. *Ha, this time, I caught her with her mouth hanging open.*

I take quick steps toward her. With my fingers on her chin, I close her mouth with a massive grin on my face. "Morning, Lanie."

She swallows visibly, looking embarrassed to have been caught in her version of a dance-off. When she scans me from head to toe, I realize I'm not wearing a shirt or pants. In one horrifying moment, the situation becomes clear. I am standing a foot away from my new nanny in nothing but black boxer briefs and a raging hard-on. *Jesus.*

Now it's her turn to smirk. There's no way she didn't notice. Lanie stares at my junk for just a minute too long to be polite.

"Morning, Dex," she says with laughter in her voice. "Ah, it looks like you're having a hard morning." She winks at me, and I involuntarily groan. "We were letting you sleep because Tate thought you were tired. Breakfast is almost ready. Why don't you go, ah … get dressed? Then you can join us. Tate made pancakes and bacon!"

"Yeah. Sorry, I'm not used to someone else getting up with the kids. I thought I overslept. I panicked a little and just ran down here," I explain, and she gives me a dimpled grin.

"It's fine. Hurry up before the food gets cold," she tosses out over her shoulder.

I glance down at Harper, then grab Lanie's arm gently to turn her sideways so I can see Sara, who peers up at me with a chubby fist in her mouth and giggles. That's when I notice Lanie's back is soaked. Sara must have been drooling all over her for quite some time. I rub Sara's cheek and laugh.

At least I'm not the only one drooling over the new nanny. Shaking the errant thought from my head, I turn and walk to my room. Upstairs, I'm still hard as a fucking rock. Climbing into the shower, I set it as cold as I can handle. No matter what I try to conjure up, my mind keeps wandering to Lanie. Her tempting round ass, her perfect, sassy lips, and tits I want to suck.

Fuck it. Giving up, I grab body wash in my hand and roughly rub it all over my cock. I close my eyes and brace myself against the tiled wall with one hand. Then I stroke my shaft harder and faster while a montage of Lanie runs through my mind like a movie.

Lanie dancing, those long, lean legs that were swaying side to side. I stroke faster. Her smart mouth that I can't help but imagine devouring. Faster. Her goddamn fingers closing my mouth, and I picture them on my cock. I feel my balls pull up and my spine stiffen as I shoot my load all over the shower.

What. The. Fuck.

I'm panting and doubled over. I haven't come that hard in years. Leaning against the shower door, I try to catch my breath. When I come to my senses, I smile and think about her smart mouth, asking if I've had a hard morning. She thought she got the upper hand, and I admit, she had me off balance for a while. But two can play at this game, and fuck me if I give a shit that it could all blow up in my face.

I took longer than I planned to get back downstairs. I had to have my wits about me before dealing with Lanie again. By the time I return to the kitchen, she and the kids have finished eating.

"We made a plate for you. It's in the warming drawer," Lanie says, never taking her eyes off of my kids.

I take the plate and turn off the oven. Sitting at the table, I watch as Lanie plays a board game with Tate, still wearing the girls. Her hair is in some sort of messy bun on top of her head. She looks like there is pancake-batter on the side of her face and she is most definitely wearing a ton of flour. Still, she's beautiful. I smile to myself and tuck into my food, trying to eat quickly.

I'm putting my dishes in the dishwasher when I hear Lanie come up behind me with Tate and the girls.

"Lanie," I say by way of greeting, "I'll finish getting everyone ready so you can shower before we have to leave."

I turn to Tate, who's smiling broadly. "Hey, buddy, it's time to get ready for school. What do you want for lunch today?"

He raises puppy dog eyes to Lanie.

"It's all right, buddy, we can save this game for after school. I'll leave it right here all set up for when you get back. I'll even make sure your dad doesn't peek and try to cheat," she stage whispers with a smile and a wink.

Before I can stop myself, I take a step closer to her and lower my voice. "Oh, Lanie, I've never been a cheater, but when I decide I want something, I don't let up until it's mine."

Realizing Tate is still watching us, I take a step back. "Okay, bud, what about lunch?"

He gives me a grave look and then glances at Lanie.

Shit, what was I thinking?

"It's all right," Lanie tells me. "I already made his lunch.

Tate-o-nator, why don't you get dressed and brush your teeth? I'm excited to see your school today."

He gives her a smile and heads to the hallway. I turn to Lanie and see her regarding me with something I can't quite place.

"Sorry, you had such a *hard* morning, Dex." She puts extra emphasis on the word hard. I can see the humor in her eyes. The expression I couldn't place? Mischief, pure trouble. "I hope my presence here isn't putting you in a *hard* place." She says it innocently enough, but then laughs. "I told you not to fall for me. I haven't been here for twenty-four hours, and it already seems like this could become quite a *sticky* situation."

She smirks and turns her back to me.

Does she know I was jerking off in the shower? With the hard-on I had, I'm sure there's no doubt what I was doing. Somehow, that turns me on even more. I know I shouldn't engage, but she said she'll only be here a year, right? Living in my house. Sharing a wall with me. It's most definitely the worst idea in the history of bad ideas. Still, I can't help myself. I'm drawn to her in a way I can't explain, so I make a rash decision to shoot myself in the foot and go for it.

"Lanie, Lanie, Lanie," I say, stalking her slowly. "A little flirting could make this year a hell of a lot of fun." *Or I could end up with the world's worst case of blue balls,* I think to myself. Either way, at some point this morning, I've already decided I don't give a fuck. I want her. Finally admitting that to myself, I walk over to her. "However, the only sticky situation was in my shower ten minutes ago, and I can promise you, I won't be falling in love with you. My heart is on permanent lockdown. I can't help it if my cock has other plans."

I wink at her, and she gasps, turning a blazing shade of crimson. I realize I just crossed so many lines that I positively shouldn't have. I can't have her quitting before I even get to London, but her body language tells me she's enjoying our banter. After all, she started it.

I shrug my shoulders and lean into her. Lanie tilts her head, and her lips fall open on a gasp. She thinks I'm going to kiss her, and damn if my cock isn't screaming at me to do just that, but not yet. I've got too much riding on this to make that move right now. Instead, I reach down and pat Harper's sleeping head. Lanie frowns, and I wink as a chuckle escapes from deep in my throat.

"Okay," I say, trying to ease the tension we just created. "Please explain to me how and why you have two kids strapped to your body."

I scan her from head to toe, painstakingly slowly, and I see her shudder. Good. I like knowing she reacts to me in kind. When I finally make her mine, it's going to be fucking amazing watching her body respond to me. I almost can't believe I'm not scolding myself, but the thought of making her mine floods my chest with a warmth I haven't felt in a long time. Somewhere, my inner voice is reminding me I haven't known her a week, so *slow the fuck down.* But twenty-four hours in, I just don't have it in me to care.

"Well," she starts, and I wonder if she can even control the sass that shines from her, "I woke up because I heard Tate singing to the girls. He was on the floor with them reading books and singing."

I stare at her, stunned. I don't think I have ever heard Tate sing, and certainly not in the last year.

"Anyway," she continues, "I walked in and started talking to him, well, maybe at him since he didn't reply much, but I found out he was letting you sleep because he thought you were tired." She shrugs. "I asked if I could help."

She says that like it explains everything.

"I've never heard him sing. I'm sorry I missed it," I tell her, sincerely feeling sad.

"He's a great big brother. He loves these girls so much," Lanie's voice drifts, as if she's lost in thought.

I smile because, really, there's nothing to say to that. The one bright spot in his pain has been loving on his sisters. "That doesn't explain why you're all harnessed in, carrying two babies."

She blushes, and my balls tighten.

"You know a lot about harnesses?" she teases, looking up at me through her thick eyelashes.

Allowing a small groan to escape my lips, I close my eyes briefly. *This is going to be a hell of a year.*

She seems to sense my distress and laughs. "I tried putting the girls in their high chairs so we could cook, but they were not having it. I asked Tate if you had any baby carriers, and he showed me your closet that could rival any baby registry. I found these, and tada."

I smile at her sheepishly. "I bought all that stuff and couldn't figure out how to use half of it. I guess I never had the time to return anything. It's just been sitting there. I'm glad something is finally getting used. Let's get you out of them so you can get cleaned up, though. I'm an expert at harnesses now, by the way."

She sucks in a breath, and it's my turn to laugh.

I reach in to unbuckle Harper from her front, and my hand accidentally brushes the underside of her breast.

"Sorry." It comes out in a hoarse whisper.

I quickly move my hand and stare into her blue eyes. Her face is bright red, and she has her bottom lip between her teeth. I unhook the other side of the baby carrier, holding Harper in my left arm. Then, I put my thumb on Lanie's chin, effectively releasing her lip from her teeth.

"Don't do that," I tell her. "It does things to me."

I turn away, but not before I see the heat in her eyes.

I lay Harper down on her playmat. Once she's settled, I head back to Lanie and twirl her around.

"I'm going to unhook Sara now and lay her down next to Harper. Then I'll help you out of these things."

After laying the girls on their playmat, I lift my gaze to find Lanie is still standing in the middle of the room. I walk back to her and start undoing the hooks and buttons that hold the baby carries to her front and back.

"What do you mean it does things to you?" she asks, trying to meet my eyes. Her voice is a breathy whisper.

As much as I would love to show her just what it does to me, I know I have to rein this— whatever *this* is—in. *At least until I get back from London.*

Instead of answering, I let my hands graze down her arms while removing the carrier from her back and am fucking delighted when goosebumps rise all over her soft body. She's so responsive I almost break.

Leaning down, so my mouth is just inches from her ear, I whisper, "Go get dressed. We have to take Tate to school shortly. I need to introduce you to everyone."

She shivers and takes off, not looking back once.

CHAPTER 11

LANIE

I walk to my room as quickly as I can on shaky legs. *What the hell happened today?* One minute I'm making pancakes with Tate, and the next? Bam. I'm flirting with Dex. I haven't even been able to speak to a man in the last eighteen months. Now I'm okay aggressively flirting with one? At least, I think it was flirting. It's been a long time. Too long, in fact.

After my shower, I smirk as I remember Dexter's heated gaze when I mentioned he had a hard morning. I can't help it; I break out into a full belly laugh.

This won't be so bad, right? I told Dex I would stay for one year. With the attraction between us, maybe it wouldn't be such a bad thing to explore. We have an end date already; he doesn't do love, and I want to find a way to have it again. It should be a win-win.

Even though I have to be downstairs any minute, I know I need a check in with my best friend. Pulling up her name, I hit FaceTime, and wait for it to connect.

"Jules," I hiss when I see her smiling face. "I haven't been here a week and we're already flirting. *Me*, Jules, I'm flirting with a man!"

"O-kay," she says, slowly trying to contain her amusement. "I know there are a million ways this could go sideways, but you're consenting adults. As long as you both agree to put the children first, I don't see why it's such a big deal. I'm actually freaking ecstatic for you. You're finally on the road to recovery, my friend. If that hot specimen of a man can help you move on, I say go for it."

"It's not that easy, Jules," I complain.

"Answer me this," it's how Julia starts most of her interrogations. "How would you feel watching Dex leave on a date with someone else? He's the first man in almost two years you've had any kind of chemistry with. Would you honestly be okay with him dating someone else if you didn't at least explore it first?"

A sadness that makes no sense considering I just met the man washes over me as I picture Dex on a date with someone else. Since I don't want to answer Jules, I tell her a different truth. "I know, without a doubt, I'm in for heartbreak with this guy."

"Sometimes, we have to have a little heartbreak to get where we need to be. Maybe a little heartbreak will be worth it if he can help you get past what happened to you. Remember, you're the one who keeps saying you'll only stay a year. You have to remember that. Your heart isn't the only one risking heartache if you take things any further with him," Jules informs me.

"You're right, as always. Lord knows if I don't do something, I'll end up as alone as my mother has always been," I say morosely.

"Lanie Kathleen Heart. You listen, and you listen good," Julia scolds. "You are not, nor will you ever be, alone."

"Thanks, Jules. I have to get going. Tate has to be at school soon. Luvs." I send kisses through the phone before hanging up.

Luvs. Never alone. Remember that. With that sobering

thought running through my head, I get dressed and run down the stairs to help load the kids into the car.

~

Tate's school is surprisingly traditional. I'm not sure what I was expecting, but as we pull up to the brick, L-shaped building that says 'Waverley-Cay Elementary' on it in bright green letters, I smile. Glancing back at Tate, I notice he has a nervous frown on his face. I wish I knew why. He should be loving school at this age.

We park in front of the building, and I start unbuckling the girls while Dex gets out the monstrous double stroller. Tate stands beside the car, wringing his hands.

"Hey, buddy, what's up? Are you nervous about school today?" I ask.

He shakes his head and stares straight ahead, but I sense something is amiss.

Dex locks the car, and I reach out to Tate, not sure if he will take it or not, but smile when he slips his little hand into mine. I give him a small squeeze of encouragement.

"Tate will have to head straight to his class while we check in at the office," Dex starts. "Tate, you go ahead to your classroom. Lanie and I have to fill out some paperwork. When we finish, we'll come down to your class and introduce Lanie to Mrs. Williams."

Tate nods, squeezes my hand, then slowly walks down the hall with his head hanging low.

"Has he ever said anything to you about not liking school?" I ask when Tate is out of earshot.

Dex shakes his head, appearing sad. "No. I know he's different lately, though. He used to love coming to school. This year has been tough on him. He never complains, but he doesn't ask to play or see anyone outside of school. To be honest, I'm not even sure who his friends are or who they used to be. The other nannies were never very good at giving me details," he says as though it's just occurred to him, and he scowls. "Turn left here and show them your license at the desk. You'll have to sign a document and some permissions, then you can head to Tate's classroom. I'll fill out the necessary forms. It'll be faster this way. I have a meeting at ten-thirty. I'll meet you in the classroom as soon as I'm done here."

I do as he asks, and I'm directed down the hall to the last door on the right. I walk the halls slowly, looking at all the happy artwork lining the walls. The school has done an exceptional job of making it feel homey and cheerful. Although made out of what looks like cement blocks, the walls are painted a light, airy blue. Each classroom has a section with bulletin boards, classwork decoratively displayed.

I stop to study one self-portrait that is so insane I try not to laugh when I hear a commotion. Turning, I realize it is coming from the boy's restroom. I know I can't go in. Well, until I hear the taunting.

"Tate, Tate, you're always late, so now this is forever your fate," a boy standing over Tate is singing.

I'm through the door before I even realize I am moving, frozen by what I see. Tate is being held down by a rather large kid who has what appears to be soap stuck on a stick. I stare at it carefully and realize it's not a bar of soap, but a urinal cake and the little asshole is trying to rub it all over Tate's face and clothes.

"What do you think you're doing?" I yell as I rip the kid off Tate. I have the little bully by the arm and am picking Tate up with my other hand.

"Lanie, please don't," Tate whispers.

I see he has tears coming down his face, and I turn to the

bully, doing my best not to throttle him. "You," I point menacingly, "what is your name?"

"I don't have to answer you. I'm going to get you kicked out of here for entering the boy's bathroom," the little shit says.

"You listen to me, you little punk, you ever touch Tate, look at Tate, talk to Tate, or even think about Tate again, I will make your life a living hell. I don't care what you think you can do to me; I will make sure you get what's coming to you tenfold. Do I make myself clear?" The vitriol in my voice is unfamiliar.

He rolls his eyes while I turn to Tate.

"Hey, buddy," I say, trying to inject every ounce of sweetness I can into my words for him. "You take a few minutes and get cleaned up. I'm taking this kid to meet your teacher. You come to find me when you're ready, okay?"

He answers silently with a nod of his head but won't make eye contact with me.

I turn to the bully. "You, move it. *Now!*" I yell.

By the time I reach Tate's classroom, I am shaking with rage. During the short walk across the hallway, the bully informs me that Mrs. Williams already knows. And because of who his father is, she won't do a thing. We make our way into the classroom, and he heads straight for the teacher.

"Mrs. Williams, this crazy lady just escorted me out of the restroom. I think I should call my father now," the conniving little ass threatens.

I catch the momentary fear cross her face before she rises from her desk to walk into the hallway with me. She immediately starts as if she's going to direct this conversation.

Oh, hell no, lady.

"I'm assuming you're yet another new nanny for Tate?" she asks, barely hiding her disgust.

"Yes, as a matter of fact, I am. Lanie Heart." I reach out my hand, which she chooses not to shake.

"Yes, well, Ms. Heart, we have rules in this school. I'm afraid we're going to have to call the school officials. Parents are not allowed in the children's restrooms. Ever," she informs me in the most demeaning manner.

"You know what," I begin, barely containing my anger, "that's a great idea. I would like to file a complaint. Do you know where all of your students are, Mrs. Williams? Do you know I had to enter that bathroom because that bully in there was holding Tate down on the bathroom floor, trying to force-feed him a urinal cake?"

She pales but doesn't respond. That's when I realize the bully was telling the truth.

"This isn't the first time this has happened, is it, Mrs. Williams? This behavior has been going on for quite some time, yet you've done nothing to stop it, have you?"

"Ms. Heart, you don't understand," she says, her voice shaky. "Jake just has a way about him. It's not only Tate that he teases. It's not that big of a big deal. His other nannies never said a word."

I see red. "I don't give a flying fart what his other twit nannies have or haven't done." I'm yelling now, and I can't seem to stop myself. I'm vaguely aware of someone coming down the hall, but I'm on a roll.

"I'm here now. I will be here. Every. Single. Day. I will be checking on Tate and his classmates. I will be making calls and hounding this school day and night until Jake faces the consequences of his actions. I don't care who his father is. He. Will. *Not*. Hurt. Tate. Again. Do you understand me? You'll be lucky if you get to keep your job when I'm through with you."

Just then, a hand lands gently on my shoulder. I turn to see Dex with Tate at his side, both of them eyes wide and mouths agape. If I wasn't so mad, I might laugh.

"Mrs. Williams, I'm not sure what's going on, but I suggest you call the office and have someone cover the class.

I think we need to have a meeting right now." Dexter's voice is deadly calm, but I can see the vein in his temple throbbing.

I get on my knees so I'm at eye level with Tate. "Hey, Tate-o-nator, everything's going to be just fine. I promise you. Are you good to go into the classroom?" I ask, holding him securely. "I was hoping you could show me your desk. I'll help you get settled while we wait for Mrs. Williams' helper to come from the office."

He seems to be slightly in shock but walks with me into the classroom.

We get him set up at his desk, and I'm relieved to see that Jake is across the room. He still looks evil, but I can see he's at least a little worried. Even from here, I can hear the controlled venom spewing from Dexter.

I crouch down beside Tate's desk and raise my voice slightly while speaking to him. "Bullying is never okay, under any circumstances. You understand that, right?" I want to make sure he knows, but also that all the other children here realize it, too. "I meant what I said. I will be here every single day, Tate. I will make sure you're safe. I promise you. I will not let this continue."

He has gone a little pale. When he moves, he's so fast, I almost don't see him when he barrels into me for a hug.

I kiss his head and whisper, "Everything's going to be fine. I promise you."

Peering around the room, I spot Dex by the door. His face is bright red, hands clenched into fists. We make eye contact and have a whole conversation without ever saying a word.

"I'm going to go to the office now to fix this. I'll be back to pick you up today so I can check in. Are you going to be okay?"

Tate gives me a small smile and pulls away. He doesn't make eye contact with anyone, but he pulls out a folder that says 'morning work' and gets to the task.

I stand up and glare at Mrs. Williams, then follow her to

the office with Dex guiding me by the elbow. The way he is hanging on to me, I briefly wonder if I'm the one about to get into trouble.

∾

*T*he ride home from Tate's school is quiet. Both girls have fallen asleep in their car seats. Having lost his temper in the meeting with the principal and Mrs. Williams, Dexter seems to be lost in thought as he pulls the car up to the house and shuts off the engine. Slowly, he turns to me with a pained expression.

"I had no idea. I'm his father, and I had no idea this was going on for so long." He has tears in his eyes.

During the meeting, we found out that Jake has been tormenting Tate and a few other children all year. Mrs. Williams did the best she could to keep them separated but couldn't always succeed. It turns out Jake's father is also a bully. The school called him numerous times before he started threatening Mrs. Williams.

"Tate's a smart kid. He probably didn't want you to know. Listen, part of me feels bad for his teacher, but a bigger part feels like the suspension is justified. She's tasked with keeping children safe in her care, and she failed. As for Jake and his dad? All I can say is karma. US senator or not, karma has a way of catching up."

As the story unfolded in the school office today, I saw so many expressions cross Dexter's face. Luckily, Jake and his father were not present because I think Dexter would have ended up in jail.

I gently place a hand on his. "There are several reasons you didn't know, but you do now. How we handle it going forward is what matters."

"How am I supposed to go to London? I can't leave him

like this. I've already failed him in so many ways." Dex's voice breaks, and he looks away.

"I meant what I said to Tate today. I'm here now. I promised him I would make sure he's all right and I will make good on that promise. You can trust me. We'll fix this together. Isn't this trip something you can't put off? It's imperative for your company, right? You said it has to be successful so you can continue to provide for your family and employees. Not to mention, continue to pay me," I say with a wink.

He cracks a smile but silently agrees with me.

"Well, then let me do what you're paying me the big bucks for. You take care of what you have to do and trust me to handle all of this. I promise I won't let Tate, or you, down." I reach across and place my hand on his forearm. "Do you trust me, Dex?"

Dex turns in his seat, angling his body toward me. We're so close I can feel his breath on me. The smell of him—clean, crisp ocean, and all-male—instinctively cause my thighs to squeeze tightly together. I'm so nervous about what his answer will be that I feel myself begin to sweat.

Real classy, Lanes, ugh!

"For some reason, I do trust you, Lanie. I can't thank you enough. You've been here for less than two days, and I already feel like I've known you my whole life," he admits. "How is it you come into our lives and make us feel like you were supposed to be here all along?"

My throat is thick with emotion, and I have to work to swallow it away. Dexter seems to be leaning even closer like he wants to kiss me, and oh God, how I want him to kiss me. But it's been a tough morning, so I go for humor instead, trying to break the tension. "Just call it the Mary Poppins effect."

The bark of laughter that falls from him is surprising

because it seems to happen so infrequently. It startles the girls who both burst into tears, and our moment is lost.

Dexter heads to his home office while I tend to the girls. The rest of the afternoon goes by quickly. Before I know it, I'm packing the girls into the car Dexter insists I drive when I have the kids and head back to the school to pick up Tate.

When I arrive in the pick-up line, I am relieved to see Tate sitting with a little boy and smiling. I can do this after all. I can make a difference for this family even if it may end up breaking my heart when I have to leave them.

~

The next couple of days go by in a blur. Dex is working a lot, getting ready for his trip, while I settle into a good routine with the kids. Mrs. Williams has been suspended with pay while the school advisory committee looks into the complaint we filed. Jake has received an out-of-school suspension for the time being, and the change in Tate is remarkable. I've never seen him so calm and carefree.

Jake will likely be back to school in a week or two, but the school has promised us he'll be placed in a different classroom. I would have preferred a different school, but I'll take what I can get for now. I'm still picking up Tate from school every day, arriving fifteen minutes early to make my presence known.

Today is a beautiful day, so I'm sitting on a bench outside of the school. The girls are sitting in their stroller with some teething cookies. They're a mess but happy, so I let the mess go.

"Excuse me? Are you Tate's nanny?" someone asks me in a deep, rumbly voice.

Instantly, my spine straightens, and I push the girls'

stroller behind me. I'm not expecting to see Jake's father, but I have to be prepared since I don't know what he looks like.

I stand up and cross my arms over my chest. "I am. Who are you?"

"Sorry, I should have started with that." He laughs, putting me at ease. "I'm sorry if I startled you. My name is Jamie. I'm Connor's manny," he says with another hearty laugh. "Connor and Tate are friends." He frowns. "Well, they used to be. Connor said Tate hasn't played with anyone for a long time and hadn't wanted to talk to him anymore. I told Connor that Tate had a lot going on, but he came home yesterday and said Tate sat with him at lunch. He was hoping they could start playing together again. I used to pick them up from school a couple of times a week before his parents got divorced, and I'm happy to do that again. I know his mom never wanted to take them to their house, and that's fine, but I know Connor misses his buddy."

I'm so shocked it takes me a minute to answer. "Um, yeah, I'm sure Tate would love that. If it's okay, I'd like to talk with him first. He's had a tough week, so I just want to make sure he's up for it. Did you say his mom never took them herself?"

"Yeah, between you and me, she never seemed very friendly. My boyfriend and I thought he would be better off when she left. Then he had this string of self-obsessed nannies. To be honest, I'm not sure which was worse. I don't mean to pry ... oh hell, yes, I do! I love the gossip." He laughs again. "Connor told me what went down with Jake a few days ago. Props to you! I'm glad Tate has someone on his side. I would have loved to take that little prick out myself, but it seems like you handled it much better."

I laugh out loud and immediately know he and I are going to be friends. "I think you and I are going to get along just fine. Let me talk to Tate tonight. If he's up for it, why don't you guys plan to come over after school one day next week? It sounds like it's our turn to host a playdate anyway!"

"We would love that, thanks. And yes, I think we'll be excellent friends!" He winks at me, and we exchange numbers.

When Tate and Connor come walking out of the school together, Jamie nudges my shoulder with his. I can't help the happy feeling that takes over my heart. Tate is going to be just fine. I can feel it.

CHAPTER 12

DEX

After the incident at school, the rest of the week flew by in a whirlwind of meetings, kids, and flirting with Lanie. Before I know it, I'm landing in London. My heart is still heavy over Tate. Parent guilt is eating me alive, but Lanie promised to be on top of things. I trust her completely, and that's a weird feeling for me. I don't know if I ever trusted Bitchzilla this much, and to be honest, that really scares me.

In just a week, Lanie's taken up residence in my mind and I can't see that ending anytime soon. For now, I have to focus on this deal. I'll be working twelve to eighteen hours a day just to make this deadline. Failure isn't an option. Knowing Lanie has the kids covered makes this so much easier.

As much as I trust her, I still have a past that won't let go of me. *It seems like something Lanie and I may have in common.* The guys are doing as promised by checking in on her every day. They had better keep their goddamn hands to themselves. They've all been warned.

I also had the security system upgraded before I left, installing cameras inside and outside of the house. I know I should have told Lanie, and I will when I get home. I just couldn't come to London without being able to check in on them.

Loki warned that it's an invasion of privacy, and Lanie will be pissed when she finds out. He's probably right, but I did it anyway. Hopefully, she'll understand.

Unfortunately, watching Lanie with my kids is quickly becoming an obsession. I reason doing it by telling myself I need to keep an eye on my kids; it's not like I put one in her bedroom. I groan silently because holy hell would I have liked to, and yes, I'm fully aware of how creepy that makes me.

I'm in my hotel room waiting on room service so I take a seat on the couch to FaceTime the kids. The time difference has been difficult for us, but they're my priority. I'll always make it work. I promised Tate I would FaceTime him at least once a day; I have to come through on that no matter what.

Lanie picks up after the second ring, and my breath catches. *God, why does she have to be so fucking hot?*

"Hey there, boss man! How's London?" She's smiling, her hair's a mess, but she has never looked better. Instantly, I'm hard as fucking granite.

"Cold," I answer, "and wet. Very, very wet." I shouldn't do this with her, this weird back and forth we sometimes have. I often wonder if she knows how sexually charged our conversations are. She seems so innocent, yet her eyes dance with mirth as she answers.

"Well, Mr. Cross, sometimes I find I enjoy being wet." She winks, and I can only nod. "Tate is dying to talk to you, but first, I wanted to ask you something."

Nothing like throwing my kids out there to deflate a boner. "Yes, Ms. Heart?" I force out.

"Remember how I was telling you about Tate's friend, Connor? I met his nanny, Jamie? They're coming over for a playdate this week. Tate is so excited, by the way. Jamie seems sweet as well, and I was sort of wondering …" She breaks off, visibly nervous about continuing, and she has me intrigued.

"What are you so nervous to ask me, Ms. Heart? Now you have me so very curious." I grin into the phone.

Relaxing slightly, she says, "Fine. Do you care if I have friends over when the kids are in bed? Jamie's sister is also a nanny in town, so I thought I would have them over one night to try and make some friends down here."

I want to tell her that I'll be her friend, but I don't. Nor do I even have to think about her request. "Lanie, it's your home, too. As long as you're not throwing a rager while my kids are sleeping, I'm more than happy for you to have a friend or two over. I want you to feel at home, but thank you for asking. I hope you guys have fun."

"Thanks, Dex." There's something about her voice in moments like this that thaws a deeply buried part of me.

"You're more than welcome ... and, Lanie?" I feel my voice softening to match hers.

"Yes, Dex?" Her sass is returning.

"Thank you ... for everything. I truly don't know what I would have done if I hadn't found you." I let my emotions play out through my words.

"You're welcome." Her smile is so honest, so pure, and gone far too soon. "Here's Tate."

The call with Tate is brief. He still isn't talking much, but the look of pure joy on his face when I asked him about his upcoming playdate loosened a little more of my blackened heart.

I spend the next few days working, FaceTiming with Lanie and Tate, and obsessively watching the security cameras at the house. Every morning, Lanie dances around the kitchen, making the kids breakfast, and every morning, Tate leaves the house laughing. She's good for him, I realize. I go to bed at night watching recorded clips of Lanie interacting with the kids, and thank God they're in the videos, or I'd be jerking off to home movies like a creeper.

Thursday, in between meetings, I get about thirty pictures from Lanie of Tate and his buddy. She's thoughtful in a way I've never encountered. The next morning, I order room service and settle down to FaceTime home.

"Hello, boss man. How's London?" Lanie asks with a smile that brightens her whole face.

"The same as yesterday, and the day before." This has become our conversation every time I call. "Tell me about Tate's playdate?"

"Oh, my God! It was great. They played together for three hours, and he did better than I could have hoped. I was super proud of him. Connor's a talker, so I don't think he felt pressure to say much, but I did hear him answer questions a few times." She's so animated as she speaks that I have trouble tracking her through the phone with all her wild hand movements.

"That's great, Lanie." I can't explain the deep sense of gratitude I have for her. All the other nannies we've had combined didn't have the compassion or love for Tate the way Lanie does.

If I didn't know better, I would think I was developing feelings other than gratitude for her, too, but I haven't known her long enough for that, so I quickly push that thought aside. Insta lust is one thing. Insta love doesn't even belong in the English language. Plus, I've turned into a bit of a creeper. I had my assistant order me another laptop so I could have the live feed from the house going all the time while I worked on my other one. Her voice relaxes me in a way I've never felt before. Even when the girls are crying and it's complete chaos, she's calm and loving—everything their mother was not.

"Dex? Did you hear me?" she asks, calling me out of my thoughts.

I'm watching her sitting at the kitchen island while talking to me. She has little jean shorts on and a tank top that hugs every curve. She doodles on a piece of paper as she speaks; I wish I could see what she's writing.

"Uh, sorry, bad connection. What did you say?" I lie.

"I said you just missed the kids. They were exhausted. Tate was so tired, he put himself to bed early. We'll have to try to catch you in the morning. Also, Jamie's going to be here soon, so I should go. Is it okay if we open one of these bottles of wine on the island?" Lanie asks, and I can't help but notice how comfortable she seems to be in my home. *Or how much I like that she does.*

"Sure, whatever you want, Lanie." I hate that at that moment I know it's true. I'd give her just about anything I could.

"Okay, have a good night ... er ... day, I guess. I'll have Tate FaceTime you in the morning." She laughs, still not having mastered the time change between us.

"Goodnight, Lanie. Have fun with your friend," I tell her.

Realization hits like a punch to the throat. I need her to feel comfortable in my space more than I've wanted anything in a very long time.

"Goodnight, Dex," she says quietly, in a tone I'm starting to realize is just for me.

I stare at the phone long after she hangs up. Then I remember Preston called me earlier today, so I move to the desk and call him back.

"Hey, asshole, how's London?" he answers my call.

"Nice greeting, dickhead. What if it had been Molly on the line?" I ask, not waiting for his answer. "London's fine," I tell him. "Deals are almost done. I can't wait to get home. You guys still checking on Lanie?"

"Of course I have been checking her out. She's hot, man!" Preston says to piss me off.

A growl escapes my throat. When I speak, my voice has turned to gravel. "I told you, she's off limits."

"Yeah, you tell her friend, Jamie, that?" He's laughing so hard now, I almost missed what he said.

"What do you mean, Jamie, her nanny friend?" I ask, and Preston laughs even harder.

"You mean her *manny* friend? He's a dude, you know! And a good looking one. They seemed to be getting along really well when I stopped by earlier. He's a very touchy-feely kind of guy."

I'm out of my chair so fast it flips over behind me. Fuck. The one day I couldn't watch the live feed.

"What do you mean, he's a dude?" I yell.

"I mean, he has a dick, and if I were a lady, I'd probably think he was hot," Pres enlightens me.

"What the fuck? She never said anything about Jamie being a guy. He's coming over tonight for wine. What the actual fuck?" I say, and begin to pace.

"You jealous, bro?" he asks me, and I have to stop for a second.

Am I jealous? I run a hand through my hair and pace the room. I'm angry. I don't want her going out with anyone but me.

She's mine. Mine.

I slump onto the bed. "Fuck. I think I am."

"Well, you better make a move. I'm not saying this to be a jerk, Dex, but she's hot and sweet as hell. I know one of the single dads at Tate's school already asked for her number," he tattles.

My stomach clenches. "What? How do you know that?"

"She told me. Jamie thought it was hilarious. He is a pretty good dude; I think you'll like him."

"The fuck I will," I grumble. "Well, did she give it to him? The phone number, I mean?"

"Not sure, but listen, she's doing great. The kids are as

happy as I've seen them in a long time. Tate even gave me a fist bump when I was leaving. He didn't talk, but he made eye contact with me the entire time I was talking with him. That's a huge improvement, man. Don't screw this up with Lanie." He's quiet for a few beats. "I think you all need her."

I hate when Pres is right, but I can't argue. "Okay, thanks for checking in on them. I've got work to do."

"Anytime … and, Dex? Don't go crazy and do something stupid. Just because she has wine with Jamie tonight, in your house, doesn't mean anything is going on between them."

I can't tell if he is laughing at me, but I growl and hang up on him anyway. Immediately, I start flipping through the feeds on the home cameras until I find them in the kitchen. She has her feet curled under her on the stool. Her hand is on his arm, and she's laughing. My gut clenches as I call her.

"Oh, hey, Dex. Everything okay?" she asks without a care in the world.

"Are you on a date?" I blurt, unable to contain my jealous tone.

Through the security camera I can see the confusion written on her face as she answers, "What? What are you talking about?"

"Jamie. Are you on a date with Jamie? You didn't tell me Jamie was a *he*, not a *she*," I bite out.

I'm watching her on the video feed when I see her roll her eyes to Jamie.

"Don't roll your eyes at me. Answer the question." As soon as I say it, I wish I could take it back.

Her head swivels all around the room until she lands on the camera above the cabinet. Her voice is low and heated. "Are you watching me?"

"Damn right I'm watching you! Now answer the question. Are you on a date with him in my house?" I'm not sure if it's hurt, betrayal, or anger she hears in my voice, but none of it is enough to tame her rage.

"You psycho creeper!" she shrieks. Her emotions take over, and she can't control herself. "It's none, you hear me ... *none* of your business if I'm on a date. I told you, I *asked* you if I could have friends over. You told me this was my home, too. You have no say in who or what I do!"

"Lanie—" I realize she's hung up on me. I glare back at the monitor and find her giving me the finger as she drags a chair over to the counter. Before I can blink, she has ripped the camera from the wall.

Fuck! I call her back, but she doesn't answer. A few minutes later, I get a text.

Lanie: I am too mad to answer your call right now. If you have a question about the kids, then ask it via text. I will not answer your calls. We will talk about this when you get home.

Dexter: The fuck we will, that's in four days. I want to talk now!

Lanie: I don't. Do you need anything concerning the kids?

Dexter: Lanie, don't push me.

Lanie: Yes or no, Mr. Cross?

Dexter: Ms. Heart, I'm furious.

Lanie: Good. Me too. Tate will call you tomorrow. Good-bye.

She doesn't answer my messages for the rest of the night, so I finally give up. He better not be touching her, or I will break his legs. Knowing there's nothing else I can do right now, I finish up work.

In the next few days, there's very little communication from Lanie. She texts me pictures of the kids and answers direct questions about them when I call. Most of the time, when she answers, she immediately puts Tate on the phone.

Finally, my deal in London wraps up. I head to the airport, calling Trevor on my way.

"Hey, Dex, congrats on the deal! You must be so relieved?" he says, pride evident in his voice.

"Yeah, I am. Thanks. Have you been by the house lately?" I ask, unable to focus on anything but Lanie.

He chuckles while answering, "I was there yesterday. Lanie has everything covered. Why?"

"She's pissed at me about the cameras. I kind of messed up. I lost my shit when she had a guy over and let it slip that I could see her rolling her eyes at me."

His laughter fills the air, and I have to pull the phone away from my ear.

"Yeah, I know. Jamie and I had a good laugh about you yesterday."

"What the fuck? Are you friends with him, too? Jesus, can't anyone be on my side? Why does everyone have fucking eyes for my girl?" I growl.

He goes silent. "Your girl? What are you saying, Dex?"

"Jesus, I don't know. I can't get her out of my head. I'm fucked up," I admit.

"You like her," he states plainly. "You wouldn't be possessive like this if you didn't. I've never seen you like this, Dex. I'm a little worried, dude. She's good with your kids; you guys need that stability right now. Are you sure this is something you want to pursue?"

Sighing, I run a hand through my hair. I'm going to go bald if I don't stop pulling at my hair because of her. "Fuck, Trevor, I don't know. My head is saying not to rock the boat; we need her just like you said. A bigger part of me is out of control and has been since the first moment I saw her. At first, I thought it was just lust. I needed to get laid. I'm not so sure anymore. I want her in my bed, but I feel like I just might want her, all of her, and it scares me."

Trevor is quiet for a long while.

"Trevor? Are you still there?" I ask, staring at the phone screen.

"Yeah, I'm here, just thinking," he replies, softening his voice. "I'm not going to tell you what to do. You know how I feel about love and shit, but ... I do think you deserve to be happy, Dex. You always believed in love, even before Anna. It's what made you different, better. You've lost that part of you. It's a part I always admired, and if you have a chance to find it, really find it, I think you should go for it. Perhaps it won't work out in the end, but don't you think that maybe you deserve to try?"

"I'm afraid to mess things up with her the same way I did with Anna," I admit.

"You asshole!"

I'm so shocked that I pull the phone away from my ear to check the caller ID again to make sure I didn't accept another call by mistake.

"Excuse me?" I say incredulously.

"Get your head out of your ass," Trevor yells. "*You* didn't mess anything up with Anna. She was always a selfish bitch. We all saw it but wanted you happy, so we kept our feelings to ourselves. We won't make that mistake again, by the way. Lanie is different; we can all see it. Figure out what you want and go for it, but for Christ's sake, don't let the fears of your past ruin your future."

"You know my track record, Trevor. What if she leaves me, too? I'm not sure I would survive her." Even putting a voice to my concerns causes my hands to shake.

"I don't know what to say to that, man, other than you know we'll always stick by you. You have to decide if she's worth the risk."

"Preston said I might already be too late. Guys are asking for her number, and she was on a date with Jamie at my house," I grumble.

He forces the issue. "As I said, figure out what you want, Dex. Is it her?"

"I think she might be."

"There's no in between with her, dude. Even I can tell that about her. You're either all in, or you walk away. If Lanie is what you want, then go for it." He chuckles, and I know I'm not going to like what he says next. "By the way ... Pres is an asshole. He was just trying to get your ass in gear. Jamie's gay."

"What the *fuck*?"

Trevor just laughs and hangs up. Now I have to get through airport security trying to look like I won't kill someone.

CHAPTER 13

LANIE

It's been a long week, so I am happy when Friday arrives. Dexter should be home tomorrow, and thankfully, we've made it without any significant incidents, but I'm exhausted. I can't imagine Dex doing this by himself for so long.

I'm sitting at the table doing a puzzle with Tate when a massive yawn hits. "Hey, buddy? How about pizza and a movie tonight? Just you and me?"

He turns his grin up to me and nods.

"Okay. Go change into your pjs while I order the pizza. Then you can pick the movie."

Tate heads down the hall to the stairs when the doorbell rings. He stops, frozen in place as he stares at the door.

"Who's at the door, Tate? Your Uncle Preston is supposed to stop by, is it him?"

He doesn't answer me, but I can tell from the kitchen that he's shaking.

What the hell? I rush down the hall toward him and find tears running down his face. Tate's pointing at the door where I can see a woman through the glass wearing a harsh expression on her face.

"Jesus, Tate, open the damn door for your mother," she shrieks.

Tate's little body shakes uncontrollably, so I step in front of him while she continues banging on the door. Never have I been so glad for my need to lock, check, and relock doors.

Crouching down to Tate's level, I turn his body so the door is no longer visible.

"Hey, buddy. Look at me, just me, okay?" I tell him as calmly as I can manage.

His mother's angry curses echo through the walls.

"Remember the promise I made you? No one is ever going to hurt you again. Not as long as I'm around. Remember that?"

The poor kid doesn't make any moves, although I can see in his eyes that he hears me.

"Is that your mom over there?" I point behind him.

Tate's eyes travel toward the door again, and he pales but nods.

"Well, she seems a little scary right now, but I've got you," I tell Tate, drawing him in for a hug. "I'm going to send her away and let your dad handle it. I need you to help me with the girls while I do that. They're in the family room sleeping in their pack n' plays. Can you go in there, close the door, and sing them a song, very quietly, so they stay sleeping? Can you do that for me?"

With one shaky look at the door, he turns and heads to the family room.

What the hell do I do now? Where is Preston?

I know I can't let her into the house. She's terrifying.

What did Dex ever see in her? I wonder. Pulling out my phone, I do the only thing I can think of; I FaceTime Dex. He doesn't answer.

Come on. Please answer the phone. I try three more times before he finally picks up.

110

"Lanie? Sorry, I was going through customs. Everything all right?" he asks, sounding out of breath.

"I, well—" I begin, but he cuts me off.

"What's that noise, Lanie? What's going on?" Concern is lining his questions.

"We have a visitor," I say, walking to the front door and slipping outside. I quickly close the door behind me so I don't let Tate's mother in the house while hopefully keeping whatever will happen now from reaching Tate's ears.

"Who the hell are you?" she screams. "Why didn't you let my son come to the door?"

My face is ashen as I turn the phone around so Dex can see his ex-wife face-to-face.

"Answer me, goddamn it," Tate's mother yells.

Before I know what is happening, she slaps me across the face with enough force to send me reeling back into the door.

"Anna, that is enough!" comes Dexter's angry, pained scream. "Lanie, are you okay? Let me see you."

I'm dizzy but manage to turn the camera on myself in time to watch his eyes fill with a rage I've never witnessed from him before. I look up, trying to keep tabs on the woman who will likely strike again, when I realize Preston has pulled into the driveway and is sprinting toward us.

"Anna, what the fuck are you doing here? Lanie? What the hell? Did you hit her, Anna?" Preston looks as wild as Dexter, who's now shouting through the phone. Preston finally hears him and grabs the phone from me.

"Preston? Thank fuck. Get Lanie in the house, please. Keep her phone though, I need to deal with Anna."

"You and me both," he grumbles.

"Deal with me? Me? I'm their mother, you assholes," she shrieks, sounding slightly unhinged.

Preston ignores her, turning his back to talk to me. "Lanie, go inside, okay? Check on the kids."

I nod and rush through the door, but not before I hear Dexter's dangerously low voice. "You gave up the right to call yourself a mother the minute you walked away. If you ever come near my kids or touch Lanie again, I'll kill you myself."

I run to the kitchen, pausing at the family room door to listen for Tate. He's still singing to the girls and sounds calm. After hurrying to the kitchen for an ice pack, I head back to Tate. The poor kid, that bitch did something to him. I can just feel it. He was so stricken when he saw her through the window. I know that fear.

I slip into the room, but when Tate sees me, he bursts into tears.

"Hey, buddy!" I say, trying to fake a calm I don't feel. "It's okay, I'm fine. I was in such a hurry to get to you I ran into the door. You're okay now; I'm here."

He raises his hand to remove the ice pack.

"Hey, I'm fine. Preston's here. He's sending her away and letting your dad deal with her. Do you want to talk about what just happened? You didn't seem very happy to see her."

Tate shakes his head and quietly says, "She doesn't like me."

My heart breaks for him. He buries his head into my neck and cries just as Preston slips into the room, a furious expression on his face.

When his eyes land on mine, he swears. "Fuck!"

My eyes dart in his direction, giving him the slightest nod of my head. "I'm good. I was in such a hurry to get back to Tate I ran into the door." I implore Preston with my gaze to go along.

Preston narrows his eyes, but nods once.

"So, Tate-o-nator, what do you say we both get changed and let Uncle Preston order the pizza for us?" I look at Preston. "Are you staying for dinner?"

"Yup, I'm staying. I think we'll have a big sleepover

tonight so we can all be here when your dad gets home. Trevor and Loki want to come, too!"

I peer up at him questioningly, but he gives a look that says, 'Do not argue with me.'

"Wow, that sounds like fun, doesn't it, Tate? Let's go get ready!" Taking his hand, I lead him upstairs.

Comparatively, the rest of the night goes smoothly. I have to admit, it's nice having the guys here to help with the babies, even if their skills are more than unconventional. Tate has stuck close to me since his mom showed up, but I haven't pushed him to talk, not yet anyway. It was a tough day for both of us. If he needs to just cuddle into me, I won't complain.

After we finish a movie about toys, the guys put the girls to bed. Yes, it takes all three of them. Somehow, they manage so I can put Tate to bed.

"Lanie? Can you lay with me?" Tate asks with the voice of a lost, little boy.

Usually, I would encourage him to sleep alone, tell him he's a big boy, but right now, he just needs comfort, so I climb into bed next to him and snuggle. "Sure, buddy, I'm here for you. Try to get some rest."

We're both fast asleep before I realize I never said goodnight to Dexter's friends.

CHAPTER 14

DEX

"Where is she?" I burst into my house, knowing all three of my friends stayed here last night to watch over Lanie and the kids.

I round the corner to the kitchen and see Trevor with Tate pouring something into a frying pan. All the anger leaves my body the second I see my little guy. Tate runs to me, wrapping his arms around my legs in a death grip. I scoop down to pick him up into a hug and never want to let him go. His little body is trembling, and I realize he's crying.

"Hey, hey, don't cry, Tate. I'm here. I'm so, so sorry I wasn't here yesterday. I'm so sorry."

Tate hiccups and pulls back to look into my eyes. "It's okay, Daddy. Lanie saved me again."

He lays his head on my shoulder, and I squeeze him even tighter. The lump in my throat is so big, I can't swallow and can't stop the tears flowing down my face.

Someone walks up behind us and places a hand on my shoulder, then I hear Loki speak. "Hey, Tate! Think you can help Pres out with the girls? He's in the nursery looking a little lost."

Tate looks at me, then at Loki. After placing him on the

floor, he shrugs his shoulders and heads off to join his sisters.

"Where is everyone?" I ask, staring Trevor in the eyes. He knows what I'm asking. Where's Lanie? Is she okay? Is she still here? *Please don't let her leave us.*

"Lanie's still asleep, but she's going to have one hell of a headache today," he whispers. It must be worse than I thought.

I turn to Loki. "Get Ryan from EnVision Securities on the phone now ... please." I lower my voice. "Tell him I want eyes on Anna, then I want him to get her to a meeting with me as soon as fucking possible."

I turn to head upstairs when Loki holds up a hand to stop me.

"Just give me five minutes, then you can go be the knight in shining armor. Lanie told Tate the door hit her pretty hard. He asked her to sleep with him last night because he was afraid ..." The way he said *door* lets me know nothing has gotten past Tate. The fact that he was afraid has my insides twisting in a way that's so painful I'm not able to breathe.

"Afraid of what?" I finally ask. "You were all here."

"That she'll leave," Trevor all but whispers.

I hate that Tate's finally talking, and this is what he has to say. My throat is too dry, and it hurts to reply. I give a curt nod to them both and stare up at the ceiling. What can I say? The truth is, I'm afraid of the same thing.

Loki clears his throat. "Listen, man, if you're going to set up a meeting with Anna, we need to talk. You'll have to do it at your office where we can install cameras in case she asks for something crazy. You don't know what she's been up to all this time, so you have to cover your ass."

None of us know exactly what it is that Loki does. He's never been allowed to tell us. For that reason, we all have our theories. Most likely something in the government, the CIA, or some sort of special agent. Until he can open up, I'm just happy to have him on my side.

"Thanks, guys. I'm going to head up and check on the girls." I give them both a heartfelt slap on the back and head upstairs, Loki following closely behind.

I stop off quickly in the nursery, kissing each girl, breathing them in. I can't help but chuckle as I take in Preston and Tate. Preston looks like he stuck his finger in a light socket. My friends have no idea what they're doing, but they're here, trying, and I'm forever grateful.

"Tate," Loki says behind me. "Trevor's ready to finish breakfast, and I'm back for diaper duty. Wanna trade?"

Tate gives him the biggest smile and darts past us down the stairs.

"I'm going to go check on Lanie. Thank you both."

They each come in for a one-armed hug and pat on the back, neither of them saying anything. They don't have to. These guys are my family.

Entering Tate's room, I freeze. Lanie's asleep on her left side with her hands tucked under her face. I notice the bruise on her cheekbone and I feel murderous.

Slowly, I make my way to her. Even with the bruised face, she's gorgeous. My chest aches with an unfamiliar feeling as I carefully sit beside her and watch her sleep for a few long moments. When I reach out to softly brush her hair away from her face, she startles awake.

"Hey, it's me, Dex. Sorry to wake you," I say gently.

"Oh my God! What time is it? The kids—" she starts, flustered, but I cut her off.

"The kids are fine. The guys are taking care of them ... for the most part." I try to smile for her sake. "Are you okay?" My throat feels like I'm swallowing a hundred angry bees. I feel shame deep in my gut for not protecting her. "I'm so sorry I wasn't here to protect you."

Lanie smiles sleepily. "I don't need protection. I'm fine. I admit I wasn't expecting a boot slap from her, though. She's stronger than she looks."

I chuckle at her use of boot slap and shake my head. It's just another thing to love about her. Now it's my turn to startle. It's way too soon for love. Even when I believed in love, I never really bought into love at first sight.

Realizing I've been staring at her for too long, I move to stand. Before she can protest, I've scooped her in my arms and am carrying her to her room.

"Wait, put me down. I can walk!" she exclaims loud enough that both Preston and Loki stick their heads into the hallway, snickering.

I narrow my eyes at them, and she laughs.

"Not today," I grumble in response.

We move in silence until I reach her bed, pull down the covers, and gently lay her down. I'm so close I smell the light floral scent of her shampoo. Her hand skims my jaw as I tuck her in, and she thanks me.

I want to ask her why she's thanking me, but I'm caught in her gaze; I feel lost. Slowly, I lower my mouth to hers and kiss her like my life depends on it. I don't know if I can ever come back from this kiss. Her lips are so soft and gentle. My need for her is intoxicating. My tongue teases her seam, causing her to gasp. And when she opens those delicious lips for me, I dominate her mouth. I don't pull away until we're both breathless and maybe a little less lost.

"What was that for?" she asks in a whisper as her fingers reach up to touch her swollen lips.

"Me," I answer honestly. "Thank you for saving Tate again. Stay in bed. He wants to bring breakfast up to you. I'll get you some ibuprofen and an ice pack, too."

Lanie sits up in the bed, staring at me with heat in her eyes. I have to look away before I take her right here.

"Honestly, I'm fine. I don't need to stay in bed," she protests.

"Please?" I ask quietly. "It'll mean a lot to Tate." I turn and head for the door. "We'll have to talk about Anna later. I want you to file a police report, but we can do that after the kids are in bed ... if you don't have any plans tonight."

"No plans. I'm not sure about the police report, but we can talk."

∽

Downstairs, I find Tate and Trevor plating a tray of food for Lanie. Preston and Loki are on the floor playing with the girls, looking a little ragged but still managing to make the girls laugh. I peek at the tray and turn to Tate.

"Hey, buddy, do you think you can carry that up yourself, or do you want me to help you?" I ask gently.

Very quietly, he replies, "I'd like to do it myself."

I smile and can't help but notice how fast he's growing up. "Okay. That's a very nice thing to do. I know Lanie will love it. How about we put covers on the cups so nothing sloshes around, then you can take it up? Sound good?"

Smiling, he gives me a nod.

I put the covers on the cups, hand him the tray, and then watch him walk down the hall. I'm lost in thought for a minute when I realize Trevor is beside me trying to hand me something. Glancing down, I'm shocked to see a child's handwriting on a very old envelope. I take a closer look and realize that it's mine.

"Is this the letter I wrote to you the summer you got sent to the camp in England?" I ask incredulously.

"It is." Trevor grins. "We were about twelve at the time. I think it's time you read it. Remember who you used to be. Who you should be. Then think about everything going on right now and make a choice."

I try to wrack my brain but cannot for the life of me remember what I would have written so long ago that made such an impact he kept it for twenty years. Preston walks over and joins us; they have clearly discussed what's in the letter.

"Why don't you head to your office and read it?" he suggests. "I'll head up to check on Tate and Lanie. Trevor can clean up here while Loki watches the girls."

I feel a little ganged up on, but I know they love me, so I head to my office and do as they asked.

Dear Dex, June 28th, 2002

Dude, camp here sucks. I haven't found anything I can eat. The people all talk weird, and they're so formal I want to poke my own eyes out. I miss being at home. Please send me some snacks! Anything American will do. Seriously, anything!

The only thing that hasn't sucked is a girl I met here. She's super cool, I think I might like her, like really like her but I don't know. How do you know? You're the sappy heart of our group. Tell me how you'll know when you love someone? I'm not sure I believe in love anyway, thanks to my parents, but, dude. This girl! She makes me feel different, so I need some advice ... and snacks, don't forget the snacks.

See you in a couple of months,

Trev

I can't help but laugh. I remember that summer. It royally fucking sucked. That was the only summer we ever spent apart. Our only means of communication was through snail mail. I go to slip the letter back in the envelope and realize there's another page. I pull it out and am shocked to see my handwriting.

Dude, July 10th, 2002

Why so formal? Are they monitoring your letter writing, too? It wouldn't surprise me. I looked up the camp yesterday. Who has a dress code for summer camp? It must be so stuffy and boring as hell.

I've included as many snacks as I could fit in the box. I hope they get to you, and they don't confiscate this stuff. It cost me a small fortune.

Okay, about the girl. Do you realize you never even told me her name? I need names and descriptions to give you proper advice, but this sappy heart will improvise just this once. Here are Dexter's rules for knowing you're in love:

Are you willing to do anything to keep her safe, like from snakes and big ass spiders?

To see her happy?

Can you always put her first, even if that means leaving in the middle of the most epic game on X-box?

Think about her dating someone else. How does it make you feel?

Are you happier around her than when you're not?

Does she make you want to do better? Be better?

I know we aren't old enough to have fallen in love a bunch of times, but I know you, dude. You're always going to run from it. When you find the girl that makes you feel all the feels, don't be an ass. Go for her.

You deserve to be happy. You always have. When we grow up, we'll make sure we're all happy, always. We're family, remember that.

Pretty deep for a couple of twelve-year-olds, right? I believe in love, Trev. I have to. I know we'll all find it someday. If I ever forget, you remind me, and I'll do the same for you.

Get your ass back to Waverley-Cay. Summer sucks without you.

Dex

Well, fuck! I guess this is Trevor reminding me.

Does Lanie make me feel all this? My heart says, *YES, YOU FUCK*, but my mind is a mess. I know I want to date her, but where could it go? How could we do it without hurting her relationship with the kids? Will I be strong enough when she leaves us?

Too many questions are running through my head. I slip the letters into my desk drawer and lean back in my chair. I've got a lot of shit to think about.

CHAPTER 15

LANIE

Tate has barely left my side all day. We've snuggled, watched movies, and played game after game. As much as I love it, I'm itching to get out of bed.

"Hey, buddy?" He stares up at me with the same deep green eyes as his father. "I'm feeling a lot better, but I think I need to take a shower. It would also be good for me to walk around a little. Can you go down and help Daddy come up with a dinner plan? I'll be down as soon as I'm showered."

He looks at me skeptically, but agrees and heads out of the room.

In the shower, I finally have time to think about that kiss. *What did it mean? Did I like it? Can I handle a no-strings hookup?* The one thing I do know is that I can't stay forever, even though the longer I'm here, the more my heart falls.

That was one hell of a kiss though. No one has ever kissed me like that. I have a feeling if anyone could help me get past my insecurities to be intimate with someone again, it would be Dexter Cross. The thought is both terrifying and exhilarating.

My heart beats rapidly as I tuck a towel around myself and head into my room. Somehow, I miss Dexter sitting in the chair in the corner. I'm just about to drop my towel when he clears his throat.

"Ah, Lanie?" His voice is hoarse.

I jump right out of my skin and the towel lands on the floor. I dive-bomb to crouch on the opposite side of the bed, raising myself just enough for him to see my head and maybe my shoulders. "What the ever living helpers are you doing in here?"

I know the deep chuckle he lets out is at my expense, and I feel my cheeks flush.

"Well, Lanie, I didn't know you would come out here and just drop your towel. Not that I didn't enjoy the show, but I figured sitting directly in front of your bathroom door, you would notice me. You seemed lost in thought ... something on your mind?"

"I, oh, well ... geez, no! Nothing. I was just daydreaming, I guess." It's a little white lie that has my face flushing hot. I quickly change the subject when I realize a) I'm still naked, and b) he is still sitting there like the cat that got the cream. "Seriously, what are you doing in my room?"

He shifts and then sits up. "Well, Tate insisted I come up and carry you down for dinner."

I notice the seriousness in his face, but I can't help but laugh. "Dexter, I got hit in the face. My legs are perfectly fine."

Dexter clears his throat uncomfortably. "Yes, I can see that they are."

The heat in his eyes is unmistakable. He doesn't look away. "Lanie," he sighs, "Tate's pretty shaken up. He begged me to come up here and get you. It's the most he has spoken to me in months. Please, just let me carry you down to the family room."

The sincerity in his voice tells me I can't say no. "Can you just give me five minutes ... you know, to get dressed?"

The smirk on his face says he doesn't want to go

anywhere, but he stands. "You sure you don't need any help? I wouldn't want you to get dizzy and fall over. I'm more than happy to help you dress."

I don't know what the hell comes over me. When I'm with Dex, I feel like the confident girl I used to be, not the shell I've become. I used to be somewhat of a flirt, but nothing like this, and definitely not since I was released from the hospital. I stand up, completely naked, throwing a pillow at him. With my hand on my hip, I point to the door and tell him, "Out."

He stands there, mouth agape for a moment too long, before striding to my side of the room. There's a starved expression in his eyes that darkens when they land on my lower abdomen.

What was I thinking? I don't have the same body I used to have. My stomach that's now covered in scars. No man like Dexter is ever going to think that's sexy. I make a move to cover myself with the second pillow on the bed.

"Don't," he warns. "Don't cover your scars for my benefit. We all have scars, Lanie. They make us who we are. They don't make you any less beautiful. One day you'll tell me how you got them. One day I'll tell you about the scars that mark me here." He points to his heart as he says it. Then he turns. "Get dressed. I'll be back in five minutes."

What did I just do?

~

Dexter

I'm sweating like I just ran a goddamn marathon. What the hell just happened in Lanie's room? Holy shit, I saw her completely fucking naked. My God, I don't think I've ever gotten hard so fast in my entire life. Now I'm pacing the hallway trying to calm my dick the hell down, but it seems to have a mind of its own.

I hate the way she reacted when I noticed her scars. I know it was my fault. I must have looked murderous when I finally saw them, but fuck, she was so stunning, I honestly almost missed them completely. That fucking monster really carved her up. Still, I was honest when I said it didn't make her any less beautiful.

The letter from my twelve-year-old self comes to mind. I know right then I am going to make her mine, but for how long? She's gun-shy and has been adamant about only staying a year.

Will I survive if I fall for her? What if she leaves me, too?

What I need is a plan. Tonight, we'll talk about goddamn Anna. Tomorrow, I'll call in reinforcements and develop a plan to make Lanie mine forever.

~

Lanie

Precisely five minutes later, Dex is knocking on my door. I open it, unable to keep my snarky comments to myself.

"Sooo," I drawl, "you do know how to knock?" It's a shitty thing to say, I know, but I'm feeling shaken and a little lost after our naked ... well, my naked encounter a few minutes ago. He leans in and picks me up like a baby who weighs nothing.

"Honestly, at least let me walk down the stairs, so you don't kill us both. You can pick me up at the bottom if it means that much to Tate."

"Not going to happen, Lanie. I promised Tate, and I never go back on my promises." Something about the way he says it while staring into my eyes with such open honesty makes me shudder. I know he's talking about more than his promise to Tate.

Dex carries me down to the family room, where I see Tate has set up a makeshift hospital tray on the couch. He has the girls in their high chairs on either side of the sofa, and a chair for Dex in the middle. My throat feels too tight. I can't speak for a moment. Dexter seems to understand and takes extra time tucking me in, allowing me to collect myself.

"Tate? You did all this for me, buddy?" I eventually ask him.

He nods his head, and I can't stop the tear from rolling down my face.

"Come here, buddy," I choke out.

Tate walks over to me slowly, unsurely, and I grab him into a fierce hug. He sags into me, burying his face in my neck when I feel his tears.

"Hey, hey, look at me," I coo.

He tilts his face up, but not before trying to wipe away his tears.

"Are you crying for me or because you were scared?" I ask gently.

"Both," he sobs, and my heart cracks wide open.

"Listen to me right now, okay?" I tell him, my voice finding strength for him. "Do not cry for me, you understand me? All adults should always protect you, no matter what. You matter to me, Tate. You, your sisters, even your cranky old dad matter to me."

I hear Dexter snort, and a short burst of laughter erupts from Tate.

"I will never let anyone hurt you. I promise you that. As long as I am around, I will always keep you safe. That's what your dad and I are here for," I tell him. "To love you. To protect you. To make sure your days are filled with love and laughter. If we get a little banged up in the process, we did it to keep you safe. That's the only thing that matters to me. I will always protect you."

He doesn't say anything but nods, so I keep going. "Crying because you're scared is normal. There have been many times in my life when I was scared. Sometimes crying makes you feel better. But having someone you can turn to, someone you can trust is always best. And, Tate, you can always come to me. No matter what or where or when, I'll always be here for you," I promise him.

He looks at me with big, sad eyes, and his voice is low and shaky when he says, "But who will protect you, Lanie? Who's there for you?"

I'm so affected by his words that a small sob gurgles in my throat. I try to speak but choke a little. Before I can say anything, Dex comes forward.

"I will, Tate. I'll protect Lanie just like I protect you and the girls. Lanie's part of our family while she's here," he looks over to me and adds, "a part of our family as long as she wants to be. Lanie has proven her love for you time and time again, so I promise you, little man, I will protect her."

The sentiment scares the hell out of me. I'm so shocked I can't say anything at all.

How could he tell Tate he will protect me? He has no idea what my life is like. He knows I can only stay a year. That's why I told Tate no matter where or when he can always come to me.

So, why is Dex making it sound like forever? I can't do forever. I certainly don't have a good track record. Not to mention he doesn't know the permanent damage Zachary did when he cut me open. There's no happily ever after for me. The sooner he realizes that, the better.

CHAPTER 16

DEX

The rest of last night was slightly off. We ordered take-out and Tate made sure to stay as close to Lanie as humanly possible, but she was quiet, subdued. Nothing like the Mary Poppins cyclone I've grown to really fucking adore.

I'm not sure what upset her. Was it me promising to protect her? Was it Tate, so wise beyond his years that threw her off? Maybe it was our argument about Anna.

"Listen, Dex, I just can't. I can't go to the police station, please don't make me. I'll be more prepared if she comes back. Please, can we just try to forget it happened?"

"Lanie, you cannot be serious? She assaulted you. Who knows what she would have done to Tate."

"Nothing would have happened to Tate. I meant what I said. I will always protect those I care about."

"But don't you see, Lanie? That's exactly what I'm trying to do."

It went on like that for an hour, and we still didn't come to a conclusion we agreed upon. She looked exhausted, and after a while, I told her I would figure out what to do with Anna and sent her to bed.

Whatever it was, Lanie seems to have swept it under the

rug today. When I came down this morning, she was dancing around with a giggling Tate while making breakfast. *She is so fucking adorable.*

I interrupt only briefly to tell her I have a little work to do, and I'll be in my office. She nods in understanding without making eye contact. *Hmm, maybe it's not all back to normal.* Regardless, we'll get there as soon as I come up with a plan.

~

Two weeks later, I was up half the night making lists. On paper ... like a pussy teenage girl, but whatever. Trevor is always making goddamn lists. He swears by it. The first one I made was for Anna and how I will handle the situation, which didn't take long to complete. I know I can trust Loki and Ryan on this.

The list for Lanie was a lot more work-intensive. I've made a list of everything I know is essential to her: the McDowells, Julia, Vermont—for whatever reason—North Carolina, family, kids, loyalty, honesty. The things she doesn't seem impressed by—money. It took three hours and a plethora of safety features for her to agree to drive the damn SUV I bought explicitly for carting around my kids. She's also apparently not a fan of fancy, always preferring her T-shirt and jeans. I have to admit, I love that about her.

During this process, I realize there's so much I have to learn about her, but I know, without a doubt, the answer to all my twelve-year-old self's questions is yes. The past two weeks we have spent every night talking after the kids go to bed. More than once, she's fallen asleep, and I carried her to bed. Not that it's a hardship. Having her so close to me feels right.

So, what the hell am I going to do? How am I going to get her to agree to at least try a relationship with me?

I stare at my list while listening to Lanie laugh and play with my kids. *I want her here.* Hell, I probably even need her here, so how do I figure out my next moves?

Then it hits me.

All my answers are in Vermont. I rush from my desk so quickly, I almost forget to put my Lanie list away. I quickly tuck it into my back pocket, along with the letter I wrote to Trevor. Not that I think she would ever snoop, but the last thing I need is one of the guys to fucking find it. They would never let me live it down.

I run up the stairs to my room and call Trevor.

"So, you're finally headed to Vermont or what?" he asks, answering his phone.

I'm struck dumb. "What? How? Seriously, Trev, are you watching the video feeds at my house?"

He laughs. "No, you dumb ass. It would be the only logical answer if you decided you want Lanie in your life long-term. Go to her source and make some allies. She won't give in easily, not with her background. I take it that is why you're calling, right?"

I sigh. "Yeah, I can't tell her, though. She'll freak out. I'll tell her when the time is right."

"Okay, so what do you need?" Trevor asks, getting right to the point.

"Addresses. The McDowells, Julia McDowell, anything I need to know about the town, I'm going to try and get a flight out tonight, so I need it soon," I tell him.

Trevor laughs at me but comes through like I knew he would. "Consider it done. You'll have a file in Dropbox by five."

I thank him, book a flight, and then head down to talk to Lanie and Tate.

Ten hours later, I'm crammed into the smallest plane I've ever been on. They say it's because the airport in Burlington, Vermont is small. I'm coming to realize I have no idea what I'm in for. Molly rented me a car because, apparently, Lanie's little town is an hour and forty-five minutes north-east of Burlington. *Jesus, it has to be up near Canada.*

She also got me the best hotel she could find but warned me not to get my hopes up. *It would not be up to my standards.* Then she laughed, which made me seriously reconsider my plan. If Trevor hadn't been on board with it, I might have turned around. *I can handle a small motel for two nights, right?* I give myself a pep talk the entire flight.

When we land, I realize it actually is a small airport, smaller than even some of the tiniest Caribbean islands I've been to. I wander around, searching for the rental car place. It takes me fifteen minutes to even find another person.

"Excuse me. Do you work here?" I ask when I finally find someone. "I'm looking for the rental car window and can't seem to find it."

The older man laughs. "You have to go outside, take two rights, then enter next to the deer head. You better hurry, though. They're closing soon."

Is he serious? I glance at my watch. It's seven p.m. I realize he is, in fact, telling the truth.

"Thank you," I tell him, taking off at a jog in the direction he sent me.

Almost an hour later, I'm on my way. They talk about the south being slow, holy hell.

By the time I pull into the motel, it's almost ten. I put the car in park and look out over the steering wheel. Molly cannot be serious. I pull up her name and press send. She answers on the second ring.

"You're joking, right? This can't be where I'm supposed to stay," I tell her, slightly annoyed after my long day.

"Mr. Cross, I told you, things are different up there. You knew Lanie grew up in a very poor and rural area. All the ski lodges were full at the mountain. This was the best I could do. There aren't even any VRBOs available up there this time of year. I'm sorry, Mr. Cross, that's what you get."

I'm about to say something when I realize she hung up on me. *Damn it, maybe Lanie is rubbing off on her.* The thought, although it should piss me off, makes me smile.

After climbing out of the car, I grab my bag and head to the front door. I open it slowly and take one tentative step inside, pausing to inspect the place.

"Well, sonny, get your ass in here and close the door before you go freezin' us all out." I move quickly to shut the door behind me to find a woman who has to be ninety sitting behind the counter with a Miss Rosa name tag.

"Um, hi. I'm Dexter Cross, I'm … checking in." I look around a bit before returning my eyes to Rosa. She has a mischievous gleam in her eye.

"First time to Burke Mountain, is it, son?"

"Yes, ma'am, it is,"

"And I'm a guessin' it was planned last minute?" she asks, not even trying to suppress her snark.

"Yes, ma'am," I answer again.

Then she cackles, actually cackles. "I just a knew it. You suits are all the same. End up here when you don't plan well enough. I know it ain't much, sonny, but I can promise you a clean room and a comfy bed. There are only two other guests right now." She pauses, tapping her chin. "I reckon you can have breakfast just about any time you feel like it."

I'm an asshole.

"Thank you, ma'am. It's my first time in Vermont," I tell her. "I wasn't sure what to make of it. I'm here to surprise some, ah, people. I want to talk to them about a mutual friend."

"Well now, is that right? Who you hopin' to sneak up on? I can probably help. GPS don't work for most folks out this way," Miss Rosa informs me with a devilish smile.

I think about it for a minute and figure it's too late for her to ruin any surprises, and she does genuinely seem interested, so I find myself talking. "I'm here to see the McDowell family. Do you know them?"

"Sonny, I've been livin' here my whole dang life. I know everyone and everything. If you're here to see Maxine and Pete, you're either Julia's long-lost baby daddy or you're here about our sweet girl, Lanie, so which is it, huh? You the shit baby daddy or someone else wantin' something from our Lanie?" she asks through narrowed eyes.

"Ah, no, ma'am. I do have three kids, and while their m-mom is not around, she ah, she is accounted for," I stammer.

"So, it ain't Julia, bless her heart, such a sweet girl and that Charlie of hers, such a little looker that one. What is it you want with our Lanie?" Miss Rosa asks, even more mistrusting than before. "Our Lanie-girl has been through quite a time lately, you know. She don't need no more heartbreak. The only good thing that ever happened to that girl was the McDowells. If you're here to cause trouble, you should know no one in this town will think twice about shootin' your ass."

Startled, I cough. She's dead serious. "No, ma'am. No trouble. She's living with me right now. She's … ah, she's my children's nanny. I just want to get to know the people she cares about so I can make her more comfortable with us."

"Mhmm. You like that girl. No use in denyin' it, sonny. I can see it all over your face," she states as if it's the law. "Maxine will, too. Now, off you go. When you git to your room, you think on if you're willin' to put in the work before you go see those good folks. Our Lanie has had a rough life. I can tell you she's going to need some convincin' if you want her to love ya. Knowing her, she already cares and probably loves your kids, but lovin' you? That's going to take hard work, so don't go after her if you ain't cut out for it. Now git." She shoos me away like a fly, and I feel the same way I did the first time I met Lanie.

What the fuck just happened?

~

The next morning when I stop to get coffee, I finally realize just how small of a town this is. Walking into the local coffee shop, I'm surrounded within minutes.

"So, you're Dexter, huh?" the girl behind the counter asks.

"I thought he would be smaller, more like a pencil pusher," says an old man sitting by the door.

"He's got some balls coming here unannounced," comes from a guy about my age. He definitely works with his hands, I notice.

I wonder what he does? I'm so far out of my element here.

I put my hands up in surrender. "I'm sorry," I say, turning to the young guy first. "How did you know who I was?"

Everyone laughs.

"Man, this town is as small as it gets. By eleven-thirty last night, you were on the town group chat. You're here to get some info from the McDowells. I have to tell ya, Julia will not be impressed with you going behind Lanie's back."

Shit, I hadn't thought of it that way.

"Listen, I just want to get to know the people that matter to Lanie. I really like her and want her to stay and feel comfortable with my kids and me." *I can't believe I am explaining myself to strangers.* "We all feel like she's family in the short time she's been there. I didn't realize this would seem like a betrayal."

A small, boney hand lands on mine, and I turn to my side. *Miss Rosa. Of freaking course.*

"Hi, Miss Rosa. I guess I have you to thank for this welcome party?"

She has the grace to look chagrined for a moment before answering. "Sonny, we all just want what's best for our Lanie, after everything that's happened to her and all. We are ... well, we are very protective of her, but if you explain to Maxine what you did to me, you'll be just fine. Julia, ah, she's as smart as they come, socially a little off that one, but my money's on you. If anyone can win her over, you can. Good luck. Now all you skit, let the man be to go about his business. He has his work cut out for him."

Loosening the collar of my shirt, I head back to my rental with the directions Miss Rosa slipped under my door sometime last night. I study them skeptically and decide to use my GPS instead, but soon realize Miss Rosa was on to something.

Following the handwritten directions, I turn left at my third cow farm, go half a mile, and turn where the barbed wire ends. I'm thankful it's daylight because this is some *Children of the Corn* shit right here. Miss Rosa says the driveway is about two miles long, so I take my time on these two miles to pull myself together.

Here goes nothing.

CHAPTER 17

DEX

Rounding the bend in the driveway, I pull up in front of an old but well-kept farmhouse. It has a wraparound porch you usually see in movies. Rocking chairs line the exterior of the house as far as the porch goes. And at the top of the stairs to the right of the doorway is an older man with a shotgun.

I swallow thickly. *So he knew I was coming.* I guess I should expect that with this town from now on.

After putting the car in park, I turn off the ignition. The man hasn't moved but is watching me. I notice he's dressed in a polo shirt, jeans, and work boots. A little bit city, a little bit country. Fascinating. This has to be Mr. McDowell. I climb out of the SUV and hold my hand up in a wave.

He doesn't say anything as I approach, but he does move the shotgun into his lap. Listen, I grew up in the south. Everyone had guns, but not once have I been to see about a girl and had one pulled on me. *This is something new.*

I land at the bottom of the steps before I speak. "Mr. McDowell, sir?" I ask in question.

"You must be this Dexter Cross that has my wife's phone buzzing like a hive full of bees," he answers.

"Yes, sir. I didn't realize I would cause such a commotion coming here. I apologize for that. May I sit?" I ask, suddenly feeling uneasy. "I'd like to talk to you a bit."

He doesn't answer but nods and points to the rocking chair beside him with the shotgun.

Jesus, I might pass out. This is harder than I thought ... Maybe I should have made a better plan. Tentatively, I climb the steps and take a seat.

"I take it you're here about our Lanie? She isn't in any trouble, is she? It doesn't seem like something our girl would do, but luck never has been on her side," he tells me.

"No, sir, she isn't in any trouble, but now that I am here, I'm having a hard time finding the words to explain why I came," I admit bluntly.

"Well, Counselor, I suggest you approach it like you would a case in court. I know you weren't in trials often, but surely you had practice in law school," he answers, letting me know he's on to me.

I can't help but smile at that. A lawyer through and through. "I see you did your research, sir."

"Always. Don't you?" He smirks.

I grin again. "Yes, sir, that's part of the reason I'm here. And while I would love nothing more than to present a case in front of you, Lanie deserves more than that, so if you don't mind, I'm just going to lay it all out there."

"Good answer, Dex, good answer." Smiling, he waits for me to proceed.

"You see, I think Lanie's amazing. I have from the first moment she walked into my house like she owned the place. She closed my mouth when my jaw hit the floor from something she said. Twice." I can't help the smirk that comes over my face, and Mr. McDowell chuckles.

"I take it that doesn't happen very often to you these days, does it, young man?"

"No, sir, it does not," I answer truthfully. "But here's the thing, she came into my home, cuddled my daughters who I never thought would stop crying. She got my son to speak when he hasn't since his mother left almost a year ago. She has me smiling even when I think I might be losing my mind. I know it hasn't been long at all, but I think I could fall for her."

"You think, or you know? Those are two very different things, young man. With Lanie, you have to know." He peers down for a moment, then back up at me. "Her story is not mine to tell, but I will say, if you want something with her, you have to be all in."

I sit in silence for a moment remembering Trevor had said the same exact thing.

"Well, sir, there's another issue. I know all about her past. How her mother's boyfriend put her in the hospital when she was ten, the years of neglect and abuse she suffered. I even know about what Zachary did to her and how tough her recovery has been."

He looks shocked, possibly mad, so I quickly continue.

"Please understand, I didn't do it to go behind her back. I was hiring her to take care of my children. With an eighteen-month gap in her work history, I had to dig into her a little. Now that I know her, I hate that I broke her trust that way, but my children have been through so much I had to do more than due diligence," I plead my case.

Mr. McDowell stares at me for a long moment, then bows his head and sighs. "I probably would have done the same thing. In fact, when she told us she was going to work and live with you, I may have done some digging of my own. She may not be my blood, but she is my daughter. So, tell me, son. What did you hope to get from coming all the way up here?"

"Honestly? I think some advice," I tell him. "She's going to hate what I know when she finds out. I do plan on telling her when the time is right. I could probably use some advice on how to go about that." I smile at him. "Also, maybe some allies when she turns me down again and again because I know getting her to trust me as anything more than a boss, even as a friend, is going to be an uphill battle. Getting her to give me a chance, or at least admit she wants to, is going to be even harder."

"She hasn't been in North Carolina long. How are you so sure this is what you want?" he interjects.

I stand and take the old worn envelope out of my back pocket and hand it to him. "I wrote this when I was twelve. Somewhere along the way, I lost that part of me when I started dating my ex-wife in high school. Then, Lanie came into my life and cracked my battered heart wide open. I can honestly answer yes to every one of those now."

He takes a few minutes to first read Trevor's letter, then my reply. When he looks up, his face has softened. He lays the shotgun down beside him.

"Well, I never have been one to interfere with the girls' love interests, but I think it's safe to say you've got me rooting for you as long as you don't hurt her. I'll be honest with you, it's the two McDowell women you have to win over," he tells me with a wicked grin.

He stands up and yells through the door that it's safe to come out. I brace myself for what comes next.

Whatever I was expecting was not this pixie of a girl standing in front of me with a baby on her hip, who she eventually hands off to her dad. Her son is oddly familiar. While I'm staring at him, trying to place the familiarity, I realize I missed a question from who can only be Julia.

"I'm sorry, your son's adorable. I missed what you said," I tell her.

Her lip twitches like she is trying not to smile. "His name is Charlie, and he is, thank you. What are you doing here, presumably behind Lane's back?" She makes a strange little clicking in her mouth, something I come to find is a nervous tick of sorts, but right now, she has her hands balled into fists, ready to strike.

"Julia, just calm down a minute and let him explain. I think you'll be happy with his answers," Mr. McDowell tells her.

I give him a grateful smile.

"Just because you pulled the wool over my dad's eyes, with lawyer-speak I would imagine, does not mean I'll automatically trust you. I have FaceTimed Lanes every single day since she has been there. I've said hi to your children multiple times, and they love her. If you're here to try and send her packing or something, you're making a huge mistake. I have the money and resources to make sure you regret it every day of your life."

I should be pissed. No one threatens me. However, it warms my heart to see how much these people genuinely love my Lanie. Their Lanie, too, it seems.

"I'm not here to fire her," I say, slightly offended. "I'm man enough to do that to someone's face, not run to their family to do it."

Julia puffs up a little at my acknowledgment of her being Lanie's family.

"I'm here for back-up as strange as that sounds. I want to have a relationship with Lanie. Whatever she can give me, and I know it's going to take work and a lot of convincing. I'm committed to that. My kids are committed, but I know I need more. I'll need all your support when she comes running home because I do think she will fight it. Fight it until she can't face it anymore and comes home to you." I say it because it's the truth. "I'll be honest, though. I want her with me always, and I need help to make that happen."

Julia speaks more softly than before when she replies, "You sound like you love her. You haven't even been on a date yet. One kiss cannot have you head over heels already." She turns bright red when she realizes what she said.

"Well, it was a perfect kiss." I give her a wink, and I think she's ready to implode. "Look, I know I haven't taken her on a date yet. However, I know how I feel. I know how hard it will be to convince her to give us a shot, but I'm committed. I'll put in the hard work. Will you help me?"

The smile that takes over Julia's face is pure trouble. "On one condition," she says.

"Anything, name it!" I answer before I can think better of it.

"Tell me what you're doing to keep Bitchzilla away from our Lanie?" Julia asks with the expression of a true troublemaker.

That's when I know this trip was a success. We spend the next day and a half concocting plan after plan, then back-up plans for our back-up plans. By the time I land back in North Carolina, I feel ready to take on the world.

CHAPTER 18

LANIE

Dexter's recent trip was unexpected. Luckily, he said it was a quick trip and his last one for a while. When he texted an hour ago to say he'd landed, I felt a sense of relief I wasn't quite ready for. Tate and I are finishing the last of our preparations for dinner, while the girls, for once, sit happily in their high chairs watching us.

A few minutes later, the front door opens, and Tate goes barreling toward Dex, who picks him up quickly, swinging him upside down in a fireman's hold.

"Hey, buddy! Did you have fun with Lanie?" he asks with a lightness about him.

When he replies, "Yes," I watch the tension in Dexter's shoulders relax a little. Just one word, but I know he'll take whatever he can get.

"Hi, Dex. How was your trip?"

He sets Tate down and stalks toward me. I back up until I'm against the sink and look around nervously. Tate has returned to making his crescent rolls while the girls are conversing in their own language.

"My trip?" he repeats. "My trip was very ... enlightening." Something about the way he says it makes my spine tingle in anticipation ... or fear, I'm not sure which. "And you, Lanie Heart? How were you while I was away? Did you miss me?"

The naughty gleam in his eye has me stammering. "Ah, I-I-I know the kids missed you very much."

"I'm sure they did, Lanie. However, I'm asking about you. Did you miss me?"

I'm not sure how to answer that, so I duck out of his arms that have caged me in without me noticing. I scoot to the other side of the island, putting Tate between us. Like a tiger stalking his prey, he comes to my other side and turns my face to his.

Leaning in, he whispers, "Lanie, did you miss me?"

I bite my lip without realizing what I've done. Before I can release it myself, Dex has my chin between his thumb and forefinger, removing my lower lip from my teeth with a growl.

"I ... um. Yes, I guess you could say I missed you, too," I gasp.

"Hmm, I like that answer, Lanie. I like it a lot, but next time you won't have to guess because you'll know!"

He takes a step back, and I feel like I can breathe again. My panties are soaked, my head is spinning, and my hands are shaking.

Dexter notices and wraps his big hand around mine. "Calm down, Lanie. I won't hurt you. Ever. Please don't be scared of me. Let me look after you, just a little."

With no answer for that, I drop my head and slip my hands from his. "Dinner's ready. Tate, why don't you go wash your hands while I set the table, huh?" My voice is shaky. Dex has thrown me entirely off my game.

"Okay, Lanie!" Tate's response is strong, natural, and so happy.

Dex whips his head to Tate in confusion.

"He's been talking a lot today," I tell him. "He's been really happy and is starting to come out of his shell. Even his new teacher said she saw such a difference in him when we talked yesterday."

Before I can say anything else, Dex catches my face between his hands and kisses me. Not frantically like last time, but gently, almost lovingly. After a few seconds, he places his forehead on mine so we are nose to nose. "Thank you ... for everything, Lanie. I don't know what any of us would do without you in our lives."

Trying not to make eye contact for fear of what I'll uncover there, I quietly whisper, "You're welcome." Deciding to go for a bit of humor, I add, "Remember, Mr. Boss Man, don't fall in love with me." I give him a saucy wink and am startled by the emotion I find in his eyes.

"It might be too late for that, Lanie Heart. It just might be too late," he growls, shaking his head.

I make it through dinner, barely looking at Dexter from across the table. Luckily, the girls keep us so busy feeding them it's not uncomfortable. Surprising us all, Tate is a chatterbox, telling us all about school today and how he played with Connor at recess. The expressions of pure joy, relief, and happiness I find on Dexter's face in the brief moment I allow myself a glance at him cut right to my heart. That's the way a parent should look at their child. Something I never had until Mimi and Pawpaw. The thought makes me sad.

"Uh, Dex? I forgot I planned to FaceTime with Julia and her parents tonight. Will you be okay to clean up or should I text to postpone it?"

Dex stares at me for a minute, skepticism radiating off him in waves, and I know he's not buying my bs. "I can handle it, Lanes, but just so you know, we're your family now, too. You can always come to me. For anything." His eyes penetrate deep into my soul, and I struggle for breath.

I note the seriousness of his tone and am grateful, except I can't exactly talk to him about him. Making my way upstairs, I misstep when I realize he called me Lanes.

Weird. No one but Julia calls me that.

⁓

Dexter

Dexter: I messed up and kissed her already. I know. I know! I fucked up within the first five minutes of being home. But Christ. This is going to be hard. Help!

Julia: Seriously, man! Check yourself. If you want the girl, stop being a tool and get your shit together. Our plan is good. She's FaceTiming me now. I'll try to do damage control, but she's going to hate us both if this backfires. You know that, right? I'm ONLY doing this because I want her to be happy, and for some godforsaken reason, I think you might be the one to do it. So, MAN THE FUCK UP!

Dexter: Will do.

Jesus, that girl has a mouth on her. I know from my research that she's obnoxiously smart, although a bit socially awkward. *Kind of like Trevor,* I think to myself. I can't help but laugh at what a pair they'd make if they didn't kill each other first. Now I just have to hope that Julia is right about our plan, and this all doesn't come crashing down.

⁓

Lanie

"Jules, I can't see your face. What are you doing?" I ask, trying to figure out where the hell she has the phone pointed.

"Sorry, Lanes, I just had to finish up a text. What's up with your Irish face?" Finally angling the camera so I can see her, she winks like the troublemaker she is.

I freaking luv her, and my laugh is instant. "I'm just missing your Irish face, I think. Oh, and Dexter kissed me again."

Julia makes a surprised face that, after fifteen years of friendship, I know is completely fake.

"Okay, Jules, spill. You're a terrible liar. How did you know he kissed me when it only happened an hour ago?" I command, scrutinizing her phone through the small screen.

"Well …" She looks totally uncomfortable.

"Spill it, Jules." My expression leaves no room for argument.

In true Julia fashion, she tries another tactic. "I hear Charlie crying … do you hear him? I'll have to call you back."

"Don't you dare. I'll get GG to your house before you can even blink," I threaten. She knows I would.

"Fine, but you have to promise not to be mad. And not to leave your room until morning so you don't say something you're going to regret. And promise not to be mad at anyone."

Goosebumps form all over my arms at her pleading tone.

"Julia? You're scaring me. What the ship are you talking about?" I can't hide the anger and fear taking over my body.

"Ugh! This is not supposed to be how you find out. We had a whole plan. An awesome plan, Lanes. It would have worked if I wasn't such a shit liar," she admits in defeat.

"God, Julia, why would you lie to me and *what are you talking about*? I'm totally freaked out now."

She lets out an enormous sigh, which I know is another ploy to stall for time. "Well, you know how your boss just got back from a trip?"

"Yesss?" I drawl. Those butterflies in my stomach from when Dex kissed me? Yeah, they're an angry hive now, missing their queen.

"Well, did he ever actually say it was a work trip?" She's

not making eye contact and staring anywhere but into the screen.

"Holy hot pocket. Just spill it already, Julia!"

She slaps her hands to her head, then slowly peeks into the camera through her fingers. Within seconds it's like she has diarrhea of the mouth, and I can't even be sure I understand everything.

"Well, he came here," she begins, "to Burke Mountain. He stayed at the Wagon Wheel, *the Wagon Wheel*, Lanie. He met eighty percent of the town getting coffee, then came to Mom and Dad's house. He wasn't trying to betray your trust. I made sure of that. I really put him through the paces, I swear. We honestly think he cares about you. He wants to date you. Weirdly, he wanted Mom and Dad's approval, and I guess their support because he knew it would be a hard, uphill battle to get you to agree." She finally sucks in a breath before delivering the final blow. "He cares about you, Lanes."

I'm pacing my room. Swinging my arms wildly, but I can't seem to form any words.

"Lanie, for fuck's sake. Stop swinging the phone around before I hurl all over my room."

I stop and glare into the phone. "Why, Jules? Why would you all gang up on me? You're supposed to be *my* friend. *My* family. Were you even going to tell me?" My voice breaks as I fight back the tears.

"Lanie, I'm sorry," she wails. "Yes, I was going to tell you but not right away." She cringes, waiting for my response. When one doesn't come, she continues, "We had a plan. Mom, Dad, me, and Dexter, who is as hot as you fucking said he was." Her grin is honest, but it's her waggling eyebrows that irritate me.

Rolling my eyes so I don't say something I'll regret, I realize I'm shaking with rage. At Julia? Her parents? Dex? I'm not even sure.

"Listen to me very closely, Lanie. We love you, but you've

had a fucked-up life. My parents always wished they could do more for you, but your douche-canoe of a mother wouldn't give up her parental rights. We've always felt like we failed you in some way." She glances away as she collects herself.

"Then, well, then Zachary happened, and none of us were there to protect you. You almost died, Lanie. I promised myself the second we found out you would pull through that I would find a way to help you heal. To have a happy, whole life. I think if you can give Dexter a chance, you have a shot at all of that and more ... with him."

Her love for me outshines her words. This girl. My family. They all just want what's best for me, and I don't even deserve her kindness.

Through my tears, I stare at my best friend. "Julia. How can you even stand me? It's because of me you left that conference in Boston without getting that guy's name. For crying out loud, we call him Boston because you never found out his real name. It's my fault Charlie will never know his dad. So much is my fault. How can you care so much about me being happy? I ruined your happily ever after by being there the night Zachary attacked me," I cry.

"Now you listen here, you asshat. You ruined nothing. There's no way of knowing if Boston would have even given me his real name after the game we had been playing all week, let alone his number. You know I'm not an easy person to get along with sometimes, Lanes. And I don't know how else to tell you this, but what happened? It happened *to* you, not because of you. No one's to blame but Zachary." Julia implores me with sad eyes to finally believe her.

"I don't know if I can tell him about the attack, Jules. I'm no good for anyone. If I can't tell him about my past, how can he ever really know me?" I whisper.

"Honey, I know you're hurting right now, and it feels like we all betrayed you. But trust me, it wasn't like that at all. We all, Dexter included, just want what's best for you. I only spent one day with him, and even I think you need to give him a little more credit than that. I think you'll find out that he isn't that much different from you under that alpha male thing he has going on. We all have scars, Lanes. Some are just better at hiding them. Now, promise me. Pinkie-swear, you won't go barreling out of your room and spew venom all over Dexter?"

I give her my best angry face. "That I can't promise. I'm also mad at you guys, too, you know?"

"I know, but we're family, *real family*. You can't be mad at us forever. And to hear Dexter talk, it sounds like you just might be part of his family as well. Get some sleep, Lanes, okay? I'll talk to you in the morning?"

"Sure. Night, Jules. Luvs."

"Luvs you, too."

I throw my phone on the bed and start pacing. I'm spitting fire. What was he thinking, inserting himself into my life like that?

Oh God, what if someone told him about my attack? My mind is whirling in a hundred different directions, worried about everything and nothing at the same time. Julia's right, though ... I can't go out guns blazing, not just yet. I have to get my thoughts together, so I continue to pace.

CHAPTER 19

DEX

*J*ulia: Abort! Abort! Abort mission, for now. Sorry, dude. She dragged it out of me. I can't lie for shit, and she's pretty pissed, but I think she will calm down. Wherever you are, hide. Now. I don't think she'll come out of her room for at least an hour, but you never know. She's probably collecting her thoughts, but you do not want those conversations right now. In the morning, it will be better. Hide.

Dexter: What the actual fuck, Julia? I thought you were rooting for me. Then you go and sabotage me the first chance you get? This isn't a fucking game to me, Julia. I want a real shot at this. If you ruined my chances, I-I don't even know what I'll do. FUCK!

Julia: Calm down, asshat. I'll help you fix it. But for tonight, lie low. I'll help smooth it over in the morning.

Dexter: Fucking hell.

Julia: Double fuck, but we'll fix it. I got your back, buddy.

I grab the baby monitors and head to my room. Thankfully, it's already pretty late. *I cannot believe I am fucking hiding like a little boy.* What else can I do, though? Julia knows her best, even though this is all her fault. I roll my eyes and hear Lanie in her room, mumbling and ... pacing? Yup, definitely pacing. Holy hell, this is going to be a long night. I'm leaning against my door just as my phone rings.

Julia.

"Hello?"

"Listen, I know I'm breaking all kinds of girl code here, but I have to tell you something." The way she says it gives me an immediate sense of dread.

"What is it?" *Deep breaths, Dex. In and out.*

"Well, here's the thing. For the last year or so, Lanie has been having nightmares. Usually only when the power goes out, which happens a crazy amount here in the mountains. I have to tell you now because you have to look out for her. When she's stressed or overwhelmed, they tend to happen, too. I'd say finding out about your little excursion is overwhelming for her."

I'm about to tell her it is, in fact, her fault that Lanie knows I went to Vermont, but she rambles on like the pink bunny with endless energy.

"The problem is, you won't hear her. She always leaves her door open, and the light on so it should be easy enough to peek in on her," she explains.

"Julia," I grumble, "I'm not sure that's such a good idea."

"Listen, jerk off. I'm not there, so you have to do it. If Lanie has a bad one, it'll be tough for her to wake on her own, but whatever you do, don't put your meaty paws on her. If she feels your giganotosaurus sized hands, it'll be even harder to bring her out of the nightmare. Just walk into her room and loudly but kindly tell her who you are and that you need her to wake up. Keep saying it over and over again until she comes to. Kindly though ... got it?"

My mind is overflowing with emotion right now and I don't speak right away.

"Dexter! Do you hear me? You need to watch out for her. You said you were going to protect her, correct?"

That shocks me into action. "Yeah, I'll take care of her. I promise."

"Good. I'm sure we'll talk soon."

I go to say good-bye, but she's already hung up. This night just brought insane to a whole other level. Now, I'm really in for a long night.

Crossing the room toward my bathroom, I rake a hand roughly over my face. I get ready for bed, but I know no sleeping will take place tonight. When I'm finished, I settle into a chair that sits against the wall I share with Lanie. Sitting vigil was not in my plans, but it makes me realize just how far I'm willing to go to keep her safe.

After a while, my head bobs. I'm in that state of awake, but only barely. Rubbing a hand over my face, I sit up taller, searching for the clock. Lanie stopped pacing a couple of hours ago. It's probably time to check on her.

There's no way to do this without feeling like a complete ass. Trust me. I've tried to think of any scenario where I'm not some creeper watching her sleep; I found none. Now, I'm standing in the hall, ready to peek around her door like a Peeping Tom.

Julia said I have to do this. Yeah, I'll just blame it on Julia if Lanie wakes and freaks the fuck out. Pep talk complete, I take the final step into Lanie's doorway.

At first look, I'd think she was sleeping, but there's something about her face. It's contorted in pain. Stepping closer, my stomach wretches. Tears stream down her face. Slowly, almost imperceptibly, she's rocking from side to side, reliving the most devastating situation of her life.

"Lanie," I cry out desperately. "It-It's me, Dex. You're having a nightmare; you have to wake up. You're at my house, and you're safe, but you have to wake up."

I get no reaction, so I take a step closer. Her pain is so

visceral I'm having a hard time not breaking down myself. Knowing Julia said not to touch her, I raise my voice. "Lanie. Lanie, it's me, Dex. Wake up for me, Lanie. Wake up right now. You're safe."

Sucking in the air like it might be her last breath, Lanie jolts up in bed. Her eyes are unfocused, and I'm so far out of my element I might as well be on Mars. Watching as her tears slowly dry, I realize something else. Julia didn't say what to do now.

"Lanie?" I question quietly.

She turns her head, but I don't think she's seeing me. It's like encountering a sleepwalker, and my heart hangs heavy in my chest.

"Lanie, it's me, Dex. You had a bad dream. You're in my house, and you're safe."

Her eyes are wild but slowly coming into focus when she bursts into tears. "I'm safe. I'm here, not at Zachary's. He can't get me here," she repeats, gasping for air while cradling her midsection.

I don't think I've ever witnessed something so gut-wrenching. "Lanie," I say again, cautiously. "I'm going to walk toward you now. I'm going to sit next to you on the bed. If you don't want me to, just say no, and I won't move."

She doesn't respond, so I walk ever so slowly to her and sit on the bed, where she flings herself into my arms. "Oh God, I'm so sorry, Dex. I'm so, so sorry. Did I break something or-or wake up the kids?"

Putting my hand on her head, I smooth out her hair, hoping the gesture is comforting. "Shh, Lanie. Shh. You didn't do anything."

On a hiccup, she asks, "H-How did you know?"

I give her a sad smile. "I told you my trip to Vermont was enlightening."

She cries harder. "Oh my God, you must think I'm crazy. I swear, though, it usually only happens when the lights go out, and when you were in London, I slept with a flashlight on." Lanie tries to hide her face. "I'm so embarrassed."

Grabbing her chin, I lift her face to me. "You have nothing to be embarrassed about, Lanie. I'm glad I can be here for you. I want to be here for you. Julia told me how to wake you up, but she didn't tell me how to comfort you now."

"That witch! Whose side is she on, anyway?" Lanie says through her tears, but there's no malice behind it. I doubt she has a wicked bone in her body.

"Lanie, I'd say the entire McDowell family is on your side, always. She was worried about you, sweetheart." The endearment slips off my tongue and feels so right. She blushes, but I don't back down. "Tell me, sweetheart, what usually happens now that you're awake?"

She tries to pull away, but I keep her locked firmly in my arms. Turning her face from me is as much as I'm willing to give right now.

"It-It's stupid, really. Julia normally climbs into bed with me. We've done it since we were little. She used to say body heat keeps the monsters away. B-But I'll be fine, honestly, Dex. You can go back to your room. I've got this."

Peering down at myself, I take in my appearance, though I'm not sure why it matters. I'm fully dressed in sleep pants and a T-shirt, but when I feel her shaking again, I know I'm all in. Julia will no doubt have my balls for this, but there's no way I can leave her alone and frightened. Sleeping with the lights on is not a habit of mine, so I kiss her head gently and move to stand. Before I can walk away, she's clutching my hand in her cold, trembling one.

"Hey, Lanie. Look at me," I plead.

She sniffles but doesn't raise her head.

Crouching down in front of her, I pull Lanie's hands into mine. "I'm not going to leave you. I just have to grab something. I'll be right back."

Lanie's eyes finally meet mine. The same bright blues I'd

recognize anywhere, but tonight they're haunted. Hollow. Terrified. I feel her pain like it is my own, and it's devastating. Giving her hand one last squeeze, I enter her bathroom. I bought out the drug store as I'd promised, so I know she has a bright pink sleep mask in here somewhere. It only takes a moment to locate it since almost everything is still in the bag. *Stubborn woman.*

With the item in hand, I walk to the opposite side of the bed. Lanie has scooted herself up to rest against the headboard and is watching me like a hawk. Without preamble, I walk to the bed, making my intentions known.

"Dex. Y-You really don't have to do this. I promise I'll be fine. I'll just read a little."

Her voice quivers, and without even looking, I know she is lying. "Lanie, it's the middle of the night. You, sweetheart, have just had one hell of a nightmare. What kind of an asshole do you think I am? I am going to lay right here with you so you can sleep, nothing else."

She seems lost in thought but doesn't argue. Instead, she slides down into the bed and turns on her side. Just before I pull the sleep mask into place, I reach over, grab her around her middle, and tug her back into my front.

The gasp she exhales is my new favorite sound. Leaning over, I kiss the back of her head and whisper, "Sleep, sweetheart, you're safe." Within minutes, she's relaxed, but I can tell she isn't sleeping.

"Lanie? Can I ask you something?"

"I-I guess that depends on what it is," she answers honestly.

Hating that I need this answer, I ask, "You had this nightmare because of my trip to Vermont, right?"

Exhaling slowly, I feel her take a deep breath before answering. "It wasn't necessarily the trip. I felt blindsided. It was something I couldn't control. I haven't had very good luck with things I don't have complete control over the last few months."

I swallow thickly, not entirely sure I want the answer to my next question. "Did you have one after Anna hit you?"

"No. I don't think so." Her voice is stronger than before. "I slept with Tate. Body heat keeps the monsters away, remember?"

"Okay." I pause, thinking about my trip to Vermont and all that has happened since. "You know, we're all on the same side. The McDowells, the kids, me. We're all on your side. Just let me be here for you. You told me you were recovering. We can talk about that another time because I do want to be there for you in every single way." Biting my lip, I glance around the room, then pull her even closer. "Lanie … I'm sorry you had a nightmare because of my little stunt. I didn't do it to go behind your back or to have you lose faith in me. I guess I just wanted to talk to the people you love the most. I wanted their perspective, their advice. I really like you, and I'm going to spend every day showing you just how much."

A sob escapes as she tries to speak. "Don't fall in love with me, Dex. I'm too broken. I'll never be what you need."

"Oh, pretty, pretty woman. By the time I'm done, you'll never want to let me go." I have to tamp down the urge to pound my chest when I get the reaction I was hoping for.

"Did you just give me a line from *a hooker movie*?" Lanie asks, not able to control her giggle.

"Paraphrased." I smirk. "You get to be Mary Poppins. I'm the white knight." I'm not ashamed in the least that I know my chick flick trivia.

"Maria, remember? I'm more Maria, and you do realize it was the hooker who said that, not the knight?" she schools me.

"Lanie, it's called creative liberties." We sit in silence for a few moments, but it's not uncomfortable. "Lanie? Do you know the difference between Mary Poppins and Maria?" She stays silent. "Maria's the one who stayed."

Her gasp tells me she got my message loud and clear.

"Go to sleep, sweetheart. I've got you."

CHAPTER 20

LANIE

I wake slowly, a distinct difference from my usual morning routine. Not startling awake is something I could get used to. Gradually, my body catches up to my brain, and I realize I have a sense of calm that I'm not sure I've ever had before. I'm also all kinds of hot. My eyes open like a slingshot when I realize why I'm so warm.

My body goes stiff as I take stock of everything around me and silently groan while last night's events come rushing back. I'm going to disown Julia the second I can sneak out of Dexter's strong embrace.

Trying not to move too much, I glance down and realize he has one hand wrapped securely around my boob. *Just freaking great.* I feel his other arm tucked under my pillow. He genuinely must not have moved a muscle last night.

Gently, I try to wiggle out of his embrace but stop abruptly when I feel his cock—long, hard, and thick—standing at full attention against my ass. His arm around me tightens its hold, and I hear him breathe me in. Slowly, he releases my breast to rest his hand on my ribcage.

"Morning," he says, his voice gruff with sleep. "You can't keep moving on me like that, sweetheart. I'm trying to be a gentleman, but your tight, little ass rubbing against me is making it really hard."

"I can tell." I snort. *So ladylike, Lanie, geez.* "I should get moving. Tate will be up soon. We have a breakfast routine now, so I know he'll be waiting for me."

"Soon." He leans up on his forearm, rolling me onto my back. "I'm not going to lie. I've dreamt about waking up with you like this. Does that scare you?"

I press a hand to his chest and push slightly. I'm not ready for these conversations. "Dex, please. I-I was honest with you. I'm a mess. I can promise you that this kind of damage is not what you want."

"We'll see, Lanie. I'm going to show you that you're wrong every day. I'm going to ask you out every chance I get, and when you're ready, you'll say yes," he informs me.

I roll my eyes, but he doesn't seem to notice or care. "Thank you for last night. I know it's probably a shock to see me like that." I glance down, ashamed. "I never wanted you to witness it."

Dexter leans down and kisses my forehead. "I want to see and know everything about you, Lanie." Before I can respond, he climbs over me to get out of bed. "I'm going to need a long shower. A long, cold shower. I'll meet you guys in the kitchen." He gives me a lopsided grin, making him appear more like a man in his late twenty's trying to make it through life than the million-dollar business mogul I've come to know.

Taking the pillow he used last night, I place it over my face and groan loudly. *"Maria is the one who stayed."* His words echo in my head. Ugh. If he understood the degree of damage done to my soul, he would never ask me to stay.

∼

"Lanie! Today's the day, right? We're meeting Connor for pizza, parks, and play. Right, Lanie? Can we go now? Is it time?" Tate asks impatiently. It's almost shocking that this is the same kid who barely spoke only a few short weeks ago.

"Whoa, slow down, buddy. Yes, today's the day! I know you're excited, but you do have half a day of school today. Jamie and I will pick you up and we'll have an entire afternoon of pizza, parks, and play," I tell him, laughing at his excitement.

"Awww, man," he drags out. "That's hours and hours and hours from now," Tate whines.

I've never seen him this excited, or this animated. Judging by the expression Dexter's wearing walking down the hallway, it's been a long time for him, too.

"What's up, Tate? I haven't heard you this excited about anything in a long time. You guys have something fun planned today?"

"Lanie's picking me up from the early-release day and taking me for pizza, park, and play with Connor. Jamie's coming, too," Tate explains in one long breath.

"Jamie, huh?" I hear Dex grumble. "Just great." At least he tries to sound a bit more cheerful for Tate's benefit. "You guys will have fun."

"Dexter," I scold. "I know we haven't talked about it with … everything that's been going on, but Jamie is a very nice man. He's become a great friend. He is also terrific with Tate, so take it easy, huh?"

Appearing properly chastised, Dex goes about getting his coffee.

Tate and I finish up breakfast with the music back to full volume. Dexter watches on with his signature crooked grin while the kids and I all dance to the beat. Some country singer is crooning about the girl that got away.

"I'm working from my home office today, so I'll take care of dinner. What time will you be home?" Dex asks me.

"You're taking care of dinner? Can you cook?" I know I sound skeptical, but seriously? I've never seen him in the kitchen doing anything you could consider cooking.

Stalking me slowly and watching the whisk I'm holding, he stops just inches in front of me. He reaches up and tucks a stray hair behind my ear, then whispers, "I have lots of talents, Lanie. Today is day one of making you never wanna let me go." He winks and walks away, and I'm left wondering what the heck I've gotten myself into.

∽

In the time it took to drop Tate off at school, Sara and Harper fell asleep in their car seats. *This might put a damper on Tate's big plans.*

Deciding to drive to the market on the opposite side of town, I hope that might be enough of a nap that they'll cooperate with our afternoon fun. Knowing it'll take at least twenty minutes to get there, I use this time to catch up with Jules. Pressing the fancy button on the car Dex insists I drive, I say, "Call Jules."

She picks up on the second ring. "Ahh, hi, Lanes. How's your day going?" Julia asks in a phony, innocent voice.

"Cut the baloney, Jules. I know you told Dex to babysit me last night," I whisper yell so I don't wake the girls.

"It wasn't like that, Lanie. You know I was just worried about you. Plus, I told him to check on you, not cop-a-feel by sleeping with you," she groans.

I suck in a breath so exaggerated you'd think it came from a Saturday morning cartoon. Then I start to hiss.

"Oh, fuck," Julia says.

"Yeah, I'd say that, Jules. What the heck? You already talked to him this morning? Do I need to remind you that you're *my* friend? Why are you pushing this? Why are you helping him?" My emotions are unraveling quickly.

"It is not like that. Not exactly," she hedges. "I only texted him to make sure you were okay. I didn't want you to think I was hovering."

"You realize how messed up that is, right?" I keep the anger in my voice, but I'm running out of steam.

"Yes. I also decided I'm not going to apologize," she says so matter-of-factly I don't respond. "You gave me the push I needed a year and a half ago. It may not have ended the way we would've liked, but it gave me a kick in the ass. I also got the best thing that has ever happened to me out of it. I wouldn't trade Charlie for anything in the world."

I grumble incoherently, but she talks right over me.

"So, consider this your proverbial kick. The whole town is rooting for Dex. You might as well give him a chance, or you won't be able to show your face back here for some time. GG has a betting pool going, but I'm not allowed to place a bet. She claims I have insider information. Can you believe that, Lanes? Total bullshit."

"Julia," I groan again. "Last night, he asked me if I knew the difference between Mary Poppins and Maria from the *Sound of Music*."

"What? That's random."

I love Julia. She's the smartest person I know, but she couldn't catch a social cue if it smacked her in the face. "It's because he called me Mary Poppins on my first visit here, remember?"

"Oh yeah! And you told him you were more of a Maria." She laughs. "Well, don't leave me hanging. What's the difference?"

"Maria stays," I tell her.

Julia's silent.

"Hello? Jules? Did I lose you?"

"I-I-I'm here," she sniffles.

"Are you crying?" I ask, in shock.

"He's worth the risk, Lanie. Please, at least think about giving this man a chance," Jules begs.

"I'm not sure if I can." The lump in my throat feels like it's trying to choke me, so I attempt to swallow the emotion lodged there. "I have to go. I have to get some stuff from the market. I'll call you later. Luvs."

"Luvs, Lanie. Bye."

Banging my head on the steering wheel, I let the tears flow. I look like a crazy lady, I'm sure, but I feel so out of control.

Give him a chance. "Can I do that?" I ask aloud.

I'm answered by noisy gurgling sounds in the backseat. I'm not sure if it was my head banging or my one-person conversation that woke them, but both girls are babbling happily now. *Might as well get our shopping out of the way.*

CHAPTER 21

DEX

Julia: Soooo, it turns out I'm not a great wingman. Sorry.

Dexter: Wtf, Julia? What now?

Julia: She knows that I know that you slept in her bed last night. She's kinda pissed you spoke to me before she did.

I can't deal with this girl. I press the call button.

"Well, hello, Mr. Cross," Julia answers like she didn't just throw me under the bus. Again.

"Don't, Julia. What kind of cockblocking did you do this time?" I bark.

She scoffs, "I hardly cockblocked, you douche-canoe. I told her to give you a chance, but you may want to rethink your method of asking for help. Not sure she appreciates the little camaraderie we've got going on."

Pinching the bridge of my nose, I take a calming breath. "Did you at least tell Lanie I only told you so you wouldn't crush my balls when you found out I slept in her room last night?"

"Nope. Didn't get the chance, Cross. She had me tearing up over the little Mary and Maria lesson you gave her."

I shrug my shoulders—not that she can see me. "What do I have coming my way?"

"Not sure, honestly. She's grocery shopping with the girls right now. Did you decide on a plan?"

Sitting on the corner of my desk, I smile. "I did. I told her I'm going to spend every day treating her so well she won't ever want to give me up. Today is day one of my Make Lanie Mine plan."

"All right, big guy. Good luck. We're rooting for you. Miss Rosa's got a betting pool going ... most bets are on you. No pressure or anything."

Chuckling at her antics, I say good-bye.

There's something endearing about Julia. Strange, annoying, but endearing just the same.

～

The doorbell rings, and I run to get it. He's a little late. I hate late, especially for this project.

As I open the door, he asks, "Mr. Cross?"

"Yes. You must be Richie?"

"Sure am. Heard you have a project for me and need it done by this afternoon?" He glances around the house.

"That's right." I usher him inside, looking around the driveway like I'm about to get caught. "She'll probably be home around four p.m., so it has to be completed before then. Will that be a problem?" I ask, escorting him toward the stairs.

"Sir, for what you're paying me, it'll be done before four, and you'll never even know it's there." He chuckles.

"That's what I like to hear. Right this way, Richie." I'm grinning like a fool, and I don't give a shit.

～

Dexter: Day 1 of MLM: Mission in process. LED floodlights are being installed in her room as we speak. She never has to worry about the lights again.

Preston: It's a little early in the day for word games. What's MLM?

Julia: Obviously, it's Make Lanie Mine. Should I expect these updates daily?

Trevor: Who has the 802 number?

Trevor: Also, little bit creeper-ish here, man. What happened to chocolate and flowers?

Julia: A guy gives me flowers and chocolate, and I'll kick him in the taint all the way back to his car.

Trevor: Noted. Again, who is 802?

Dexter: 802 is Lanie's best friend, Julia. Julia, meet the guys; Trevor, Preston, and Loki.

Preston: Is she hot? The friend?

Julia: Another douche-canoe? Come on, Dex. I thought you were better than this.

Trevor: I think I'm in love.

Loki: I'll be MIA for a couple of months. I'll be on the lookout for my invite to the wedding.

Dexter: Be safe, man.

Trevor: Check in if you can.

Preston: If Julia's shooting me down, Loki, will you be my date to Dexter's wedding? Be safe, bud. We'll be thinking of you.

Julia: Definitely missing something. But hey, be safe!

Loki: Take care of the girl. Guys, take care of Dex. Julia? Hell, good luck!

Trevor: Will do. Dex, keep us updated.

Preston: What's step two, lover boy?

Dexter: I'm making dinner tonight.

Trevor: Jesus, don't burn the place down.

Dexter: Your confidence in me is overwhelming.

Preston: Dinner, got it. What else? Doll, do you have any suggestions? I think it's going to take more than dinner and some floodlights to win over your girl.

Julia: I'm going to assume you're calling one of the guys *doll* and not me. If you're talking to me, watch your balls when we meet in person.

Preston: Noted.

Preston: So, any suggestions?

Trevor: Dex, lead with your heart. The rest will follow.

Julia: Get Maria to stay!

Dexter: Will do.

Preston: Who the fuck is Maria?

Slipping my phone back into my pocket, I walk up the stairs to check on Richie. He's been up there longer than I thought he'd be, and I'm starting to get nervous. "Hey, Richie, how's it going?"

"Ah, it's going okay. Ran into a bit of a snag with some wiring, but I'm back on track now. Can't say I've ever had anyone ask me to put backup floodlights in a bedroom before, though. I definitely haven't been asked to hide them, but whatever floats your boat, dude."

CHAPTER 22

LANIE

"What the fiddlesticks are you doing in my room?" I know I'm shrieking, but if he's doing what I think he's doing, I'll kill him.

"Jesus Christ, Lanie. You scared the shit out of me." Dexter holds a hand to his heart, but he's shifty. He's guilty of something, I know it. I'm living with a total creeper.

I stare from Dex to the portly man on a ladder in my room, then back to Dex. Hands on my hips, face flaming red, I wait for him to explain. The stout man quietly climbs down the ladder, giving Dexter one of those *man* looks. You know the ones, they say, 'good luck to you.'

"You gosh dang creeper. Are you putting one of your cameras in my room? Why? Why would you do that?"

Dexter looks mad, and the portly man's face turns as red as a raspberry.

Good, I ruined his plan, but what kind of pervert is he? Let him be angry. So am I. Three quick strides are all it takes for him to cross the hallway to meet me, and I feel my outrage slipping.

His voice is dangerously low, and I shiver. My body is a

stinking traitor, too. "Let's get one thing clear right the fuck now, you hear me, Lanie? I am not now, nor have I ever been a creeper. Have I done anything, anything at all to make you think you couldn't trust me?" he asks, inches from my face.

"You did put cameras all over the house when you were in London," I point out.

"Dang, she got you there, boss," the burly man observes.

Dexter gives him a deathly glare, and he goes back to work.

"Lanie," he sighs, "I'm not putting cameras in your room." He glances away and grips the back of his neck, seeming more unsure of himself than I've ever seen him.

I let out a long breath. "Then what are you doing, Mr. Cross?"

"Fuck, Lanie. Are we back to Mr. Cross?" He raises my face to his. "I'm installing emergency LED floodlights in your room. If the power ever goes out, they kick on within two seconds. I-I just didn't want you to be afraid anymore."

My world spins, and all I can hear is my heartbeat whooshing in my ears. *Did he really just do this for me?*

A second later he's cradling my face in his hands, thumbs wiping away tears I didn't even know had fallen. "Lanie. Sweetheart, look at me."

It takes a herculean effort, but I raise my gaze to his.

"I'm going to do stuff like this for you every day. Every single day you're going to be treated the way you should've been treated your entire life."

Without another thought, my hands wrap around his neck, and I kiss him. I kiss him with every piece of my heart I can give. I'm greedy in my pursuit, a feeling I've never experienced with a man before. When his lips comply, my tongue asks for entry, and he gives me a moment to lead, then takes over.

His kisses leave me breathless. He tastes of mint and

coffee. His lips are soft and sweet. His tongue dominates mine with his hands entangled in my hair. Somehow, he has walked us backward. I'm up against a wall, but I don't feel trapped. I don't feel scared. I feel wanted, needed even. *I feel whole.*

Dex ends the kiss much sooner than I would have liked, resting his forehead against mine. "Lanes, we have to take this slow. I want you to trust me completely." He kisses my forehead, then hugs me close. "Have dinner with me tonight. We'll put the kids to bed, then have a dinner date here at home. What do you say?"

I'm still breathless. My brain isn't working correctly. "Dex, I don't know." *Feelings are so freaking confusing.*

"Just dinner, for now." He gives me a sly, little smile while kissing my forehead once more.

"Just dinner," I repeat.

"I can't wait." His voice takes on a husky edge, and it sends shivers down my spine. Dex chuckles just as someone clears their throat. "Shit, I forgot he was here." He laughs again.

"Mr. Cross, you're all set. I'll just ... ah, send you an invoice?" He's clearly embarrassed by our little show.

"That would be great, Richie. I'll walk you out." Dex winks at me on his way by, and I remember why I stopped back at home in the first place.

"Dex? I have to get Tate from school soon. Can you help me grab the groceries? I don't want to be late."

"Whatever you need, Lanes. Always." His crooked smile beckons, and he pulls me into his side.

~

"Julia," I hiss into the phone, "we just put the kids to bed. He wants to have an ... um, hmm ... I don't even know what. A date? At home? He says it's just dinner, but come on. He isn't playing fair. Plus, he flat out told you he wants to date me."

"Lanie, it's dinner. Get to know him," she tells me like a child, and I have to take a calming breath.

"Okay, maybe you're right."

"I know I am. Now go bone him." Julia cracks herself up.

"Julia! There will be no boning, I promise you that." My voice is sharp, but I haven't mastered the scary, angry tone yet.

"You're no fun, Lanes. Luvs."

"Luvs," I say, rolling my eyes.

Beep. Beep. Beep

"What the heck?"

Running down the stairs, I head toward the sound. Dex is in the kitchen flapping a sheet pan around, trying to clear the smoke away from the smoke detector. His hair's disheveled, his shirt untucked. Perfectly imperfect.

"Lanie, thank God, open the back doors. Please? I need to get this smoke out of here." He sounds desperate.

Laughing, I run to the doors and sweep them open wide. "Dex, what happened here? I was only upstairs for twenty minutes."

"I guess that's twenty minutes too long," he mumbles.

As the smoke clears, I glance around the kitchen while he sinks down onto a stool. There are three bowls of thick, gooey sludge on the counter. It kind of resembles pancake batter, but it's lumpy with lots of spices. The sink is full of what I can only imagine is every utensil he owns. The counters are covered in flour, the stove is covered in batter, and what I think are splatters of grease. Anyone walking in would assume we set the twins loose in here.

"Seriously. What were you doing?" When I turn, I find him blushing, and it makes me smile.

"Julia said you liked chicken parmesan. I looked up a

recipe, and it didn't seem too hard. News flash, it's a fucking nightmare," he grumbles.

I'm belly laughing now. Not only because of the disaster he made in the kitchen, but because if he knew the reason I always ordered chicken parmesan, he wouldn't have attempted it.

"Come on, let's get this cleaned up, then I'll let you in on a little secret," I whisper conspiratorially as I move to throw the mess on the stove into the trash can. "Julia thinks chicken parmesan is my favorite because I always ordered it when I would go out to dinner with her and her parents. The truth is, it was usually the only thing on the menu I recognized. The places her parents would take us to were nicer than anywhere I'd ever been to. The chicken parmesan was also usually the cheapest. I would try to get plain pasta, but Mimi insisted I needed protein." I shrug at the memory. "So I picked chicken parmesan, never wanting to rock the boat or embarrass them."

"From my time with the McDowells, I don't think they would have cared. Did you ever tell them?"

"Gosh, no! Mimi would kill me. When you grow up poor the way I did, you just kind of learn how to blend in, not make a scene. I loved them so much even when I was young. I was always afraid they'd stop taking me in." I've never admitted that to anyone, but it slipped out so easily with Dex.

He regards me as I clean, and I feel my body flush.

"Can I ask you something?"

"Dex, you can always ask, doesn't mean I'll answer." I give him a sassy smile.

"Why social work? I saw your grades, you're brilliant. Something must have made you choose such an emotional profession." His question is innocent, but I need a moment to answer.

Turning my back to him as I wipe down the counters, I

collect myself. When I speak, I know he must be struggling to hear me. He moves closer but makes no move to touch me.

"My mother was an alcoholic. She wasn't always abusive, but when she was, she was smart about it. Her favorite punishment was of the verbal variety. It took a long time and a lot of coaxing from Mimi for me to even begin to understand my worth. I think I chose social work so I could do better than all the ones that couldn't help me. Mimi always took me in, no questions asked. When my mother went on a bender or with another new boyfriend, I knew I could seek refuge with the McDowells, or my grandmother, GG. I think that's the only reason my mother never tried to move me to another town. Whenever she tired of me, she knew Mimi or GG would take me until she needed me for something else."

He doesn't say anything for a beat, and I bite my lip, wondering if I've scared him off. A moment later, he takes my hand in his and leads me through the kitchen to the family room—the mess he created forgotten as he sits me on the couch. "I'm going to grab us some wine and crackers since I messed up dinner. Get comfortable. I'll be right back."

I settle into the deep cushions, but it doesn't seem like Dexter. *I wonder who picked it out?* It's large, and made out of the finest leather, with those brass tacks running all along the seams. It's the only piece of furniture that doesn't fit with the rest of the house. He did an excellent job making a massive property feel like a home. I'm running my hand along the seam when Dex returns.

"It doesn't fit here, does it?" he asks, watching my hand caress the leather.

"How did you know what I was thinking?" I'm trying really hard not to laugh.

"I think the same thing every time I walk in here." He hands me a glass of wine and takes a seat next to me. "I bought it after Anna left. She would have hated it, which made me love it even more." He laughs, but there's no humor in it. Scrubbing a hand over his face, he leans back into the couch.

"Short version of where Anna went?" I ask, and immediately feel like a jerk. "Dex, you don't have to ... I shouldn't have asked."

He stares straight ahead, not acknowledging my comment, and I wring my hands together. "About a month after we found out she was pregnant with the girls, my dad was in an accident. It was a drunk driver—they say he never felt a thing." He swallows once, twice, three times before continuing, "I had him on life support, but after two weeks with no brain activity, the doctors said I was only delaying the inevitable. All the guys were with me when I had to pull the plug. Until that moment, it was the worst day of my life. If I had only known it would get so much worse." He takes a long drink of wine, encouraging me to eat a few crackers and some cheese before he continues.

"I went home that afternoon. Trevor wanted to come with me, but Anna never liked any of my friends. As I pulled up to my driveway a man was walking out. I didn't really think much of it at the time. I went to her, needing comfort, but she was more distant than normal, even for her. She said she was sorry about my dad at the same time she handed me divorce papers. She left that day with the man waiting on the road. After that, I only saw her the day she gave birth. I gave her a check; she gave me all parental rights. End of story. I'm not sure why she showed up here after all this time, but I am sorry for what she did to you. I'll fix that, I promise."

I'm numb. I'm not sure what I was expecting, but that definitely wasn't it. After setting my wine on the coffee table, I slide in next to him and rest my head on his shoulder.

"I'm so sorry about your dad." He wraps his arm around me, and I melt into him. "Were you close to him?"

"I was. It was always just dad and me. My mom left when I was five, and I never saw her again. It's probably why I was so angry with Anna. We met in high school. She knew all about my mom, and she did the same thing to Tate. I can never forgive her for that."

"I don't blame you. I can't imagine having such a fantastic child and walking away. How can she take that for granted when people like me will never have the chance?"

CHAPTER 23

DEX

Lanie immediately tenses and tries to slide away from me. I hold her tighter. "Lanie, please. Don't pull away. You don't have to talk, but please do not pull away."

She sits frozen for a few minutes before melting back into my side. We stay like this until we empty our wine glasses. We're sitting in companionable silence, both so deep in our own heads that I almost don't hear her when she speaks.

"I've told you I'm damaged. I-I …" she starts and stops multiple times. "Dexter, I was attacked." She cries silently in my arms.

"Lanie, shhh, baby. Don't cry. I know." I swallow thickly as my own tears fall. I'm not sure if she'll feel relief that she doesn't have to say it out loud or pissed that I went behind her back. Either way, I owe her the truth. The kindness of not making her re-live such a despicable act.

"I know about your attack. I know all about your injuries, and how strong you are. I know you protected Max by enduring every abuse imaginable. And I know that you have come out of it even more beautiful than you were before," I tell her, meaning it with my whole heart.

It's then that she hits her breaking point. Lanie's sobs are deep, painful, full-bodied ones. *Has she never allowed herself to let go before?* It makes me realize, no matter where this goes, I will be here to hold her for as long as she lets me.

~

The sun breaks through the drapes. I've angled Lanie so she's laying across me, hoping she'll be more comfortable that way.

Last night, she explained how her attacker thought she was his wife, who was pregnant with another man's baby, because he was so high and drunk he couldn't see straight. Once he knocked her unconscious, he tried to cut the non-existent baby out of her. When she told me she could never carry a child, she cried herself to sleep in my arms.

I've spent the entire night holding her, not taking my eyes off her once. I know this is not how she wanted to tell me. Hell, she probably thought she would never tell me, so I'm not sure what will happen today. Anxiety rolls in my gut at all the ways this could go sideways, but I try to push it aside. I want to spend these last moments holding her before she inevitably tries to shut down again. Just before six, she stirs.

"Dex?" she says sleepily but not making eye contact. "I'm so sorry I fell asleep. I'm going to run up and shower before Tate wakes."

I don't let her go right away. "Lanie, do you remember what I said to you that day you came out of your shower?"

She still won't look at me, but I hold her steady to hear my words.

"Your scars make you who you are. They show how much you've overcome. They do not make you any less beautiful. Just remember that. Please, don't run away from me. I know we both got a lot of pain out in the open last night. Let me be the one to help put you back together."

"Richard Gere and Humpty Dumpty? You have quite the repertoire there, Mr. Cross." It's not the answer I was looking for, but she's smiling, so I take it.

My chuckle rumbles from deep in my belly as I help her to her feet. "I know last night was a lot to take in. I definitely never thought I would rehash my shit with Anna, but I want you to understand that you will not scare me away. Take your time. Let everything sink in. We'll take this slow, okay?"

"Okay," she agrees quietly, but rushes out of the room like her ass is on fire.

I sink back onto the couch and put my head in my hands. *Fuck*. This was way too much, way too soon. I haven't prayed in a very long time. Not since I used to pray for my mother to come home, but I find myself praying now. I pray to God that Lanie doesn't run. Checking my phone, I decide it might be time to call in backup.

Dexter: Day 1 didn't go the way I planned. We laid all our ghosts bare. I'm afraid she's going to run.

Julia: Wtf, Dexter? How did that happen?

Dexter: I burned the chicken parmesan.

Julia: Hey, dipshit? How do you go from burning chicken to baring your souls?

Trevor: It's a little early for this, but can I just point out, I really like Lanie's friend.

Trevor: She has a point, though. How did you get from point A to point B?

Dexter: I don't know, guys. I burned dinner. We talked. I told her about my dad and Anna and ended up telling her the whole damn story.

Silence. For ten damn minutes. Nothing.

Dexter: Hello? I told Lanie everything.

Julia: Dexter, what happened after you told her?

Dexter: She let it slip that she couldn't have children. Then she tried to tell me about her attack. I couldn't stand to see her in pain, so I told her I knew all about it, and it

didn't make her any less beautiful. Then we sat for a long time, not talking. She cried herself to sleep while I held her. She's spooked this morning, I can tell.

Julia: You're a good man, Dexter Cross. Your bros will be at your house in twenty minutes. I'm going to call Lanes.

∽

"*D*ex? You here?" Trevor lets himself in through the front door.

Standing, I greet him in the foyer. "Hey."

"Lanie here?" Trevor scans the hall.

"No, she left a little while ago to take Tate to school. Come on in." I lead him to the kitchen and put on a pot of coffee.

"I'm a little shocked that you let Lanie in so quickly. You told her everything?" he asks.

"Everything. Dad, Mom, Anna. I gave her all the dirty details. Now she knows I looked into her attack, too. I'm not sure how she's going to take it," I admit.

"I'm proud of you, Dex. I wasn't sure you'd ever get to this point again. It's good to see, man. It gives assholes like me hope."

"What gives you hope?" Preston walks in, holding a box of muffins. As much as Preston has changed over the years, he's still a good guy at heart. He tries to hide it. None of us are sure why, but I recognize the pain in his eyes. Whatever he has kept from us since college haunts him to this day.

"Dexter letting his girly side out again and going after love."

They both laugh, and I feel my lips twitch. Girly side or not, I'm happier than I've been in a long ass time.

Catching Trevor's eye, the laughter fades. "I'm really nervous she's going to run. What do I do?"

"Day two of MLM? I'd say you have to tone it way the fuck down tonight," Preston says.

"Thanks, Pres. Any advice to go with that, or are you just stating the obvious?" Trevor has always pulled Preston's strings; it's their own kind of love language.

"Go for humor. Humor and a movie with minimal talking. Let her relax tonight. Just be together without any pressure. Does that make sense?" Preston asks me.

Smiling like the Cheshire cat, I look at him. "It does, thanks. It really does. Who knew the manwhore had a sensitive side?"

"Hey, I let him out everyone once in a while. What do you need from us?" Preston asks, pretending to be taking notes.

"T-shirts. I need to have a couple of T-shirts made today and some matching pajama pants." Trevor and Preston are thoroughly confused, and I laugh, picking up my phone.

"Good morning, Mr. Cross. What can I do for you?" Molly asks on the second ring.

"Hello, Molly. I have a rather odd request. I need a couple of T-shirts made and some matching lounge pants in the next few hours. Can you take care of that for me?"

She clears her throat but doesn't bother hiding her amusement. "Yes, sir. Send me an email with the details and I'll have them delivered by two p.m."

"Thanks, Molly." I'm thankful every day that woman didn't quit.

Since returning from London, I've tried to go easy on her, even insisting she take a vacation that I paid for personally. She's a great assistant, probably the best I've ever had. I can't lose her.

Turning back to the guys, I inform them day two of MLM is in full swing.

CHAPTER 24

LANIE

I've been out of sorts all day. I'm not sure if I'm happy my past is out in the open for Dex, pissed that he dug so deep into such sensitive information, or a mix of both. Sitting in the car pick-up line at Tate's school, I realize I have a full half hour before he comes out. Instead of allowing myself time to have an internal war, I call Jules.

"Lanes! I've missed you," she answers in greeting like we didn't speak at seven o'clock this morning.

"Hi, Jules. Where are you? Is that Mimi in the background?"

"Sure is," I hear Mimi say. "Let me see my girl.

"Oh, Lanie, don't you look good. I miss you, my sweet girl. How are those beautiful charges of yours? Julia showed me pictures of you with them this morning, and they're just precious. I haven't seen you looking that happy in a long, long time. It made this old woman's heart jump for joy."

"Hi, Mimi. I miss you so much." I can't hide the tear that falls down my cheek.

"Now, you listen to me, young lady," Mimi scolds. "You deserve to be happy. Don't you dare be your own worst enemy. Pawpaw and I really liked that young man when he came up here, you know. That's a big gesture on his part. I'll never force your hand at anything, but if Pawpaw approves, I think you ought to at least think about unlocking a little piece of that big heart you have."

"Thanks, Mimi." I sniffle. "It's just terrifying. I already love these kids so much. What happens when things don't work out? I'll never see them again."

"Give me that phone," I hear Pawpaw say. "Honey, did you listen to what you just said? If you spend the rest of your life expecting things to end, you'll miss all the beginnings, all the good. I know you haven't experienced much of that goodness yet, but I'm guessing that your luck is about to change. I think you can finally experience all the love this world has to offer if you just open your heart to it."

"What if I get hurt again?" I whisper.

"There are no guarantees in this life, Lanie. You of all people know that, but if you don't at least try to embrace the good after all the bad you've endured, are you really even living?" Pawpaw asks. "Locking your heart away will ensure you don't get hurt, but that's not the life you deserve. It's not the kind of life we want for you. Just think about that, okay, honey? Think about what you and you alone want out of this life, then make it happen. If you get hurt, you'll do what you always do. You'll come home to your family. Then you'll pick yourself back up like the strong, independent, beautiful, young woman we have watched you become. We couldn't be prouder of you, sweetie. We love you, and we'll talk to you again soon, but think about what I said."

He doesn't give me a chance to argue, so I say my goodbyes. "I love you, too, Pawpaw. Tell Julia I'll call her later."

"Will do, kiddo. Be safe."

I end the call and peek into the back seat. Both girls are still sleeping, so I have a few moments to collect myself before Tate comes running out.

Pawpaw's words run through my head. *"Are you really*

living? It's not the kind of life you deserve. Think about what you and you alone want out of this life and make it happen."

"What do I want?" I ask the silent car, the answer coming to me like an electric shock.

I don't want to end up alone like my mother.

"It looks like you have some decisions to make, Lanie. What do you want out of this life?" I'm met with silence until I hear the school bell ring, and kids come tumbling out of the double doors.

~

Dex

MLM Group Text

Dexter: I left her outfit and snack basket on her bed after dinner. She's been up there for half an hour. What if she doesn't come down? I'm standing here looking like an asshole.

Preston: Did you honestly name this group text the MLM group? When did you become such a pussy?

Dexter: Shut up, asshole. Help me or move along.

Trevor: It's a solid plan. Just give her time. Julia's on the phone with her now.

Dexter: How do you know that?

Trevor: ...

Trevor: ...

Dexter: Now who's being the pussy? Trevor? What's going on?

Trevor: Okay, fine. Julia and I have been texting in the background, trying to make sure neither of you fucks this up.

Preston: Trevor and Julia sitting in a tree, k-i-s-s-i-n-g.

Trevor: How long did it take you to text that with all the hyphens, you dick? We're just trying to help.

Dexter: Not to be a prick, but this is about me, guys. ME!

Julia: Chill out man-lady. She's coming down. Try—I know it's tough for you—but please try to be cool tonight. Don't push anything. Don't talk about anything. Just be.

Dexter: Got it. Gotta go get set up.

Trevor: Good luck.

Julia: Keep your hands to yourself.

Preston: Completely ignore the advice to keep your hands to yourself. I'll be waiting with bated breath to find out how this plays out. (Eye roll emoji)

∽

Lanie

"Lanie!" Julia's voice comes through the computer screen. We decided on a Zoom call tonight to see each other better. I'm sure she's really just checking up on me.

"What?" I ask.

"Don't get snippy. Are you going down there or not? It seems like he went to a lot of trouble to make a relaxed night at home special," she tells me, obviously still team Dex.

"Ugh, Jules. Why is he doing this?" I say, more to myself than to her.

"You know why. You also know why our entire town is invested in where this relationship goes. We all want you to have the best life you can. GG said odds are ten to one right now in Dexter's favor." Julia laughs.

I roll my eyes at her but secretly love that my hometown cares so much about me.

"Okay," she says, "show me your outfit again. Keep this a secret, but I think he has something special on, too."

Laughing while I imagine what he could possibly be

wearing, I stand in front of the screen again. He had someone make me a T-shirt in the most hideous pattern meant to look like the curtains Maria cut up in the movie. In large letters across the chest, it simply says, 'Maria.' He picked lounge pants in the softest material I've ever felt. They're a deep navy color to complement the ridiculous pattern of my shirt.

Julia has tears running down her face. "It's both the sweetest gesture and ugliest thing I've ever seen. What else is on the bed?" She sniffles, and I know she's trying to keep the tears at bay.

"He left a massive bucket with some packets of popcorn, every kind of movie theater candy you can imagine, and a note telling me the movie begins as soon as I'm ready to join him," I tell her.

"You have to admit, Lanes. That's pretty romantic," she says, all googly-eyed.

"It is," I admit, "but I've spent the last year convincing myself romance would never be a part of my life, Jules. I'm so scared. I-I think I'm starting to care for him, and I love his kids so much. If I keep going down this route, how am I ever going to survive when it's time to come home?"

"I'm not sure, Lanes," she says truthfully. "I think you should stop worrying about the future for now and live in the present. I really shouldn't tell you this, but I'm a terrible wingman so screw it. Dexter's downstairs pacing, completely freaking out that he's scared you away. If you're not going down, you should at least put him out of his misery."

"Julia, are you still talking to him every day?" I screech.

"Oh yeah, we have a group message going. Dexter, Preston, Trevor, Loki, and me," she says proudly. "Hey, do you know what Loki does? He told us he was going *MIA* for a while, and he hasn't responded since."

"Oh my God," I say, face planting into the palm of my hand. "No, I don't know what Loki does. That sounds like some kind of spy crap, though. Are you seriously telling me that not only is our entire hometown taking daily bets on my love life but that my best friend is plotting behind my back with a bunch of guys she's never met?"

"Yup, it's awesome. We even have a club name, but I can't tell you what it is yet. And Dexter's friends are fun to rile up. Preston takes my shit like a champ, and Trevor … well, Trevor's pretty interesting, actually."

My head whips up to the screen, and I notice her flushed cheeks. "What? What do you mean, Trevor is *interesting*?"

Julia is definitely blushing, and she never blushes. Not once in twenty years of friendship have I seen her blush. "Oh, nothing," she sing-songs. "Story for another time. We're talking about you. Are you going down there to put that poor man out of his misery?"

Reluctantly, I agree. "You tell Miss Rosa this doesn't mean anything. It's just two friends watching a movie together."

"Mhmm. Gotcha. Totally platonic. Have fun and hurry up! The poor man is down there, breaking out in a nervous sweat." She laughs.

"You're so ridiculous." I giggle. "Okay, I'm going. Luvs."

"Luvs, Lanes. Talk to you tomorrow."

After checking my hair one more time to make sure it looks perfectly messy, I grab our bucket of snacks and make my way to the family room.

Walking through the door, it takes me a second to process what I'm seeing. Dexter is standing in the middle of the room, hands on his hips, smiling as broadly as I've ever seen. Uncontrollable laughter hits me as I stare at him. He's in a bright red T-shirt with 'White Knight' written in bold with, 'Baby, I'm gonna treat you so nice,' underneath. As if that wasn't enough, his lounge pants are the same hideous pattern as my T-shirt. It isn't until I notice the windows that I completely lose my mind, laughing so hard I'm afraid I'll pee myself.

Covering every window is a large piece of fabric in the same pattern as my shirt. In the center of each one, there is a hole cut out in the shape of a T-shirt.

When I'm finally able to compose myself, I turn to him. "You're taking this whole Maria thing a bit far, don't you think?"

"It was easier than getting chimney sweeps to jump out of the fireplace." He shrugs, but I can feel him watching me out of the corner of his eye.

We're both laughing, but he's pinching the back of his neck. He does this when he's unsure of himself. *I've already learned his tell*. Smiling, I walk to him, telling my brain to shut up for once and let my heart lead. It's in there. I just have to learn how to listen to it again.

Reaching him, I don't hesitate. I wrap my arms around him, and his arms clamp around me the second we touch. His strong arms are holding me, making me feel safe. It's a foreign feeling for me, I realize. Even when I was with the McDowells, I always waited for the other shoe to drop. I knew it would only be a matter of time before my mother would show up to use me as a prop for whatever scam she had planned next.

"Thank you," I say into his chest. "Just, thank you for going to all this trouble."

"Sweetheart, it was no trouble. My mission, remember? Make it so you're never gonna wanna let me go."

Unsure of the emotions I'm feeling, I gently pull away. "All right, what movie are we watching?"

"I'm offended you even have to ask," Dex scoffs. "*The Sound of Music*, duh." He smiles like I carry all the sunshine on my shoulders as he searches for the movie.

"Uh … okay, I'll go make the popcorn." I practically run from the room. I need a breather.

Calm down, Lanie, I tell myself, clutching my racing heart. No one has ever gone to this much trouble for me before.

The McDowells always made my birthdays and holidays special, but they said that's just what parents do. Outside of my adoptive family and GG, not one person in my life has ever done anything to make me feel as I do now.

I take the few extra minutes I need while making the popcorn before I head back to find Dex. He's propped up on the couch with pillows and blankets all around him. His arm is raised as if waiting for me to climb in at his side. At this moment, there isn't anything I've ever wanted more. Feeling contentment I never knew existed, I relax into Dex as the movie starts. We don't speak much, just hold on to each other. When I glance up, I find him watching me instead of the movie.

"You're missing all the best parts," I whisper, adjusting myself in his embrace.

Staring me straight in the eyes, he declares, "I disagree." He continues watching me as he rubs gentle circles on my back. Feeling too warm, I turn my attention back to the TV.

When the movie ends, neither of us move, and eventually, I'm lulled to sleep by the rhythmic way he's been massaging my back. I don't wake until Dexter's tucking me into my bed.

"Shh, don't get up." He kisses my cheek. "I had an amazing time with you tonight, Lanie. I can't wait for our next date."

I wake the next morning feeling lighter than I have in years, unable to remove the smile on my face for the rest of the day.

CHAPTER 25

DEX

MLM Tactical Group
Dexter: Day 2, extraordinary success! Seriously, *the* best date I've ever had in my life.

Preston: Dude, you changed the group name again? Did your balls shrivel up and die?

Preston: Why was it so good, you finally got laid?

Julia: Do I need to remind you yet again to watch your balls when I meet you in person, Preston? Don't be a dickwad.

Trevor: Hahahaha

Trevor: Glad it went well. Our girl had fun?

Dexter: Watch it. Lanie isn't "our" anything.

Trevor: Jesus, you Neanderthal. When you get the girl, she will be part of our messed up little family. Therefore, she will be "our" Lanie.

Julia: You all need to stop getting your panties in a twist. We're all on the same page. I'll also remind you that Lanie was mine first. (I'm imagining Dexter growling right now, and I am LOLing)

Dexter: Whatever.

~

MLM Tactical Group
   Dexter: Day 12, game night.

Julia: So, not only are we getting the play-by-play of the plan, but we're also getting a rundown after it happens?

Preston: I'll send everyone some beer and popcorn.

Dexter: Fuck off all of you...

~

MLM Tactical Group
   Dexter: Day 21, wine tasting.

Julia: hahaha

Trevor: (Laughing emoji)

Preston: Good Lord, you have lost your balls.

~

MLM Tactical Group
   Dexter: Day 32, another success.

Preston: (Clapping hand emoji)

Trevor: Happy for you, man.

Julia: Not sure I can reply to this every day. It's becoming a bit nauseating.

~

MLM Tactical Group
   Dexter: Day 45. The plan is on hold. Girls came down with a cold. Re-do tonight.

Preston: I don't even know what to say to you anymore.

Julia: Any chance we can skip the daily check ins and move to weekly or, better yet, monthly updates?

Trevor: I'm with Jules.

Dexter: No can do, my friends. You're in this for the long haul with me.

Trevor: At least you're happy.

~

*J*meet Lanie outside of the nursery. She looks exhausted; the girls have been extra needy today. I wrap her in a hug, loving how normal this has become for us.

"Hi."

"Hi," she replies into my chest.

"It's a beautiful night out. Let's grab the baby monitors and sit on the deck with a glass of wine. I won't keep you up late. I know you're tired."

"That sounds great, actually."

I grab the bottle of wine while Lanie retrieves the glasses. At the last minute, I snatch a throw blanket off the back of the couch. It's warm out, but I've noticed Lanie gets cold easily. I find it funny since she grew up in Vermont. *How quickly she has adapted to the south.*

Making my way to the lounger, I settle in, motioning for Lanie to sit between my legs. She hesitates for only a second. When she leans into me, I wrap my arms around her, loving her scent that washes over me. I pour us both a glass of wine, enjoying holding her with the sound of the ocean in the background. It's hard to see from here, but on nights like this, you can hear it without having to make your way through the dunes. For the first time, I'm thankful the interior designer convinced me to string Edison bulbs out here all around the patio ceiling. The dim lights give Lanie an ethereal glow. The fire pit in the corner will have to wait for another time. We won't be out here long enough for it to be worth it tonight, but I tuck the fire pit idea away for another time.

"It's so peaceful out here," she sighs.

"It's probably the only thing about this house I liked when I bought it," I admit.

Her perfect nose scrunches up as she asks, "Why did you buy it then?"

Eesh. How do I explain this without sounding like a pretentious asshole? "My board members thought I needed to uphold a specific image to get that London deal done. I knew after all the papers were signed, I would make a lot of money. More than most would ever see in a lifetime. Security and the safety of the kids became something I had to seriously consider. I figured the gated community was as safe as I could get."

Almost hesitantly, Lanie chooses her words carefully. "So, you didn't live here with Anna?"

"Fuck, no." It comes out harsher than I intend, so I soften my voice. "No, I'm not sure how she even got the address."

"Have you found her yet? To see what she wanted?" she asks, staring straight ahead.

Wishing like hell I had, I shake my head. "No. It's almost like she's hiding. I can't figure out her game, but she was never very good at being patient. I suspect she'll find me again soon enough."

"Do you think sh-she's dangerous?" Lanie's body goes rigid, and I hate the fear in her voice.

I turn her face to mine so she can see how serious I am. "No, Lanie. I don't. She may be a bitch, but she had never been violent before she struck you. I haven't figured out what she's after, but I promise you I will. She will never come near you again, I swear."

She nods, turning back to the ocean.

After a while, Lanie shifts so she's lying on her side

between my legs. From this angle, I can't help but see her cleavage pressed between her arms as she places her hand on my thigh. She's very rarely made the first move, and I've had a severe case of blue balls for the last month. I've endured it because I want her to know I'm doing this at her pace, but I lose all my brainpower when she angles her body against me like this. That's precisely why I'm caught off guard when she suddenly moves to straddle me.

"Ah, Lanie?" I question, my voice so deep and husky I hardly recognize it as my own. She doesn't answer. Instead, she very slowly and gently kisses my lips. It isn't the same type of kiss we've shared in the past. This kiss feels like she's trying to tell me something. I feel her heart and soul in this kiss, and it scares me a little. It feels like good-bye. I don't take control, even though it's killing me. I let her tell me everything she can't say with words and hope to God I'm not translating this kiss correctly.

Eventually, she pulls away and lays her head on my chest. I feel my shirt getting wet, and I realize she is crying. "Sweetheart, what's wrong?"

"N-Nothing," she manages.

Her tears gut me. "If it's nothing, then why are you crying?"

"I just wanted to say thank you. This has been the best month of my life. You have made me feel special and loved. You've done everything I could ever hope someone would do." Her voice is strangled with emotion.

"Lanie? Why do I feel like there's a but coming?"

"Dex, I just don't think I can be what you deserve," she sobs.

"What? What are you talking about? Lanie, you've made my house a home. You've made me happier than I have been in years. Where is this coming from?" I'm desperate for her answer.

She hiccups as she tries to control her tears. "Dex, I feel

your reaction to me."

Embarrassed, that's what I am right now. "Yeah, well, that little asshole has a mind of its own. I told you I can't always control it, but I've never acted on it. Have I made you feel pressured to do something you're not ready for?"

"No, it's not that at all."

"Then what, Lanie? What's bothering you?"

She tries to stand, but I hold her to me, loving the way my hands fit on her hips.

"Please, Dex, let me turn around. I don't know if I can say this to your face."

My stomach knots painfully. It's a heavy, solid feeling that makes me feel like I might be emptying all its contents before this conversation is over. It takes all my willpower to let her move. Once she's settled, I wrap her in an embrace. With her back to my front, I rest my chin on the crown of her head and wait. It feels like an eternity before she speaks.

"When I was in the hospital, those first few days, I wasn't fully awake. I would hear bits and pieces of conversations but couldn't open my eyes."

Scared of where this is going, but not wanting her to get off track, I give her a gentle squeeze of encouragement.

"The first thing I remember is someone telling Mimi they ordered a rape kit."

I suck in a breath, not sure I'm strong enough to hold it together for this.

"When I came to, everyone tried to tell me, but I wouldn't let them. I didn't remember it. I didn't want to know. I didn't want to know anything about my attack. In my head, it was just easier to pretend it never happened. I-I was a flirt when I was younger, but I was never one to just hook up. I had one boyfriend my senior year of high school. We broke up after a couple of years, and I just focused on school."

She pauses and nibbles on her nails. It's a habit I haven't seen her do before.

"Whatever it is, Lanie, I'm here for you. I'm not going anywhere," I whisper.

"That's what I'm afraid of," she cries. "You don't understand. I don't know if I can ever be intimate with someone and not have flashbacks to what might have happened. I don't know if I can ever look at my body and not be reminded of my attack every time, but I don't think I'm strong enough to find out the truth either. I don't know if I'll ever feel comfortable being with anyone sexually ever again. You deserve better than that. You deserve more than a damaged freak. You deserve someone more than me."

I try to interrupt, but she steamrolls right over me. "I love your kids, Dex. They give me a purpose I haven't had in a very long time. I'm terrified if whatever this is between us doesn't work out, I'll lose them, too. I'm scared that if it does work out, I'll mess them up.

"Do you know the first question I asked Mimi when I was coherent enough to speak in the hospital?" With my chin still resting on her head, I shake my head no, and she continues, "I asked if my mom knew what happened. I wanted to know if she had visited me. Turns out, she knew and chose not to visit. I found out later she told people at the bar that I must have *done something* to provoke the attack. That she always knew my slutty looks would bite me in the ass."

I'm silent for a long time. Part of me wants to make sure she's done, and part of me needs a minute to process everything she just said.

Fuck, I really wish I could consult Julia right now.

I'm on my own, and I know this is a make-or-break moment for us. I dig deep and go with the only solution I can come up with. I gently slide Lanie forward, standing up and walking to the front of the lounger. I take her hand in mine and pull her to standing. Not saying a word, I guide her through the house and up the stairs. I don't stop until we're standing in my bedroom at the foot of my massive bed.

"Dex, didn't you hear anything I just said to you? I—"

I cut her off. "Lanie, we aren't going to do anything but sleep. Stay right here while I get some stuff from your room. I just want to hold you tonight." I know she's confused by my lack of response to her confessions. The truth is, I need a few more minutes to gather my thoughts, but I'm not willing to let her go for the night.

When I return to my bedroom, I have a few of her things in my arms. Taking her hand in mine, I guide her to the bathroom, where I lay her stuff out on the second sink.

She's in a daze. Confused, possibly hurt, but I'll fix that soon.

Leaving her on one side of the vanity, I move to my side and brush my teeth, never taking my eyes off hers in the mirror. After a while, she breaks eye contact to brush her's and wash her face. I left her a choice of pajamas and one of my large T-shirts. It's up to her what she feels comfortable sleeping in. But I'd be a lying bastard if I said I'm not ecstatic when she enters the bedroom wearing my T-shirt.

"Come here," I tell her, needing to be close. "I'm just going to hold you tonight. Come." I lead her to the bed and tuck her in. Walking to the other side, I take off my watch and set it on the nightstand. As I slide in beside her, I pull her as tightly into my side as I can. When I feel her shoulders shaking, I know she's crying, and it causes a terrible ache in my chest.

"Lanie?" She rolls to face me, but I hug her tightly. "Stay," I command, knowing that if I look at her, I'll never get this all out. It's too important for her not to hear. I'm holding onto her so tightly I'm worried she won't be able to breathe, so I force myself to loosen my hold. "I told you I saw your report. I'm sorry again for going behind your back, but I hope you understand I only did it to protect my kids."

She's eerily still.

"Lanie, I-I have to tell you—"

"Please, Dexter. Please, I don't know if I can handle this."

"Lanie, the rape kit was negative. He did unspeakable things to you, but rape wasn't one of them." I let her cry for minutes, maybe hours, I'm not sure, but I hold her praying to any higher power I just made the right decision. That I can help extinguish this one demon. When her cries have subsided, I give her a squeeze and roll her over to face me.

"I don't know if I did the right thing by telling you, but I want you to know something. I will wait for you forever, however long it takes. We'll move at your pace or stay as we have been. I just want you here, like this, being able to hold you. You told me all the reasons I didn't deserve you. Let me prove that you are everything I deserve, and more"

"Dex, I—"

I place my fingers on her lips. "I mean it, Lanie, this is your world. I'm just lucky enough to be a part of it. If at any point you decide you're ready and want to try for more, I'll be here with open arms. Remember, I've already had the pleasure of seeing you naked, and it was the hottest fucking thing I've ever seen in my life. If I get that chance again, I'll spend every ounce of energy I have proving just how gorgeous you are to me, scars and all."

She places a hand along my jaw, and I sink into her touch.

"No matter what happens, you will always be welcome in my children's lives. And in whatever manner you choose because they love you, too. I'll never ask you to be more to them than you're ready for.

"As far as your mother, Lanie? You have to let her go. She doesn't deserve you, your pain, or your happiness. Sometimes the best families aren't the ones you are born into. They're the ones that take you in even when you're broken."

Rolling her back over, I kiss her temple and snuggle into her back, silently hoping I never have to let her go, knowing without a doubt I'd never recover from it.

CHAPTER 26

LANIE

Dexter: Day 67 plan in place. Sylvie will arrive at the house at six p.m. ... Best MLM plan to date.
Lanie: Ermmmmm???
Dexter: FUCK! This wasn't for you. Don't worry, I'll explain it all when I get home.

I call Julia immediately and she sends me to voicemail. I call again and again with the same response. That ass wipe. She's ignoring me, which means Dexter got to her before I did. What the hell? He's like a ninja texter or something.

Lanie: I know you're avoiding me. Just tell me who Sylvie is? Do I have anything to worry about?

She replies immediately, of course.

Jules: Not a thing. Try to go with the flow, Lanes. Loosen up a little.
Lanie: You! Are you telling me to loosen up?
Jules: The irony is not lost on me. Gotta go. Luvs.

I don't bother replying. I'm coming to terms with everyone in my life ganging up on me, but I refuse to let them off the hook too quickly.

*D*ex has been avoiding me all day, probably at Julia's instruction. If I didn't love them both so much, I'd be pissed.

Holy fuck.

Thank God I'm not holding a baby right now, because I may have dropped her. *Did I really just say that I love Dex?*

I'm on the floor playing blocks with the girls, trying to figure out what I'm feeling when the front door flies open. In an instant, I'm standing up, herding all the kids behind me. I'm shooing Tate into the kitchen when he darts past me.

"Nanna Sylvie, you're here! I didn't know you were coming."

"Well, just look at you, darling! I can't tell you how good it is to hear your sweet voice again. This must be the lovely, young lady we can thank for that." She comes to me, hand outstretched, Tate glued to her side. "You must be Lanie. I'm Sylvie Westbrook."

I know Dex said Sylvie was coming over, but I don't know her from Adam, so I'm trying desperately to pull Tate back to my side. Dex said he hasn't seen his mother since he was five, and there's no way this woman is related to Anna. I go to voice my concerns when Preston walks in, leading a pack—yes, a pack— of men.

"What the holy hockey is going on here, Preston?" I'm overwhelmed by the amount of male laughter that erupts. I look all around. I'm surrounded by Preston and four almost identical versions of him. They all have their unique way about them, but I swear, each is a carbon copy of the next. Standing before me are five insanely attractive versions of the same man.

"Holy geez, your dad must have had some strong genes," I let slip before I can sensor myself.

Sylvie bursts into a peal of very dignified laughter. "That

he did, my dear, that he did. I take it you haven't met Preston's brothers yet?"

"Ah, definitely not, ma'am," I say in shock.

"Oh, forget that ma'am business. Sylvie is just fine. Now, manners, Preston. Make the introductions," she orders.

"Hi, Lanie, I'm Preston, the best looking and oldest brother. Then there's Easton, Halton, Colton, and Ashton here is the baby." He points to each in a line.

"Wow. Hi, I wasn't expecting you. Does Dex know you're coming? Can I get anyone something to drink?" I'm entirely out of my element here, and thankfully, Preston can tell.

"Relax, sweet thing. Dex will be here any minute to explain. It's all taken care of," he coos.

I don't get to ask what it is that's taken care of because I hear the door shut again and in walks Dex, smiling without a care in the world. He makes the rounds, greeting each Westbrook in turn.

When he reaches me, he says, "Surprise!"

"Oh, dear. Dexter, this is not the kind of surprise you spring on someone," Sylvie tsks him in a way I have often heard from Mimi, and I feel immediately at ease with her. Turning to me, she explains the situation before me. "Since none of my boys have managed to give me any grandchildren yet, I like to borrow Dexter's whenever I can."

I give him the side-eye, but he's still all smiles.

"After that dreadful woman left, you know who I'm talking about, dear, I made sure my trips to visit happened more regularly. When the girls were a few months old, I began taking them to my house one weekend a month, so Dexter could have some time to himself. Truthfully, it's so I can spoil the kids rotten," she adds under her breath. "I haven't been by lately because I was trying to let you settle in, but Preston told me it might be time for another visit. Let's get these kiddos packed up, and we'll be on our way!"

"But, but I don't understand. What's with all the muscle?" I ask, staring at all the Westbrooks.

"Oh, don't mind them. These boys have known Dexter almost as long as Preston has. When they heard what I was up to, they just couldn't pass up the opportunity to see the girl that caught Dexter's heart," she says slyly.

Dex clears his throat uncomfortably. "Right, okay. Sylvie? Let's go. I'll help you pack a bag. Lanie, you'll need to pack, as well. Just a few things, bathing suits, shorts. Just the essentials, and nothing fancy."

"Oh. Oh geez. Okay."

I guess I'm going to the Westbrooks, too. It would have been nice of him to give me a little heads-up. I try not to be bitter, but this will be the first time in months we haven't spent the night together in some way. The realization makes me sad.

"Hey, sweet thing, why so glum?" I don't know how he does it, but Preston is always sneakily perceptive.

"Oh, nothing, just thinking about what I should pack," I tell him.

Preston watches me for a few minutes, and I see the wicked gleam in his eye. "Pack whatever you want, darling. It'll just be you and Dexter on the yacht. The six of us are on kid duty all weekend." He winks and walks away, leaving me feeling like I just got bulldozed by a Westbrook truck.

~

"That's a whirlwind of a family," I comment as the Westbrooks make their exit with kids and gear in tow.

"That they are, but they're some of the best people I've ever known. Sylvie loves the kids, and the boys all love it because, at least for a few days, she stops nagging them." He laughs and pulls me down onto the couch with him. "So, you ready?"

"Ready? For what? Am I going to Sylvie's to help with the kids?"

"No, Lanie. We're going away for the weekend. On a boat, just the two of us. Well, plus the crew. Did you pack?" he asks, staring me down, daring me to disagree.

"Dex, I don't know. This sounds like a lot," I say honestly.

"Just because we'll be on the water and not land doesn't mean any of our rules change, Lanie. This weekend is just for you. Plus, I already got permission from Pete and Julia. Mimi sends her love, too." He winks.

I roll my eyes. "Of course you did."

He's yanking me from the couch when he smirks. "Come on, let's get you packed. We leave in twenty."

"I don't even know what to pack. Seriously, this is so far out of my element." I'm whining, but I can't help it.

Coming up behind me, he wraps me in a hug that calms every nerve ending in my body. "Don't worry so much, Lanie. I'm here for you. Come on, I'll help. You really don't need much."

～

Almost an hour later, we're settled into the cabin of the *boat.* "Dex, where I come from, this is more than just a boat. This is massive, like super star massive."

"Only the best for you, sweetheart. Now, come on, get unpacked. Dinner will be served soon."

"Dexter!" I screech. "I didn't bring anything to wear to a sit-down dinner."

"Sweetheart, this is just about you and me. There's staff on board, but you'll rarely see them. Their job is to make sure we have everything we need without ever being in our way or making you uncomfortable. You could go to dinner in your pajamas and it would be fine. I just want you to relax and have fun. Have you ever had a real vacation? An adult vacation that didn't include Maxine and Pete?"

Embarrassed, I look away.

"Lanie, that didn't come out right. I didn't say that to embarrass you. I can't tell you how much it means to me that they always included you in their family. With all the shit in your life, they were the one consistent bright spot, and I'll be forever grateful. I just want you to experience a few days where you have absolutely nothing to worry about except what you want to do, eat, or drink next. Can you do that for me?"

Throwing myself at him for the millionth time, I hug him, letting all the words I can't say show through my actions.

"Come on, I'm starving."

~

Dinner was incredible. I don't think I've ever eaten such delicious food in all my life. Dexter arranged for all my favorites, leaving out the chicken parmesan, and made sure our first meal was something I'll never forget. Laying on the deck of the boat, we're side by side with our heads angled toward each other. Hands entwined, Dex raises them to kiss each of my knuckles.

"So," he begins, "this is day sixty-seven in my plan to make you never wanna let me go. How's it working so far?" His eyes dance with humor, but his voice is laced with love.

True to his word, he's done something every single day. Some days it was a simple flower or a candy he thought I'd like. One day it was a book he found in an old bookstore. Other times, they're over the top like this.

Never once have I felt pressure from him. Never once has he initiated anything intimate without asking me first. As I peek over at him, I see the nervousness he holds. He's always worried I'm going to run. After everything he has given me, all the kindness he's bestowed, I give him as much as I can.

"Honestly, I don't think I've ever felt more loved than I have these last couple of months." I don't look at him, I can't, or I'll break. It's as honest as I can give him right now.

He rolls to his side, running his fingers through my hair. "I do, you know."

It's not a question. There's no doubt what he means, but he clarifies anyway.

"I love you, Lanie. I love you like I never imagined possible. When you hurt, I feel it deep in my soul. When you're happy, I feel like I could float away. When you smile at me, I feel like the king of the goddamn castle.

"I am not expecting anything in return right now, Lanes. I just want you to allow me to be a part of your life, so if or when you're ready, we'll be together forever. I have no doubts about that, Lanie. You're it for me. I know I'm scaring you, that's why I got you on this boat, so you can't run away from me." He laughs. "I'm kidding … sort of." He winks, kisses me gently on the lips, and lays back down beside me.

He loves me. Just me. Not what he can get from me. Not what he expects from me, just me. Pawpaw is the only other man to ever love me unconditionally, and as much as he loves me, it's different from Dex. I don't know how to explain it. I definitely can't describe it.

"I always loved to lay and look at the stars," I tell him. "No matter how bad things got in my life, I knew I was always connected to Julia through the stars."

Dex reaches over, taking my hand in his once again. "I'm so glad you had them in your life, Lanes. They're as much a part of you as any of the bad. I'd say they're even more you than your mother. I see how you are with the girls. God, Lanie, how Tate took to you, how you got him talking almost immediately. You have so much good in you. I wish you could see how much you still have to offer."

When my gaze finds him, I see the love behind his words.

We're silent for a while, side by side, holding hands. "When I first came home from the hospital, I moved in with Julia. She had to change my bandages every day. As they started to scar over, we would talk about connecting them like the stars. As the scars healed, they looked worse. At least to me, so I stopped trying to connect them. I stopped looking at them all together. I would turn away when Jules would tend to them."

I pause for a moment, not sure how to share the rest. Counting to ten, I figure it's best to just get it out there, so I do.

"After plastic surgery, I knew the scars were as good as they were going to get, but it didn't matter anymore. I couldn't have children, so it didn't matter what the outside looked like, anyway. I try not to touch them when I'm in the shower. I pretend they don't exist. You're the first person to see me besides Julia, and as much as I know you care, even you couldn't hide your disgust. I don't blame you …"

"Wait a minute, Lanie. Just wait a minute. When I saw you naked, I was not disgusted. I was pissed, Lanie. That's a huge difference." He sits up to face me straight on. "I wanted to tear that guy apart with the dullest pair of scissors I could find, and that's what you saw on my face. I've gotten off to the image of you naked more times than I care to admit. If you think anything other than that, I've failed you."

He takes my hand and places it on his dick. "This, Lanie. This right here is what happens every single time I think of you. Every single time I imagine you or hear your voice. Do not for one minute mistake my hatred for what happened to you for anything other than it is. Everything I feel for you, I feel because of you. Who you are, what you do, what you stand for, and yes, even your scars. I go to bed thinking of you. I wake up thinking of you. Every single inch of you."

I sit up, searching his eyes, and at this moment, I know I

want him. I turn slightly, lifting my leg so I'm straddling him. His startled eyes never leave my face.

In a husky voice, he asks, "What do you want, Lanie?"

"I-I want you to show me what you see. Show me how you see me," I plead.

"Lanie, you have to be very clear right now. Are you asking me to touch you?" His voice is rough and raw.

Biting my lip, I nod my head.

"Lanie, sweetheart, I need you to tell me. I need to hear you say it," he says softly.

"I want you to touch me, Dex." My voice is as confident as it's been all night.

"Out here? Right now?" His voice is so close I can feel it vibrate through my chest.

"Are we alone?" Glancing around, I search for the crew nervously.

"We're alone. The crew is in their cabin for the night, so I'll ask you again, Lanie. Do you want me to touch you out here?"

"Yes," I whisper.

"Anything you don't like, anything you're not comfortable with, just say stop, and I swear to God I'll stop immediately, no questions asked. I'm dying, literally sweating like a teenager at the thought of finally touching you. Most importantly, though, I want you to understand you'll always come before my needs, you hear me? The second this," he says, pointing between him and me, "isn't what you want, just say stop."

"Dex, I trust you."

"Sweet Jesus, Lanie, you have no idea how long I've wanted to hear that. Come here." He lays me out on the top deck of the boat, gently placing me on cushions. When he moves to lift his shirt over his head, I feel so wanton that I squeeze my thighs together.

"I'm going to take your shirt off now," he informs me.

Once it's off, he sits back on his feet and looks at me while slowly lowering my shorts. I'm left in nothing but my bra and panties.

Hovering over me, he growls. "You're the sexiest thing I've ever seen, Lanie." Painfully slowly, he lowers his mouth to my neck. "I'm going to kiss every inch of your body, then I'm going to do it again and again. By the time I am done with you, you'll never think of your scars again." He gently nibbles my neck, making me shiver.

My hands go to his shoulders, and I take in his massive body. He's unbearably beautiful. Running my hands down his chest to his abdomen, I feel every flex of muscle. Every time he breathes, I feel his body rippling. I don't know when he goes to the gym, but he has very clearly never missed a day.

"Lanes." His voice is strained, and I realize he's working extremely hard at staying still to allow my exploration of him. Dropping my hands to my sides, I bring my eyes back to his. "Sweetheart, I'm all for you touching me wherever the hell you want, but right now, all I really need is to show you, to let you feel how much you mean to me."

I nod my head and bite my bottom lip. I'm not positive I'm ready for this, but I want it more than anything.

"Lanie, are you okay?" The concern in his voice wrecks me.

"Yes," I say, more confidently than I feel. "I-I …"

"What is it, sweetheart? Tell me what you need?" he repeats, letting me know I am in control.

"I think I have to close my eyes," I say, suddenly feeling so ashamed.

"Whatever you need, baby, but I want to make sure you stay here with me. At this moment, can you promise me your head won't wander to anything but what you're feeling, right here, right now?"

I hadn't thought of it that way.

"Baby, I want you aware of who you're with every minute

of this. I think you should keep your eyes on me and only me. Can you do that? I won't force you, but I'm worried if you close your eyes, this might not end well."

"Okay, eyes on you." My words are shaky, letting Dex know just how nervous I am.

"I'm going to kiss you now, Lanie. From here," he kisses the base of my neck, "to here," he touches the instep of my right foot, "and back again," his fingers are ghosting over my entire body, sensitizing me in ways I never imagined.

"O-Okay," is the only word I can form.

"Keep your eyes on me at all times. Understand?" he whispers against my skin.

I can no longer form sentences, so I nod my head.

His lips make their way across my collarbone. Then he slides his tongue back across the skin he just kissed. The ocean air feels frigid against the wetness of his hot tongue. My entire body quivers beneath him.

"I'm going to unhook this now." Pulling at the strap of my silk bra, he lowers it down my arms.

"Mhm ... yes," I add when I remember he wants words, not incoherent blubbering. Closing my eyes, I feel him reach in between my breasts to the tiny clasp holding both sides of the purple fabric together. But he doesn't release them.

"Open your eyes, baby, look at me," he commands.

My eyes fly open, not remembering when they had closed.

"You good?" he asks, searching deep into my eyes.

I smile at him. "I'm good. I want this, Dex. I want you."

"That's what I want to hear, sweetheart."

With the flick of his wrist, my breasts are freed. I'm a C-cup, so there's definitely some spring when they're released. My gaze drifts from my nipples to Dexter's eyes. He's licking his lips and his eyes have darkened as he sits back to take me in. Slowly, showing me what he's doing, his hands move to cup each breast.

"God, Lanie. You're perfect. So fucking perfect."

His fingers knead and pull at the flesh, rolling one nipple then the next. I've never known how sexual this could feel. His hands lightly pulling and pinching my erect nipples have me moaning and writhing.

Sweet baby Jesus, he's barely touched me, yet my belly is coiling and tensing like I'm going to explode. I feel a light sheen of sweat appear all over my body.

Leaning down close to my ear, he asks, "You like this, Lanie? Does this feel good?"

"Yes, God, yes," I moan, unable to keep my voice down.

He growls loudly in response and moves to straddle me. I feel how hard he is beneath his shorts. Without thinking, I reach for him, but he swats me away.

"Not yet, sweetheart. You touch me now and I'll never last. Just let me explore you for a while. I want to know every inch of your body, Lanie. Every dip," his hands run over my hip bone to my navel, "every valley," his finger trails up my sternum, "every peak," his hands rest once again on my pebbled nipple.

Dex leans down and kisses the most raised of my scars, the one that crosses from my left rib cage down to my right hip. I shudder beneath him, not from his touch but by fear of what he must be thinking, being so close to those jagged marks.

"Lanie?" he whispers, sliding his tongue along the bottom scar that runs hip to hip just above my pubic bone. "These," he pauses, kissing the third and final abrasion on my abdomen, "are just marks. They're just parts of your skin, parts of you, and trust me, baby, there's nothing I don't find sexy about you. Every single inch of you is delicious, and I'm going to have so much fun tasting and touching and teasing as often as you'll let me."

My breathing is ragged. I've never felt this exposed, or this wanted. The smell of salt air, the sounds of waves hitting the boat, and the feel of Dex when he lowers his mouth to my nipple once more, is more than I can bear. I combust. I see stars. I feel like every muscle in my body is spasming. When I can finally breathe again, I open my eyes to see Dex resting over me with a self-satisfied smirk.

"Holy shit, Lanie, that was the hottest thing I've ever seen in my life."

"I, um, well ... sorry?"

He creases his brow and looks as confused as I feel.

"Lanie, have you never had an orgasm before?"

I might die. Right here, underneath Dexter Cross, I just might die of embarrassment.

"Of course ..." *Wait, is that what just happened?* When I don't continue, he leans in closer to my mouth again.

"Good Lord, Lanie. Who the fuck was your last boyfriend?" His growled words vibrate through my overly stimulated body.

Mortified is the only word that describes me right now, though. Completely and totally humiliated. I try to cover my eyes with my arm before he can see the flush I feel creeping across my entire body.

"Oh no you don't, Lanie Heart. Look at me."

Lowering my arm, I bring my eyes to his, willing myself not to cry.

"Lanie, don't ever be embarrassed about coming from my touch. I'm fucking ecstatic I got you there so quickly. I swear to God, I almost came in my shorts watching you. It was the sexiest thing I've ever experienced. To know I'm the first one to make you orgasm like that? Fuuuck, it does wicked, wicked things to me. Terrible things I can't wait to show you, but we have all the time in the world. So, you tell me, Lanie ... do you want me to continue exploring, or do you want to stop?"

Holy shit, I don't want to stop. *Do I?* Hell no, I don't. *I don't know if I can handle another orgasm like that, but I think I'm willing to try.* I almost laugh at the thought. "No, no, I don't want to stop," I all but scream.

"Thank fuck!" His voice is gritty and strained. "I want to taste you and I want you to watch me."

What did he just say? I pick my head up off the boat to stare at him as he moves down my body, kissing every few inches. He hooks his thumbs into the strings of my panties and pulls them down in one fluid motion. *Holy geez, is he really going to—*

"Ahhh," is all that comes out. "Dex, Dex, I don't think I can ... Ohhh my God."

He looks up at me and smiles before lowering his mouth once more. With one long lick, he has me open for him, his tongue pressing and licking and teasing. I feel a rush of heat flood me, making him groan.

"Fuck, Lanie, you're so wet."

I feel like I should be embarrassed, but I don't have it in me. I can't do anything but feel Dexter's body, his fingers, his tongue making my body sing. He sucks my clit into his mouth and my body arches off the boat. I'm panting, unable to catch my breath.

"Lanie, now that I know your sweet pussy tastes so fucking good, I'm never going to want to eat anything else ever again." He dives back in, flicking my clit faster and faster. Adding pressure in all the right places. Just when I don't think I can take another second of him sucking and flicking my clit with his tongue, I feel a finger enter me. I thought I'd come before, but this time, my body truly explodes. Wave after wave hits me, and I have most definitely never felt anything like this before. My body shakes violently as Dexter continues his ministrations. I feel his finger enter again, this time with a second added, and my body reaches its highest peak. White-hot heat leaves me shuddering for air.

"Dex, holy, holy, Dex, I-I ..." I honestly don't know what I want to say. Stop? Don't stop? My body's throbbing in all the best places, one pulse away from breaking me in two.

"Holy hell, Lanie, you're so tight," he says as his fingers continue to work me.

I'm not a virgin, but I've only ever been with Rob, my boyfriend from high school and partway through college. Nothing with him was ever like this.

"Baby, I'm not small. I'm afraid I'm going to hurt you. Are you sure you want to do this tonight?"

I look down, his fingers still working me, but I stare past him to his dick that is very clearly standing at attention in his shorts. I'm trying very hard to form a coherent thought right now when all I'm thinking is, *Dear God, don't let this stop*.

"I-I don't want to wait, Dex, please."

Slowly, he eases his fingers out of me, bringing his other hand to cradle my face.

"Lanie, we have plenty of time, I promise. We don't have to rush anything. Don't worry about me. This right here," he gestures between himself and me, "is enough to get me through the next several months, I promise you that."

I'm contemplating voicing my concerns when he raises my chin. We're eye to eye.

"Tell me what you're thinking, sweetheart?"

On a sigh, I let all my insecurities out. "Did you, did you change your mind? Did I do something wrong, and you don't want me anymore?"

"Christ, no, Lanie. Baby, you were perfect. Everything about you and about tonight has been absolute perfection. I just don't want to mess that up by possibly hurting you." A smirk plays against his beautiful face. "I'm not bragging, but I was honest when I said I wasn't small. I'm terrified I might hurt you and ruin everything we've done so far. Plus, well, honestly? I didn't think this would happen tonight. I really didn't expect anything. I didn't come prepared. I don't have any condoms."

Peering up into his eyes, I sense his sincerity. I know he sees the relief wash over my features when he speaks gently. "How could you ever think I wouldn't want you, Lanie? I have never wanted anything or anyone as much as I want you. That's never going to change for me either. I hope you know that. If you don't, I need to work harder at proving it to you."

Searching his face, I make my decision. "Dex ... I can't get pregnant. The doctors said the probability of it happening is so low that there wasn't even a point in putting a number. I haven't been with anyone since I was in the hospital, and they ran every test imaginable while I was there. Before that, well, there was just one boyfriend."

"He was a dumb shit," Dex grumbles before he can think better of it.

"I trust you, Dex," I tell him just above a whisper. "I want you."

He stiffens beside me, realizing what I just told him, and I wish I could take it all back. I try to stand up, but his strong arms pull me back into his lap.

"Don't go anywhere, Lanie, I'm just thinking. I always want to do the right thing where you're concerned. Are you sure, one hundred percent sure, this is what you want? That I'm what you want?"

"Yes," I answer without even having to think about it.

Dex nods his head once. "All right, then. But not here. Let me take you to our room. I don't want to hurt you, and I want to take my time," he finishes with a wicked smile I won't soon forget.

Our room, I think, while at the same time, saying, "Okay."

CHAPTER 27

DEX

Sliding my large button-down around Lanie's shoulders, I make sure she's covered while I collect all her belongings. The last thing I need is for one of the crew to find her panties. *Those are mine.*

After shoving her stuff into my back pocket, I lean down and pick her up, cradling her to my chest like I've done so many times at home. I don't tell her I intend to carry her like this one day across the threshold, as my wife, even though I think about it often.

Walking into the main cabin, I take in our opulent surroundings before heading straight for our room. Lanie's in awe of the place, and I'll admit, I am, too. The boat is a beautiful backdrop for our weekend. Or a yacht, as everyone likes to remind me. It's a floating luxury hotel from the crown molding to the solid gold accents and nautical themes everywhere. Every inch of the place screams money. It's the exact opposite of the one I'll buy for us in the future. Ours will be usable, more family-friendly, less pretentious.

When we finally make it to our room, I kick the door shut behind me and lay Lanie down on the king-sized bed.

Climbing in beside her, I lean in for a kiss. Not a kiss intended to lead anywhere, just a kiss to show her I love her.

When I pull away, tension tugs at my gut. I have to be sure this is what she wants. "Are you sure about this, Lanie? I swear to you we don't have to rush into anything. This whole weekend is just about you."

Truthfully, I had to take a minute to calm myself the fuck down. The image of Lanie coming on the deck of this boat will forever be my favorite fantasy. Even now, I'm trying to think of wrinkly balls and poopy diapers so I don't come just from the image ingrained in my brain.

"All about me?" she parrots.

"Yes, of course. I want you to trust me completely, Lanie. When you give your body over to me, I want to make sure it's because it's what you want, not because you think it's what I expect."

She watches me closely. "This weekend is all about me? And what I want?"

"That's what I said." I smile to lighten the mood. I never want her to feel pressured.

"Then what I want, Dex, what I need, right now, is you." The confident sass, although a bit shaky, is coming back. I see it in her eyes.

I exhale a long breath I wasn't aware I was even holding. "You hold all the cards here, Lanie. If you change your mind, I want you to tell me. I'll go back to just holding you all night and be the happiest man on the earth, I swear to you."

She nods in understanding, gripping the sheets below her so tightly her knuckles are white.

"Lay down, baby. You need to relax. You said you trust me, so let me take care of you. Let me show you what you've been missing."

"Yes." It escapes on a breathy exhale.

Slowly unbuttoning the shirt she's wearing, I take it off one shoulder at a time. When she's naked again, I immediately feel all the blood run to my shaft, and I have to take a calming breath. "Tell me what you want, Lanie."

"I want to see you, all of you."

And my dick tries to explode.

"Do you now?" I can't help but smile. "What the lady wants, the lady gets."

I stand, and in one swift move, kick my shorts and boxer briefs to the floor. Standing next to the bed, I drink her in.

Her hand darts out to envelope my cock, and I hiss. "Fuuuck, Lanes."

With soft, delicate strokes, she runs her palm up and down my weeping member while I struggle for control. After a few minutes, I have to step away. She looks nervous, and I realize this beautiful creature is all kinds of insecure. I should have figured that out much sooner than now.

"If you keep that up, we won't get very far."

A blush crosses her face, and her mouth forms a perfect O as understanding hits.

Climbing onto the bed, I hover over her, resting on my forearms so I don't crush her. Gently, I lean down to kiss her while I snake my right arm down her body to cup her pussy. She moans into my mouth, and my control is quickly slipping.

"I have to make sure you're ready for me, Lanes. It'll hurt if you're not ready," I warn her.

"I'm ready," she protests, and I chuckle. "I'm really, really ready."

"Let me be the judge of that, sweetheart." Slowly, I insert one finger, then two. She inhales sharply. "Baby, we are going to have to work at this. Fuck, Lanie, you're so wet, but I still think it's going to hurt."

"It's okay, I want this. I want you, please, Dex."

Lowering my body, I drop my mouth to lick her clit, loving the sounds coming from her beautiful mouth. She tastes sweet, her smell so uniquely her own. If I'm not careful, I'll be drooling all over her. I can't imagine myself ever getting enough of this, enough of her.

Glancing up, I see her belly quivering, and I know she's getting close. Sucking her clit into my mouth on a groan, I capture it between my teeth, flicking it fast and hard. As she lifts off the bed, I insert a third finger, knowing stretching her now will be my best chance of making sex less painful for her.

Fuck, if I'd known how inexperienced she was, I would have brought supplies. Just thinking about how tight she is has me humping the bed like a horny teenager.

I need her to come again. Now. With one last flick of my tongue, I angle my fingers up and stroke her most sensitive spot. She goes off like a rocket. While her body is convulsing, I slide up her body and position my head at her entrance.

My entire body is pulsating with a need for this woman, but I refuse to just push into her so I can get off. When she's able, she opens her eyes, bringing me into focus. Making eye contact, I'm caught in her spell and forget to breathe. Face-to-face, I search for any indication that she isn't ready for this. I see none and exhale sharply.

"Are you ready?" I ask, my voice cutting through the silence. I'm resting on my forearms, cradling her face in my hands.

"I'm ready, please, Dex."

Lowering my eyes to the point where we're almost connected, I shift my hips forward. Placing just the tip of my cock to rest in her channel, I quickly scan her face for approval. The smile I see there breaks through to the rest of my heart. This girl now has the power to break me, and she has no idea.

The head of my cock seems huge at her swollen, wet entrance, and I have a moment of panic. Hurting her would kill me. Staring into her eyes one more time, I tell her, "I'm going to push in, one quick thrust, then let you adjust. Are you ready?"

"Yes, yes, please." Watching us connect, I thrust in as far as she can take me right now. She moans, partly in pain, I know, but the heat in her eyes tells me that's not all she feels.

Struggling to maintain my composure, but coming close to my breaking point, I inhale deeply. "Lanie? Sweetheart, tell me when you're ready for me to move," I grind out through clenched teeth. She feels like nothing I've ever experienced before. A tight, wet glove squeezing my cock like it was made for me. If I've wondered what heaven was like, I know now. This right here, buried so deep inside of the woman I love. This is heaven.

"I'm ready, Dex. I'm ready." She claws at my chest, urging me to move.

I swear I might hear angels sing as I sink in just a little more. "Lanie, holy shit. You. Feel. So. Damn. Good." Each word is punctuated by a thrust and a grunt. The effort of not blowing my load right now is immeasurable.

"Dex, oh God, oh, Dex, I think ... I think—" A throaty moan cuts off her words as her body tightens all around mine.

"Lanie. Holy shit."

Her body continues to pulse around my cock, and I think I blackout. Her pussy is gripping me so tightly I can hardly think. Every inch I slide in deeper, and it's like coming home.

"Goddamn it, Lanie," I choke out. She's out of focus, and I worry for a moment that I might actually lose consciousness.

My spine has never been so stiff, every muscle in my body is screaming for release, but I want to hold on to this feeling for a few moments longer. I plunge into her harder, faster, deeper, and I feel my control break. I'm lost. Lost in Lanie, a montage of her greatest hits flashing through my mind until I focus once again on the face staring at me in bliss.

"I'm coming, Lanie, fuuuck I'm coming." Stream after stream flows out of me. I don't know how long I keep pumping my hips before coming to rest above her.

"My God, Lanie. It-It's never been like that before. I've never come so hard in my life. You're amazing, baby." My breath is so erratic that my chest heaves against hers. Leaning in, I kiss her softly. "Stay here. Let me clean you up."

Rushing into the bathroom, I grab a cloth, running it under warm water. Then I search for a glass of water and some ibuprofen before returning to her.

"Here," I say, handing her the glass of water and pills. "These will help with the pain."

I glue my gaze to her throat as she works to swallow the pills. Then I lay her gently back down. Leaning on the bed, I move forward and spread her legs slightly. With the warm cloth in hand, I clean her up. My seed mixed with her love, and fuck if I'm not hard as a steel beam again. Tossing the rag to the floor, I slide in beside her, pulling her tightly against me.

"Are you okay?" I ask. Worry that I've hurt her is still swirling in my brain.

"Mhmm," she says sleepily.

I roll over and hold her face in my hands, forehead to forehead.

"You're so amazing, Lanie. I don't think I can ever get enough of you now. So, tell me ... are you gonna let me go?" I cheekily add some levity to a night I know I'll never forget, but as soon as it leaves my mouth, I know it was a mistake. "Lanie, I just meant—"

She cuts me off by putting her delicate finger to my lips. "Shh, Dex. This has been the most amazing night of my life, don't ask me to make promises I don't know if I can keep."

My euphoric state takes a hit, but only briefly. I knew

going into this it would be a long road. My Lanes is going to need more than one incredible night of lovemaking. And make no mistake, what we did was make love. MLM just took one giant step forward.

I fall asleep with a smile on my face and that thought running through my mind while holding the most incredible woman I've ever met.

~

MLM Tactical Group

Julia: alert*alert*alert* Dexter got laid this weekend!

Dexter: Jesus, Julia! I don't kiss and tell, wtf? (angry face emoji)

Trevor: No, you just give us every. Single. Detail. About everything else.

Preston: Way to go, asshole. Was it everything you hoped it would be? Fuck, man, I'm with Trevor on this. We have to listen to DAILY updates, sometimes multiple times a day, and you were going to leave out the good stuff? Not cool, man. Not cool.

Dexter: You're a real piece of work, Julia, you know that?

Julia: *Takes a bow*

CHAPTER 28

LANIE

Our weekend on the *boat* was the start of me sleeping in Dexter's arms more times than not. I know I shouldn't do it. I remind him every chance I get that I have to leave when our contract is over. I can't admit that it's getting harder and harder for me to remember that myself. I've never slept so peacefully as I do in his arms. I've never woken with such hope and happiness.

Tate has become a different child right before my eyes, too. He's now, I believe, the kid he was always meant to be. I still don't know what Anna did to him, but I'm done asking questions I'll never get answers to. My job is to help him move on, let him feel love, and I do that every day.

"Tate," I yell up the stairs, "we have to get going, or we'll be late."

"I'm coming, Lanie. I want to make sure I look good," he says, flying down the stairs.

"Whoa, whoa ... hey, kiddo, the last thing we need is for you to break a leg before your big night." I smile.

"Lanie," he draws out, rolling his eyes in the process. "It's not just my night, it's the end-of-year school party, that means it's for everyone. Everyone graduates to the next grade today. There's going to be popcorn and pizza and cotton candy, Lanie. Cotton candy!"

"I know, I know! It's so exciting. But what were you working on up there?" I ask holding in a laugh, as I eye his hair suspiciously.

"I wanted my hair to look cool like Dad's," he admits shyly, and I notice he's added gel in all the wrong places.

I try not to laugh. "Can I help you? I think we just need to comb out a few places and you'll be all set," I tell him, attempting to tame the piece standing straight up at the back of his head. "All set, buddy. Daddy will be here in five minutes. Let's pack the girls up in the car so we can leave the second he gets here."

"I'm super happy you're coming, Lanes. I made something special and I can't wait to show you."

This kid. He beams rays of sunshine straight through my heart.

I crouch down to eye level. "I can't wait to see it, Tate. Do you know how proud I am of you? You've come so far these last few months. I hope you're proud of yourself, too. You've done all the work. Your dad and I just supported you. This is your night, Tate. We're all going to celebrate you, little man."

He smiles, loving being called a little man.

Shortly after we load up the girls and all the supplies they require for two hours outside of the house, Dexter pulls into the driveway. We try really hard not to show affection in front of the kids, but the longer this thing between us goes on, the harder it becomes. When my phone dings with a text, I pull my phone out of the diaper bag.

Dexter: Day 86, Tate's school show, then fire pit under the stars.

Lanie: Are you seriously still sending these text messages to our friends?

Dexter: Fuck!

Lanie: (Laughing tears emoji)

Walking into Waverley-Cay Elementary feels so different today than it did a few months ago. I no longer feel the need to keep my wits about me, peering around every corner for Tate's bully. Even though Jake is still in the school, they've made every effort to keep them on opposite sides of the building. According to Tate, he's only seen him once, and Jake never looked in his direction. *Hopefully, the little shit learned his lesson.*

We gather in the gymnasium, where the principal will give a short speech. When he's done, we'll be free to explore the school and Tate can show off his work before ending in the courtyard for food and games.

"All right, Tate. You ready to show us this big project you've been working on?" Dex asks.

"Oh yes. It's outside of my classroom. Come on."

We're walking through the halls when we hear the telltale sound that can only mean one thing.

"Gross, Dad. Did she really just poop like that in my school?" By the expression on Dexter's face, I would say yes. Harper's known for her repulsive diarrhea. I have an iron stomach, and the girl has even made me gag a few times.

"Good grief," Dex says, rolling his eyes. "Give me the diaper bag. I'll change her and meet you guys in Tate's classroom."

Laughing, I hand it over. "Okay, Tate. Just you, me, and Sara, for now. Lead the way." I take his little hand, and he guides us down the hall, pointing out various artwork displayed on the walls.

Tate stops and fidgets nervously.

"What's up, bud? Is this what you want to show us?" I glance around, then notice the artwork in front of us is family portraits made by Tate's classmates. "These are amazing, little man. Where's yours?"

He walks me down the hall a few steps and nods. Peering in the direction he's pointing with his head, I gasp. My eyes are misty, but I don't get a chance to respond because we're interrupted.

"Well, who do we have here? The little mute is talking now, I see?" The voice is low and menacing.

Turning slowly, I place Tate behind me and wrap a protective arm around Sara, strapped to my front. At first, I see Jake and my open hand balls into a fist. When I lift my gaze, I realize it was his father who spoke. There's no one else in the hallway. *How can that be?*

"I suggest you move along and check out your son's artwork. There is nothing here for you to see," I say, hating that my confidence sounds shaky, even to my own ears.

The man takes a step toward me. "I have to disagree, Ms. Heart. Because of you, my son has a blemish on his record. That's going to reflect very poorly on my upcoming campaign," he seethes.

"I have nothing to do with that, *Senator.*" The word comes out like a curse. "Had your son not been bullying Tate, none of this would've happened."

"Poor Tate." His condescending tone grates on my already frayed nerves. "His mother left him, and what's this? Is that you in his portrait?" He tries to get a glimpse of what's behind me, directing his next words to Tate. "Do you think your little nanny is going to love you when your own mother left you?" the man spits.

"Yeah, dummy, she isn't your mom," Jake chimes in.

"That is enough. Walk away, right now." There's venom in my voice and it's louder this time.

The senator gets right in my face. "You do not call the shots around here, Ms. Heart. Understand this; it would be a real shame if Zachary were free now, wouldn't it?"

Ice floods my veins.

"Do you know who has the power to make that happen?

Me, that's who. Before you make demands, you'd better have a handle on who has the real authority around here."

I feel all the color drain from my face. He knows he landed a dagger right to my chest. Then I feel a shaking little hand grab hold of my shirt. *Tate. I need to focus on Tate.* Turning my back to the asshole, I lower myself to the ground.

"Tate? Did you draw me in your family picture?" I ask him, desperate to gain control of my emotions and his.

He stares from me to the retreating forms at my back.

"Look at me, Tate. Just at me. Did you draw me into your family?" I try again now that Jake and his dad are out of sight.

He nods his head and rushes me. As I'm holding him to my side, he cries.

"Lanie? Tate?" I hear Dexter's voice, but I can't move. Tate and I are both in shock. I can't speak. "What the hell happened here?"

I stare up at him, but no words come. It's Tate who finds his voice first. The irony is not lost on me.

"I drew Lanie in our family. Jake and his dad said ... they said she isn't my mom," Tate chokes out. "Daddy, who's Zachary? Why did Jake's dad say he could get free?"

"What?" Dexter yells, breaking me out of my trance.

"Please, Dex. Don't. Not here. Tate, is there anything else you want to see? Do you want to go out to the courtyard for cotton candy?"

"No. Can we just go, Lanie?"

My heart breaks for this little boy who had been so excited about something so simple. *How can adults be so cruel?*

"Yeah, we can go, buddy. Do you want to grab some dinner somewhere? Anything you want, just name it."

"Lanie, can I talk to you for a minute?" Dexter's voice is low and full of rage.

"No, Dex. Please. This is Tate's night. Let's just make the

best of it and do something special for him, okay? We can work out all th-the *details* later."

Sighing, Dex nods. "Come on, Tate. What do you feel like for dinner? We can go anywhere you want."

"China Moon," Tate says cheerily.

Ah, to have the attention span of a six year old. If only it were that easy for me.

~

China Moon is exactly what it sounds like—a little hole in the wall restaurant that has the best Chinese food in all of Waverley-Cay. The car ride here was silent, except for the happy babbles of the girls. Once we're inside, Tate's attention is drawn to the koi pond they have running through the entire restaurant. Jumping up and down, Tate begs for quarters to feed the fish. After the night we've had, I'll give him a hundred quarters if it makes him happy.

"What do you want tonight, Tate?" Dex asks, still watching us closely and unhappy with this detour.

"Sesame chicken and pancakes." Tate grins, dripping wonton soup down the front of him.

"I'm with Tate, some fried rice and egg rolls, too, please." I'm trying so hard to turn this night around. I want it for Tate. I need it for all of us. Focusing on Tate and his feelings is the only thing holding me together right now. I'd be willing to bet by the expression on Dexter's face that he knows it, too.

Cheerful. Be cheerful, be happy, for Tate, I repeat in my head.

CHAPTER 29

DEX

The ride home from China Moon is silent. My eyes dart every few seconds from the road to Lanie sitting beside me, then to the backseat where Tate is. It's killing me that I don't fully understand what happened at his school tonight. I'm more than a little pissed that Lanie made the decision to let it go without even filling me in. I know she did it to salvage the night for Tate, but I understand her now, and whatever happened in that hallway has her scared.

Please don't let this be what has her running.

I pull into the garage, shutting the door behind us, and grab Harper while Lanie gets Sara from their car seats. Tate isn't as talkative as when we first arrived at the school, but he's bouncing back much better than I expected him to. A hell of a lot better than Lanie seems to be doing.

"Tate, why don't you go get washed up for bed? I'm going to put the girls down, then I'll come to tuck you in. Say goodnight to Lanie. We'll let her get ready for bed now, too." I don't actually know if this is what she will want, but since she's hardly talking, I figure it's what she needs.

"Okay, Dad." He runs into Lanie's arms for a hug. "Goodnight, Lanie. Love you."

"I love you, so much, little man. Goodnight." Lanie's voice is barely audible as she follows Tate up the stairs.

～

*P*utting the girls to bed is a hell of a lot easier these days, thanks to Lanie. She has them on a schedule that works so perfectly that now, I just lay them in their cribs and they fall asleep within minutes.

I'm walking down the hall toward Tate's room when I hear Lanie speaking. She must be in Tate's room, so I come to a stop just outside. I don't intend to eavesdrop very long, just enough that I can be sure they're both okay. Then I'll come back to say my goodnights.

"Can I sit with you for a minute?" I hear Lanie ask.

The squeak of Tate's bedframe tells me he's said yes.

"Do you remember how I went back to see your teacher before we left tonight?"

Again, he must respond because she continues, "Well, I went back to ask her if I could take this with me."

"You don't like it, Lanie?" Tate's voice wobbles. "You don't have to be my mom. I just want you to be my family." I can hear the tears in Tate's words.

"Oh, no, Tate! You don't understand. I asked if I could take it because I want to hang it in my room if that's okay with you. You see, I never really had a family like this. I love seeing how you drew me. I look so happy standing here holding your hand. I want you to know that I don't have to be your mom to love you. You have such a big piece of my heart that no matter where we are, you'll always be a part of my family."

"You mean it, Lanie?" Happiness radiates from his little voice.

"I do," she says. "Have I ever told you about my mom?"

"You have a mom?" Tate asks, and I almost laugh, giving away my location.

"I do have a mom, but she wasn't like any of the moms I knew. My mom had some problems, and she was mean to me. A lot." Her words are soft, like she's filtering her sadness.

"Wh-What do you m-mean?" Tate stammers.

"It took me a lot of years and a lot of help from Mimi. Remember Mimi? Julia's mom?"

"Yeah, she said she's going to bake me lots of cookies." He giggles.

Lanie laughs. "You bet she will. She makes the best cookies ever. Anyway, Mimi helped me understand I didn't have a healthy relationship with my mom. My mom was … well, she was mad all the time. She thought everything bad that happened to her was my fault, but I was just a kid. She was the adult. She should have protected me, not blame me."

"What did your mom say to you?" Tate asks just above a whisper.

"Let's see." Lanie pauses. "One time, she told me I ruined her life because she had to buy me underwear."

"How can you ruin someone's life by needing underwear?" Tate laughs.

"My mom told me because she had to buy me underwear, she didn't have enough money to go out with her friends. Not going out with her friends ruined her life. That day anyway. A lot of times, she would say that being born destroyed her life. She liked to tell me all the time that I ruined everything. That's really hard for a kid to hear or understand. I felt terrible about myself for a really long time."

"That sounds like it would be hard." The sadness in Tate's voice causes a lump in my throat.

"It was, Tate. Especially since none of it was true. What she didn't know is that I was a gift. A gift not everyone gets to have. She wasn't a very good mother."

"Did she die?" Tate asks, sounding unsure if he should feel sad or not.

"No, she's still alive, but I had to decide not to let her lousy behavior influence my life or the way I felt about myself anymore. Her nasty words were her issue, not mine. It's taken me years to learn that. She walked away from me as soon as she could, and I ended up with Mimi and Pawpaw. As an adult, I decided I was better off without her in my life.

"I guess what I'm trying to tell you is, sometimes, the best families aren't the ones who share the same blood. Sometimes the best families are the ones who choose to stand by you. The ones who choose to love and care for you. The ones who choose you, always. I want you to know, Tate, even though I'm not your mom, I will always choose you. Even if I'm not living here someday, it will always be my choice to love you. Do you understand that?" Lanie asks gently.

I know Tate is crying even before he speaks. His sniffles have been filling the air for the last five minutes. "I do, Lanie. I love you, too."

"You don't have to tell me anything until you are ready, Tate. I just wanted you to know if something happened between you and your mom, I promise you it wasn't your fault."

"Okay, Lanie. Can I tell you a secret?" Tate whispers.

"Of course, bud. You can always tell me anything," she says, sounding unsure of what he will say next.

"You're going to be a great mom someday," Tate says genuinely.

The sob that escapes Lanie is one I know she couldn't control. I know she won't be able to hold it together much longer. Not after Tate's secret. So I quickly but quietly make my way down to my office. I need backup.

Pulling my phone from my pocket, I send a text.

MLM Tactical Group
Dexter: I need help.

Before I even hit send, Trevor comes walking into my house. "Just relax, Dex. It's going to be fine."

He must see the confusion on my face because he grimaces.

"Shit. Julia told me. She doesn't think the senator spooked Lanie. Having something to focus on has been good for her. You and Tate are good for her. She just wanted me to let you know to give her some space for a couple of hours, but not all night. Lanie will need you tonight," he says in a whoosh.

"How often are you and Julia talking?" I ask curiously.

"We aren't really talking, just texting," Trevor says, shifting his weight from foot to foot.

"How often?" I repeat.

"A few times a day, probably. She's a really cool girl." Now his cheeks turn a shade darker, and I smile.

"You two are very similar. I picked up on that the first time I met her. Are you talking or FaceTiming?" I'm intrigued by his behavior, and it's nice to have him in the hot seat for once.

"No. Come on, man," he says defensively. "I just said she's a cool girl. She's fun to talk to because she isn't like all the others, but you know my situation. I can't be involved with anyone without putting them in harm's way. She also doesn't want to do anything other than text. She has her own reasons, I guess. We're just friends."

Holding up my hands in surrender, I tell him, "All right, but I think you need to figure this stuff out with your dad soon. You can't live in your bubble forever."

"I know. Listen, you all set here now?" He's already inching toward the door.

"Yeah, thanks for stopping by. I'm going to go tuck Tate in, then check on Lanie."

After giving me a hug, Trevor walks out the door, and I turn for the stairs.

While tucking Tate in, he told me all about the senator and Jake. I'm so pissed off but unsure of what to do next. The fucking senator knew too much about Lanie and about Anna. I need to find the connection. After setting a reminder on my phone to call Ryan in the morning, I knock on Lanie's door.

"Come in," she says, sounding exhausted.

Looking around, I walk into her room, still ashamed I haven't done anything to personalize this space for her. *It's because you keep hoping she'll move into your room permanently, asshole*, my damn conscience whispers in my ear.

"Hi, sweetheart. You look tired."

"I am. It's been a long day." She shifts on her bed, keeping her gaze on her hands.

"I heard," I inform her. "Tate told me everything. I wanted you to know that I heard some of your conversation with him earlier. Thank you for being there for him like that. You might be the only one who understands him right now." I sit next to her on the bed.

"Maybe." She shrugs. "Did I hear someone downstairs?"

"Yeah." I chuckle. "Trevor stopped by. Apparently, he and Julia have been texting. A lot. She told him what happened tonight and sent him over here to check on us."

Now Lanie's laughing with me. "What? How long have they been talking?" she asks, sounding surprised.

"Not talking. He was pretty adamant about that. It sounds like they set ground rules. They're strictly friends, which, in their world, means no phone calls, no video calls, just texts."

"Julia does like to set parameters for everything in her life."

"Trevor too. They're so similar I often wonder if they'd be the best match in the world or if they'd kill each other before their first date even started." Glancing over, I find Lanie's eyes drifting closed. Leaning over, I whisper, "Sweetheart? Come to bed with me? Let me hold you tonight."

"Mhmm," she murmurs.

Reaching around her back, I pick her up off the bed and carry her to my room. *I really fucking like holding her like this.* I'm expecting a nightmare tonight, and I want her close by when it hits.

Waking up with Lanie in my arms the next morning, I'm shocked to find she slept through the night. She stayed, and she didn't have a nightmare. I wonder if she also realizes this when her eyes flutter open suddenly, looking surprised.

"You didn't have a nightmare last night," I say, stating the obvious.

"I didn't have a nightmare last night," she repeats, "Julia must be right about body heat keeping the monsters away after all."

"Baby, if my body heat keeps your monsters at bay, I'd like to offer it up every night."

Smiling, she reaches up to kiss me, then jumps out of bed to start her day.

MLM Tactical Group

Dexter: Day 98, Lanie has a cold so tonight I'm bringing her homemade chicken soup (hand-made by the restaurant around the corner)

Julia: (hand clapping emoji)

Trevor: (kitten emoji)

Preston: (middle finger emoji)

Dexter: Fuck off, all of you.

LM Tactical Group

Dexter: Day 121, Ryan found Anna. He scheduled the meeting at my office on August 27th, at one p.m.

Trevor: Wtf, finally. Why is the meeting so far out? I'll be over later today to install the cameras Loki left.

Preston: What Trev said, and no bleeding heart bs. Nice change, bro.

Dexter: She told Ryan she's out of the country for a couple of weeks. He verified, she's in Mexico (rolling eyes emoji)

Julia: I'd love to kick that twat right in the teeth. Make sure she stays away from Lanes.

Dexter: That's the plan.

∼

LM Tactical Group

Dexter: Day 136, pool party.

Trevor: Wtf, dude? We're literally sitting right next to you.

Preston: In our swim trunks, about to tell Lanie about the meeting with Anna. Stop texting!

Julia: That bitch, she's so fucking dumb.

Preston: How does Jules know already if Lanie doesn't?

Dexter: Trevor, want to answer that?

Trevor: Fuck off.

Julia: Fuck off.

Preston: I see, match made in text messages (laughing emoji)

Julia: (middle finger emoji)

Trevor: Grow up.

Preston: Julia and Trevor sitting in a tree, k-i-s-s-i-n-g.

Trevor: Proof. That asshole just spent a full minute typing out that message (eye roll emoji)

"What are you all doing on your phones?" Lanie asks, looking annoyed. "Tell me what happened while Tate is upstairs getting his swimsuit on. She just wanted more money?"

"Yes, that bitch," Trevor answers before I can. "It seems like her rich boyfriend left her high and dry. He didn't think a mother abandoning her children would be suitable for his image. She even threatened to get custody back, claim it was postpartum depression that had her signing her parental rights away. It's like she completely forgot who she's dealing with," he says, looking at me, so I cut in.

"We talked in circles until I finally agreed to give her a check if she told me why she was really doing this." I don't bother hiding the disgust in my voice. "She let it spill like a waterfall. She told me how she never wanted kids in the first place. That she didn't want them now but would go after them if it meant she could get her hands on my money."

"She even said she would work the judge, get him to see things her way, then not only get the kids but make sure Dex has to pay for the nanny so she doesn't have to waste her precious time on them," Preston chimes in.

"No judge in the world will give her any face time with my kids once they see the video," I tell Lanie.

"So, she knows you videotaped her?" Lanie asks.

"That's the best part," Trevor tells her, laughing. "Dexter made a big show of telling her not to steal anything from his office because the cameras will catch her. She either didn't believe him or got so caught up in her plan that she forgot. Regardless, he told her as soon as she walked in, meaning she has no legs to stand on, and she knows it."

"I can't imagine that went very well?" Lanie says with an uneasy smile.

"Not at all," I tell her, wrapping her in a hug. "Luckily,

Trevor came out just in time to escort her out of the building. She won't be coming back, I'm sure of it. She wouldn't dare let her reputation suffer more than it already has."

We hear Tate making his way down the stairs, so we quickly change topics.

"Lanie, let's go! The neighborhood pool party is starting soon. I don't want to be late," Tate squeals.

"Hey, what about me?"

"Aw, man, you still have to get the girls ready. I wanted to get to the clubhouse so we can pick the seats next to the splashing mushrooms," he explains.

I can't help but laugh at his enthusiasm. Our neighborhood has a pool with a clubhouse—most communities in the south do—but ours is pretty spectacular, even I have to admit. They have gone all out for the Labor Day end of season party, and Tate has been talking about it non-stop for weeks.

"Okay, big guy. Why don't you and Lanie drive over? Trevor, Preston, and I will pack up the girls and walk them over in the wagon." I love the smile he flashes at the news.

Turning to Lanie, I add, "That way, we'll have a car there in case we have to get the girls home early."

"Sounds good to me. Ready for some fun in the sun, little man?" Lanie says as she chases Tate down the hall.

"Yes," he screeches, running for the door.

Laughing, Lanie shouts over her shoulder, "See you over there."

～

A full forty-five minutes later, we finally have the girls packed up, sunscreen and hats on, loaded into the little red wagon Preston insists on pulling.

"Thank fu– udge Lanie brought the cooler in the car,"

Trevor says, putting his beer in a koozie. "That would have been a nightmare to carry."

"No shit." Preston laughs.

"Dude, language," I tell him. "The girls are starting to form words. Lanie will have my head if their first real word is a curse."

"Things seem pretty good between you and Lanie, huh?" Trevor asks, gazing past me.

Looking out at all the houses we're passing, with perfectly landscaped yards and smiling, happy families, I tell him the truth. "I think it is. I'm not going to lie, I keep waiting for her to run. I'm terrified actually that she'll run."

"You've still got plenty of time with her," Preston points out.

"I know. I'm all in with her, though. She could break me more than Anna ever did."

The clubhouse comes into view as we round the next corner. It's not as busy as I expected, but even taking as long as we did, we're still early. The party doesn't officially start until four.

Trevor slaps me on the back. "Whatever happens, we're here for you. For what it's worth, Julia says she hasn't ever seen Lanie this happy."

Pride fills my chest, but then something catches my eye. I'm not sure what I'm seeing at first. Then I hear Tate crying out for me to hurry.

"Dad, Dad, help ... Lanie," is all he gets out. His tear-stained face is pressing up against the fence surrounding the pool.

Dropping all the shit I was carrying, I take off at a dead sprint with Trevor on my heels. That's when I see Lanie. A man is holding her upper arms so tightly that even from this distance, I know he'll leave bruises. I can't hear what he's saying, but I can see the spittle flying from his mouth.

Trevor veers to the left, running around the length of the

fence to the gate. I don't have the luxury of that time wasted. Running as fast as I can, I propel myself at the wall, scaling it easier than I thought I'd be able to. Adrenaline at its finest. Hauling my legs up and over, I jump to the ground on the other side.

We're behind the clubhouse, near the entrances to the bathrooms, and I feel like, for the first time in my life, I might be capable of murder. I yell at the man, telling him to let Lanie go as I run toward her. That's when I see him yank her left arm with such force, I swear I hear the pop.

Lanie crumples to the ground.

CHAPTER 30

LANIE

*L*ifting my head from the pavement, I know I didn't lose consciousness, but a pain this intense is bound to knock even the toughest men off their ass. I'm no exception. Without even attempting to move it, I know the *senator* dislocated my shoulder, possibly my elbow, too.

Clearing the fog from my brain, I realize Dexter's hunched over a body, throwing blow after blow with his fists. I try to yell out, tell him to stop, but my words don't penetrate his anger. *I don't want Tate seeing him like this.* Thankfully, Trevor gets to him a second later, pulling him off the bleeding man.

I'm still trying to locate Tate. I had him in my sights the entire time until the asshole yanked me forward. Looking around wildly, I find him standing with Preston. *Thank God.*

"Dexter," Trevor yells. "Enough. Lanie and Tate need you."

Dexter's head whips around like he's just realized where he is. He stares at me, and I nod my head toward Tate, silently telling Dex to check on Tate first, and watch as he hurries toward him.

"Come here, baby doll," I hear Preston say. "I'm just going to lift you onto a lounge chair until the ambulance arrives."

I can't speak. I simply nod my head in agreement. Tate and Dex have moved closer to me, so I can hear them talking now.

"Daddy, please. Please don't let Lanie leave me, too. I promise. I promise I'll be better. I won't bother her as much. I'll pick up all my toys. The girls' toys, too. I'll be quieter. I won't give her headaches. Tell her. Please tell her I'll do anything. Don't let her leave because I'm so bad. I'll be better. I won't cause her this trouble anymore, please, Daddy, please."

Tate's sobs wreck me.

"Hey, Tate …" I hear Dex clear his throat, trying to compose himself. "Why would you think any of this is your fault? We all know what a good boy you are. It has absolutely nothing to do with if you pick up your toys or if you're too loud. Why would you even say that?"

Tate's sobs hurt worse than any pain I've ever felt. "Mommy told me she was leaving because I was bad. I was too loud and gave her headaches. She said I hurt her head because I asked too many questions," he wails.

Dexter seems lost. I see him looking at Tate and Trevor, then me. The anger that has lived inside of me since the first time my mother told me I was worthless explodes.

"That fucking bitch." I'm not quiet. I know I just swore out loud, in front of children, no less, but they're the only words that adequately describe what I'm feeling.

Stunned, Dex jumps back, staring at me.

I try to shoo him away, but my arm hangs uselessly at my side. "Tate, come here, buddy," I tell him, calming my voice. With my one healthy arm, I clutch at him, trying to hold him tight.

"Tate, your mother is broken. You have to believe me

when I say you could never do anything that would make me leave. My love doesn't come and go when it suits me. My love for you is real, it's honest, and no one can ever break it. You, Tate, can never do anything that will make this love leave my heart. There is a Tate-sized space in here," I say, pointing to my chest, "that is always, and will always be just for you."

"Please don't leave me, Lanie. Please don't."

Knowing I can't promise I'll never leave, I swallow thickly, holding him by my side for as long as I can.

In the background, I can hear the men yelling at each other. Glancing up, I see the *senator* is standing, issuing threats left and right. Tate must be listening, too, because he moves quickly to his father's side. With only one arm, I wasn't quick enough to catch him.

"Daddy," Tate begins.

"Buddy, you have to sit with Lanie for a minute," Dex replies.

"No, Dad! Here." He raises his little hand, and I see my phone. "Before he got Lanie, she was letting me use her phone to take pictures. When he started yelling at her, I changed to video." The smile that takes over Tate's face is priceless. He knows he just did something big.

We all stare at Tate for a moment before the *senator* lunges at him. Thankfully, Dex is faster.

"You ever lay a hand on Lanie or my child again, and I will kill you. I don't care what title you've held previously. I can't imagine this video will get you reelected anyway," Dex fumes.

If looks could kill, we would all be dead right now.

Thankfully, Trevor steps in just as we hear sirens in the background. "Senator, you had better get out of here unless you want all these people who are gathering around to speak up as witnesses."

The man with eyes that are already bruising, no doubt

from Dexter's balled up fists, straightens immediately. Noticing the audience, he snaps at his son to move along. They're gone before the EMTs reach me.

"Tate," Dex starts, "are you all right to go home with Trevor and Preston? I'm going to go to the hospital with Lanie, but if you need me, I'll ask Trevor to go with her."

"No, Dad. I'll go with Uncle Trevor. Please bring Lanie home." I know he wants Dexter to go to the hospital with me, but he also wants his dad there to make sure I come home to him.

"Tate, I love you, little man," I tell him with as much energy as I can muster. The events of the last fifteen minutes are finally catching up to me.

"I love you, too, Lanie. See you at home. Right? I'll see you at home?" he begs.

"I'll see you at home, buddy," I say. What other choice do I have?

~

Dex

LM Tactical Group
Dexter: The doctors just took Lanie back to reset her shoulder, elbow, and thumb.

Preston: Fuck, man. Is she okay?

Dexter: She will be. They just gave her a heavy dose of pain meds. She won't have use of her arm for a few weeks, though. That's if she doesn't need surgery.

Trevor: Freaking hell.

Julia: Should I come down there?

Dexter: I won't tell you not to, but I will tell you I'm afraid this will be the final straw for her. I think she's going to want to go home.

Julia: Her strength will surprise you. So will where she considers home these days. Call me when you have more news. For now, I'll stay by the phone and give the two of you some time.

Trevor: Kids are all in bed. Tate's having a hard time sleeping, so I let him lay in Lanie's bed. It made him feel better to be closer to her.

Dexter: Him and me both.

Preston: On the bright side, the little man over here recorded the entire fiasco with the douche-canoe. He's our little hero. I can all but guarantee you won't have any more trouble from him or his son ever again.

Julia: Tate might be my new hero.

Preston: Sorry, Trevor. Looks like Jules has a new "buddy."

Julia: Watch your balls when I come down there, asshat.

Trevor: (Middle finger emoji)

~

Lanie

*O*pening my eyes, I immediately sense something's off. My head is fuzzy and feels heavy. I try to look around, but everything is blurry. I don't even attempt to raise my head as I take inventory of my body.

Instead of flashbacks from my attack, I hear Dex. I see Tate's worried face. I hear Tate crying, and everything becomes clear. Even after everything that just happened, I'm not focused on Zachary, the attack, or even the *senator*. All I'm focused on is this family. This family that's trying so hard to claim me as their own.

I can hear Dex and Trevor talking.

"Can you believe Anna?" Trevor asks. "I can't believe she

left you for the senator. The same senator whose son was bullying Tate."

"I know," Dexter says, sounding sad. "She knew it was going on. She just didn't care."

Preston chimes in, "At least now it makes sense why she was hitting you up for money, though. He was afraid she would ruin his already tarnished image, and he left her with nothing. Could you imagine if the press found out he was with a woman who left her children and that his son was bullying the son she left behind? It's a PR nightmare right out of the tabloids."

I know I'm missing a lot, and I want to catch up. I try desperately to open my eyes.

"Hey, Dex? I think she is waking up," I hear Trevor say.

"Lanie? Sweetheart? Can you open your eyes?"

Slowly, and with great effort, I open them. I'm surrounded by all these big, handsome men in Dexter's room with the dark gray walls and light aqua curtains that I can see swaying from a breeze.

"Preston, can you get her some water, please?" Dex asks.

"You got it." Preston jumps to get the water. If I wasn't so confused, I would probably laugh. Preston isn't someone who jumps to do anything.

"I'm okay," I choke out, my throat unnaturally dry. "Where's Tate?" I ask, searching the room for him.

"Shh, Sylvie just came and picked up all three kids. She's going to keep them for the week so you can rest," Dex informs me. He looks tired, all the guys do.

Staring down at myself, I see my arm in a sling and a big bandage covering my thumb. "Geez, I look like the Terminator or something. What is all this?" I search Dexter's eyes for answers.

"Hey, guys? Could I have a few minutes alone with Lanie, please?"

"Sure. Lanie, do want something to eat? Some soup, maybe?" Trevor asks.

"Just water is great, thank you." Thankfully, my voice is a little stronger after some water.

Trevor nods his head and leans in to kiss me on the cheek.

Preston does the same, then they both walk out the door.

"What's going on, Dex? Is something wrong with me?" It isn't until that moment I notice the tears in Dexter's eyes.

"No, baby. Nothing's wrong with you ... nothing long term, anyway. He dislocated your shoulder and your elbow, and your thumb was broken. The doctors were able to put you back together again, but it'll hurt for a while."

"Then why do you look like your dog died? Is it Tate? Is he okay?" Panic rises in my voice.

"Tate's wonderful, sweetheart. After he saw you arrive home safe and sound, he was excited to go to Sylvie's for a few days. He's worried you would try to do too much if they were home."

I smile and feel it in my heart. Even little Tate is worried about me.

"Then why are you so upset?" It has to be something big. I see nothing but pain in his eyes.

One tear, then two, falls down his chiseled face. "I'm so sorry, Lanie. I keep failing you. I want to be the one you can count on, the one you can lean on, and I keep failing you. You keep getting hurt because of me."

"Dex, you can't be serious? Nothing that's happened to me has been your fault," I tell him, shocked by the emotion I see on his face.

"I should have been there yesterday. I should have been with you so he couldn't ambush you like that." His words are angry. He's angry with himself.

"There's no way you could have known he'd be there. It

was a coincidence that he took advantage of. If he was out to get me, he would have found me at a grocery store or the school parking lot. For whatever reason, he was at the pool, saw me, and took advantage of an opportunity," I try to reason.

"An opportunity that I allowed." Dex's voice rises in volume and emotion. "Had I just been with you, you wouldn't be in pain now."

"Dex, you have to stop thinking this way. I don't blame you for this, and you can't either. You won't be helping any of us if you do," I say truthfully.

Staring at me with a vulnerability that reminds me of Tate, he moves to lay his head in my lap. When he's settled, his voice trembles and he doesn't look at me. "Are you going to leave?"

I feel like a thousand-pound weight just hit my chest. "No, Dex. I'm not going to leave. I can't promise what will happen when our contract is up, but this will not make me run," I say, shocking myself with that truth.

He exhales an audible breath. I run the fingers of my able hand through his hair. *When have I ever given and received comfort like this? When have I ever felt safe and content in the presence of a man like this?*

Never, Lanie. You've never had this before.

Turning to face me, he grins. "Lanie, you swore. Out loud. A bad one, too."

"I guess I did."

Is that one more demon this man is helping me slay?

"No one messes with my Tate—mother or not," I tell him, wondering if it might be possible to break free from my past after all.

"I love you, Lanie. We're lucky to have you."

I'm not able to speak, so I don't, and we both eventually fall asleep.

"*L*anie? What do you think you're doing?" Dex asks, alarmed.

"I need to take a bath, Dex. I feel gross," I tell him, making my way to the bathroom.

Coming up behind me, he grabs my breast. "You feel anything but gross, sweetheart," he says in that low, sexy voice of his.

Argh, this damn man. I've never felt horny before, but since experiencing Dexter Cross, sex with him is the only thing I seem to think about.

"Seriously, Dex. I need to get cleaned up." Without missing a beat, he removes his shirt and pants, standing beside me in navy blue boxer briefs.

Holy shit, he's so hot.

"Then I'll help you," he says with a grin.

Giving him a skeptical look, I watch as he holds up his arms in mock defense.

"Lanie, you're going to need help. You're telling me you can wash all that hair with one hand?"

I groan because I know he's right.

Wearing a wicked grin, he comes at me with a husky voice. "All right, sweetheart, let's get you naked." He watches me because he knows I'll shiver at his words, and like a Pavlovian dog, I do. Turning away from me, he draws the bath.

I've been wearing Dexter's button-up shirts because they're the easiest thing to get on and off. Once he's undone the buttons, he gently slides it down my arms, one at a time. "Come on. I'll help you step in so you don't lose your balance." He offers me his hand, and I take it without hesitation.

Usually, I would hate feeling like an invalid, but for some

reason, here, with Dex, it makes me feel cherished. Once I'm in, Dex guides me to the bench in the tub big enough for six people.

"Why do you have a bathtub this big, anyway?" I ask.

Shrugging, he tells me, "It came with the house. This is the first time I've used it."

As he steps out of his boxer briefs and into the water, I eye him curiously. I'm not entirely sure how he plans for this to go. I should have known he'd have a plan, though. Sloshing through the water on his knees, he reaches over the side to grab a loofah and some shower gel. It smells like lilacs.

"Have you always had lilac-scented shower gel?" I ask him playfully.

"No, Lanie. I have not. I purchased this just for you," he says seriously.

My playfulness vanishes as I look him up and down in the water.

"Lanie, don't stare at me like that. What did you expect? We're in a bathtub together. Naked. You can't seriously think I'll be able to control him with you sitting there looking at him like a piece of meat."

I'm not sure what to say, so I just watch as he moves in the water, his cock thick and long, bobbing around the tub as angry as I've ever seen it. Dex comes closer and gently runs the loofah over my injured arm, carefully gliding it across my collarbone and down my right arm. My breathing is labored as I stare up into Dexter's eyes.

"O-Oh, Lanie, I'm trying to be good here. Don't look at me like that," Dex says, closing his eyes and aiming his face toward the ceiling.

I can't help but mess with him a little.

"Like what, Dex?" I ask coyly just before I reach out with my good hand and wrap it around his base. The groan that erupts starts in his belly, working its way up his chest until it rumbles in the back of his throat.

"Good Lord, Lanie. You have to stop," he says, placing a hand over mine.

Instead of stopping my movements, though, he guides them, showing me the pace he prefers. He allows me to stroke him for a few minutes, right until he is about to lose control, then he backs up out of my reach. Watching me, he laughs at the pout I'm sure is forming on my face. "I have to get you cleaned up, sweetheart, remember?"

Reaching behind me, he grabs a shower hose I hadn't noticed. He turns it on, then wets my long, blonde hair. Walking behind me to sit on the ledge I was resting on, he straddles my body. My back to his front. I'm resting between his legs. Feeling the cold gel of shampoo being squeezed onto my head, followed by strong fingers massaging my scalp, I moan. I cannot control the sounds coming out of me. Unless you have ever had your scalp massaged by thick, sexy fingers, don't judge.

After a few moments, I feel him lean into me. "Lanie? If you keep making those noises, I am going to come all over your back."

I suck in a breath, letting it hiss through my teeth. He takes the hose and rinses out my hair. Once clean, he adds the conditioner and comes back to kneel in front of me. Reaching for my leg, he runs his hand from my ankle to my thigh. Just when I think he's going to touch me *there*, he places my leg back in the tub.

When he turns to grab something on the sink, I get the perfect shot of his ass. I never thought I'd be attracted to an ass—after all, it's an ass—but good Lord, his is perfect.

"Did you get a good enough peek, Lanie?" Dex makes eye contact with me in the mirror.

Shit, he totally just caught me ogling his ass.

Leaning down to whisper in my ear, he says, "It's okay, sweetheart, I love looking at your ass, too."

He lathers my leg with shaving cream.

"What are you doing?" I shriek.

"I'm taking care of you, Lanie. All of you."

Mesmerized, I watch as he gently runs the blade of his razor from my ankle to my knee, then starts the path all over again. With my lower legs complete, he takes my ankle and lifts it to rest on the edge of the bathtub. In this position, I'm completely and totally open to him. By the heated smile in his eyes, it hasn't gone unnoticed by him either.

Gently, he lathers my upper leg, moving it how he pleases to shave whatever he deems necessary. On his last pass, he grazes my pussy with his knuckles, and we both groan.

"Dex, please," I beg with a voice hardly recognizable as my own.

"What, Lanie? What do you need?" His nose grazes the side of mine.

"I need you, Dex. Please, I need to feel you." My desperation seeps into my words.

His low groan tells me this is torture for him, too. "Lanie, we can't. I'll hurt you. We have to wait for your arm to heal."

"I can't wait, Dex. Please." I search my reflection in the mirror, not entirely sure the person begging for this man right now is me.

"Fuck, Lanie. Do you know what it does to me when I hear you beg for me like that?"

He pulls away, searching the bathroom. His eyes are slightly crazed, which makes me laugh. I know his brain is working overtime, trying to find a solution that will allow him to touch me without hurting my arm.

"Stand up," he commands, and I do without hesitation.

He quickly rinses the conditioner from my hair, wraps me in a towel, and carries me to the foot of his bed. Once I'm on my feet, he makes quick work of drying me, his knuckles once again grinding lightly where I need release. Then he places me on his bed.

"We can't have sex, Lanie." He sounds wounded. "Not until your shoulder is more stable, but if you can keep it still in your sling, I'll take care of you." His words are filled with dark promises.

Not understanding what he means, I say, "You always take care of me, Dex. I want you to touch me."

"Lanie." My name's a painful groan. When he speaks again, it's torturously slow. "When I say I'll take care of you, it means in every way. Emotionally." He kisses my temple. "Physically." His hand tweaks my nipple, rolling it leisurely. "Mentally." Dex licks a line from the base of my neck to my earlobe, where he bites down gently, making me squirm. "And sexually, Lanie. Lay back and let me take care of you, sexually," he all but growls.

Once he has me supported on both sides with pillows, he makes good on his word. "Do you want my hands, Lanie? My lips? My tongue?"

Unable to choose one, I simply reply, "Yes," making him chuckle.

"Your wish is my command, sweetheart. Hang on." Slowly, he makes his way down my body. Sucking my right nipple in his mouth, using his tongue to flick the hardening peak. "Oh, sweetheart," he moans against my skin. "I can't get to your other tit tonight because of your arm. Looks like this one will get all the attention," he tells me devilishly.

"Th-That's okay," I pant.

Dex smirks against my heated skin. He releases my breast with an audible pop and kisses down my scars. True to his word, he does this every chance he gets, and I notice I cringe less each time he does. Reaching my hip bone, he nips it with his teeth, making me squeak.

"Stay still, sweetheart. We can't do this if you're moving.

I'm afraid we'll hurt your arm." He runs his nose along my pubic bone, inhaling deeply, and I blush everywhere. I try to twist away, but he gives me a warning growl.

"Stay still! Got it?"

I stupidly give him a thumbs-up with my one working hand and want to smack myself. He laughs and lowers his mouth to my mound.

"Oh, Dex."

"You like this, Lanie?" he asks, his warm breath adding extra sensations to my swollen nub. Reaching up with one long arm, he finds my nipple without even trying. He rolls it in time with his tongue.

"Yes, yes, yes, I love it, I love—" I break off quickly, realizing what I was about to say.

Dex smiles like he knows what almost slipped out and roughly sucks my clit between his teeth. With methodical movements, he flicks, licks, and rolls it with his tongue. He knows when I'm about to explode, and he backs off, once, then twice.

"Dex, please, not again. I need to come. Please …" I'm whimpering when he goes all in.

"Fuck me, Lanie, you taste so damn good." He laps at my folds like a man dying of thirst.

I feel the stubble of his chin against my core, his face moving side to side, causing friction on my most sensitive area. Slowly, Dex strokes me with his fingers while his tongue does wicked things to my clit.

Spreading me, Dex slides a finger into my heat. Making eye contact, I decide I've never seen anything so erotic. Smiling up at me, he asks, "Do you trust me, Lanie?"

I don't have to think. "Yes, yes, I trust you."

"Stay still, sweetheart, and relax," he tells me.

I'm not sure how I could be more relaxed, but then I feel pressure at the entrance to a hole I wasn't expecting. "Dex." I tense.

"Shh, Lanie, just trust me. I won't hurt you," he promises.

As I lay as still as I can, Dex continues to lick and suck, moving his magical fingers in and out of me when I feel the pressure again.

"Just relax, Lanie, let me in."

His tongue flicks over my clit, and I feel my stomach fluttering. I'm close. His fingers work my pussy at a pace I can't keep up with. I prop my head to watch his mouth on my clit, and he gives me a naughty grin just as he slips the tip of his other finger into my ass. The carnal sensations overwhelm me. Pleasure I have never known ripples through every inch of my body, and I erupt, hurtling through space.

I know he said not to move, but holy fucking hell. It's too much, all the stimulation at once. My arm could be broken in a hundred places, and I wouldn't feel anything but this wonderful man currently fucking me with his mouth. I'm panting and screaming incoherently. My body goes taut, my thighs are shaking. He doesn't stop until he has drawn every last spasm out of me with his naughty mouth.

Crawling up my body, kissing a path, he finally lands on my lips and asks, "Do you taste yourself, Lanie? Do you see how we taste together? Your pussy on my lips?"

I almost come again just from his words. "Oh Mylanta, Dex. How? How does it keep getting better?"

"That's the way it's supposed to be, baby," he says, laying down beside me, taking my hand in his and kissing across my knuckles with one hand, his other gliding over my sensitive flesh.

If that's true, I don't know if I'll survive another round with this man.

"Wait, Dex," I say, trying to sit up, but he holds me down.

"Don't move," he tells me, kissing everywhere he can reach. "I'm not going anywhere."

"But what about you?" I ask self-consciously.

Kissing my forehead, he whispers, "We have plenty of

time for that, Lanie. Tonight, I just want to take care of you. I'll be fine. Watching you come like that is my new favorite activity."

Sliding in as close as he can get without fear of hitting my arm, we both fall into a peaceful sleep.

CHAPTER 31

DEX

MLM Tactical Group
Dexter: Day 190, I have the perfect costumes for Lanie and me. Date 190 (trick-or-treating) and 191 (costume party) will be epic. Pictures to follow.

Trevor: Dude, you know we love you, but we have been getting these messages for 190 days STRAIGHT, multiple times a day.

Preston: If this keeps up, I might be forced to block you.

Julia: How long do you plan to keep this up?

Dexter: As long as it takes.

Julia: And is there a reason you text us your plan and review every single day?

Dexter: Yes. I'm saving them all in Google.doc. When the time comes, I'll print them all in a book for Lanie. I know she'll have to come to terms with everything before we can truly move forward, though. When that happens, I want her to have a reminder of all our days together. I don't want to leave any room for her to doubt how much I love her.

Julia: ...

Trevor: ...

Preston: Damn, man. If you set the bar this high, us mere mortals will never measure up.

Julia: Thanks a lot, dickhead. You made my eyes leak, and I don't cry. Ever.

∽

"*L*anie? Are you home?" I yell as I walk through the front door and head for the kitchen.

"We're in the playroom," she answers. "I'm helping Tate with his costume."

Entering the playroom, I see Tate standing there in a full astronaut costume. Lanie spent the past two days making it after he changed his mind at the last minute. "I can't believe you made this, Lanie. It's incredible."

"Isn't it awesome, Dad?" Tate screeches. "No one will have a costume like this one. I bet I win the best costume award, don't ya think?" He's so excited he's bouncing all around the room while Lanie patiently follows him, trying to add the final touches.

"It's awesome, buddy. Lanie did an amazing job. I hope you've thanked her because I happen to know she's been up very late the last couple of nights to finish it."

Running from the room, he whizzes past me and is back before I can comprehend what's happening.

"I did, Dad, see? I did." He's waving something around in his hand, but it's moving so fast I can't see it.

"Hold still, buddy. What is that? What did you make?"

He stops bouncing for a second to hand me a card. "It's my thank you card to Lanie. I told her thank you, thank you, thank you. Then I told her I love her so much, and this is the best Halloween I've ever had."

Opening the card, I see that's precisely what he did. Fatherly pride consumes me. "I see, Tate. I'm so proud of you, buddy. This was a lovely thing you did for Lanie. I'm sure she appreciates it a lot."

He nods so fast I have whiplash. I watch as he goes back to bouncing while talking to me, making poor Lanie contort on the floor to get his left pant leg.

"She does, Dad, she does. She already asked me to hang it on her wall so she can see it every day. She even cried. I might make one every day. If Lanie gets used to them then she won't cry anymore." Lowering his voice to a whisper, he says, "I don't like it when she cries."

"Me either, buddy. We'll have to make it our job to make sure Lanie never cries." I give him a little fist bump.

"Deal, Dad."

"Tate, I told you, they were happy tears. It's okay to have happy tears sometimes. It means something was so special you didn't have enough room to hold all your happiness, so the extra comes out in tears." By the tone of her voice, I can tell she's had this conversation a lot.

"Nope, Lanes. I don't like it. Happy smiles, sad tears," Tate says matter-of-factly.

Deciding to help Lanie out, I put my hands on his shoulders and hold him still.

"How much candy have you had today, Tate?" My gaze shifts from him to Lanie, who looks guilty. *I thought so.*

"Only five pieces. Lanie even let me have the big ones," he reports happily.

Lanie raises her hand as if to ward me off. "I know. I learned my lesson, trust me," she says, making me laugh.

"All right, bubs, you're all set! Let's get a look at you," she tells Tate, raising to her feet.

He whirls around, arms flying wildly.

"You're like a real astronaut, Tate," I tell him. "Now that you're all set, should we give Lanie her costume?" Lanie's attention is suddenly on me.

One hand on her hip and the other pointing directly at

me, she says, "Oh, no. I didn't agree to dress up. Tonight is for the kids, Dex. Not me and not you."

Ignoring her completely, I take Tate by the hand. "Come on, Tate. You and I can get the girls dressed, then you can help me put the finishing touches on my costume." Winking at Lanie as I walk by, I tell her, "Your costume is waiting on your bed. *Spit-spot.*"

"Well, aren't you cheeky," she replies with a laugh.

~

Tate and I are leaning against the door in my bedroom, waiting for Lanie to walk into her room where she'll find a very authentic Mary Poppins costume.

"Shh," I tell Tate, "I hear her coming up the stairs." Her door opens and her laughter fills the hall. Good, just as I'd hoped. "Okay, buddy. Now, help me dirty up my face."

Meeting Lanie in the kitchen, I love how carefree she appears in her Mary Poppins costume, tending to the girls. I walk up behind her, whispering into her hair, "I've never found Mary Poppins so fucking sexy in my life."

Turning to look into my eyes, she tells me, "Behave."

"I will, but first, I want a selfie. While we're out, we will ask someone to take a picture of all five of us." Holding my phone out, I snap at least ten pictures.

Picking the best one of Lanie, I send it to MLM.
MLM Tactical Group
Dexter: Mary Poppins and Bert (photo sent)
Julia: Smashing.
Trevor: Cheerio, mate.
Preston: You all have mental issues.

~

"Tate had an amazing time trick-or-treating last night," I say to Lanie, who's sitting at the kitchen island, her hair all askew, looking sexy as hell.

"He really did," she agrees. "It was fun seeing him interacting with all the kids in the neighborhood. He has come so far, Dex."

"Because of you, sweetheart. You've been our angel, fixing us, making us smile, sharing your kindness. I don't know what we would have done if you hadn't come to us." I'm about to lean in for a kiss when the doorbell rings, startling Lanie.

Glancing over her shoulder, Lanie asks, "Are you expecting someone?" She looks over at the clock. "It's pretty early."

Smiling at her, I nod and go answer the door. Tate comes up beside me, knowing who's arrived. He gives me a sly little smile and a fist bump. My big guy kept the surprise a secret for three whole hours. That might be a record for him, so I let him open the door.

"Nanna Sylvie, you're here!" He leaps into her arms.

"Oh, my sweet boy, I am. I'm so happy to see you."

I hear Lanie's bare feet coming down the hallway.

"Hi, Mrs. Westbrook. It's so nice to see you. I didn't know you were coming."

"Oh, I know you didn't, dear. That's the point." She winks and sweeps past her in search of the girls.

"Dex? What's going on?" Lanie looks around as Sylvie, followed by Preston, Easton, Halton, Colton, and Ashton, walk past her. "Do they always travel like this?" she asks, pointing at the rather large family parade that just went through the house.

"Not always," I laugh, "only when they come to pick up the kids, but tonight, they're all staying over. We're the ones going out."

"What do you mean? What's tonight?" she asks, scrunching up her nose.

"Don't worry about it. Just pack an overnight bag. Whatever you will be comfortable in. I've taken care of the rest."

She starts to argue, but Preston cuts in.

"Don't bother, doll. He's been working on this for weeks, trust me. We've heard about every single detail. Multiple times." Preston hooks his arm with hers and walks her to the stairs. "I think you have about twenty minutes before you need to leave. Better hurry."

Lanie glares at us both but admits defeat. Shaking her head, she walks to her room.

MLM Tactical Group

Preston: Cutting Dexter off at the nuts on this one. Lanie's packing. My mom, brothers, and I have the kids. I'm sure we can all expect pictures and updates soon.

Julia: Is it really necessary to rain on his parade?

Trevor: Yes.

Julia: You guys are ridiculous. You did good today, Dex. Good luck.

Preston: Trev, have you lost our Jules to the dark side so soon?

Trevor: Fuck off.

Julia: Fuck off.

Preston: Two peas in a pod, those two.

For once, I don't reply; I don't need to. They've said it all for me.

Two hours later, we've checked in to a hotel uptown and are heading to the spa. "I booked a couple's massage, then you have hair, nails, and make-up after a late lunch. They know what you'll need. Julia called and filled them in, so just enjoy the day, okay?"

"I feel like I should be nervous. Should I be nervous?" Her eyes sparkle with worry.

"Never with me, sweetheart. I've always got you."

~

*M*LM Tactical Group
Dexter: Lanie is getting her hair and make-up done. I'm starting to second guess this. Maybe I should just cancel and take her to dinner.

Julia: You can't. She's spending all this time getting ready, and she's getting excited. It's a solid plan. Just go with it.

Trevor: I agree with Jules.
Preston: Of course, you do, Trev.
Julia: Fuck off.
Trevor: Fuck off.

~

"*H*oney, I'm home," I hear Lanie call out as the door closes behind her.

Walking out of the bedroom, I snatch her around the waist. "I love hearing those words come out of your mouth," I say, nipping at the base of her neck. With her hair all twisted up in some fancy knot on the top of her head, I have complete access. "You look beautiful, Lanes."

"Thank you." She turns to look at me. "What the heck? Why are you in a tux?" Lanie asks, shocked.

"We have plans tonight. Your dress is on the bed. I'll wait for you out here." She looks adorably confused. "Well, let's go. We have reservations before the party."

"Dex, what are you—" I cut her off with a kiss.

"Don't argue, Lanie. I've spent a lot of time planning tonight. Please, for me, just go get dressed."

She gives me a smile that could light up the darkest sky and walks into the bedroom. I stand just outside to hear her unzip the garment bag.

"What the hell?" she screams.

"Tsk, tsk, Lanie. You're becoming quite the potty mouth."
I quickly close the door and go grab part two of her gift.

~

*T*hirty minutes later, Lanie opens the bedroom door and I run to take my place by the mirror. I'm doing everything I can to recreate this iconic scene for her. She walks out and almost runs into me. She's so beautiful that I drop the necklace box. "Fuck."

"Dexter Cross, what are you doing? This is the exact dress, or at least it seems like the exact red dress she wore in the movie."

I bend to pick up the necklace.

"Lanie, you're so fucking beautiful." I shake my head. Hearing her call me Dexter Cross usually means I'm in for some sass, but I try to focus. "This is not the exact dress, but it was made to look exactly like it."

"Dex, I ... why are you doing all this? And I swear to God, if that is some crazy diamond necklace you have on loan, you can forget it. I'm not wearing two houses worth of diamonds."

This makes me laugh, a full, hearty belly laugh, and immediately shakes off my nerves.

"No, Lanie. This isn't all diamonds, and it's not on loan." I open the box, knowing she fully expects me to snap it on her fingers. However, after all the injuries this beautiful woman has suffered because of me, I won't take that chance. Instead, I hand her the box.

"Tate and I had this made for you. He chose the heart. I chose the inscription." I watch as she carefully lifts the pendant out of the box to examine it. "Sweetheart, don't cry. You just spent all that time getting your make-up done," I scold her teasingly.

Lanie turns the pendant over in her hand, examining

every inch of the platinum and diamond heart we chose for her. The front is sparkly and beautiful, just like her. The back is what I hope will be our truth. *Maria stayed*.

Walking over to her, I ask, "May I?"

Taking the pendant from her delicate hands, I motion for her to turn around so I can clasp it around her long neck. From my jacket pocket, I retrieve the small matching earrings. Tate and I both decided Lanie wouldn't like anything too big. The simple posts suit her perfectly.

"Dex, this is all too much. I can't accept this." She tries backing away, but I step with her, keeping our bodies close.

"You can, Lanie, and you will. Now put them on. We have a schedule to keep. Would you like to know what I have planned?" I coo.

She slides the stud earrings into her perfect ears as she nods yes.

"First, we're going to dinner. There will be nothing slippery on the menu." I wink at her. "Then, we're going to a costume gala my company is sponsoring. It's a charitable event, all proceeds going to various therapies for abused children. Eventually, we'll start our own charity with the same goal, but until we have someone to head that endeavor, we'll donate to various foundations." As I speak, I watch her carefully for a reaction.

This right here is what I'm not sure about. I know it's a lot for her to take in, but she gives me the most brilliant smile when she does. "You, Mr. Cross, are certainly unexpected."

What I don't tell her is that I hope to name the foundation in her honor someday.

CHAPTER 32

LANIE

"Jules, the months are flying by so quickly. I can't believe it's almost Thanksgiving," I whine. "I don't think we've ever been apart for this long."

"I know, Lanes. But can I be honest with you?" she asks like there's any other way.

"You know you can."

"I've never seen you so happy, Lanes. Mom and Dad see it, too. GG's making plans. I think Dex and North Carolina have been good for you. Before you go making any permanent decisions, I hope you really think about how your life has been these last eight months."

Woosh. She really hit the nail on the head this time. Sighing because I know she's right, I prop my phone up on the nightstand and lay on my side to see her. "I know, Jules. I don't know what to do. It's not like he's come right out and asked me to stay, though."

"I'm sorry, Lanes, but that is a pretty bitchy thing to say." Her words shock me. "That man has a running commentary on every nice thing he's done for the last two hundred and fifty plus days, and you don't think that's screaming at you to stay?"

"I'm so confused, Jules. I've never felt like this before," I confide.

"I know, sweetie, but do you know how I knew you might have finally found your place?"

I shake my head.

"You've been there eight months, and not once in that entire time have you been tempted to come home. Not when Bitchzilla slapped you, not when asshat threatened you at the school, and not when he roughed you up at the clubhouse. None of that has sent you running."

"Hmm," is all I can manage. She's right, of course. I'd just never thought of it like that. "I guess I haven't felt threatened here."

"Or, you knew you wouldn't be in serious physical danger because Dex was always there for you," Jules counters.

Unconsciously, I thumb my pendant. *Maria stayed.*

"Just don't make any rash decisions, okay? Thanksgiving is three weeks away. Have you decided what you're going to do?"

"I'm not sure. Tate has been begging me to stay and celebrate with him. I don't want to let him down, but I'm missing you guys so much." It's true. I've never been away from them this long before.

"Want my opinion?" Julia asks.

"Always," I reply in my best *duh* tone.

"I think that kid has had a hell of a time in his short life, and without even realizing it, you're both healing something in the other. If it were me, I'd do whatever will make him happy and plan to come home for a weekend after Thanksgiving."

"That's a lot of thoughts," I joke. "So, you think I should stay. For Thanksgiving," I add quickly.

"I would," she says.

"I'll think about it and let you know soon. Luvs, Jules."

"Luvs, Lanes."

"*L*anie! Thanksgiving is next weekend. Are you going to stay with me?" Tate asks, full of hope.

"Tate, I told you not to hound her. Lanie has a family, too, you know, and she hasn't seen them in a very long time. This has to be her decision, right?" Dex warns him.

"Okay, Dad." Then, lowering his voice so only I can hear him, he says, "But Dad and I are really hoping you stay." He gives me a quick kiss and runs off to the playroom.

"Hey, sweetheart. Sorry about that. I told him we had to let you make your own decisions. We can't hold you prisoner … although I would really like to see you in handcuffs," Dex whispers right before he leans in for a kiss.

"Handcuffs, huh? Who knew Mr. Cross was so kinky." I smirk. Walking to the island, I grab a bottle of water. "I already made my decision, anyway."

He chokes on his drink. Pounding on his chest, he tries to sound casual. "You did? What did you decide?"

"Well, Tate seems like he'd be pretty heartbroken if I didn't celebrate Thanksgiving with him, so I thought I'd stay."

Dexter's grin outshines the sun. "That seems like a very thoughtful decision, Mrs. Cross."

I look up at him right after he says it. I don't think he even realizes the slip.

He stares at me, puzzled. "What? Do I have something on my face?"

"No, n-nothing like that. I was just thinking I should go tell Tate. He's probably a nervous wreck."

Dexter watches me retreat, wondering what the hell just happened.

"Thanksgiving is in two days. Thanksgiving is in two days," Tate sings throughout the house.

"You seem very excited." I exaggerate my words, but he doesn't notice.

"Oh, I am, Lanie. All my favorite people will be here. You, Dad, Sara, Harper, Nanna Sylvie, Preston, and all his boys."

I laugh because I wouldn't want to name the long list of Westbrooks either.

"You've never had Thanksgiving at your house before?" I ask.

"No, not that I remember, anyway. We usually go to Nanna Sylvie's. I can't believe we're finally going to fill our big table." The energy this boy has is shocking.

"That's awesome, Tate. I'm so happy for you."

"For us, Lanie, remember? You're part of me, too, now." His words are so innocent, but my throat is thick with feelings.

"That's right, buddy. How about if we get the girls to the table? Dinner's ready. Can you go tell your dad?"

"Sure, Lanie. I'll even wash my hands."

"Thank goodness for that," I reply with a smile.

A few minutes later, we're sitting around the table. Harper to my right, Tate to my left, with Dex and Sara across from us. Tate's chattering away about his teacher and his friends. He has had a fantastic start to the year. Now that Jake no longer attends Waverley-Cay Elementary, Tate has really blossomed. Dex and I alternate bites for ourselves and nibbles for the girls. For the most part, they feed themselves now, but they wear more than they eat, requiring a little guidance occasionally.

I'm bringing a spoon to Harper's mouth when she swats me away, raising both arms in the air, saying, "Up, up." And I smile. She can be a hellion, but a cute one. They don't have much of a vocabulary yet, but they can both say up.

I lean in to kiss her messy face when she grabs my cheeks with her filthy hands, holding me captive. "Momma. Momma, up."

I'm so shocked, I pull away instantly, scaring the poor thing. Now she's crying for me. "Momma." I look to Dex for help, but he seems as shocked as I am. Then, to top things off, Sara starts crying. "Momma, up." She lifts her arms in the air, waiting for me to pick her up, too.

Tate's beside me, laughing, but I can barely hear him through the blood pumping in my ears.

"Ah, I'll take them up for a bath. You two finish eating," I tell Dex and Tate.

Dex nods his head, but stares at me with concern. He lifts Sara out of her highchair and puts her in my left arm.

"Hey," he starts, pulling me away from Tate's little ears, "are you okay?"

"Me? Yeah, totally. I'm totally fine, why do you ask?" I sound hysterical, there's no doubt about it.

"I'll finish dinner with Tate quickly, then come up to help with the girls. You sure you're all right?"

"Yup, just dandy, take your time." I ease out of his grip and practically run down the hall with a girl in each arm yelling Momma.

Holy shit.

CHAPTER 33

DEX

MLM Tactical Group
Dexter: Mayday. Mayday. Mayday.
Preston: A little dramatic, even for you, don't you think?

Dexter: The girls started calling Lanie Momma, and she freaked the fuck out. She hasn't come out of her bathroom in over an hour.

Julia: Really? She hasn't called me. I'll try her now.

Trevor: I'm sure she just needs to process, that's all.

Julia: Okay, so she isn't exactly answering.

Dexter: What do you mean exactly?

Julia: I mean, she's sending me to voicemail, repeatedly.

Dexter: Fuck.

Julia: We knew she was due for a freak-out, okay? Maybe this is it, but you have to remain calm. We'll all help you out. Miss Rosa is so invested she might fly down and marry you guys herself.

Preston: Who's Miss Rosa?

Dexter: Focus, Preston.

Julia: Seriously, Dexter. She's been doing so good, but

you know she still has some things to work out before she thinks she can ever fully be whole. My guess is someone calling her Momma is bringing up all kinds of scary shit for her. Not to mention the fact that it probably reminds her she can't have biological children of her own. That was really important to her at one time.

Dexter: I feel like I'm losing control.

Trevor: I'll be there in half an hour.

Julia: You have to stay calm. Let her do what she needs to do, no matter what. We'll work around whatever hare-brained scheme is cooking in that pretty little head of hers.

Dexter: Okay, thanks, Julia.

Julia: For the record, I want this for her. I want you for her. You make her happy, Dex. That's what is important to me. She just has to get out of her own way, and she has to do it in her own time.

Dexter: Thanks, Jules.

Julia: Just keep making her happy, that's all I ask.

Dexter: Always.

~

*I*t's been three hours and Lanie still has not come out of her room. Julia keeps checking in, letting me know she hasn't heard from her either. I think that's what has us both concerned the most.

Trevor has come and gone. There wasn't much he could do for me, so I sent him home. The kids are all in bed, and I'm pacing my room wishing I knew what to do when my phone buzzes.

Ripping the phone from my pocket, I press the accept button. "Hi, Julia," I say with a sigh. I know Lanes wouldn't call me from the next room, but I'm on edge.

"Hey." She's subdued, not a great sign for me. "Lanie's

going to talk to you early in the morning. She's coming home for Thanksgiving. I want to give you a heads-up so you can react calmly. I bought her a ticket, so she'll fly instead of drive. She won't be here forever."

I sink down onto my bed feeling broken.

"Dex, she's just confused. It's been a strange year for her, but I promise you, she'll come back."

"I would have gotten her a ticket." It's a strange thing to say, but it's all that comes out.

"Dex, it isn't about the money. Lanie could have bought the ticket. She's just too frugal to spend the money. I bought it, knowing she wouldn't be able to let it go to waste. You have to support her. Help her make Tate understand. I'll talk to her the second she lands and report back to you. She wouldn't say much on the phone. I'm sure I'll get it out of her on the drive back to the mountain."

Tate. This is going to crush him, and as much as I want to be angry, the only emotion I feel is sad.

Sighing, my voice thick with unshed emotion, I tell Julia, "I'll do my best."

An hour later, I'm lying in my bed, staring at my ceiling when a soft knock comes from the doorway.

"Lanie? You don't have to knock, come in." I wave her over with one hand, lifting the covers for her with the other.

She doesn't move and isn't looking at me.

"You're going back to Vermont, aren't you?" Slowly, I lower the covers back to the bed. My words catch her by surprise, and she finally lifts her head.

"Just for a few days, I'll be back on Monday. I'm leaving early in the morning, but don't worry, I'll make sure I talk to Tate myself before I go. I'll make him understand I'll be back on Monday." Her voice is soft, and her head bowed once again.

"For how long, Lanie? How long will you be back for?" I know it's a shitty thing to say to her. She's vulnerable right now, but she isn't the only one hurting. I'm scared to death something so innocent will be what takes her from us.

"Dexter, that's not fair. I never made any promises to you or anyone else. I-I'm doing the best I can. I feel like I'm drowning, and I can't break the surface. I just need a few days at home to sort things out," she explains.

"I was hoping this was becoming your home, too, Lanie." I lay back down on my pillow, trying to keep the bitterness from my voice. "We'll drive you to the airport whenever you're ready."

She doesn't say anything, and when I look up, she's gone back to her room.

"Fuck," I yell to an empty room.

~

This morning was brutal. An awkwardness settled over me and Lanie that had never been there before. I fucking hated it.

As promised, she spoke to Tate in private, and I was surprised when there were no tears from him. Tate sat in the back of the car the entire way to the airport, chatting happily away.

Lanie's departure is quick. She gives all the kids kisses, giving me one on the cheek while never making eye contact.

On the way home, I check the rearview mirror to see Tate smiling. "What are you thinking about, buddy?" *And how do I get some of that happiness?*

"What kind of cookies Mimi will make me." He smiles. "Lanie's going to bring them back, just for me." Suddenly serious, he says, "Don't worry, Dad. She's coming back. She didn't take our family picture with her, she showed me. She said wherever she was living, she'd always take that with her. So, see? She'll be back. She even made all the pies last night and told me the food is all ready so we can still have everyone over tomorrow."

Completely shocked, I ask, "What do you mean, Tate? What food?"

He smiles. "Lanie said you might be mad. She stayed up last night to make four different kinds of pie and got all the food ready. She said she left instructions on everything, and all you have to do is turn the oven on."

I'm speechless.

Tate talks away again in the backseat, but I only hear bits and pieces. My mind is on the woman boarding a plane right now, headed for Vermont.

We walk in through the front door, and I hear Trevor and Preston bickering. Rolling my eyes, I follow their voices to the family room where a college football game is on. "What are you guys doing here?"

"Hi to you, too." Trevor smiles. In a kinder voice, he says, "Jules texted. Said you might need some help getting ready for tomorrow."

Tate comes running in behind me, almost knocking a lamp off the table he collides with. "Hi, Uncle Trevor. Hi, Uncle Preston. Nope, we don't need help. Lanie made everything last night."

They both look from Tate to me.

I just shrug. "I don't know. Tate says she told him it's all done. It just needs to be put in the oven. I haven't had a chance to check."

Preston jumps over the back of the couch, running for the kitchen. "Holy shit, she did. Score!" His excited voice echoes in the hallway. "I was not looking forward to peeling freaking potatoes today."

We all laugh, but I don't feel the humor. The guys make small talk around me for the next few hours, but I don't join in. I stare, unseeing, at the television all afternoon.

~

Sitting on my couch, the very one Lanie often comments on, my phone rings. It's Julia. "Hi, Jules—"

She cuts me off. "I don't have long." She's out of breath and has me leaning forward. "We just got to my house. Lanie's in the bathroom. All I can tell you is get your ass on a plane now. She's going to need you if she's going to do what I think she is."

My heart races, and I feel sick. "What do you mean, Julia? What is she going to do?"

"I don't have time to explain. A plane. Now. Bring the whole damn family. My parents will help. Just get here, ASAP. Go straight to my parents' house. You can all stay there."

I'm looking at Trevor when Julia hangs up on me. There's something seriously wrong with this girl.

"Preston," I shout, not realizing he's behind me, "anyone using your mom's plane right now?" I've never called in favors like this before, so Preston and Trevor's concerned expressions are warranted.

"Not that I know of. What's going on?" Preston asks, peering around the room.

"We're going to Vermont," I inform him. "Well, the kids and I have to go to Vermont. If you guys want to come, we need to leave as soon as possible," I tell their shocked faces.

"Okay, dude. I'll call my mom and see how fast we can get the plane up and running. You coming, too, Trev?"

Looking at him for the first time since I said we're going to Vermont, I notice he seems a little pale.

"Trevor? What's up, man?" I ask, walking closer to him.

"What? Oh, nothing. No, sorry, I can't. I can't go to Vermont right now. I've got some things at work. I can't leave at the moment."

He's lying. Preston and I both know it, and it worries me. Trevor's the most honest guy I know.

"Does this have anything to do with Julia?" I ask.

He rakes a hand through his hair and swears under his breath. I've got my answer.

"No," he says. "Maybe? I have too much shit in my life. Plus, she has her own baggage. We're just friends, but I do have something I can't leave right now." I'm not sure I've ever seen Trevor so unhinged.

"Are you all right?" I ask him again. "Is something happening with your dad and all his ... *stuff?*"

He turns his back to me, effectively blocking me out. "Drop it, Dex, okay? Just drop it. Let's get the kids packed up; I'll help. You'll need an entire plane for all their crap." He isn't wrong. *Who knew little people required so much shit?*

"Plane is all set. It'll be ready to leave in an hour," Preston informs me.

"Thanks, buddy, I owe you."

He ignores me, saying he'll be back soon.

Two hours later, I'm sitting on a private plane with Tate, Sara, Harper, Preston, Sylvie, Easton, Halton, Colton, and Ashton. Jesus, I hope Julia knew what she was getting when she said to bring everyone.

"Thanks, Julia." I hear Preston say, one of the perks of a private plane, I guess.

"Why were you talking to Julia?" I ask.

"Dex, you know I love you, but if you think I'm going to sit in a car driving old mountain roads looking at cow pastures for two-plus hours after this plane ride, you've lost your goddamn mind. Somehow, Julia got permission for a chopper to land at their local hospital and she'll have rental cars waiting there for us."

"Preston Westbrook," Sylvie scolds. "That's a bit excessive, don't you think?"

"No way, Mom. Not the way Colton is prone to getting

car sick. Those mountain roads would do him in for sure. I looked this town up. It's seriously in the middle of nowhere. If he was in the car for two hours, he would definitely hurl."

Sylvie tsks at him but doesn't complain further. I'm not about to complain either, since that means we will arrive much earlier than planned.

"Does that mean Julia knows to expect all of us?" I ask.

"It does. Her parents are setting us all up. She said it might be tight, but we can make do for a couple of days."

"Maybe it'll be like camping," Tate says happily. "That would be so awesome."

"Yeah, awesome," Preston grumbles, always the pansy.

Less than two hours later, I'm walking through the McDowells' front door, making introductions. Sylvie and Mimi, who I now have permission to call Mimi, are in the kitchen with Tate and the girls. All the Westbrook boys, Mr. McDowell, who I can now call Pete, and I are in their large great-room that looks over the small ski mountain.

"All right, son," Pete starts, "last I heard, our Lanie was staying with you for Thanksgiving, then all of a sudden, she's at Julia's, and you're all on some fancy plane chasing after her. Do I have to take the shotgun out again?"

Preston and Colton, who are squished together in a double chair, throw their heads back in laughter.

"He isn't joking," I say as Preston's eyes light up with mischief. "Don't start, Pres. I mean it." Turning my attention back to Pete, I explain why we're here. "No, sir. It wasn't my doing." I pinch the back of my neck, peering down. "Everything was great. Then we were having dinner, and the girls started calling her Momma."

Pete nods his head solemnly. "I see, and shortly after, she was running for home. Is that it?"

"That's about it, sir."

He leans back in his rocker, running a hand through his

hair. Glancing around the room and into the kitchen, Pete takes stock of everyone in his home.

"To be honest, I'm not sure how she's going to react to us being here. If Julia hadn't told me to get my ass on a plane, I would have let her have her space. It would've killed me, but I'd do it if that's what she needs."

"Mhm, I do believe Julia made the right call. It's about time we knock some sense into that girl." Pete smiles, and hope fills my chest.

These may be Lanie's people, but they're my allies. The thought makes me laugh.

Walking toward the kitchen at the back of the great room, I hear Tate talking with Mimi and Sylvie. I pause, pretending to look at the pictures lining the walls. The smile Mimi flashes my way tells me I'm not fooling anyone.

"Mimi, why does Lanie call you Mimi? Is that your name?"

She laughs at such an innocent yet direct question. Grabbing the stool across from Tate, she takes a seat, motioning for Sylvie to choose the one next to him. I notice they have the girls set up in the portable highchairs with some crackers. *Two grandmothers in their glory.*

"No, handsome. My name's Maxine, but you know, I met Lanie when she was just a bit older than you. I don't know how much Lanie has told you, but she didn't have the easiest of childhoods. When she was young, Pawpaw and I just decided she needed to have some people in her life to count on. I had called my grandmother Mimi, so I had Lanie call me that as well. I wasn't her mother, but I liked to show her what a mother could be any chance I got. I wanted her to have a familial feeling with us, so I guess that's why we always had these nicknames."

"If Lanie wanted to call you mom, would you let her?" Tate asks, surprising us all.

Mimi raises her head in question, and I motion for her to answer honestly. Tate has had a rough go, but he's always had the guys and me. Maybe some insight from Mimi will help him.

"Hoo-we, that's a tough question right there, little man." I laugh as Mimi uses the nickname Lanie uses so often.

Does Lanie have any idea just how much Mimi she has in her?

"It's tricky because even though Lanie's mom wasn't always good to her, she was still around."

"Not like my mom," Tate mumbles, and I suck in a breath.

Preston's brother, Easton, comes up beside me, putting a hand on my shoulder. He obviously just heard Tate's words, too.

"My mom isn't nice at all. She doesn't love me like Lanie does. She doesn't even like me very much." All the air I was holding in is now suffocating me, but I can't walk away.

"You know what, Tate? Lanie's mom didn't much like her either; perhaps that's why the two of you get along so well. I'm glad that you have your dad and Nanna Sylvie here and all those boys out there watching out for you, though. Lanie only had us when her mother allowed it. I have to imagine it was pretty lonely for her sometimes."

"I was lonely before Lanie came to live with us."

Ouch. Sucker punch right to the gut. I cannot believe he's so comfortable with Mimi. However, it helps me understand how she could get so close to Lanie all those years ago. It's an innate skill she has so obviously handed down to Lanie.

"I bet that was hard for you. You know, Lanie told me you didn't talk for a while. She probably doesn't remember, but there was a short time where Lanie didn't speak much either.

It's one of the reasons I'm so happy she found you. It took Lanie many, many years to understand the true meaning of family because it's different for everyone. Did you know that?"

"Lanie didn't talk either?" Those are all the words Tate can focus on.

Mimi gives him a sad smile and pats his hand. Looking at me, I see the sadness wash over her face. "She was about ten when something scary happened to her. She didn't talk for a couple of months after that, but do you know what I did?"

He shakes his head, enrapt by Mimi's story. "I showed her love. As she got older, I taught her it was okay to choose your family. I think that's an important lesson for you, too, handsome. Lanie's mom was not good to her; it's taken Lanie a long time to fully understand what having a family means. I'm willing to bet you've had a big part in teaching her what family should be." Mimi's still holding Tate's hand.

I see Sylvie wiping a stray tear before speaking. "Tate, you know everything your mom said to you?"

"Yes, Nanna Sylvie," he says sadly.

"None of that was true, you know that, right? Those ugly words were her problem, not yours. You're an amazing kid that anyone would be lucky to have as a son," Sylvie tells him.

Tate interrupts, "I know, Lanie told me, a lot." He laughs. "I wish Lanie could be my mom," his voice is quiet, "but I don't think she wants to be mine."

I hear a loud gasp. Shifting my gaze, I see the last person I was expecting tonight. Glancing around the room, I realize everyone's gone silent, all of us eavesdropping on Mimi and Tate's conversation.

CHAPTER 34

LANIE

Tate wishes I were his mom. *Me.* And he thinks I don't want him. Bile rises in my throat. I won't be the cause of that kind of pain.

Dex tries to speak, but I hold up my hand to cut him off. I only stopped by to give Mimi the pies I made earlier, but running into Dex and all the Westbrooks almost had me pissing my pants. Maybe I'll be mad later, but right now, my only priority is Tate.

Passing Dex, I enter the kitchen and stand just behind this sweet little boy.

"Tate?"

The kid must be attached to a spring, because before I say another word, he's launching himself at me, knocking my blueberry pie to the ground.

"Oh no, Lanie. I'm so sorry. I didn't see it in your hand." Tate pales, and I comfort him the only way I can.

"Shh. Shh, it's okay, buddy. We'll clean it up later. I want to talk to you." We walk together to a window seat on the opposite side of the kitchen.

I sense Dex taking a few steps forward, probably to hear

us. "When I was little, this was my favorite spot in the entire world," I tell Tate. "I've missed you so much."

"Then why did you leave, Lanie? I thought we were going to have a party. Oh, but guess what? It's okay because we brought all your food here on a big plane that was just for us. It was so cool." He smacks me with a smile right before leaning in for another hug.

"I know, Tate. I'm sorry. I-I heard you talking to Mimi and Nanna, though. I want you to understand, it's not that I don't want to be your mom. Being your mom is something I would love more than anything in this world, but I-I'm a little bit broken, buddy. I can't be your mom if I can't be sure I wouldn't break you, too. Does that make any sense to you?"

"Oh, that's fine, Lanie. My dad is really good at fixing things. I'll help, too. Together we can fix you for sure. Just come back home, Lanie, and we'll fix you. Then you can be my mom." Tate says it so earnestly that I fight to swallow the lump in my throat.

Dex must sense my distress because he walks over then. "Hey, Tate? It looks like Mimi needs help cleaning up that pie. Do you think you can help her?"

He leaps out of my arms. "Sure, Dad." He turns his attention to me again, staring me straight in the eye. "I love you, Lanie."

I kiss his head. "Love you, too, buddy."

"Hey," Dex says, sitting in Tate's seat.

I'm suddenly exhausted. "What are you doing here, Dex?" I don't sound sad or angry, I realize, just tired. I feel like I've been running my entire life, and I have to either cross the finish line or give up on everything.

"I was worried about you, Lanie. We all were," he says, waving his hand around the room, at all the Westbrooks. I laugh. I don't want to; it's just what happens when someone finally admits defeat.

Everyone in this house loves me. *Me!* Lanie Heart, the lost girl with a broken soul. For a moment, I wonder when I became this girl. *When did I let the pain of others dictate my future?*

"Lanie?" Dex asks, looking concerned.

Crap, he must have kept talking, but I can't keep my mind from wandering. I study all the faces now staring at me with worried expressions. *This could be my family. The family I choose.* But I wasn't kidding when I told Tate I'm a little bit broken.

Why? Why are you so broken, Lanie? What makes you this way? In my head, I can only think of one person. One person who's always held me back. One person who always set me up to fail.

My mother.

Glancing around the room once more, I come to rest on Dexter's anguished gaze. *He makes me happy. He loves me, and he's shown me in over two hundred ways. Why do I keep this wonderful man at arm's length then?*

Because you can't love him fully until you know you won't break him. The voice in my head sounds suspiciously like Mimi's.

I suddenly understand, without a doubt, what I have to do. I have to say good-bye to my mother for good. I rush to stand, but my stomach doesn't get the memo. I don't know if it's nerves from what I'm about to do or the fact that I've eaten my body weight in chocolate chip cookie dough today, but I know at this moment that cookie dough is searching for an exit. I run in circles with a hand over my mouth, trying to find the best place, but I don't see one quickly enough.

Doubled over, I know we're about to have a second mess to clean up.

Dex

LM Recovery Plan

Dexter: She's in the bathroom with your mom. Wtf am I supposed to do? She threw up all over the goddamn floor, Julia! Is that my fault? Am I upsetting her that much?

Julia: Stop being a drama queen. Not everything is about you. Get your shit together because you have to talk her into letting you go with her tonight.

Dexter: Go? Go where? Why aren't you coming over? Shouldn't you be here helping me?

Preston: Yeah, Julia! You really should be here. I'm not good at all this girly shit.

Julia: Shockingly, you're still single.

Preston: (Rolling eye emoji) I'm adding Colton to this group; he's good with girly shit.

Colton added at 6:25 p.m.

Dexter: Wtf. Julia, where am I supposed to convince Lanie to go and how am I supposed to do that? She just vomited after talking to me.

Colton: I'm definitely in the dark here. Let me add Halton, he picks up social stuff faster.

Halton added at 6:28 p.m.

Dexter: What the hell? STOP adding your brothers, Preston. This is serious.

Halton: What's going on? You realize I'm in the next room, right?

Dexter: For fuck's sake. Everyone STOP texting. Let Julia answer me.

Julia: I think you're one step closer to getting the girl, but Lanie just told me she has something to do to make sure she doesn't break your family like she was broken.

Dexter: WTH? She isn't broken. Why the fuck won't she listen to me on that? What is it she has to do?

Colton: Wait, is MLM: Make Lanie Mine? So freaking cool, man. How long has this group been scheming?

Preston: Too fucking long.

Dexter: I'm going to grab all your fucking phones in two seconds if you don't shut the hell up and let Julia explain this to me.

Easton added 6:42 p.m.

Ashton added 6:42 p.m.

Dexter: That's it. Hand over your phones. NOW.

Julia: She didn't say Dex. But my guess? If she has to fix something to be whole again, she's going to talk to her mom.

Dexter: Oh hell no. She's not going without me.

Julia: That's what I was hoping to hear.

Ashton: Can someone send us the transcripts? I have a feeling we've missed a lot of great stuff.

Julia: Fuck off. This is Julia btw. Say hi to my mom and dad for me.

Julia: Dexter, I'm out of commission tonight. Charlie's sick, so it's all up to you, dude.

Dexter: Great.

~

Lanie

"There's an entire family out there that loves you, Lanie. You don't owe your mother anything," Mimi says, helping me wash my hair in the sink. The unfortunate vomiting accident in the kitchen landed mostly on the left side of my head.

"I know, Mimi. I still can't believe they all came and brought the Westbrooks, too."

"Seems to me, Dexter has his own chosen family out

there. If the situation were reversed, do you really think we'd let you go without us?"

I hadn't thought of it that way, but she has a point.

Standing up, I wrap a towel around my head. "You're right, Mimi. But I have to do this, I-I just have to. I need the closure it will bring."

"Honey, you know she'll be at the bar tonight. Do you think you'll get the closure you're looking for if she's been drinking all day?" Mimi asks skeptically.

Staring at Mimi, I know I want to be a mom like her, however that comes to be. I also know it can't happen unless I cut the strings of my past.

"Honestly, Mimi? This isn't about the closure she can give me. It's about the closure I need by speaking my truth, out loud, to her. I know she won't remember and will very likely cause a scene, but I need it. If I want to move on, if I want a chance of inheriting that large group of crazy men out there …" I laugh because there's no other way to explain the Westbrooks. "If I want those amazing babies, I already love so much, and a man who cares so much more for me than I ever thought possible, I have to do this."

Mimi takes me in her arms, tears running freely down her face. "We've been waiting for this day, Lanie. The day you would see how special you are. How easy you are to love. How much you have to offer the world if you could only open your heart. I don't think I've ever been prouder to have you as a daughter as I am right now." She pulls back and looks me straight in the eyes. "You know, I can't let you go down to that bar alone. I insist on someone going with you. Pawpaw will go if that's what you're most comfortable with."

"Okay. I'm sorry to leave you with a house full of man-babies." My cheeky comment makes her laugh.

"Oh, honey. They're a group of very handsome men. I think I'll survive. Plus, Sylvie is excellent at keeping those boys in line."

"No kidding." I grin. "Sylvie might be the only one who can."

After a few minutes, we walk out of the bathroom to a room full of laughing and yelling. Sylvie and Pawpaw have taken the kids to the solarium, where it's a little quieter. Dexter is yelling at Colton. Halton has Easton in a headlock. Preston is taking pictures, and Ashton is spinning in circles trying to calm everyone down.

"What the heck is going on here?" I yell, louder than I knew I could.

Everyone freezes, even Preston, who's standing on Mimi's couch with his phone high in the air, trying to get everyone in the frame.

"You, young man, can get your feet off my couch." Mimi scolds, and Preston immediately jumps down.

"Sorry, ma'am. I was trying to get pictures for the MLM," he says as if that explains everything.

"Oh, well then, carry on. Everyone else can stop the yelling, though." I stand corrected. Mimi can also corral this crew with just her voice.

I stare at her like she's crazy, though. *What the hell is the MLM?*

Dexter points to each one of the guys. "Not another word or text from any of you, or I swear you won't like what you'll wake up to."

He stalks toward me with my jacket in hand. "It's not up for debate," he says, helping me into my coat. "I swear to God, Lanie, not a single word. I spoke to Julia. I spoke to Pete. If you're seriously going into that bar, I'll be going with you. I'm happy to drive, but if you insist on going by yourself, know this, I will follow you."

Looking at Pawpaw, I mouth, 'Traitor.'

The old man just blows me a kiss and winks.

"Dex, I really don't want you to see this," I say quietly. "She's going to be a mess, and it won't be pretty. She definitely will not be kind. I-I don't want you to see me this way."

Lifting my chin so I have to look at him, he stares at me, and I feel like he can see straight into my soul. "Lanie, just because this woman birthed you or because she'll likely display abhorrent behavior toward you does not, in any way, change how I feel about you. Now that we have that out of the way, let's say good-bye to the kids and get this over with, shall we?" He speaks as if he has no idea we're about to enter the seventh layer of hell.

We say good-bye to the kids, and I promise Tate I'll be back in the morning, then we walk toward the door.

Just before we leave, Sylvie stops us. "I'm proud of you, Dex. Your dad would be so happy to see the man you've become."

His eyes pool with unshed tears. "Thank you, Sylvie. That means a lot. More than you could know, actually."

She smiles and gives him a kiss on the cheek. "I love you, Dex." Four little words and they hit him hard. I see the emotion written all over his face.

"I love you, too." He leans in for another hug, then we make our way out the door.

Stepping outside, we see the wet, heavy snow that covers the vehicles in the driveway. "Tate is going to love this tomorrow," Dex says, smiling like a teenager. "He hasn't ever seen snow before."

Shocked, I ask, "How is that possible?"

He shrugs his shoulders. "Anna hated the cold, and honestly, after Tate was born, she never wanted to go on vacation with us, anyway. She made a few girls' trips, but now I wonder if she actually went with her girlfriends."

I hate the way he looks when he talks about her. I know in some ways Dex feels as if he failed. Someday, I hope he realizes he didn't.

I point him in the right direction, and we slowly make

our way down the mountain. There's only one bar she would be at. It's a few towns away and has dollar drafts of the most disgusting beer I've ever tasted. She lives for deals when it's her money on the line.

The drive would take us twenty minutes in good weather, but with the snow, it might take closer to forty. "Are you sure you don't want me to drive? I did grow up in this stuff, you know. I've been driving in it for years." When I get a glimpse of his white knuckles with hands at ten and two, I know he's struggling. His eyes never leave the road.

"Ah, I don't want to sound like a sissy, but since our lives are at stake, I'm thinking that might be a good idea."

I laugh at how easily he consents, but I direct him to the next pull off. Some things in this town never change. For the first time in my life, I like the monotony of my tiny town. Getting behind the wheel, I force my focus on the road and not what kind of hell I'm walking us into.

CHAPTER 35

DEX

Lanie is quiet the rest of the drive. I don't talk either because I'm too worried about her attention remaining on the road. I can't believe people live out here and drive in this shit regularly.

What happens if you break down? Do you even get cell service out here?

Having been here once before, I know the town is small, but in the snow? It's like my own private nightmare. I never realized how much of a city boy I am until right now.

Lanie slows the car as the town come into view. It looks like a ghost town at night. All the buildings look like they're at least a hundred years old. It gives it a quaint feeling that I'm guessing is much less creepy in the daytime. She takes a left down Main Street, and I feel myself pumping an imaginary brake. Lanie's driving slowly enough, but the steep incline of the road has me on edge. Shocking me completely, she pulls over halfway down and puts on the emergency brake.

"What are you doing? We can't stay here; the car will slide down the road." She laughs at me and puts her mittens back on after opening the car door. Gaping at her, then the snow-covered road in front of us, I clench my teeth. "Are you serious right now? This is where you're going to park?"

"Yes, Dex. This really is where I'm going to park. The bar is right over there." She nods with her head, and I follow her line of sight.

I try not to make a face, but it takes a lot of work. With an old barber sign out front, I can tell the bar is in the basement. Steeling myself for what we're about to walk in on, I work to relax my face. "I trust you, let's go."

Walking around the front of the car, I notice Lanie has stalled in her seat, and I quickly round the corner. "Hey, sweetheart, are you okay? We don't have to do this if you're not ready, you know that, right?"

She nods but doesn't answer, so I lean in and hold her tightly in my arms. After a few minutes, she mumbles into my jacket.

"I-I'm ready. Let's go."

I pull back just enough to look her over and pray to every God out there that she's ready for this. Taking her hand, I lead her across the slippery street.

"Laa-nie Heart, is that you?" I hear a woman slurring her shouted words as we land on the opposite sidewalk. Then I hear Lanie mutter something under her breath, but I don't catch it. I glare up at the drunken woman and I'm relieved to notice she's way too young to be Lanie's mother. This young woman is about Lanie's age.

"Hi, Jillian. How are you?" Lanie's words are clipped, and she keeps walking.

"I'mmmm good. How is you? Who's this? Not your boyfriend obv-obviously," the drunk girl blurts out.

"Obviously," Lanie mimics. "Good to see you, Jillian. Have a good night."

"Always did thinks you was better than us, didn't you, Lanes?"

Jesus, are we going to get into a fight before we even enter the building? Thankfully, Lanie ignores her and drags me into the bar.

Pulling open the door, I immediately have to duck. I may have an inch of clearing before my head hits the drop ceiling. *Shit, I hope we can get a seat soon.* Peering around, I'm surprised by how packed it is.

Lanie leads us through the crowd, yelling over her shoulder as we go. "The Wednesday before Thanksgiving is always crazy because all the kids that left for college are back. Everyone goes out to catch up," she explains.

Walking through the bar, I take note of all the different people here. Young professionals, old farmers, kids that are home from college, the ones who float around, it really isn't that much different than some of the bars at home.

We're halfway through the crowd when Lanie stops so suddenly, I run right into her back, almost knocking her over. I'm about to ask if she's okay when I glance up and notice a woman sitting with her back to the bar, staring straight at Lanie, a look of disgust all over her aging face.

Instinctively, I know it's her. Not because Lanie looks like her, but because I recognize the hatred in this woman's eyes. It's the same loathing Anna had the last time I saw her.

I would imagine in her younger years, Lanie and her mom could have passed as sisters. Now she looks like a woman who has led a hard life of drugs and alcohol. Placing a hand on her shoulder, I lean down to her ear so she can hear me over the noise of the busy bar. "Are you ready, sweetheart?"

My words spark Lanie to life because she moves again. This time, she's dropped my hand, but I work to keep pace with her and keep her within arm's length.

When we reach her mom, Lanie stops a few feet away and surveys our surroundings. As if sensing trouble, the woman to the left vacates her stool, and I guide Lanie to sit. It takes all of five seconds for her mother to start in.

"Well, if it isn't my selfish, piece of shit daughter. Where you been, *kiddo?* Momma could have used some help with the bills the last couple of months, but those assholes up the mountain refuse to tell me where you'd gone. I figured after that Zachary set you straight, you'd stop slutting it up everywhere, but considering who you just walked in with, I'm guessin' I was wrong. Tell me, sir, how much you paying her for tonight?"

I'm beyond pissed. I've never hit a woman before, but I'm seconds away from knocking this bitch out.

Lanie, seeing my hands balled into fists, places her palm on my knee. One shake of her head is all it takes to tell me not to make a move. She'll handle it. Feeling proud of my girl's strength, I place my hand on her lower back in encouragement. To my surprise, she lets her mother continue.

The older woman leers at me. "Name's Laurel. What's yours, handsome?" She holds out her hand.

I stare at it briefly and make a show of placing my hand in my pocket. "My name's Dexter. I'm not the one here to talk to you, though."

"Shit, you got him wrapped up tighter than a willy in a whore house," she spits. "Tell me, did my dear old daughter here tell you she got a man locked up and his son taken away, all because she needed some attention? She got herself in too deep with some guy, then claimed he attacked her. Can you believe that shit? You look like you got money, too. You better watch yourself around the girl who cries wolf, or you might be in jail next."

Unable to control my anger any longer, I lean in with a voice so low and dangerous, it's hard to detect as my own. "If I end up in jail, it'll only be for putting you where you belong."

Lanie pulls me back and ushers me behind her. I know this isn't my fight, but hell if I'm going to sit by while this woman tells straight-up lies.

"Are you done, *Mother*? Or is there any other poison you want to spew my way? This is your one and only chance to get it off your chest. After tonight, we'll never see each other again," Lanie announces with an eerie calm to her voice.

"What? You givin' me ultimatums now, you ungrateful little shit?" Her mother leans in dangerously close and loses her balance on the stool.

Lanie catches her, sitting her upright and moves away quickly.

"Get your slutty little hands off me before I call the cops," Laurel grumbles.

"No ultimatums, Mother. I'm simply telling you, after tonight, you will no longer be welcome in my life."

I'm starting to get nervous at how rigid Lanie's body is, even though her voice remains steadily calm.

"News flash, smart-ass. That's not how family works. You're stuck with me just like I'm stuck with you." Laurel shoots an evil grin our way.

"Not my family. I'll ask one more time. Is there anything else, anything at all you want to say to me?" Laurel stares at her incredulously.

"Nope, I got nothin' to say to you that you ain't already heard."

Lanie nods her head, and Laurel is clearly thinking this is the end of their conversation.

"That's fine, Mother. I do, however, have one question for you. *Why?* Why have you hated me so much all my life? What could I have possibly ever done to you?" A small speck of vulnerability creeps into Lanie's voice.

Laurel's face goes red, and she slams back the rest of her beer. Laurel leans in, so she's almost nose to nose with Lanie. "Why would I ever love the whore that killed my sister? My best friend. Why would I ever love you after that?"

Lanie's face goes white. Clearly, she has no idea what her mother's talking about.

"What are you saying?" I interject. "Lanie was two when your sister died."

Seething and through clenched teeth, Laurel spits, "You think you know so much? You and your little slut here—"

I interrupt her. "I'm going to tell you one time and one time only. Do not disrespect Lanie in front of me again, or you will not like the outcome. I have the resources to make your life a living hell. Don't test me on that."

Laurel stands quickly, this time yelling. "You think I'm not already in hell, you asshole? I've been in hell for twenty-two years. If this needy, whiny, problem-causing bitch didn't get an ear infection, my sister wouldn't have gone out that night." She pushes a finger into Lanie's chest, punctuating each word with a hard poke. "My sister died because of you. It's your fault. Everything has always been your fault."

Before I can stop her, she shoves Lanie with both hands, sending her flying backward off the stool. I catch her just before her head hits the ground.

When she's upright, Lanie waves me off and stands face-to-face with her mother. "I was a child, Mother. A child incapable of caring for myself. You're the one who brought me into this world. Therefore, it was your responsibility to care for me, not Auntie's. If I had to guess, I'd say you were probably too drunk to drive to the store. That's why Auntie went out that night. Am I right? That seems the most plausible, and that would make it your fault, not mine. Even if you weren't drinking, you, Mother, were the adult. You failed me in every way possible, not the other way around." She pauses to take a breath.

"When you're old and alone, you remember that. Remember that you once had a daughter who tried everything to get you to love her. Who tried everything for you to notice her. When you're alone and dying, you remember that you did this to yourself. Not me. Do not contact me again. Do not contact the McDowells again, and do not contact GG again, or I'll be the gum on your shoe. You think you're in hell now? It'll be nothing compared to what I will do if you so much as breathe our names again. That's not a promise, Mother. That there is a threat."

Lanie grabs my hand just as I notice Laurel raising a beer bottle in the air. *Fuck no, not again.* I lunge at Lanie, covering her body with my own just as the bottle crashes down on my head.

~

A few stitches, and many hours later, we pull back into the McDowells' property. Lanie maneuvers the long driveway like she's done it a thousand times before. She probably has. We haven't talked much since arriving at the hospital. Lanie was deep in thought, and I figure after tonight, she probably has a lot to sort through.

I always thought my mother was evil for leaving, but after experiencing Laurel tonight, I realize she likely did me a favor.

After putting the car in park, Lanie turns to me. "I'll help you in and get you settled, then I'm going back to Julia's house." Her voice is strong, but subdued.

"Do you want me to come with you?" I ask, more hopeful than I should be. "I'm sure Sylvie would be fine getting up with the kids." It's too dark for me to read her face, but I sense the answer before she speaks.

"No, thank you. I'll be fine, and Tate will be sad if you're not here when he wakes up."

I sigh because she's right.

"Jules and I will be back in the morning to help get everything ready. I-I'm going to need some time, Dex. I need to fix myself before I know what I'm capable of giving."

I feel the sadness of her words deep in my chest. "Okay,

Lanes. Just know, we're waiting for you whenever you're ready."

I want to tell her how much I love her but worry she isn't in the right headspace, so instead, I tell her a different truth. "I'm proud of you, sweetheart. You were so strong tonight. You never cease to amaze me, Lanie, but tonight I saw a strength I think you've had hidden away for a long time. I'm so incredibly proud of you."

"Thank you," she chokes out. "Let's get you inside."

True to her word, Lanie gets me settled inside, then leaves. As soon as she's gone, my spot on the couch is overrun with visitors. Every single adult in the house is crowded, perched, nestled, and squished in all around me, asking for details. Once I've finally quenched their thirst for gossip, I send them to bed and lie awake for hours wondering where Lanie and I will land when the dust settles.

CHAPTER 36

LANIE

"I cannot, I repeat, *cannot* believe you got them all here behind my back, Jules." I'm slightly hysterical, but when your best friend continually goes behind your back, I think a little hysterics are warranted.

Julia was also conspicuously asleep when I got home last night. And just happened to have Charlie in bed with her this morning so I couldn't ram her room and start yelling. "And, by the way, using Charlie as a shield is low, even for you."

"Hey. He's sick. I can't help it if he needed some mommy snuggles that just happened to save me from your wrath for a few hours. Listen, I already told you, I'm not going to apologize. This is for your own good. Now, go get ready, we have to leave soon. Mom's waiting for us."

I roll my eyes but stomp past her room to get in the shower anyway. Shutting the bathroom door, I hear Julia's phone going off like fireworks, and I know it's that damn group text no one will tell me about. I'm really starting to hate them all.

Dex

MLM Recovery Plan

Dexter: How is she this morning? She hasn't replied to any of my texts.

Trevor: Just how many have you sent this morning? Give her some space, dude.

Dexter: It doesn't matter. I just need to know she's okay. Last night was rough.

Preston: Just how *rough* was it???

Colton: Rough Rider?

Ashton: Rough God Goes Riding?

Easton: Van Morrison? Nice.

Halton: Rough waters?

Colton: Ash, you lose. That sucks.

Halton: I hear you do, too, dude.

Dexter: Seriously, Preston, get these dickheads out of here. I need real help. Real advice. Not all this shit.

Preston: Now you know how we've felt for the last 9 months, dude.

Dexter: Pres, I'm begging you, please. I'm on my last nerve right now. I swear to God, I think she is going to run. I can't handle this all, please.

Trevor: Pres, he's desperate.

Preston: Okay, okay. Sorry, Westbrooks, you're getting the boot.

Colton: Wait? Seriously? I wanted to see what happens.

Trevor: You will when you get an invite to the wedding. That's how you'll know MLM worked. Buh-bye, Westbrooks.

Julia: All right, asshats. She's in the shower. We'll be over shortly. Dex, she's a little snippy today, but I think we can handle it. Don't pressure her about plans or the future, though. She still has a lot of shit to work through.

Dexter: Okay, thanks, Jules.

Julia: Shit, gotta go. She's after my phone again. FYI, hide all your phones. She's on to MLM and is making it her mission to find out what's going on.

Dexter: What??? NO. Do not let her do that. It'll ruin her last surprise.

Preston: Such a romantic.

Dexter: Shut it, get me everyone's phones, now, and I mean everyone's. You can all have them back when Lanie leaves.

Preston: Wtf, you're not serious?

Dexter: 100% Hand them over.

―

Lanie

"If you won't give me your phone, at least tell me the gist of what the messages say?" I've succumbed to begging, and I'm not ashamed of it.

"Lanes, I already told you I can't. When the time is right, you'll know everything. Just be patient." Jules attempts a soothing tone, but I know it's crap. "Now, grab the stuff from the kitchen. The car's running, so I'm going to head out with Charlie. The poor guy still had a fever all night. I'm not sure he'll make it through dinner."

"Aw, Charlie-o. I'm sorry. Anytime you need to leave just let me know. I'm happy to skip out whenever you are."

"Yeah, I'm sure you are." Jules rolls her eyes and walks out into the frigid mountain air.

Damn, I already forgot how cold it is up here. I'm really loving the weather in North Carolina a lot more than I thought I would.

That's not the only thing you're loving. Ugh, even my inner voice is ganging up on me.

Twenty minutes later, we're walking into the very full

McDowell home. Mimi is in heaven, having always envisioned a large family. The *boys,* as we're now calling the Westbrook clan, are on the couch with Pawpaw and Tate. Dex is nowhere to be found. Mimi and Sylvie are flying around the kitchen, laughing like they've been friends for years. The entire scene makes my heart happy.

Did I bring all this happiness to their doorstep?

"Mom," Julia whisper-yells behind me. "Charlie still isn't feeling well, and he fell asleep on the way over. I'm going to put him down in Lanie's room. Is that okay?"

"Poor little guy," Mimi and Sylvie say in unison. "Of course, of course," Mimi starts, "is that all right with you, Sylvie?"

Sylvie must have slept in my old room last night.

"Of course, dear, whatever you need. If anything's in your way, just push it to the side."

"Thank you, Mrs. Westbrook—"

Sylvie tsks Jules mid-sentence, "None of that. Sylvie will do just fine." She smiles warmly at Julia, and I just watch the scene unfold.

"You got it, thank you, Sylvie." Julia winks at me on her way to the stairs.

Is she feeling the happiness around us, too? Has it always been this way, or is it different? Am I different?

I have all these thoughts running through my head, confusing me at every turn, so I don't notice when Dex comes up behind me with Harper in his arms.

"Happy Thanksgiving," he says, making me jump.

Not to be outdone, Harper uses her big girl lungs. "Happapapa bababba, Momma!"

We both freeze, and the entire house instantly goes quiet.

I casually glance around, knowing everyone is waiting for my freak out. Hell, I am, too. However, it doesn't come.

Looking up at Dex, I say, "Happy Thanksgiving to you, too. How's your head? I'm so sorry about my mother."

"I'm not, Lanie. For once, I was freaking there for you, on time no less. I might even get my man-card back now."

He winks just as Harper starts screeching, "Momma, Momma, Momma," and holding her arms out to me.

Okay, now I'm freaking out a little. Once could be played off as baby babble, but four times? I'm starting to sweat, not sure if I'm ready for this when Mimi comes to the rescue.

"For now, all you have to do is pick her up and reply 'Lanie' whenever she says Momma. If at some point you both agree that Momma is a name you want to take on," she winks, "it'll be easy enough to correct. Don't tell her no, just reply with 'Lanie'."

"But we haven't, I mean, we're not ready, we, talked, haven't ... Geez, I don't know what I'm trying to say." I drop my head to my hands, feeling like I could cry. "Why am I so messed up?"

"You," Pawpaw says, pointing right at my heart, "are not messed up. I thought we talked about this, Lanie. You're a good girl who was given a raw deal. It's up to you now to make your life right. Make your life what you want it to be. You took the first step last night. Now follow through," he says, kissing my forehead in greeting. "Now, give me this little pumpkin pie. Who do we have here?"

"That's Harper, Pawpaw. You can tell because she has a little freckle on the left side of her nose," I tell him.

"What? She does?" Dex asks incredulously. He puts his face right up to Harper's. "No, shh– shiplap, she does."

"I see our Lanie girl has gotten into your skin there, sonny. No one says shiplap unless they're head over heels with my girl."

I recognize the voice immediately.

"GG," I exclaim at the same time Dex says, "Miss Rosa?"

"GG?" Dex asks. "Miss Rosa is GG?"

"Good grief, son. You need a lesson every time you're

300

coming to visit or what? Yes, I'm GG, but you don't go callin' me that 'til you've earned it, you hear?"

Dex nods and chuckles at her antics.

I know it's a lot to take in. I love GG, but she's a piece of work.

"Now, get over here and help my old ass to the table. I'm hungry and I need to get to the mountain soon."

"Yes, ma'am." Dex salutes her, and she winks. She likes him already.

Dinner goes smoothly with everyone joking and having a great time until Mimi stands to make an announcement. Clinking her glass with a spoon, she waits for conversations to die down. "Can I have everyone's attention? Pete and I have something we'd like to share."

Julia and I make eye contact across the table and realize neither of us knows what this is about.

"Originally, we thought we'd just be sharing the news with our girls, but now with all of you here, we couldn't be happier to be sharing it with the whole family." It doesn't escape me that Mimi refers to Dex and the Westbrooks as family. "After a lot of thought, Pete and I have decided to finally retire."

"What?" Julia and I yell in unison.

"Now, girls," Mimi starts, "you both knew this day was coming."

"What does this entail, exactly?" Like a cartoon, we all see Julia's brain spinning with possibilities.

"Well, for starters, we have a buyer for our practice, so we'll begin phasing out after the New Year. Once that's finished, probably in early spring, we'll work with a realtor to put the house up for rent when we aren't here unless Julia decides she would like to take it over."

Julia raises her hands and shakes her head.

"We just aren't ready to let it go yet. You girls grew up here. We like the idea of grandkids having a place like this to visit. Towns like ours build character and instill empathy. It's a good place for everyone to spend some time." She makes a pointed glare at a few of the Westbrook boys, and Sylvie laughs.

"Why are you going to rent the house?" I ask, dreading the answer.

"Oh, Lanie. You've always known we want to retire to the beach house. In the last couple of years, we've been getting it ready for us to live there at least half the year," she reminds me.

"So, you're moving to the Outer Banks?" Julia asks with a wicked grin.

"That's right," Pawpaw says. "I can't wait to wake up to the sounds of the ocean every day." He really does seem excited, but I can't help the feeling I'm missing something when I see the glances being tossed around between Mimi, Pawpaw, and Jules. This is a lot to take in, and I'm not sure what to make of it.

~

Sitting at the large table long after dessert has been served, I take the time to observe my surroundings. Mimi and Pawpaw's house is the same as it's always been. A comfort to my chaos. A safe haven in my world of hurt. They're the same loving people they've always been, opening their home to people that were strangers just yesterday. Scanning the group now, we look like a family. A large, noisy, messy, chaotic, slightly dysfunctional family.

My family, the voice in my head says, not sounding so traitorous these days.

I feel a small hand pulling on my shirt, and I look down to see Tate. He seems nervous and unsure of himself. Not at all the kid we've come to love the last few months. "Hey, Tate-o-nator. What's up?"

He shrugs his little shoulders, and I excuse myself from the table. Dex watches on with a nervous expression, but I tell him we're okay. Walking Tate back to my little slice of heaven at the window seat, we both get comfy.

"What's up, big guy? You don't seem so happy." I try to sound upbeat, but something about his posture has the hairs on my neck sticking up.

Without looking at me, he hands me a big sheet of paper. I know instantly it's our family portrait he drew at school. I swallow, trying to fight back the tears. *Why is he giving this to me?*

"In case you don't come home, I wanted you to have this. You'll always be my family, too, Lanie."

I stop fighting the tears and let them fall. "Oh, Tate, I'm sorry if I made you worry. I'm coming back, remember? I promised you," I whisper, holding him close.

"But you might not stay. I heard my dad talking to Uncle Trevor on the phone last night. He was super upset, too. If you can't be my forever, can you promise to always call on my birthday?"

I'm crying so hard now I can't breathe. Dex was upset. Tate wants me to be their forever.

What the hell am I going to do?

CHAPTER 37

DEX

It's been two weeks since we arrived home from Vermont. I haven't pushed Lanie, I know the conversation with her mother and then the McDowells dropping the bomb of their retirement on her has been a lot to process.

The first week, she was definitely subdued, retreating to her room most nights as soon as the kids were in bed. This week, I feel as though something's changed. She's welcoming my affection, sometimes sleeping in my bed so I can hold her, sometimes staying in her own room. I try to take comfort in the small victories.

Lanie has promised Tate that she will be here for Christmas, so I've decided it's time to get MLM ready for her. On my way home from the office, I stopped at a little booksmith on the outskirts of town and told him what I want. He took all the copies of the texts I have saved since the first MLM group text went out, and I explained I would like space left at the end of each day for me to handwrite a note. If he's confused by my outlandish request, he doesn't say so. He simply tells me it'll be done in a week. As far as I know, Lanie hasn't made any decisions yet, and to be honest, I'm scared of pushing the issue.

Pulling up to the house, I notice Sylvie's here. She parked in front of the garage so I can't pull in. *That's strange. Did I forget she was coming?* Parking beside her, I make my way to the front door, letting myself in.

"What the hell? Lanie?" I yell when I notice Harper sitting in the middle of the entryway. Looking past her, I see Sara sitting farther down in the hallway. "Lanie?" I yell again, picking up Harper and making my way to Sara.

This isn't like Lanie at all. Just as I'm about to panic, Trevor steps out of the hallway bathroom. *What the fuck is going on?* He points to Harper, then Sara, then himself. That's when I notice they have matching red shirts on.

"Trev, you're worrying me. What's going on and where's Lanie?" He doesn't answer, just points again to Harper, Sara, then himself.

Following his fingers, I see they have words printed on them. Harper's says 'The'. Sara's says 'Thing' and Trevor's says 'About'.

Trevor takes Harper from my arms and nods down the hall. I don't know where he comes from, but Preston steps forward, taking Sara from my arms, and I notice his shirt says 'Lanie'. I'm sweating now. I might even be trembling.

What kind of man fucking trembles?

Preston senses my hesitation and puts a hand on my shoulder. He doesn't say anything, but the grin exploding from his face puts me at ease, somewhat. He nudges me to enter the kitchen farther, where I find Sylvie. Her shirt says *Is*. She gives me a kiss on the cheek and turns me toward Tate. He's so happy he's bouncing on his toes as I walk to him. My heart rate picks up, and my stomach does a stupid little flip. Placing a hand on my chest, I see Tate's shirt says 'She'.

Holy fuck, I think I'm having a heart attack.

Tate propels himself forward, and I have no choice but to catch him. "I love you, Dad," he says right before he squirms to get away.

Setting him down, he turns me to face the playroom where Lanie is standing with her back to me. My heart is pounding so loudly in my ears, I might be deaf. I am definitely shaking now, and the sweat dripping down my spine reminds me how much I want this to be real. How much I need this to be real.

"Lanie, sweetheart, you're killing me here. I'm about to have a heart attack, I think. Please, baby, put me out of my misery."

She slowly turns her head, tears flowing down her cheeks, but she's wearing a smile that could light up the darkest of days.

"Lanie, please, baby."

Winking, she turns her body. When I see the word 'Stays,' I run to her, holding her damp cheeks in my hands.

"I need to hear you say it, sweetheart. Tell me this means what I think it does."

Lanie's still crying, and the splash that hits my arm tells me I am, too. She nods her head through her tears, but it isn't enough.

"No, Lanie. I need you to say it out loud. I need to hear it."

Through a sob, she grants me my greatest wish. "I'm staying, Dex. I'm staying for as long as you'll have me."

"As what, Lanie? What are you staying here as?" *Please say mine. Please, please be mine.*

With a wink, her sass hits me square in the chest. "What do you want me to be?"

I growl just before capturing her lips with mine. Every time I taste her, she's sweeter than the last. This kiss will forever be my favorite. It's the first one where I know she isn't going anywhere. The first one that marks her as mine forever.

Pulling back, I search her face. "Mine, Lanie. I want you to be mine forever."

Before I can finish, Tate comes tearing into the room. "Mine too, Lanie. Mine too!" he says, jumping up and down.

Behind me, I see all the red shirts lined up. *The Thing About Lanie Is She Stays.*

"She stays," I read.

"She stays," Lanie repeats.

This is a day I will never forget.

~

MLM Accomplished!

Dexter: I did it. Lanie's mine. She's staying forever. She is officially my girl.

Trevor: I'm literally standing two feet from you.

Preston: I'm blocking you now.

Loki: Good to hear, man. Happy for you.

Dexter: Loki, you're back?

Loki: I am, and I have about 4,000 texts to go through.

Preston: Don't bother. All you need to know is he got the girl.

Julia: But their story is a pretty good read if you want to spend a few hours catching up.

Julia: Congrats, Dex. I'm happy for you both.

Dexter: I know I've driven you all crazy this year, but thank you for standing by me. All these messages will be worth it when Lanie opens her Christmas present.

~

Christmas is in a few days, but Lanie hasn't been feeling well. I've spent days trying to get her to go to a doctor, but she refuses. She keeps telling me she gets this way sometimes before her period, but she has a slight fever, and the upset stomach is becoming more frequent, so I have to call in the big guns.

Putting the phone on speaker, I walk into the family room where Lanie's resting on the couch.

"Lanie!" Julia yells, startling us both.

"Jesus, Jules, you don't have to yell," I say, rubbing my ear.

"Whatever. Lanie, do you hear me?" Julia asks.

"Yes, Jules. I think they can hear you all the way uptown." Lanie's snark just proves she isn't feeling well.

"Good, then you listen to me."

"And me," Mimi chimes in.

"Me too," Pete adds.

Lanie groans. "I'm listening."

"Dex tells us you haven't been feeling well, and no matter what line of shit you're feeding him, you and I both know it isn't *normal*. We've made you a doctor's appointment, and Sylvie is on her way to watch the kids. You are going. Do you understand?" Julia scolds.

"Fine, *mom*." Lanie pouts like a sullen teenager.

"Good. Dex? I want you in the exam room with her, then call me back. Make sure you put it on speakerphone, so I can hear, too."

"Julia, I'm not a child. I'm perfectly capable of going to a doctor's appointment on my own."

"No can do, luvs. You lost that chance when you wouldn't go to the doctor in the first place." Once again, Julia confirms my suspicions. She's crazy. And I'm happy she's on our side.

Lanie sighs, but puts up no further argument.

∽

Sitting in the exam room, I feel anxiety settling in my chest. We've been here an hour, and no one has told us anything yet. The nurses have taken her bloodwork and a urine sample; since then, we've just been waiting. I'm also learning that Julia has the patience of a two year old.

"Have they come back yet? What the hell is taking so long?" she asks.

"Jules, you asked less than five minutes ago. You'll hear them come in. Just try to relax, please. You aren't making this any better with your impatience," I inform her.

"Well, excuse me, asshat. I'm not there, and I'm worried." She truly sounds upset, and I feel like the asshat she called me.

"Jules, I'm fine, I promise. I'm sure they're just backed up. We did get squeezed into the schedule today," Lanie tries to appease her friend.

There's a knock on the door, but we only hear Julia. "About freaking time."

"Julia," I hiss. "If you don't behave yourself, I'll put you on mute."

"Don't you dare," she replies angrily. "I'll stay quiet, I promise."

"Ms. Heart? I'm Dr. Bailey. It's nice to meet you. Let's have a peek, shall we?" The doctor lays Lanie down and starts manipulating her stomach. "Lanie? Would it be okay if I took a look at your scar tissue?"

Lanie's eyes dart around the room. "Um, sure. I-I was attacked a couple of years ago." She tells her story, and I try like hell to stay calm. The doctor listens patiently, nodding in understanding the entire time.

When Lanie's finished, the doctor covers her back up. "All right, Lanie. Is there any chance you're pregnant?"

I watch Lanie swallow her sadness.

"No. The attack made pregnancy impossible for me," Lanie explains.

"I see. Can you tell me where you were treated after the attack? And would you be willing to have the records sent here for me to see?"

"What for? Is something serious going on with Lanie?" Julia blurts from the phone screen, thoroughly confusing the doctor.

"Sorry, Dr. Bailey. That's my best friend, Julia. She insisted on being involved," Lanie explains, embarrassed.

Dr. Bailey smiles. "I see. It's always good to have people around who care. To answer your question, Julia, no. I don't believe Lanie is in any danger. However, with injuries like hers, I like to make sure all my bases are covered."

"I was treated at Dartmouth Hospital in New Hampshire. I grew up in Vermont. That's where it happened. Dartmouth was the closest hospital with a trauma center," Lanie explains before Julia interrupts again.

"Dr. Bailey? My dad is friends with the Chief of Medicine there. Have Dex text me what she needs, and I'll make sure you have it within the hour."

Dr. Bailey smiles. "She doesn't mess around, does she?"

That's the understatement of the century. "No, she doesn't. Sometimes it's a blessing, and sometimes it's a curse." I glance down at the phone then, thankful Jules had already hung up, presumably to call her dad.

Dr. Bailey gives me the information on where to send the records, has Lanie sign a release, and leaves the room. Fifteen minutes after sending it to Julia, she calls back.

"It's all set. Dr. Bailey should have it in her mailbox."

"How the hell did you do that so fast?" I ask.

"Never underestimate the determination of a worried father. Dad had his buddy paged out of surgery, and voilà, Dr. Bailey has Lanie's records."

"Remind me never to get on your bad side, Jules. I have a feeling you can be scary as hell." Glancing at Lanie, I find her asleep. "Jules," I whisper, "Lanie fell asleep again. I'll let you know when the doctor comes back."

"Okay, thanks."

The wait is excruciating, so I'm thankful when I get a text from Preston.

MLM Accomplished!
Preston: How's our girl?
Dexter: Sleeping. She's had bloodwork taken and given a urine sample but no results yet. The doctor was waiting for her medical records from Vermont.
Preston: You doing okay?
Dexter: I'm fine. I'm sure it's just the flu, but the doctors have to cover all the bases because of her prior injuries.
Trevor: Hang in there, man. I'm headed to your house now with pizza and to give Sylvie a hand with the kids.
Loki: I just walked in your door.
Preston: I'll bring the beer and some dessert for the kids.
Dexter: Thanks, guys.
Julia: Good job, boys. I'm proud of you.
Preston: (Rolling eye emoji)

Almost an hour later, Dr. Bailey knocks on the door, waking Lanie. "Hi, Lanie, how are you feeling?" she asks.

"Tired and nauseous," Lanie responds.

Dr. Bailey just smiles at her. "I'd like you to meet my colleague, Dr. Price. We just had a lengthy call with your team at Dartmouth. I have to say, they all took a liking to you. You have a pretty big team of fans up there," Dr. Bailey tells us, but is interrupted once again by Julia.

Why the hell did I call her back?

"Is Lanie okay? You're killing me here, Doc!"

As I said, patience is not a strong suit for Jules.

Laughing, Dr. Bailey answers Julia's rude outburst. "Yes, Julia. Your Lanie is going to be just fine. As I was saying, this is Dr. Price. He's our resident reproductive specialist."

"Hi, Lanie," he greets her kindly, shaking our hands.

Lanie remains silent. I'm not sure if it's nausea or fear, but I reach for her hand and squeeze anyway.

"I just want to take a quick look around with an ultrasound. Is that all right with you?"

"Yes," she says skeptically. "Are you sure everything's okay?"

"I believe so. Just give me a minute so I can get a feel for what kind of internal damage you have."

Lanie nods her head, but I'm so confused, and fear for her well being is creeping in.

"Why do you need to check her internal damage for the flu? Is this something we should be worried about?" I ask him, sweat dotting my brow. I only just got Lanie. I can't lose her now.

"Are you the husband?" Dr. Price asks.

"Boyfriend," I reply.

Putting his gloves on, he smiles. "I'll be able to answer all of your questions after I have a look around. Just give me a few minutes."

He drops a big glob of blue goo onto Lanie's stomach. I immediately have flashbacks to doing this with Anna. What a different feeling it was with her.

"Okay, let's get my bearings ... and ri-ight here ..." He doesn't get to finish.

I've seen that before. Then he twists the angle of the ultrasound wand, and my vision goes blurry.

"Holy shit," I say.

Julia starts screeching in the background, "What? What's wrong? Dexter, answer me, damn it."

Lanie is silent, she doesn't know what I'm seeing.

The doctor glances up and smiles. "Lanie? Congratulations. You're pregnant. With twins."

My world does go black then. Luckily, I was sitting against a wall because I came to with a nurse scowling at me, waving a smelling salt stick in front of my face. "I swear, in this day and age, you'd think you men would have learned to compose yourselves."

I immediately sit up straighter, staring at Lanie, who's white as a ghost.

"But ... but the doctors told me the chances of pregnancy were so small there wasn't even a point in putting a number to it. This can't be right." She's searching the room for an explanation, but I've seen those blips three times before. They don't lie.

"Having seen your initial reports after the attack, Lanie, I would have agreed with your Dartmouth team. I don't believe they gave you false information there. These really are miracle babies. There's no medical evidence to support why they were able to implant, but they did."

Hardly able to hear the doctor, I finally come to my senses. Placing the screeching Julia on mute, then waving the nurse away, I climb into the bed next to Lanie, balancing so I don't fall off the edge. I need to be close to her.

Clearing his throat, unhappy it seems with our new seating arrangements, he begins talking to Lanie again. "Now, Lanie, I have to be honest, this will be a high-risk pregnancy due to the internal damage and scarring you have. However, after reviewing all of your records and seeing for myself, I don't see any reason you won't be able to carry the babies close to full term. That also means you'll have to adhere to all our guidelines exactly and commit one hundred percent to bed rest when that time comes. Unfortunately for you, bed rest will arrive much earlier than it would have under normal circumstances. I know this is a lot to process, but I want to let you know, I am happy to be your doctor if you are comfortable. I'll get you through this pregnancy."

Dr. Bailey speaks next, "Lanie, Dr. Price is one of the top doctors in this field. I firmly believe in sticking with him to offer you the best chance at a happy, healthy pregnancy. Of course, you're welcome to get second opinions or go to another practice if you're more comfortable."

Lanie and I cut her off at the same time, so I tell Lanie to go first.

"I-I think we'd like to stay with Dr. Price, right?" she asks, staring at me.

"Absolutely." I kiss her forehead because I need to connect to her. Internally, I'm so happy I could burst. Externally, I curb my reaction, unsure of how Lanie feels about all of this yet.

"That's great to hear," Dr. Price responds. "As I said, this will be a rather tricky pregnancy, so starting now, I don't want you lifting anything heavier than twenty pounds. No strenuous workouts," he raises his head, "sexual activity is fine at this stage. I just wouldn't suggest anything crazy."

Lanie blushes as red as I have ever seen her.

"I would also like to see you every two weeks to start, but know that it will become weekly in a month or two. Do you have any questions for me?"

Lanie shakes her head, still in shock.

"Ah, how far along is she? When are the babies due?" I ask.

Lanie's head whirls to the doctor, realizing she wants those answers, too.

"I'd say, judging from the ultrasound, you are about four weeks along, Lanie. Making your due date around September 17th. However, we won't let you go past thirty-eight weeks. You'll likely go into labor much earlier than that, though. Also, something to be aware of, with all the internal scarring, you won't be able to deliver naturally. You'll need a C-section. The good news with that is our plastic surgeon may be able to lessen some of the scarring around your lower abdomen if you wish. That's nothing that needs to be decided any time soon. I just wanted to make you aware. Do you have any other questions?" He glances from Lanie to me.

"Doctor? Ah, I know you said this is a high-risk pregnancy. Will these complications put Lanie's life in danger?"

He places a comforting hand on my shoulder. "Lanie's a fortunate woman. I can honestly say I don't anticipate her risk to be much higher than a comparable pregnancy of multiples. With her scarring, I'd like to err on the side of caution. I know this is scary, but I do have confidence in a positive outcome for you all."

After shaking his hand, and then Dr. Bailey's, they leave the room.

"Lanie? Sweetheart, how do you feel about all this?" I ask her, unmuting Julia at the same time.

"How the fuck do you think she feels, Dex? Jesus, that was a stupid question." Without even hesitating, I hang up on Julia and turn my phone off. I warned her.

Staring into Lanie's eyes, I see her confusion. I feel her excitement, and I sense her hesitation.

"Baby, everything's going to be okay, I promise you. Lanie, I'm so in love with those little peanuts growing inside of you already. I believe this is a good thing, sweetheart. We're growing from a family of five to a family of seven in just a few short months." *Holy shit. Five kids under the age of seven.* "Tate is going to be over the moon."

"Holy hot pocket." She graces me with a smile I've never seen before.

Returning her happiness, I decide this smile of all her different ones is my favorite. This smile tells me she's whole, she's happy, and we're going to be just fine.

CHAPTER 38

LANIE

I wake up Christmas morning and run to the bathroom. Whoever called this morning sickness needs a swift kick to the throat. My morning sickness has no sense of time and happens all hours of the day. As I'm hovering over the toilet bowl, Dex comes up behind me as he does every day, placing my hair in a ponytail and rubbing my back until it subsides.

"Why are you up so early?" he asks, knowing the sickness never hits until I wake up.

"I was hoping to get the vomiting out of the way before the kids wake up and run to see if Santa came. I don't want to miss that."

Setting the cookies and carrots out last night with Tate was the beginning of many new memories I'm making with him. I'll cherish this first Christmas forever, though.

"We could have held them off, you know?" He hands me a glass of water and adds toothpaste to my toothbrush for when I'm ready.

"No way. This is my first Christmas with my own family. I will not let a little morning sickness ruin it for me—" My words are cut short when I have to fling my head back to the toilet bowl. Ten minutes later, I'm finally ready to brush my teeth, just in time, too, because Tate comes bouncing into our room as I finish.

"It's Christmas, Lanie. It's Christmas," he screams.

You can't feel anything but excitement when a child has such an innocent look of happiness on his face. I never understood the excitement people spoke of when describing the feeling of Christmas morning. Right now, though, I do. I finally feel the magic of Christmas morning. Today, I'm living it, and I don't plan to ever let this feeling go.

∽

The day goes by in a flash. We FaceTime with Mimi and Pawpaw, then with Julia and Charlie. Trevor and Loki stop by in the afternoon with gifts for the kids, and we FaceTime with the Westbrooks after dinner.

I learn Dexter usually has Christmas with the Westbrooks, but after talking, he decided he wanted to have our first Christmas together, just us, our family. I melted a little at the sentiment of it, and the Westbrooks agreed as long as they got a redo with us next week.

Around eight, the presents have all been opened and the kids are in bed. "I think we can clean up this mess tomorrow, right? I'm too tired to even think about it right now." These pregnancy hormones are no joke.

Dexter laughs but agrees. He starts a fire in the fireplace, and we snuggle in on the new sofa I got him for Christmas. This one is massive, and it's made of a soft fabric you can't help but get lost in. All seven of us will be able to cozy up on this one for years to come.

Sitting, Dex pulls me closer onto his side. Since learning I was pregnant, with twins no less, he's been fiercely protective. So over the top protective we had to have a conversation yesterday about his hovering. Thankfully, he took it in stride.

"I've got one last present for you, sweetheart. Do you want it?"

Feeling guilty because he's already given me so much today, I try to contain my smile, but it breaks through anyway. "I do," I say, clapping my hands together like a child.

Dex gets up and goes behind the fourteen-foot Christmas tree I insisted we had to have. Joining me back on the couch, he places a hefty package in my hands. It's shaped like a book, and I can't imagine what it could be. To say he spoiled me this Christmas is an understatement. I don't think I've had this many gifts in all my birthdays and Christmases combined.

"Go ahead, open it," he encourages, leaning back into the couch with a satisfied smile.

I do as he asks and gasp as I run my fingers over the leather I find inside. Taking it gently out of the box, I turn it over in my hands. Embossed on the luxurious leather front is *MLM, the story of us*. Looking at him, I see all the love he has directed at me. Carefully, I open the cover and laugh as I see the very first entry:

Dexter: Day 1 of MLM: Mission in process. LED floodlights are being installed in her room as we speak. She never has to worry about the lights again.

Preston: It's a little early in the day for word games. What's MLM?

Julia: Obviously, it's Make Lanie Mine. Should I expect these updates daily?

Trevor: Who has the 802 number?

Trevor: Also, little bit creeper-ish here, man. What happened to chocolate and flowers?

Julia: A guy gives me flowers and chocolate, and I'll kick him in the taint all the way back to his car.

Trevor: Noted. Again, who is 802?

Dexter: 802 is Lanie's best friend, Julia. Julia, meet the guys; Trevor, Preston, and Loki.

Preston: Is she hot? The friend?

Julia: Another douche-canoe? Come on, Dex. I thought you were better than this.

Trevor: I think I'm in love.

Loki: I'll be MIA for a couple of months. I'll be on the lookout for my invite to the wedding.

Dexter: Be safe, man.

Trevor: Check in if you can.

Preston: If Julia's shooting me down, Loki, will you be my date to Dexter's wedding? Be safe, bud. We'll be thinking of you.

Julia: Definitely missing something. But hey, be safe!

Loki: Take care of the girl. Guys, take care of Dex. Julia? Hell, good luck!

Trevor: Will do. Dex, keep us updated.

Preston: What's step two, lover boy?

Dexter: I'm making dinner tonight.

Trevor: Jesus, don't burn the place down.

Dexter: Your confidence in me is overwhelming.

Preston: Dinner, got it. What else? Doll, do you have any suggestions? I think it's going to take more than dinner and some floodlights to win over your girl.

Julia: I'm going to assume you're calling one of the guys doll and not me. If you're talking to me, watch your balls when we meet in person.

Preston: Noted.

Preston: So, any suggestions?

Trevor: Dex, lead with your heart. The rest will follow.

Julia: Get Maria to stay!

Dexter: Will do.

Preston: Who the fuck is Maria?

At the bottom of the page, I notice Dexter's neat, sprawling handwriting.

This is the day I decided to make you mine. Not because I had the need to own you, but because I knew my life would never be complete again without you in it. This is the story of how I eventually won you over. This is also a promise to never take you for granted. Thank you for choosing us as your family, Lanie. I love you.

"Day one?" I glance over at him. "Just how long did you harass our friends for?" Without letting him answer, I flip to the back and see Day 252. "Dexter, you did not?"

"I did, and I'm not ashamed of it either." he replies, crossing his arms over his broad chest.

Knowing I won't able to sleep until I've read it, I lean into Dexter and read through two hundred and fifty-two days of our love story. Sometimes laughing, sometimes crying, all of it having an effect on my heart. Reaching the end, I realize it has a false back.

"What's this, Dex?" I run my fingers over a thin, blue ribbon sticking out of a small, square flap in the back of the book.

"Open it," he tells me.

Pulling the ribbon, all the air in my lungs comes out in a whoosh. Attached to the silky, red fabric that says *'Lanie, will you marry me?'* is the most beautiful oval-shaped solitaire diamond ring I've ever seen. Lifting my gaze from the book, I watch as Dex drops to his knee in front of me.

"Before you, Lanie, I was sure true love didn't exist. I thought I was content living my life for my kids, never opening my heart to anyone again. Then you waltzed in here with a sass I hadn't known I was missing in my life. Slowly, you healed my broken little family, and nothing would make me happier than to officially make you a part of the family you saved." He pauses, still holding my hand. "Before you answer, you should know, this was a group effort. The day after your little T-shirt stunt, Mimi, Pete, Julia, and all the guys went with me via FaceTime and helped me pick out this ring. There was a lot of negotiating that went into it. In the end, we all decided this was the one for you. So, tell me, Lanie, will marry me and be our forever?"

Sniffling, I flop down on the floor with Dex. "You have something backward, Dex. I didn't heal your family. You were never broken, just bent a little. You guys saved me when I didn't know I could be saved. You gave me courage when I felt weak. You gave me confidence when I thought that part of me was lost forever. You gave me love when I didn't know I could accept it. You, Dex, made me whole, and there is nothing I want more than to become your wife."

Dexter doesn't wait a minute more to place the ring on my slightly swollen finger and kisses me hard. I'm pulled from the moment when I hear cheering and screaming and possibly crying.

"What the heck is that?"

Dex gazes sheepishly at the coffee table, where I see tiny faces in a grid on his phone. Everyone we love is on a group FaceTime and just witnessed the best moment of my life. "She said yes, guys." He smiles into the camera, then glances back at me and shrugs. "It was only fair. I made them all a part of our story from day one. It wouldn't have been very kind of me to exclude them from the best part."

Shaking my head, I reach for him. "Dex, I think the best is yet to come."

"I do believe you're right, fiancée," he replies.

Fiancée. Never in a million years did I think taking a nanny job in North Carolina would lead me here. Now that I am, though, I don't ever plan to leave.

EPILOGUE

DEX

A week after I proposed to Lanie, she informed me that Julia was coming to visit. Then she told me Julia was moving here permanently with her son. Lanie was hoping it would be okay for Julia and Charlie to stay in the guest house while she looked for a place of her own. Of course, I said yes. Having Lanie's family close by would be an answer to our prayers once these babies arrived. I knew that from experience.

"Honey, we're home," I hear Julia sing out as they walk through the door. Walking toward the foyer, I greet them both with a hug.

"I'm so happy you're here," I tell her. "Where's Charlie?"

"I decided to leave him with Mom and Dad for the week. I thought it might be easier to house hunt this way."

"Now that she has official permission from work, she can move any time," Lanie says, happiness filling her voice.

"We told you, the guest house is yours for as long as you want it. It just sits empty otherwise, and it's the perfect size for both of you," I remind Julia.

"Thanks, Dex. I really appreciate that." The more time I

spend with Julia, the more I appreciate all her quirks and insecurities.

"Come on, let's show you around. Lanie said you wanted to start babyproofing before Charlie gets here, so I left a box of supplies on the kitchen counter for you. It's a long story, but I had a lot of extras," I tell Julia, and Lanie laughs.

~

*F*our days into Julia prepping the guest house for her and Charlie, she comes bursting through the kitchen door. She has a way of entering a room that could rival your favorite goofball on any TV sitcom.

"Lanie," she screams at full volume before realizing we're both sitting at the island.

Shaking my head, I try not to let the groan escape. Apparently, that's how Julia always enters a room.

"Oh, I didn't see you there," she says.

"You didn't look," I mumble, resulting in a shot to the ribs from Lanie's elbow.

"Lanes, I just remembered what you need! Can I borrow your car?" The energy this girl has is shocking.

"Of course you can borrow the car, Jules, but I don't really need anything right now."

"Maybe not today, but you will soon. Just wait and see," Julia sings across the kitchen.

I toss her the keys. "I just put gas in it, so you're all set."

"Great, be back soon," she says.

"What do you think she's up to?"

"I have no idea. With Julia, it's better not to even guess." She laughs.

~

An hour later, I'm sitting in my office when Trevor comes busting through the front door, Julia-style. *What is it with these two?*

"She's here? Julia. She's here?" he asks out of breath.

Raising my eyebrow, I try to figure out what's going on. "With as much as you guys text, I figured you knew."

"No, no, I didn't know. I've been in the lab day and night finishing something. What the hell is she doing here?"

I don't understand his agitated state, but it's been a long time since I've seen him this worked up. "Yes, Julia's here, just not right at this moment. She went out to run some errands. Come on, let's grab a beer," I suggest, hoping the alcohol will calm whatever storm is brewing. He's antsy, and when we reach the kitchen, curiosity wins out. "What's the big deal? You knew she was Lanie's best friend. You had to know you'd run into her at some point. Are you telling me you're really only texting? Still? No phone calls? No FaceTime?"

"No, strictly texting. It's the best for everyone." I study him as he picks at the label on the bottle.

"What's best?" Lanie asks, walking into the kitchen.

I look to Trevor, who's quick to reply, "Nothing, Lanes. How are you feeling?" he asks, changing the subject.

"So far so good," Lanie tells him, moving to sit next to me at the island.

"Lanie, I've got just what you need, babes." Julia's voice rings loud as she walks down the hall.

Glancing up, I notice Trevor has gone completely pale and is tilting his head like he recognizes the voice. Julia enters the kitchen, her tiny body entirely covered by a grocery bag and a five-gallon pail of ice cream in one hand and what has to be a three-gallon glass jar of pickles in her other hand.

"Can you believe I had to go to five different stores for

these pickles, Lanes? But trust me, they are so—" She breaks off as she lowers the bag to find Lanie.

I quickly realize her eyes are not on Lanie but on Trevor, who has turned completely green. "Angel?" he questions.

"Charlie?"

Glancing between them, I notice Julia's body trembling.

Completely confused, I turn to Lanie, who's also pale. "Holy shit," Lanie whispers before a loud crash catches my attention.

Dragging my attention away from Lanie, I realize Julia has dropped the jar of pickles and everything else in her hands. She's backing up when I realize there's glass all over the floor and she's barefoot.

"Julia, don't move. You don't have shoes on, and there's glass everywhere," I warn her, jumping up to get a broom.

"N-No, I have, the groceries, they, but, you, not, Charlie?" she says, making no sense but visibly shaking now. Before I can reach her, she turns and runs down the hallway with keys in hand.

Trevor moves to follow her, but Lanie holds him back. "Hold on there, Boston, this is my fault. Let me explain while Julia gets her thoughts together. She won't be able to talk to you until she's cleared her head."

"What do you mean this is your fault? What the hell is going on, Lanie?" Trevor yells.

"Hey! Calm down. Yelling at Lanie isn't going to solve anything," I say, angry at his raised voice.

Sighing, Lanie says, "Come on, let's sit in the family room. This is going to take a while."

∼

Lanie

Is this real life? How is it possible that Julia's Boston is Dexter's Trevor? *Holy fuck, here goes nothing.* Sitting down across from Trevor, I try to organize my thoughts, but they come out in a rush.

"Okay, well, right before my attack, Julia was scheduled to go to a conference in Boston. I was trying to push her out of her comfort zone a little. I got her to agree to a new wardrobe and made her promise she would put it to good use. I just thought she needed a one-night stand, so I told her she didn't even have to use real names if she didn't want to. How was I to know you guys would keep the game going all week?"

"I called her Angel, so she called me Charlie," Trevor says with a crooked smile, obviously lost in a memory.

"Right ... I didn't know that part. Ah, we called you Boston when she got home. Anyway, the day she left, she was already planning to tell you her real name and exchange numbers. You had dinner plans at the hotel that night."

"Yeah, but she didn't show up. I searched everywhere for her for months. It was like she disappeared." Trevor runs a hand over his face before he glances back, waiting for me to continue.

Dexter's head is going back and forth between us like a pinball machine, all news to him apparently.

"Her not showing up was my fault, Trevor." The familiar feeling of guilt washes over me. "About two hours before she was supposed to meet with you, she got a call from her parents that I'd been injured. She wasn't thinking, she just left. She didn't even pack up her stuff from her hotel room, just grabbed her keys and took off. I'm so sorry, Trevor," I tell him. "We've been looking for you ever since, but with no real information to go on, we've had no luck."

"I'd say luck just smacked you in the face." Dexter laughs.

Then his face pales, and I know he's about to spill Julia's biggest secret.

Before I can stop him, he blurts, "Holy shit, Trevor. You're a dad. You're Charlie's dad. That's why he always seemed so familiar. He has your fucking crazy colored eyes."

I hang my head and sigh.

Trevor is up and screaming before I catch a breath. "What? Is that true, Lanie? Do I have a goddamn son no one told me about?" he yells.

"Trevor, I'm going to tell you again to calm the fuck down. Did you just hear Lanes? They looked for you. They had no way to contact you," Dex reminds him.

"She needs to come back here right now," Trevor growls, reaching into his pocket for his phone. Pressing dial a few seconds later, we hear the telltale ring coming from the floor covered in pickle juice.

"What the fuck?" Walking over to the mess he pulls out her phone. "She left without her phone? Or her wallet? What the hell?" he mumbles, staring down the hallway. "She didn't even leave with any shoes on. Where the hell could she be?"

He's pacing the floor now, looking as frantic as I've ever seen him and mumbling incoherently. "Julia is Angel. Charlie's my son. Fuck, my father. What am I going to do?" Stopping abruptly, he turns to Dex. "Is she in Lanie's car?"

"Yes," Dex replies, seeming uncomfortable all of a sudden.

"Then you can trace her car. Tell me where she is."

"What?" I screech. "You track my car?"

Embarrassed, he shrugs his shoulders. "It's a feature that came with the car," he says as if that explains everything.

We will be talking about this later, for sure.

Dex pulls out his own phone, presses a few buttons, then scowls as he follows the dot. "Ah, I don't think she is coming back tonight."

Trevor runs over and grabs the phone from Dexter's hand.

"Where the hell is she going?" he asks, looking at us both now.

I peek over Trevor's shoulder and cringe. "It looks like she's headed to her parent's beach house in Corolla."

"How in the hell is she going to do that with no phone, no money, and no goddamn shoes?" he bellows, then resumes his pacing.

"I-I don't know." And really, I don't. I'm having a hard time believing this is real, too.

Doubling over, hand on his knees, Trevor tries to catch his breath. *Oh shit, I think he's having a full-blown panic attack.*

Running to him, I rub circles on his back. "Deep breaths, Trevor. Full, deep breaths."

After a few minutes, he's able to pull himself together. Standing to his full height, resolve in place, he turns to me.

"Give me the address, Lanie. I need it now."

"Trevor, I'm not giving it to you unless you promise you're not going there to yell at her. This wasn't her fault. It was mine. She was devastated when she found out and realized she would never be able to tell you. This is as much a shock to her as it is to you," I remind him.

Sucking in deep, he softens his expression. "Lanie, it wasn't your fault either." Exhaling, he continues, "It was fucked up circumstances. No one's at fault, but I do need to talk to her as soon as possible. There are things, things about my family she needs to know." He gives Dex a foreboding glare.

"She will be safest here, Trevor. Bring her back, don't worry about Lanie's car. I'll send someone to pick it up later," Dex tells him.

"Wait, what do you mean safest? Why would Julia be in danger?" I ask, my heart racing.

"She isn't in danger ... yet," Trevor states grimly. "But if my father finds out I have a son, everything will change."

I don't hesitate. I push him to the door. Slightly hysterical myself, I urge him to move faster. "Hurry up and get Julia." Dexter's already texting him the address. "I'll keep calling the house phone until she answers."

"Please don't tell her anything about my father. I'd like to do that in person. We have a lot to talk about. Just tell her I'm on my way and to talk to me. She's only been gone an hour. I'll make up the time on the highway."

EXTENDED EPILOGUE

Extended Epilogue

*D*ex and Lanie return home to two sets of twins, Tate and more adults than they know what to do with. It isn't until Trevor's past comes for Julia, however, that the crew will have to come together in a way they've never done before! You don't want to miss this! Click below to download the extended-epilogue

Get the download here
https://dl.bookfunnel.com/qw7m10tftx
Or visit my website: www.averymaxwellbooks.com

As an Indie Author, the best promotion I can get comes straight from you, my readers. If you loved Lanie and Dex please consider leaving a review. Reviews are how authors like myself make it in this business. Thank you in advance.

Please leave a review here!

Let's be friends!
Avery hangs out in her reader group, the LUV Club, daily. Join her on FB to get teasers, giveaways and release dates first!
Avery Maxwell's LUV Club

ALSO BY AVERY MAXWELL

The Westbrooks: Broken Hearts Series:

Book 1- Cross My Heart

Book 2- The Beat of My Heart

Book 3- Saving His Heart

Book 4- Romancing His Heart

The Westbrooks: Family Ties Series:

Book .5- One Little Heartbreak- A Westbrook Novella

Book 1- One Little Mistake

Book 2- One Little Lie (Coming Soon)

Book 3- One Little Kiss (Coming Soon)

Book 4- On Little Secret (Coming Soon)

ACKNOWLEDGMENTS

Acknowledgements

There are so many people to thank for helping me with this book.

First, my family. To my husband, my daughter, and three sons, thank you for your support. Even when the laundry was piled to the ceiling and you were having to get your own snacks, you supported me. You let me sleep in when I'd pull an all-nighter writing and you very rarely complained:)

Renee, my critique partner for her many beta and alpha reads. Not to mention the rewrites. Your support and guidance through this process has been amazing. The late night texts, phone calls and screenshots are what have helped get me this far. For that I'm eternally grateful!

Beth, my dear friend who managed to complete my developmental edits in under a week while also working 12-16 hours days at the hospital during Covid-19. Thank-you. Not just for the instrumental part you played in this book but for all you do to care for and help others. At the hospital and in your personal life. XOXO

Brooke & Valerie, what can I say? I wouldn't be Avery Maxwell without you;)

Laura & Lauren & Chelle, knowing each of you has made me who I am today. Thank you for your friendship and constant support. Without each of you, I wouldn't have had the courage to ever even begin this process. Luvs.

Editor: Melissa Ringstead, https://thereforyouediting.wordpress.com/

Cover Designer: Jodi Cobb @ Dark City designs. www.darkcitydesigns.com

Denis Caron at https://www.weekendpublisher.com for all your guidance on this incredible journey.

ABOUT THE AUTHOR

A New-England girl born and raised, Avery now lives in North Carolina with her husband, their four kids, and two dogs.

A romantic at heart, Avery writes sweet and sexy Contemporary Romance and Romantic Comedy. Her stories are of friendship and trust, heartbreak, and redemption. She brings her characters to life for you and will make you feel every emotion she writes.

Avery is a fan of the happily-ever-after and the stories that make them. Her heroines have sass, her heroes have steam, and together they bring the tales you won't want to put down.

Avery writes a soulmate for us all.

Avery's Website www.AveryMaxwellBooks.com